KIDNAPPING

the

PRINCE OF ALBANY

James J Dunn

This story is a fictionalized account based on true facts of a 1933 event.

ISBN: 9780692348994

Cover design by Melissa Schropp

Acknowledgements

My thanks to all those listed below. They were a great help to me during my search for the facts.

Joe Sanchez of the National Archives (Pacific Division)

Craig Carlson and his staff at the Albany Hall of Records

Ray Joyce, son of Officer Joyce

Forensics Department of the Albany County Police

Author's Note

On July 7, 1933 the nephew of the politically powerful Dan O'Connell was kidnapped outside his home. From the recently declassified files of the FBI and TSA, it has come to light that the kidnapping began in February of 1933 with the botched kidnap attempt of Morris "Mush" Trachnier, and was financed by a robbery of the Rensselaer County Bank in which Officer James Stevens was killed.

This account is built on researched facts and visualized details by the grandson of T.W. Dunn - the Jury Foreman.

Prelude
Murder of Legs Diamond

"Ladies and gentlemen of the jury, have you reached a decision?"

A pudgy man with black suspenders and matching bow tie stood. "Ye-s" His voice cracked. "Yes, Your Honor, we have."

"On the first count of kidnapping James Duncan—how say you?"

"We the jury find Mr. Jack Diamond not guilty."

"Hurrah!" cried the spectators sitting behind Legs Diamond and his attorney Daniel Prior.

"Order, order in the Court!" Judge Peters rapped his gavel. "On the second count of attempted murder, how say you?"

The foreman pulled at his bowtie and cleared his throat. "We find the defendant not guilty."

"On the third count of aggravated assault on Grover Parks, how say you?"

The foreman glanced at his note sheet. "We find the defendant, not guilty."

Whistles and cheers resounded. Judge Peters rapped his gavel and boomed, "Order, order!" When the noise subsided he turned slowly toward the defendant. "Mr. Diamond, you're free to go."

The judge then faced the jury. "Ladies and gentlemen of the jury, thank...." He dropped his gaze and passed the gavel from one hand to the other. He looked up then and said, "Go home. Court's adjourned."

The Superintendent of the New York State Police, in his trademark pinstriped gray suit and with a face that looked set in stone, stroked his salt and pepper mustache before reaching over the courtroom rail and pulling on the prosecutor's shoulder. He demanded, "How the hell did that happen?"

"Don't know, Major." Henry Epstein shook his head. "Two eyewitnesses."

Henry stole a glance at the crowd around the defendant. One after the other they were pumping his hand. The prosecutor turned back to the Police Superintendent and said, "You got me. Prior pounded Duncan pretty bad. The kid was quivering so much maybe the jury thought he wasn't credible. Old man Parks…what can I say? Looks like they took the word of a retired sheriff over an old man. That Sheriff Pierce kept a stone calm but he spoke straightforward. Apparently his word still carries a lot of weight even up here in this county."

Epstein had started stuffing papers into his briefcase. He paused and aimed a casual glance at the plump-faced dark-haired woman giving Legs Diamond a mousey kiss. A photographer stepped forward and Alice Diamond turned and smiled for the photographer. Legs turned and shook hands with John Oley.

"Never thought a jury would take their word over two eyewitnesses." Epstein clicked his cheek with this tongue. "Just don't know, Major."

"Ease up on 'im, John," Attorney General Bennett interjected as he stepped to the wooden rail. Bennett lowered his head. "Not here. Who's the other slouch next to Diamond?"

Albany Police Chief David Smurl, next to the superintendent, lifted his chin toward the other side of the courtroom. "The small one is Oley's younger brother, Francis. Both of them were piss ants with the Dutch Schultz mob. The tall skinny guy…dunno."

Legs Diamond had begun his stroll out of the courtroom. He paused and turned back to the authorities. "Yo, Bennett, Warner—we'll be having a little celebration over at the Rainbow Room. Join us. I hear the crow is real good! Ha-ha-ha!"

On the steps of the Albany County Courthouse, Bennett

stopped his small group of attorneys. "John, David. Get your best troopers and detectives together. I want Diamond followed around the clock. We're gonna dig till we get 'im. Henry, contact New York and ask for—"

"Hey, look!" Major Warner pointed to the red two-door Ducenburg with whitewall tires and chrome wire wheels. "Isn't that Sheriff Pierce at the wheel?"

Bennett quick-turned. "Y-e-a-h, Green County must have an awful generous pension. That bastard!"

"Son-of-a-bitch," Albany Police Chief Smurl muttered under his breath. He moved down a step and stared at the four-door limo that had rolled to the curb. A chauffeur stepped out and held open the rear door. Out stepped a tall woman with flowing shoulder length blond hair, oval face with round eyes and red painted lips.

Smurl said, "Thought Alice would've had her shot by now."

"Who is she?"

"Kiki Roberts." Chief Smurl sniffed. "She's Legs's favorite squeeze, showgirl from New York. Diamond's wife swore she'd—" He stared with snow ball eyes as the pudgy jury foreman with his bowtie slipped into the limo, followed by Kiki. "So that's how…" he said.

Henry, the prosecutor, stepped to the sidewalk, "Major, Chief, I can't beat a stacked deck."

Bennett stepped down, "It must've cost him plenty. There's gotta be a trail some place. Check on Diamond's and Pierce's finances. Hell, check the whole goddamn jury." He buttoned his coat. "Christmas or no, we've got work to do. Henry, get the car?"

"Yeah, sure."

When Henry disappeared around the corner Chief Smurl stepped over near Bennett and Warner and asked, "How far do I dig?"

John Bennett, New York State Attorney General, locked his teeth. His eyes narrowed. "You don't want Diamond here, I don't want 'im here and the four kings don't want 'im here. I don't care if you dig all the way to China." He lowered his voice. "Or dig six foot, Chief. I *want* Jack…Legs…Diamond!"

Hours later a black cheese-box car with chrome grill and black tires swung to the curb. Two men got out from the front and walked to the fringe of the circle of light from the overhead street lamp on Dove Street. "That's far enough," a voice called from the opposite side of the light.

An oversized barrel-figured man stepped from around a mailbox, staying beyond the light. He tossed a newspaper into the lighted area. The Albany Times Union flopped open to the headline, 'Jack Legs Diamond Not Guilty.' Below the headline, the date: December 17, 1931. The big man said, "There's two keys inside. The brass key opens the front door of number 67. The steel key opens apartment 2-B. Take it after I leave."

"What about the cops?"

After a dull giggle the guy said, "You've got the whole night. None within ten blocks."

Some time later that night, "Ring-ring-ring!" The man in the bed beside the phone wiped sleep from his eyes and said, "This better be good." Into the receiver he said, "John Warner here."

"Sorry, Major. This is Lieutenant Thomas. Legs Diamond was just assassinated."

"How terrible."

After the Major hung up a slight voice at his side asked, "Who was that, dear?"

"Just business."

Chapter 1
Blueprint for a Kidnapping

In February 1933, Percy "Angel Face" Geary swung his car around a laundry truck and pulled to the South Pearl Street curb, splashing dirty snow slush on the sidewalk pedestrians. Before he crossed the street he looked in both directions, but did not see lady fate barreling down on him.

Geary failed to read the warning sign in the blow-up of a furnace. This failure would engulf him in a national episode, a kidnapping second only to the Lindberg case in notoriety. He was about to become involved in the O'Connell Kidnapping—a case that would lead to his suicide and a change in federal law.

Geary had begun his criminal career in 1916 when he was acquitted of burglary. His slim 5'9" body with blue eyes and light chestnut hair belied his ruthlessness. His gun battles with police and charges of attempted murder and kidnapping demonstrated that Geary was a vicious hard-core mobster. His meeting on this day with childhood friend John Oley would lead them both to hard time for "hard criminals." The justice system would break Geary. At his parole hearing after 26 years in prison he pleaded with officials not to parole him. It was ironic that in his very first job he was a laundry delivery boy and in 1959 he committed suicide by throwing himself under a prison laundry truck. He chose death over parole.

In 1933, his patent leather shoes left a trail across the slushy street and into the red brick warehouse numbered 22, home of the Fort Orange Distribution Company. Inside he called out, "Anyone home?"

"In here," came the reply from the manager's office.

Inside the office Geary hung his trench coat on the coat tree behind the door and took a seat across the desk from his friend and partner, John Oley. Geary propped his feet up on the desk and asked, "Pay day yet?"

John Oley had brown hair and was two inches taller than Geary and thirty pounds heavier, a medium build. He started his criminal career early. In 1922 he was convicted of burglary. He listed his occupation as "beer distributor" but in reality it was stolen beer. He was a bootlegger and hijacker. His methods had allowed him to work his way up the underworld ladder until he became a trigger man for the late Jack Legs Diamond.

John Oley always thought he could outsmart anyone, but before it was all over he would learn that fate is the great equalizer. He would be medically paroled in 1959 and die of lung cancer in 1960 with his wife at his side.

Oley took an envelope from the middle desk drawer and tossed it at Geary. "Here yuh go." He resumed reading the newspaper.

Geary thumbed through the money in the envelope and mumbled, "These are getting mighty slim."

Oley stretched his legs out, creating a bridge between the desk and chair.

In 1933 Prohibition was nearing its end. By the end of the year it would be over and you could brew beer and alcohol legally. With the end so close, a system that had seen bootleg profiteers paying local officials to look the other way was changing quickly. Politicians who needed money could set up their own brewing businesses. To ensure their own big profits they set up various kinds of "legislation" to stop competition— by denying a brewing license.

There were huge profits to be made, but John Oley was about to learn that money out-ranks friendship. In the coming months the O'Connell family, that had a lock on the beer business in Albany, New York, would prove the cliché that "blood is thicker than water."

John Oley rubbed his ruddy face and took another drag on his cigarette. He said to Angel Face Geary, "Everyone smells the repeal of prohibition in the air. A lot of the cops don't arrest anyone for it any more. The profit in illegal booze ain't what it used to be. Betcha booze will be legal by the end of the year."

"K-boom." The noise rattled the windows.

Oley and Geary hurried to the street-side window. What they saw did not much surprise them. Smoke was coming from a saloon down the street. Soon a fire truck raced by with siren blaring.

Oley said, "Wanna bet they didn't buy Hendricks beer?"

"No bet," said Geary. "That's the second one this month. Say, we're not going to try to horn in on Hendricks' territory, are we? I don't want my furnace to blow up—yuh know what I mean?"

Oley closed the window and went back to his seat. He said, "There's enough room in this for all of us. Besides, I know the family—worked for them for a few years." He took a deep drag of his cigarette and rubbed his face. "Dan wouldn't do me wrong."

Geary loosened his tie. He wore his trademark white silk shirt, which told everyone he wasn't a truck driver like he said he was. He shook his head, "I'd think twice before I messed with the kings."

Oley chuckled at the ceiling. "You worry too much, Percy."

The phone rang. "Oley here." He shouted his next words. "Whaddya mean 'our records'?"

Minutes later Oley slammed the phone down and Geary said, "What was that all about?"

Oley rubbed his face. He began pacing back and forth. "That was Manny. Alcohol Board turned us down flat. Said no to our application for a brewing license. Said they didn't like our criminal records."

"Hell, John. Now what the hell we gonna do?"

Oley swore and swiped the newspaper onto the floor. He began pacing again. "Manny said we gotta get some more cash to grease the skids, said if we put my father and brother on the brewing application along with some green under the table we'd be a shoe-in. Damn it! We just gotta come up with enough cash to brew beer *and* pay off the Alcohol Board."

He reached over and picked up the newspaper and did a double take when he spotted the article in the lower corner. "Hmmm," he said. "Glen Falls Girl Returned in Three Days after a Two Thousand Dollar Ransom Paid."

Angel Face Geary dashed out his cigarette. "So what?"

Oley lit another cigarette and inhaled. "I'm thinking *easy* money. We *snatch a fat cat* so we can ask for a bundle of money. Enough to pay off the Board *and* set us up to brew beer."

Angel Face rolled out his lips. "How much?"

Oley pushed his palms up his face and gave a cheesy grin. "Hundred G's. Maybe more!"

"A hundred G's!" Angel Face jumped to his feet. "Are you nuts?! Who the hell has a hundred G's?"

Oley laughed. "No one does. We ask for twice what we want and settle for half. That's business."

Geary chuckled at the floor. "I'll buy that. So who we gonna clip?"

Oley drew his palm down his face and dropped his head. "How about Johnny Amando?"

Angel Face shook his head. "Johnny's too much trouble. His speakeasy is doing great. He just took on two bodyguards."

"Probably so." Oley snapped his fingers. "We could clip Jim O'Hagan. Guys would pay plenty to get him back."

Geary pulled on his nose. "You wanna kidnap a former middle-weight contender? You and whose army is gonna put the bag on him?"

Oley paced in a circle. "Yeah, yeah." Suddenly he stopped. He picked up the accounting ledger. His fingers tapped the cover. "Why not? We'll kill two birds with one stone."

"Whaddya mean?"

Oley grinned. "Mush Trachnier is what I'm thinking."

"Ole Mush? The very dapper Mush Trachnier? Your former employer?"

"It's strictly business, Percy. I already know his routine. It'll be easy."

"Cheese-us, John. Half the guys in the county make book with Mush—or drink with him."

"That's why he's perfect. Everybody will chip in to get him back. Here's the best part. I'm thinking we put the bag on Mush and ask for a king's ransom. No one will have all the money, so we get Mush to offer up his brewery as collateral. We use the ransom to buy up all of Mush's property with his own cash. We get cash and his beer operation for nothing." Oley snapped his fingers. "We'd be in business in no time."

Percy 'Angel Face' Geary adjusted his shoulder holster then said, "Sounds jake to me. But who yuh gonna trust to be the go-between? Who's gonna run the negotiations and handle the cash?"

Oley smirked. "Me."

"You?"

"It's easy, Percy. We get Mush to come up with a list of go-betweens. All we have to do is nix each guy on the list until Mush mentions my name. We clip Mush and fix it so I'm the go-between and bagman. We play both ends against the middle."

"One thing, John," Geary said. "Everybody knows us around here. They see us bird-dogging Mush and word will get out. It'll get back to him. Mush would know something's up."

"Ah…got a point there, Percy. We'll have to use guys from out of town—guys that aren't known around her. Know anybody?"

Angel Face folded his arms across his chest. He sank his head and pulled on his lip. "Maybe. There's Leo. He does some freelance."

"Hold on now. I don't need no hayseed for this operation. This is gonna be a class act. What's his bona-fides?"

Percy's eyebrows shot up. "Leo Scarnici. Met him in the joint at Welfare Island. He's a top gun for Dutch Shultz down in New York. Everyone calls him Big Charlie Scarnici. After his first three days in the big house, no one messed with him."

"Sounds right. Know anything else about him?"

Angel Face cocked his head. "Rumor says he buried his chauffeur alive over some deal."

"You sure about that?"

Angel Face scowled. "N-o-o. Not gonna ask him neither."

Oley drew his palm across his mouth. "I see. Can yuh contact him?"

"Not directly. Have to go through Zeigler."

"Phil Zeigler? In the Bronx?"

"Same guy."

Oley waved. "Hell, I know Phil. Give him a call. Have him stop up."

***

Days later, a dark blue 1928 Nash sedan spit brown snow slush from its tires as it chugged up the State Street hill. Phil Zeigler was slim but putting on weight. There were age bags under his black marble eyes and his chin sagged. Zeigler was the go-to man in the Bronx. The only thing he didn't do was murder, but of course he could find you whatever you wanted for a fee.

Zeigler held to the dashboard of the Nash. The car fishtailed every time the driver touched the brakes or punched the gas pedal.

Zeigler said, "Downshift, Charlie—it's too slick for brakes. That's the Wellington up ahead on the right, big brick building."

Big Charlie Scarnici double-parked outside the nine-story red brick Wellington Hotel. He kept the engine running. Phil Zeigler hopped out saying, "I'll check us in."

Before Zeigler closed the door he pointed at the corner of State and Eagle and a two-story white concrete building with shops on the ground floor. Two large picture windows came together at the corner of the ground floor. He said, "That's the Waldorf Lunch Room—where we're supposed to meet."

Scarnici said, "Too far to walk in this wet stuff—so hurry up." His olive-colored skin, dimpled chin and Mediterranean features gave him the look of a movie star. He gave a cat's-eye gaze at the people crossing in front of the Nash. He was a man always on guard. He was a killer for the Dutch Schultz mob, a job role that necessarily meant he had acquired quite a few enemies. Always there was the possibility that someone close by was gunning for him.

A glimmer in the rear view mirror caught his eye. His hand slipped inside his coat to his gun. His eyes zeroed in on the speck of light reflected from the badge on the dark-blue wool coat of an approaching Albany cop. That badge made a nice target, Scarnici thought. And then he thought, this might be a short stay.

In 1935 those thoughts would become reality. Scarnici would be executed in Sing-Sing Prison for killing a Rensselaer cop. He released his grip on the gun only after the cop jumped aboard the trolley car going up the hill.

The passenger door flew open. Zeigler was back. Scarnici slipped the Nash into gear and moved forward, finding a parking space in front of Ralph's Jewelers—next door to the Waldorf.

Phil Zeigler opened the door and the two men entered into the clatter of dishes and babbling rumble of noon-hour diners. A man across the room waved his arm in the air.

"There's John Oley."

Zeigler shook Oley's hand. "Been a while, John. This is my friend, Charlie Scarnici."

"Percy's running late, stuck in the snow," Oley said. "Have a seat. Take a load off."

Zeigler and Scarnici hung their coats on the post at the corner of the booth. Scarnici slipped in first so he could put his back to the wall and keep a watchful eye on the other patrons. He drew a bead on a waitress with curly brunette hair that hung to her shoulders. She stepped over to their booth and placed water glasses and menus on the table. "Special's roast beef," she said, and hurried off to attend the next table.

Scarnici leaned forward on his elbows. He lowered his voice. "John, you look familiar. Ever been to the city?"

"Some. West Side mostly. Worked with Legs Diamonds, and dealt some with Waxy Gordon. Ever run into them?"

"Waxy, on occasion. He used to play cards with Dutch Schultz."

Oley cocked his head. "*Used to play cards?*"

"Well, uh…no one's seen Waxy in a while."

Oley stifled his reaction. Scarnici meant Waxy Gordon was dead and knew enough not to accuse anyone. Oley grinned. "Probably taking a long vacation."

The subject went no further because just then Oley spotted an old friend. "Oh, here comes Manny."

Manny Strewl was a lean five-foot-nine man with a hooknose on a bold oval face framed by wavy brown hair. He and Oley had been grade school friends and more recently criminal cohorts. They had done time at the Atlanta

Penitentiary for mail robbery and impersonating a mail worker (federal official). There was also an attempted murder charge but it was not proven.

Strewl was an individual who used his brain more than his brawn—a fact that may explain why he was the only member of the Albany kidnapping gang to die of old age, in 1995.

Strewl shook hands with everyone. "Phil, yuh made good time. This the man Percy mentioned?"

"Sure is. Charlie Scarnici. From the Bronx."

Strewl shook Scarnici's hand. "Percy's said a lot about yuh."

Strewl took an envelope stuffed with cash from his suit coat pocket and put it on the table between Zeigler and Scarnici. "This will show yuh we're serious. Should more than cover your travel expenses."

Zeigler slipped the envelope into his inside coat pocket. "I'm sure it will. Whatcha got going?"

Strewl took a seat next to Oley and leaned toward Scarnici and Zeigler. In a low voice he said, "Gonna expand our beer business. We can cut you in for a piece of the action or cash. Depends on—"

Oley interrupted. "Here comes the waitress."

"Special's the roast beef."

The waitress turned after taking the orders and bumped into Angel Face Geary. "Sorry."

Geary removed his coat. "Ok, hon. Just bring me whatever they're having."

The waitress made a note and hurried away. Geary pulled a chair from a table and sat at the end of the booth. "Didn't mean to be late. Got stuck in a hole. Did I miss anything?"

Strewl leaned forward and again spoke in a low voice. "I was just telling these guys—"

Oley nudged Strewl's arm and gestured toward the booth behind where several men had just sat down. "Too many ears, let's eat first. My brother has a place over on Market Street. We can go there, have some privacy."

***

Following lunch John Oley parked his maroon Pontiac sedan in front of 18 Market Street. Zeigler and Scarnici were behind him. Oley led the way into the speakeasy. "My brother Francis owns half this joint. Doing okay for himself."

Inside, John Oley called out to his brother's business partner, M.J. Fitzgerald, who was stacking glasses on the back shelf. "M.J., line them up for my business friends from New York."

The burly barkeeper was totally Irish with red hair, a twinge of freckles and big floppy ears. His red mustache contrasted with his white complexion and threads of gray mixed with his red hair. He popped the tops on several beer bottles and slid them down the bar.

John Oley caught the bottles. He handed them out after he glanced at the Hendricks beer label. He smirked at M.J. "Outta Barman's?"

M. J.'s voice boomed out. "Hey, Francis. Brother's here with friends." He lowered his voice. "We buy enough Hendricks beer so our furnace don't blow up, yuh know?"

The sound of gum popping announced Francis Oley's arrival. He had just turned 21, had short wavy brown hair, a mole on his lower jaw and hazel eyes on a roundish face. Francis could laugh at a good joke, but could stop the laugh as quick as turning off a light. He spoke with an Irish brogue and no one could figure out how he had picked it up. The knot in his loose fitting tie was similar to one he would tie in a bed sheet around his neck in 1937 when he hanged himself in the Utica Prison.

John Oley introduced his brother. "Francis, this is Phil Zeigler and Charlie Scarnici. Came up from the city. Need a place to talk."

Francis Oley popped his gum. "Ain't much—but my office is upstairs." He handed his clipboard to M.J. who got busy setting a bunch of beer bottles on the bar. Francis gave each man a bottle and filled his and his brother's hands with more bottles, then he led the way up the stairs next to the bar and kicked open a door. He took the chair behind the battered oak desk. His brother and Manny Strewl sat on the desk's corners. Angel Face leaned against the wall next to the door with his suit coat open so he could easily reach his gun if he needed it.

Scarnici spun a chair around and sat backwards on it and pulled his suit coat open. He waited until Zeigler settled in a wicker chair before he caught Oley's eye and flipped open his palm. "Your nickel, your show."

John Oley rubbed his face vigorously with both palms. "Here's the deal in a nutshell. We wanna snatch a guy by the name of Mush Trachnier. Runs a big brewery across the river. We want to take over his operation. We need—"

"You need us for the rough stuff," Scarnici interrupted. "Easy enough to plant him."

John Oley lit up a cigarette while Strewl lit a cigar. "Almost," Oley said. "We're pretty well known round here. We need some front men. Strangers no one knows. We'll do the groundwork. We'll back yuh up when the time comes. You guys can have a piece of the action or straight cash."

Scarnici watched as Zeigler lit a cigarette. Shortly, a dull blue smoke haze hung in the air. Scarnici rubbed a beer bottle on his cheek. "Don't know about you, Phil, but Albany's too far north for me. I'm in for cash only."

Zeigler burped. "Me too, Charlie. We're in for straight cash, John. What's the play?"

John Oley drew his palm down his face. "We play both sides against the middle. We kidnap Trachnier and ask for a king's ransom. We'll have Mush make a list of possible go-betweens and have his family code the list using numbers for letters—then have it put in the papers. Next, we, as the kidnappers, turn down each name on his list until my name comes up. I used to work for Mush, so it will be on the list at some point. We use the mail for negotiations so nothing is traced back to us."

Scarnici leaned forward. "Why don't you just volunteer as the bag man, John?"

"Too obvious. Someone might get wise. Better to have the family come to me than me go after the family."

Scarnici lit up a cigarette and spit a tobacco leaf onto the floor. "Mail's a little too slow, John. Could take a while."

"True, Charlie, but I'm guessing the cops would tap Trachnier's phone or anyone else's phone who gets involved. That's why the mail is safer." He chuckled. "And cops can't tail a letter."

You got the lowdown on this guy Trachnier?"

John Oley gave a broad grin. "Trachnier eats at Keeler's Restaurant every Friday night. Over on State and Green Streets. Mush lives on the bottom floor of a two-story house west of town on Kate Street. We just box Mush in on the road and stuff him in the trunk. Next we get all his friends to chip in for the ransom. We make it high enough so Mush has to offer his brewery as collateral. After the pay off, you guys go home. We use our share of the ransom to buy up all of Mush's debt markers and property. We get Trachnier's business and territory bought with his own money…and it's all legit."

Charlie Scarnici licked his lips. "Sounds like a sweet deal. Where yuh gonna stash him?"

"We're thinking Poughkeepsie."

Scarnici shook his head. "Too close. I got a place on College Street in the Bronx close to me. Be farther away from your friends—and easier for us to baby him."

"Charlie's right, John," said Zeigler. "If you're too well known round here you don't wanna stash the victim too close. With that in mind, how yuh gonna contact yourself for the ransom. Being in two places at once is a tough job."

"Easy, Phil. That's where the mail comes in. I write myself a letter and slip out of town to mail it. Then slip back into town unnoticed. If that don't work, I call you guys from a pay phone and have you guys mail me the ransom letter. I'll look innocent as a lamb. If we have to use more than one letter, we just use different mail drops. We'll have the cops running in circles. All's we need is a few more guys for the job."

Zeigler pulled on the back of his neck for a moment. "I can hustle up Al Fisher and have Benny Holinsky bring his machine gun. Whaddya say, Charlie?"

Scarnici sat up straight. "I'm thinking Little Charlie Herzog will throw in with us.

Tony Reino, too. Angel Face, you in on this?"

Angel Face, standing against the wall, nodded.

Scarnici tipped his beer toward Francis Oley. "What about your brother, John?"

All eyes focused on Francis Oley who said, "Nah, business is picking up. I'll pass."

John Oley slapped his thighs with both palms. "That'll do it. Don't wanna split the pie too much."

Scarnici wiped beer suds from his mouth with his sleeve. "You got a date set?"

"We got it wired. Next week. First Friday in March."

***

A week later in a red brick apartment on High Street, the air in the kitchen was rank with the same blue haze of tobacco smoke. Someone had cracked the window to let in some fresh air. John Oley had spread out a map of Albany. He pointed at the intersection of Green and State Streets. "Here's the plan. Mush eats here at Keeler's Restaurant every Friday night. Mixes a little business with pleasure. He eats late, which is good for us and bad for him. Nice and dark. He normally swings up State Street and shoots out Delaware Avenue, to Whitehall Road. It's the fastest way home for him. Kate Street is the first right off Whitehall. Mush's house is the second two-story building on the left. He lives on the bottom floor. A big number four is nailed on the porch column so you can't miss it. He parks his car behind the house in the garage about 50 feet back."

Oley drew his finger along the map. "There's a dark stretch on Delaware Avenue between Reeve and Cutler streets. Me, Charlie and Reino will cut in front of Trachnier with the Pontiac and cut him off. Phil, Al, Little Charlie and Benny can box him in from behind."

Oley rubbed his face. "Benny, you're back-up with your machine gun. Just don't fill Trachnier full of holes till after we get the money. Manny will follow Mush to Keeler's. He'll signal us when Mush is ready to leave the restaurant. Then he'll hightail it to the Elm Street garage and get the truck ready to take Trachnier to the place Scarnici has set up in New York. We'll slip Trachnier into the back of the truck then it's off to New York."

Strewl placed a shoebox on the table. He took out a roll of two-inch wide adhesive tape and gauze. "For Mush's eyes once we get him in the car." He twirled a pair of handcuffs around his fingers. "Everyone familiar with these?"

The laughs stopped after a few seconds. Strewl tossed the handcuffs back into the shoebox. "That's it till tomorrow night. Let's go get some grub."

***

The next night John Oley stood in the middle of Green Street. Steam snorted from his nose in the chill of the late night air. He gazed at the milky glow created by the streetlights and Keeler's Restaurant. He tied his beige trench coat closed before walking back to the dark blue 1928 Nash sedan. He tapped on the window.

Zeigler rolled down the window. Oley spoke in a hushed voice. "How you guys holding up?"

Zeigler started the car. "Cold. Time for more heat."

"It'll be hot soon enough."

Little Charlie Herzog pointed at the approaching shadow of a man prancing toward them. "Looks like now's the time."

Oley sprung around with a hand inside his coat. "That should be Manny."

Puffs of steam came from Strewl's mouth as he reported, "Trachnier's done. Paying the bill now. We got a problem."

"What problem?"

"He had two dinner pals."

Scarnici called out, "Not too much of a problem." He snapped the cylinder closed on his .38 revolver. "Me and Reino will handle it."

Strewl took a deep breath. "Hold on, Charlie—don't need dead bodies pointing to us. Got a better idea." He pointed to the car under the State Street lamppost across from Keeler's. The car was shaped like a half-stick of butter with a cube on top. "That's Mush's Reo. Just wait till he drops his buddies off and he's alone."

Oley tapped Strewl's shoulder. "Yuh better get to the garage and warm up the truck. Can't be much longer. Guys, let's get the cars warmed up."

Shortly, Oley bumped Scarnici's arm and pointed to three men on the sidewalk in front of the restaurant. "The taller one's Mush."

Morris "Mush" Trachnier was white-haired, pencil thin, and had a chipmunk face. He always dressed in sports clothes with a handkerchief in his breast pocket so he was prepared to hand it to any tearful woman. He was well known in political and sporting circles from Albany to Miami. His luck at the track plus bookmaking and an illegal alcohol business provided him sufficient funds to spread cash to politicians and mobsters alike.

A few minutes later one of the three men in front of the restaurant walked up State Street. The other two got into Mush's Reo coupe. Seconds later blue smoke puffed from the Reo's exhaust. Oley turned on his headlights and said, "Here we go, Charlie."

Mush Trachnier's Reo made a wide turn in the intersection of Green and State streets. The headlights came on as it headed west on Green Street.

"Shit!" Oley said. "He's coming this way. Duck!"

Crouched below the dashboard and head to head with Oley, Scarnici whispered, "Thought you said he always went up State Street. Where the hell's he going?"

The Reo's headlights bathed Oley's car in light that faded as it passed. Oley sprang up. "Beats me. Probably dropping off his friend."

Oley cranked the Buick's steering wheel hard. He punched the gas pedal. The Pontiac fishtailed away from the curb. Oley shouted out the window to Zeigler. "Come on!"

Both cars zoomed off, chasing the Reo as it faded in the distance. Within minutes Oley and his gang lost sight of Trachnier's car. Zeigler pulled alongside Oley's car and called from the open window, "Nice try, but we lost him."

Oley rubbed his face. He looked in all directions. "No we haven't—he's gotta go home. We can snatch him there."

Oley's car raced westward followed by Zeigler's car. Oley raised his voice. "If we get to Mush's house before him we'll just hide out till he shows. If he's already home you knock on the door, Charlie. When he opens it, we rush him. Let Benny hang back with the machine gun to cover us. I'll have the car waiting."

Scarnici moved his hand inside his coat and loosened his gun holster. "Straight up or feet first—he's coming with us!" A moment later he pointed at tail lights in the distance. "Careful. Company."

Oley studied the tail lights as they grew larger. "Son of a bitch!"

Scarnici looked in all directions. "What?"

"Them's Reo's tail lights, Charlie. I'd know them anywhere. We caught him!"

Oley accelerated. He grinned as the Reo turned onto White Hall Road. "That's Trachnier alright."

Oley followed the Reo onto White Hall Road and saw it turn onto Kate Street. He coasted onto Kate Street. The Reo turned toward the garage behind the house. "How's it look?" Oley said. "Is Zeigler with us?"

Scarnici craned his neck to look out the back window. "Right behind us."

Oley glided by Mush's driveway. "Whaddya think?"

Scarnici leaned back to see out the rear passenger door window as the Reo's lights clicked off. He saw Mush pull the garage door closed and begin his walk to the front of the house. "Either get him or breeze him."

Oley swung toward a bare spot in front of the second house past Trachnier's driveway and snapped off his lights. He hit the brakes. They squealed like a stuck pig.

Oley and Scarnici exchanged stunned looks. Oley opened his door. Behind them Zeigler and Fisher opened their car doors and jumped out. Reino followed.

The shadowy figure of Mush Trachnier paused in the driveway. He began running toward his house.

Scarnici yelled as they charged across the neighbor's yard. "Go! Go! Go!"

The sound of a breaking windowpane came from Mush's front porch. Scarnici yelled, "Hit the dirt!"

Light spit from Mush's gun like roman candles. "Bang-bang!"

Scarnici rolled over on the ground and pulled out his gun. He fired twice. Wood chips flew off Trachnier's porch column. It all sounded like a Western gun fight. Waking dogs added to the chaos of noise.

The neighbors' porch lights began coming on. A voice cried out, "What goes on there?" Another called, "What are you guys doing out there?"

Holinsky swung the machine gun toward the voices. Oley knew that in the dull light they might be identified so he lurched at Holinsky and yanked the barrel down. "No no!" Oley said. "We'll get boxed in. Too many witnesses."

Oley took quick aim. "Bang." A porch light went out. "Run for it!"

Scarnici shoved Zeigler toward the Nash and began running for the Pontiac. "Split up!" he said.

Oley gunned the Pontiac engine and zigzagged through the streets of Albany, hoping to shake off potential followers. Finally he turned onto a residential street and slipped into the garage behind the house at 40 Oakwood Avenue. He pulled down the garage doors and checked in all directions. "Looks like Phil went the other direction."

Oley entered his house followed by Scarnici and Reino. He pointed Scarnici to the front living room. "Get the curtains."

Oley pulled the kitchen shades down, took a fistful of beer bottles from the icebox and spread them on the table then began dialing a number on the phone on the kitchen wall. "Fran," he said, "stop over."

Minutes later a scratch at the door got their attention. A voice called, "John, it's Francis. Open up."

John Oley closed the door behind his brother. "Anyone see yuh?"

Francis Oley took off his coat. "Looks clear. How'd it go?"

"Saw us coming."

A slender woman came into the room. Her brunette hair was pulled back from her oval face, one of her front teeth was split. She said, "What happened?"

Scarnici kicked John Oley's foot under the table. Oley drew his hand down his face. "Nothing, Aggie. Go on upstairs."

Agnes Oley quietly left the kitchen as she always did, knowing her husband had been involved in some sort of criminal activity.

Scarnici growled, "No sense telling the world."

"Take it easy, Charlie."

"Easy! Take it easy? After that circus! You said he wasn't armed!"

Oley went nose to nose with Scarnici. "He doesn't carry, Charlie! Did yuh see him run for the house? He keeps a gun by the door. Hell Charlie, you were supposed to beat him there!"

"We would've, John, if yuh hadn't parked in the next county. Damn it, next time, make sure yuh got good brakes. They made enough noise to wake the dead."

Oley tossed the Pontiac keys and his gun on the table. He took another set of keys from the hook next to the back door. "Me and Fran will take Aggie's car and get a beer down at Nickey's saloon. That's the first place street news hits. We'll know what everybody thinks in short order. If we're not back in forty minutes, clear out."

To those who waited—Scarnici and Reino—the interval seemed an eternity, but John and Francis Oley returned as promised. John tossed the late night edition of the

Knickerbocker Press on the table. Both men chuckled. "The luck of the Irish."

Scarnici put his gun away. "How so?"

John Oley rubbed his face. "Ran into some of Mush's friends. News is already all over town. People think I had something to do with the kidnap attempt."

Reino shoved his gun into his shoulder holster. "And you're still standing here?"

Francis Oley laughed. "Sure enough. John convinced them we couldn't have done anything because we weren't packing a gun. Worked like a charm."

John Oley dropped a small wad of cash on the table. "That's all I got, Charlie. We lost a bundle on this one. Called the garage. Phil made it there. All Mush's friends are on the lookout for strangers driving a black Nash. Fran can drive yuh's all back to New York in the Nash. The Nash is not black—it's dark blue. And with Francis at the wheel people won't suspect a thing. Just stay low until clear of Albany. Fran can take the train back. We'll be in touch."

Scarnici placed Oley's gun on the table and scooped up the money. "Call when you're ready."

John Oley watched as his brother backed the Nash out of the garage and drove down Oakwood Avenue. The passengers had ducked down on the back seat floor. The car disappeared onto New Scotland Avenue.

John Oley dialed a number on the kitchen wall phone. "Manny, it's me. Think we're in the clear. Gave Charlie the last of our cash and sent them on their way. Now we have no beer license plus our cash is about gone. Got any ideas?"

"I'm thinking we take advantage of the situation, John."

"Advantage! Hell, Manny—every chiseler in town will be on the lookout."

"Right, John. But we try the soft sell. We threaten the politicians. Then reapply for a beer license. They'll know we're serious because of the attempt on Mush."

"And if that don't work?"

"Simple, John. We snatch a politician. They have money and don't carry guns. Maybe one that has a say on issuing a brewing license. To avoid the problems we just had, all we gotta do is wait until the snow melts."

"Any particular politician in mind?"

"Sure…he's related to the Kings of Albany."

Chapter 2
Crime to Finance Crime

A few days after the failed Mush Trachnier kidnap attempt, in his rear apartment at 95 Elm Street, Manny Strewl dropped paper and pencil in his brother's lap. "Need yuh to write something for me."

Jacob Strewl turned off the radio and put the newspaper he was reading to one side. "Why me, Manny? I'm not your secretary."

"Yeah, but I don't need this traced back to me."

"Cheese-us, Manny. What about me?"

Manny waved his arm in the air. "Don't worry, Jacob. You don't have to sign it. And anyway, the cops don't have your prints on file—there's no way they can trace it back to you. All I need you to do is write a few words to Ed O'Connell."

"Ed O'Connell the lawyer? Why him?"

"Because him and his friends are stopping me and Oley from getting a beer license. I just wanna push him a little is all. Scare him off some."

Jacob licked the pencil point. "What do I say—or should I say, what do you want to say?"

Manny lit a cigar and puffed blue smoke into the air and began dictating.

ED

JUST A WARNING FOR YOU + DAN I
AM IN A POSITION TO KNOW LIKE
MUSH TRACTIONER WATCH YOU
STEP YOU ALL MIGHT GET A
SURPLISE ANY TIME ALL ARE
MARKED JUST A MATTE OF
PROPER CHANCE YOU MAY
THINK THIS IS HOOEY THATS
UP TO YOU TIME WILL TELL
OPEN AIR + WEATHER IS A HAND
STRAIGH TIP
HOGING DAYS ABOUT OVER

Manny took the note, glanced over it and sealed it in an envelope. "This should make the O'Connells back off." He grabbed his hat. "Gonna go mail it. Back later."

***

A week later Strewl hustled up the steps of 18 Market Street and pounded his fist on the speakeasy door. Francis Oley checked the peephole and swung the door wide. "Come on in, John's here."

John Oley was sitting at a table with a cup of coffee. Strewl jammed his hat and trench coat on a chair and threw the beer application papers in front of him. Oley set his coffee down, rubbed his face and started to read.

Strewl dropped into the chair opposite and growled, "Those sons of bitches want the whole business all to themselves!"

John Oley looked up. "What the hell's this all about? Says here my brothers aren't good enough to run a beer business? Hell! Will and Ed are clean. Snyder said they'd be shoe-ins. Why'd we get cut out?"

"Keep reading, John. It says Will and Ed don't know nothing about making beer. Says they're just fronts for us."

John Oley slapped the papers on the table. "Well hell! Dan O'Connell's got a record. And Solly's no better." He rubbed his face. "Damn it! Ed and his partner, Sam Arnowitz—they don't know jack about beer but they got a license to brew."

Strewl twisted in his chair. "Yeah, they have the pull, don't they? But looks to me like we been pushed too far. Time for things to go our way, John. I say we push the O'Connells back."

John Oley folded his arms across his chest. "Legs Diamond tried to push his beer into Albany. Look what happened to him."

Francis Oley filled the coffee cups he'd put on the table. "Thought the cops hadn't closed that case."

John Oley raised an eyebrow at Strewl. "Never will, either. But everybody knows who had Diamond bumped off. They just can't prove it."

Strewl smirked. "Don't wanna prove it neither. That's another reason to clip them—pay back for the Legs Diamond murder. The O'Connells need to understand they ain't the only players in town."

John lowered his voice. "Who we gonna clip?"

Strewl bobbed his head. "One of the O'Connells, of course. It'll be easy. We'll do it the same as Trachnier—but wait till the snow clears. And this time, no squeaking brakes. We still have a few months rent left on the apartment where we planned that job."

Francis Oley paused the popping of his gum and caught his brother's eye. "Better watch it. I heard that both Dan and Solly O'Connell picked up some heaters after that Trachnier crap. Word is Solly goes through two boxes of ammo a week, can put three shots outta six in the center. Even Dan's been practicing some. If things go wrong, you'll have a bigger shootout than what you had with Trachnier."

Strewl pulled at his jaw. "Uh-huh…well then, how 'bout we nail the older brother? Packy."

John Oley pulled a cigarette from his shirt pocket and lit up. He blew smoke toward the ceiling. "That old geezer!? A pound of catfish is worth more'n him."

Strewl grinned and reached in the inside pocket of his suit coat for a cigar. He pointed the cigar at Oley. "You're forgetting his last name. The O'Connells will pay plenty to get their own flesh and blood back. It'll work just like what we planned for Trachnier. We use the ransom to buy up all the O'Connell property and debt markers—and put the whole clan out of the brewing business."

Strewl leaned back in his chair and smiled big like he'd just eaten the canary. "And it'll all be legit."

John Oley stroked his jaw. "Manny, I've known Dan O'Connell and his family a long time. Going after one of them is like poking a sleeping bear—yuh know what I mean?"

"Only if they find out, John. If we use the same guys to front for us, the O'Connells will never know it was us."

John Oley clutched his coffee with both hands and peeked over the rim of the cup. "What bothered me was, Holinsky was ready to cut loose on the whole neighborhood with that confounded machine gun. If it'd been up to him there'd have been a flood of bodies—just like Capone's Saint Valentine massacre. Last thing we need is Holinsky and that damn gun of his tipping the scales."

Strewl drummed his fingers on the table. "Good point. We need some cool heads." A few seconds passed in silence then Strewl looked up. "Say, Francis—you needing some extra cash?"

Francis bobbed his head. "Wouldn't hurt none. The newborn's costing more than I expected. I'll throw in for a cut."

"Good. We can bounce Holinsky and you take his place."

John Oley tapped his cigarette ashes into the ashtray. "I'll buy that. And Angel Face will kick in. What about the rest?"

The cigarette and cigar smoke grew thick as Manny and the Oley brothers came up with a plan. The blue haze of all that smoke, evidently, kept them from seeing the consequences the future held for the design they set in motion that day.

They faced one immediate problem: seed money for putting the plan in operation. The Trachnier job had left them short on cash. John Oley said, "Barely enough to cover the gas bill."

Strewl countered with, "Yeah, but we got guns, we got ammo. We can get what we need, John. Let's run this by Zeigler, pick his brain. We can worry about expenses later."

Strewl turned toward Francis Oley. "I want you and Angel Face to start checking out Packy O'Connell. By the time me and John here get back from New York, I wanna know what brand of shorts he wears. I'll call Zeigler, tell him we'll be down this Saturday."

***

The Saturday morning traffic on New York City's Broadway was light. A drizzling April rain was melting the remaining snow and passing cars splashed it onto pedestrians who did not take care to stay back. Manny Strewl and John Oley jaywalked across 46th Street and entered the Century Hotel. Oley pulled his coat close and shivered. "Can't wait till May gets here, this kind of weather chills me to the bone."

The hotel lobby was busy, people checking in and out. The slush and mud tracked inside kept the hotel janitor busy mopping but his efforts were futile. Strewl stepped carefully on the wet surface as he approached the front desk. He removed his trench coat and rapped his knuckles on the counter to get the clerk's attention. "Excuse me. Would you ring Miss Margaret Campbell's room, tell her that her visitors from Albany are here?"

The clerk dialed, then pointed to the black lacquered doors between the brass frames. "Take the elevator to the eighth floor. Room 812."

A dark red carpet muffled their steps as they neared the room. Strewl knocked. The peephole darkened for a second and the door swung open. The face of the man before them broke into a grin. His hair was black as coal and his eyebrows just as dark and thick as caterpillars. His eyes were dark too, like black marbles.

Benny Holinsky reached his huge hand to the visitors and called out, "Phil, company's here!"

They found Phil Zeigler taking a hit from an opium pipe. When he finished he set the pipe on a black box in the middle of the bed where Al Fisher was sitting. Zeigler cautioned Fisher "not to use it all" then rubbed at his blood-shot eyes and pointed to a table laden with liquor bottles. To the newcomers he said, "There yuh go, it'll take the chill outta your bones."

He turned some glasses right side up and began pouring drinks. As he handed one to Strewl he said, "So tell me about this new plan."

Strewl tossed back the drink and gulped air. He said, "Same plan, Phil. Just a different slouch."

John Oley took a handful of ice from the ice bucket, dumped it in his glass and squirted seltzer water into his whiskey. "Some slouch! Wait till you hear who it is, Phil."

Strewl sat down in a straight chair and crossed his legs. He touched his fingertips together. "Phil, I'm thinking Packy O'Connell. The family's got bucks. Should be easy pickings."

"Easier than Trachnier?" Holinsky asked.

Strewl mused for a moment. "Yeah, easier than Trachnier."

Zeigler wiped his blood-shot eyes with his long black tie. "You guys ever think about taking Solly O'Connell? Or maybe Dan. Solly drops a bunch of cash here in New York. And he's got a lot of markers out. Comes down here quite a bit. We could snatch him here—not have to run to Albany and back."

"We thought of that," Strewl said. "Heard on the street that Solly bought a gun, and so did Dan. Good chance Benny there would have to fill 'em full of holes, which wouldn't do anybody any good. Besides, Dan's the banker in the family. He's the one that'll have to raise the ransom. Ed—"

Laughter interrupted him. Oley said, "Hell, nobody'd pay to get a lawyer back."

Zeigler pulled at his nose. "Yuh know, there's a bigger fish to hook."

Oley and Strewl exchanged glances. Oley said, "Bigger fish?"

A knock on the door prevented the answer. John Oley's brow wrinkled and his hand slid inside his suit coat to the gun in his shoulder holster. "You expecting someone else, Phil?"

Zeigler pointed at Holinsky and the door. "Sam Gross called last week with a problem. Something about some furs. Asked if I could help."

Holinsky checked the peephole. The man at the door was short and chunky with smoke-colored receding hair and a drawn face. His tight necktie forced his skin to lap over his high starched shirt collar. "It's Sam alright."

Holinsky took Sam Gross's hat and coat and said, "Sammy...heard you showed Phil and the others here a good time last summer."

Zeigler called out. "He sure did! Come on over here, Sam. Have a drink. Remember this guy?"

John Oley shook Sam's hand. "If you're not locked in a Canadian jail, July in Toronto beats July in Albany anytime. Say Sam, this is my partner—one that sent the bail money."

Gross shook Strewl's hand. In a Polish-Russian accent that Strewl had difficulty understanding Sam said, "You did my friends good. Next time you're in Toronto, it's on me."

Zeigler slapped a drink into Sam's hand. "Gimme a few minutes, Sam."

Oley swiped his face with his hand. He liked Sam Gross ok, but he had gone on alert. He feared any slip of the tongue that might tip off the O'Connells or sink their plan before it got started. Their plan would have them dealing with the powerhouse of Albany, New York. Wise thing was to keep the deal quiet.

He reached for his hat and coat. "Say guys, I need some grub. Gonna grab a steak."

Al Fisher pushed his glasses up and set the opium pipe aside. "Hold on, John. Let me show yuh Anna Belle's Steakhouse—just around the corner."

Strewl rubbed his cheek with his glass while Fisher and Oley slipped their coats on. Turning to Phil Zeigler he said, "I'll pick the place and set it up. You just get the guys and pick him up is all."

Oley followed Fisher out of the room and closed the door. Zeigler put one hand on his back pocket and pulled at his nose with the other. He watched as Strewl draped his coat over his arm and headed for the door. Strewl was about to open it when he said, "What the hell you want the old man for? Get the kid. He's the prince among three kings. They'd pay plenty to get him back—no questions asked."

Strewl nodded his head. "I'll think on it, Phil." He held his hat and pointed it at Zeigler. "I'm talking more than a hundred G's. If you can't find the right mob you let me know and I'll get another."

***

Minutes later Strewl entered the steakhouse and was hit with the pleasant aroma of grilled steak. The place was cozy because the kitchen ovens kept it warm on a cold damp day. Waiters were scurrying about with trays.

He joined Oley and Fisher who were already seated. The contrast between the men was striking. Fisher wore a drab gray suit. Black-framed glasses sat on his thick nose, and his dark hair was cut squirrelly smooth on the sides. He looked like an accountant. His companions looked like lower-middle-class businessmen.

When John Oley finished eating his plate held only a bare bone and an empty potato skin. He wiped his mouth with a white linen napkin and lit up a cigarette. "You're right, Al. Best steak I ever had."

Leaning close to Fisher, Oley lowered his voice. "We lost a lot on the Trachnier deal. A bit low on cash right now. Know where we can get some quick?"

"Such as?"

Oley scanned the surroundings to make sure no one was listening. "We know a bank close to Albany but we got the same problem as before. We're too well known. Need some outsiders. Me and Manny can do the ground work but we need some trigger men. We'd split 50-50."

Fisher removed his glasses and began cleaning them with a linen napkin. He dropped his chin and said in a low voice, "Big Charlie is…busy. Have to be after April."

Oley blew smoke into the air. "No problem. It'll be warmer in May."

***

On a sunny day in May, Manny Strewl was at the wheel of a Willy-Knight. John Oley, in the back, slid forward and leaned close to Big Charlie Scarnici in the front passenger seat. Oley raised his voice above the hum of the tires as they rolled across the steel slats of the Hudson River drawbridge in Albany.

"Don't worry, Charlie. They only raise the bridge early in the morning and late in the afternoon."

Manny Strewl turned left off the steel drawbridge onto Broadway and zipped west along the river road. Before long they spotted the sign: 'City of Rensselaer.' They crossed over a small hill and the main attraction came into view: a big red lollipop-shaped sign on a large building of gray stone. Arched over the rounded top of the sign was the word 'Rensselaer.' Beneath it, along the stick of the lollipop, the sign read 'County Bank.'

The Willy-Knight waited at the stoplight at the intersection of Partition Street and Broadway. Big Charlie Scarnici told Strewl to pull in at the store next door to the bank.

The light turned green. Strewl made a left from Broadway onto Partition and parked in front of the General Store. Tan bricks framed the store's display window. Above the store were three more floors that housed apartments.

Scarnici poked Strewl's shoulder and gestured with his thumb. "Let's take a walk."

Strewl told Oley to stay with the car. "Back in a few minutes, John."

On the sidewalk in front of the store, Scarnici perused the candy and tableware and figurines in the window. His other eye studied the Rensselaer County Bank. Gray columns supported the Corinthian-style pitched roof. The bank was one story shorter than the apartments beside it. Metal bars framed the arched glass entrance.

Charlie tilted his head at the wooden doors. "Big doors. Thick, huh?"

"Two inches of solid oak," Strewl said, pretending to wipe dirt from his eye. "They keep them open in summer, only use the glass doors."

They strolled past the bank. Scarnici pulled on his lip. "Apartments mean kids. Flatten one in the street and there'll be all hell to pay."

A pedestrian approached. When they were alone again Strewl said, "You're right, Charlie, so I figure we hit the bank on a weekday, while the kids are in school, the dads at work and the old ladies doing the wash."

Scarnici turned back toward the car and dropped his voice low. "How much did you say?"

Strewl snickered. "Go on and get in the car. I'll be right back—wanna show you something."

Strewl ducked into the General Store and exited with a copy of the *Rensselaer Eagle*. He got behind the wheel and opened the paper, pointing to an advertisement. He read aloud: "Rensselaer County Bank and Trust Company. Main Office, 810 Broadway. Branch Bank at 156 Broadway. Edward J. Guilfoil, President. Assets over $3,000,000."

Strewl pushed the paper to Scarnici and started the car. "How about a slice of that? Only one small problem, which I'm about to show you."

He pulled around the corner and started up Broadway. Two blocks later, he pointed to a dirty red brick shoebox-shaped building. The door was off center, to the left, and above it cream-colored words: 'Rensselaer Police.'

Big Charlie Scarnici sat up straight. He planted one hand on the dash and one on the seat back and checked both directions. "Cheese-us! I can spit from here to the bank."

Strewl gestured toward the rear window. "The branch bank is a mile in the other direction."

Scarnici scratched his forehead with his thumb. "Branch banks don't have jack. This changes a few things."

"Another bank?"

Scarnici sucked in his lower lip and dropped his head. When he looked up he said, "No, we just need some guys with experience is all. Better use my regular guys. And maybe a bigger gun. What kinda deal we talking?"

Strewl pulled to the curb and took cigars from his inside coat pocket and handed them round. He bit the end off his and pulled his palm across his mouth. "Here's the deal, Charlie." He lit the cigar. "I figure me and John will map everything out. We'll foot the expense of setting things up. You and your guys do the job quick-like then get out of town. Me and John will take the heat, but the cops won't be able to do anything—cause we'll be clean. And you aren't known in these parts, so you'll be clear. When things cool down you come back up and we snatch Packy O'Connell. It's a cinch."

Scarnici chewed his cigar and studied the police station. "Phil's guys are light on robbing banks. I was wondering—"

Oley spoke up. "Be careful. You can only slice a pie so many ways."

"Yeah, I know, but Big Joe Poffo and Max Parkin can cut a V at 20 feet with a .38. Reino's a good inside man. Those cops—" Scarnici pointed at the police station. "I better get hold of Artie."

Oley exchanged a glance with Strewl. "Who the hell is Artie?"

Scarnici chuckled. "Charles Arthur Floyd. Papers call him Pretty Boy Floyd."

Strewl raised his eyebrows at Oley then gave Scarnici a one-eyed stare. "Helluva high stepper, Charlie." He glanced at the police station. "Just remember, we don't need a blood bath up here."

Scarnici sat back with a stone face. He lit his cigar and inhaled and exhaled. "That's up to the cops. They'd better not get in the way. When's the curtain due to go up?"

Strewl pulled from the curb, made a u-turn on Broadway and headed back toward Albany. "Couple a weeks. Thinking the end of May. Have your guys come up early to check things out. We can use the same apartment we used to plan the Trachnier deal. Can yuh be ready by then?"

Scarnici flicked ashes out the window. "Doesn't take much planning to pull a trigger. We'll be ready."

***

During the last week of May in the same apartment where the failed Mush Trachnier kidnapping had been planned, Manny Strewl shoved toward Scarnici a paper with a sketch of the inside of the Rensselaer Bank. Squares along the sides and lower edge represented teller cages and a customer work desk. The vault was clearly labeled.

Strewl said, "Alarm buttons are under the counter. As long as the tellers keep their hands up they can't sound the alarm. Herbert Burhans is the head teller. Big deposits are made directly with him."

John Oley chuckled. "Something more to boot—a surprise, Charlie. Know why we picked May 29? Cause that's when the railroad receipts come in. This is gonna be a big haul!"

Poffo sniffed. "How yuh know when the deposits are made?"

"Easy... Bill Card. He works for the railroad and he's always the one makes the deposits. Brown derby, handlebar mustache—can't miss him."

Max Parkin pulled at his nose. "Guy might get suspicious if he sees someone watching or following him. Tellers too, for that matter."

Oley pulled a bundle from under the table. He untied it and out fell a blue jacket and pants and cap. "Thought of that. Picked these up in White Plains. Railroad regulation. Just like train conductors wear. You can look around wearing these and blend in with no problem. Whoever's the inside guy can have it."

He handed the uniform to Scarnici. "When your men bust in, the inside man can make sure everyone's hands are held high and off the alarm buttons."

Scarnici flipped on the hat and slid into the jacket and buttoned the brass buttons. "Not a bad fit."

***

On the morning of May 29, 1933, John Oley answered the telephone. "Oley here." He handed the receiver to Scarnici. "Pretty Boy for you."

Scarnici said, "Hell Floyd, you're late....Ah shit! Don't bring them here....You know

Mt. Kisco? It's by White Plains. See a guy named Ralph Zucco. Tell him I sent you. He'll let you hold up there a while. Tell Zucco I'll call him later."

He hung up the phone and shook his head. "Boston cops are all over Floyd. He can't make it."

Big Joe Poffo pushed past Little Charlie Herzog (who was using the alias Charlie Shore) and stepped between Tony Reino and John Oley. Poffo pointed at Strewl. "That makes us one short. One of your guys wanna join up?"

Strewl threw his pencil down on the map on the table. "Are you nuts? Anyone sees us hanging round a bank you may as well put up a sign. Use your stupid head!"

Poffo thrust a hand inside his suit coat. Angel Face Geary, Max Parkin and John Oley did the same.

Scarnici threw up his palms. "Hold it! Just lemme think a minute."

He put his hands to his temples. After a few seconds he dropped his hands. "So we're short a guy. Same plan. I'll take the tellers and the cash in the cages. Joe, you cover me. Anyone flinches—yuh cut 'em down. We'll leave the car idling outside with Little Charlie—and Little Charlie, you be ready to back us up if we need yuh. If any slouch on the street asks, say you're waitin' while your buddy makes a deposit. Reino, you're the lookout at the bank door. Watch for the cops. Their station house is only four minutes away."

Tony Reino took his .38 revolver from his belt and clicked open the bullet chamber and pushed the bullet ejector with his thumb. He held the empty chamber up to the light and said, "Won't be a problem. We can see them coming on that long straightaway. Be real easy to stop them."

Little Charlie grinned as he followed suit and reloaded his revolver. "Only takes five pounds of pressure on a trigger."

***

Just before noon a 1928 dark blue four-door Nash, license plate 3U4299, pulled around the corner near the Rensselaer County Bank on Partition Street. Scarnici, dressed in the blue uniform, got out of the Nash and began strolling around and watching for Bill Card and the expected railroad deposit.

At the intersection a small boy saluted Scarnici—who returned the salute. A few steps later a man in a suit flashed Scarnici a big smile and said, "Afternoon, Captain."

Scarnici tipped his hat and hurried back to the Nash. He ducked beside the car to get out of sight and tossed the uniform cap through the window. He muttered, "'Blend in,' he says. Gimme my coat."

Reino stepped from the car and handed Scarnici his brown coat. Scarnici yanked off the blue uniform coat and tossed it on the back floorboard. He mumbled, "Damn it! Everybody on the street wants to know me."

Reino nudged Scarnici. "No time, Charlie." He tilted his head toward a man with a brown derby and handlebar mustache and a leather case clutched under his arm. "Looks like the deposit has arrived."

Scarnici touched Little Charlie's shoulder. "Pull around front across from the bank. Poffo, stay with him until he parks—and keep the gun under wraps till you get inside. Max, you too. Reino, let's go."

Reino and Scarnici waited until the Nash had parked on Broadway before they headed for the bank. As they walked Reino suddenly hopped in front of Scarnici, facing him and gesturing over his shoulder. A flower lady was setting up shop right by the bank entrance.

Reino hissed, "Now what the hell do we do?"

Scarnici noted that Poffo and Parkin had left the car and started toward the bank. He brushed by Reino and said, "Plug her if she gets in the way."

He waited on the bank's top step for the others to catch up then leaned his back against the door and pushed it open. They trooped in. Poffo tore the brown paper off the machine gun and swung it up as he yelled, "Nobody move!"

Poffo kept the gun aimed at the tellers while moving slowly toward the back right corner. Coins dropped from customer Mary Kirsch's hands and hit the floor. They sounded like jingle bells. Her hand reached to catch a bouncing quarter.

Scarnici pointed one of his pistols at her. "No yuh don't, honey!"

Teller Agnes Babcock withdrew her hand from the customer and the bars on the teller cage and inched her finger toward the alarm button under the counter. Scarnici aimed at her head and pulled back the hammer with a loud click. "Don't!" he said.

Poffo waved the machine gun back and forth. "Hands up! Back up!"

From the raised hands of a teller named Gladis Ivecson dollar bills floated to the floor like snowflakes.

Max Parkin aimed his gun at the head teller's desk which was situated near the open vault. The teller and the railway agent were in his line of fire. He moved closer and shouted, "Up, Buster!"

He grabbed Bill Card by the shoulder, yanked him to his feet and shoved him along. "Move!" he ordered.

A male voice said, "Mary, Gladis, ladies—do what he says."

The voice belonged to a slender gentleman who took a step around the teller cage on the far end. Scarnici raised his gun. "That's far enough!"

The man's light brown hair was parted down the middle and a gold chain lay across his gray pinstripe vest. He kept his hands held high as he side-stepped into full view. "Sir, I'm Herbert Burhans, the chief teller. I can assure you we don't want any trouble."

Scarnici waved both of his guns. "Great. Back up, join the rest of them. All of yuhs—in the corner."

Tellers and customers began moving toward the back corner. Scarnici holstered one gun, put a hand on the counter and jumped over the short gate to the back of the cages.

Burhans kept his hands high and motioned to the five tellers to move on back. "Be calm, ladies. Just do as he says."

Nicholas Walters, a bank clerk, had been at the end of
the teller cages with a ledger sheet in hand when Scarnici and
his gang came barreling in. Now he kept his hands high and
moved along with the tellers. He appeared to be corralling the
women into the corner. As he did so, he took a wide side step
and slid his foot over the newly installed silent alarm button in
the floor.

***

Clang-clang-clang. Patrolman William Castor reached up and
turned off the alarm on the switchboard. "Captain! Captain
Connery! The bank's alarm went off again."

A stout man in a blue police uniform with papers in one
hand bolted from a side office. He held his glasses in the other
hand as he pointed at the switchboard. "That damn thing. It's
the fifth time this month. Thought Guilfoil had it fixed last
week."

He glanced around the empty police station until he spotted
a balding seventy-two-year-old man in plain clothes with
scraggly gray sideburns returning his stare. "Stevens, time for
work. Go check out the bank. Tell Guilfoil if it happens again
I'll cite him for disturbing the peace."

"Excuse me, Captain," said a patrolman. "This just came in
on the wire. Boston's seen Pretty Boy Floyd and think—"

Captain Connery snatched the paper from the patrolman's
hand and said to Stevens, "Take Rabe here with yuh and teach
him something."

Detective James Stevens stifled a chuckle. "Let's make it
snappy, kid. Grandson's got a ball game tonight and I don't
wanna miss it."

Patrolman Rabe grabbed the car keys from below the
switchboard. When he turned back he bumped into a frowning
Detective Stevens who took the keys from his hand and said,
"I'll drive."

Rabe said, "This could be Floyd. Think we need the siren?"

Stevens opened the door to a car with Police painted on the side. "This town is too small for the likes of Pretty Boy Floyd. And no, we don't need the siren. After all the false alarms, why scare people?"

Detective Stevens sped the car down Broadway and swung into a parking slot in front of a brick apartment building two doors short of the bank on the opposite side. "Let's find out what's going on." He eased out of the car and checked up and down the street in both directions. There were no curious faces looking from the apartment windows. "Looks quiet," he said.

A car passed by. Detective Stevens led the way across Broadway. When he reached the other side he did a double take. A rumble was coming from the big-block eight-cylinder Nash parked at the corner. A powerful engine, yet there was no exhaust smoke coming from the tail pipe—which meant it was a finely tuned car, and that was an oddity in such an old car in a farming community.

Stevens could see the man at the wheel of the Nash turn his head left and right but he couldn't see his face. He noted the black knot of a hat ribbon on the white felt hat. Detective Stevens pulled at his jaw. The flower lady, Edna Jamell, held out a bunch of blue poesies. "Some flowers today, Detective?"

"Have to do some banking first, Edna."

At the bank's glass door Stevens glanced again at the Nash. The driver's elbow was resting on the open window but his shoulder was twisted back toward the bank. The hairs on the back of the detective's neck felt the steely gaze of the driver's eyes. Stevens slipped his hand inside his coat to his service revolver and peeped through the glass door. He didn't see anybody, which seemed odd because the noon hour was usually a busy one at the bank. He pushed the door open.

The glass in the door shattered in a hail of lead. He fell backwards onto the steps, his own gun spitting fire into the bank.

Patrolman Rabe dove right. A bullet found its mark in his thigh.

Rabe's outstretched arm knocked Edna Jamell to the ground. He dragged Edna behind a concrete column and began shooting—to the left at Reino in the bank's doorway and right toward Little Charlie across the street. Ricocheting bullets and concrete chips rattled the air.

Rabe's back was against the concrete wall. The crossfire had him pinned down. He was trapped and wounded, but kept firing.

Scarnici ran out, jumping over Stevens's body. His guns began belching fire at Patrolman Rabe. Chips sprang from the concrete column like popcorn.

Poffo swung around the bank door and pointed the machine gun at the column but Scarnici stopped him with a shout. "Save it!"

Parkin bolted from the bank and dashed across the street to the Nash. He broke a hole in the back window and began firing toward Rabe. Reino made a beeline for the passenger side where he stood on the running board and fired over the roof of the car before ducking inside.

Little Charlie Herzog was at the wheel. He backed the car into the middle of Broadway and jumped out into the street where he began shooting in the patrolman's direction.

Scarnici yelled. "Go! Go!"

Poffo darted toward the car.

Scarnici sprinted around Little Charlie and took the wheel. "Let's go!"

Parkin, inside the car, was busy reloading. As Little Charlie turned toward the car Detective Stevens rolled onto his side with gun raised. His bullet hit the car.

Herbert Burhans, the Chief Teller, ran out and scooped up Stevens's gun and fired. Little Charlie caught the lead from behind and arched his back. Hands reached to pull him into the backseat and Scarnici punched the gas pedal. The tires screamed and C-shaped tire marks traced the getaway path.

An approaching motorist coming south on Broadway saw the car speeding away. Burhans pointed in the direction the robbers took and called to the driver, "They robbed the bank!"

The motorist immediately tore after the Nash.

Scarnici was making good time. He zipped around a car then tossed his gun over to Reino and ordered, "Reload!"

Parkin was watching out the back window. After a bit he yelled, "We got company!"

Scarnici swerved around another car and straddled the white line. "Can yuh hit him?"

Parkin aimed out the back window and snarled, "Watch me!" But he soon broke into a laugh. "Hey! Looks like he's outta the game! A truck cut him off."

A voice called, "Little Charlie's not doing so well."

Reino snapped his revolver closed. "He's hit bad?"

Parkin turned Little Charlie over and examined the hole in his lower back on the left side. "I've seen worse—he'll make it."

As they neared the drawbridge leading into Albany Parkin yelled, "Look! A cop!" A police motorcycle was parked behind a car. The uniformed policeman stood next to the driver's door with citation book in hand.

The speeding Nash swerved as Scarnici reached for his gun and pulled back the hammer. He held it below the dashboard and said, "Act natural, act natural."

The motorcycle patrolman was Herbert Devlin. As the Nash passed him, Reino snapped him a salute.

Scarnici laughed at the image in the rear view mirror. The patrolman was scratching his head with one hand and had the other on his hip. The image grew smaller as the Nash zoomed over the steel drawbridge.

"No trouble now," Scarnici shouted. "We're in the clear!"

And for the time being, they were. But things were not as they seemed. For starters, Tony Reino—when he reloaded Scarnici's gun—put his own gun down and later made the error of picking up Scarnici's. The mistake would be his ticket to the electric chair.

What none of the men in the Nash understood on that day in May was that the dust cloud kicked up by the Nash's tires would become a tornado—a tornado headed straight their way. Big Charlie Scarnici had cackled with laughter when he sped by Patrolman Devlin at the drawbridge, yet six months later it would be Devlin who identified him as the driver of the getaway car and tagged Reino as a passenger.

The small town of Rensselaer on that 29th of May 1933 lost one of their finest. Detective Stevens did not survive. He had been one of the oldest active policemen in the section. The town's district attorney was a formidable character, and only seven months would pass before Scarnici would come up against him, as we will see in a later chapter.

Chapter 3
Butch is Selected

The tires of the Nash slowed to a muffled rumble after Big Charlie Scarnici made the left onto the brick pavement of South Pearl Street. From there he turned onto Catherine Street and then Morton Avenue where at number 148 he entered a concrete driveway between a pale blue single-family house and a red brick three-story apartment building. The drive led to an eight-bay single-story wooden garage. Each unit had double doors and a concrete floor.

At the sixth bay John Oley and Manny Strewl held the doors open and waved the Nash inside and hurried to close the doors behind it. The car fit inside almost as snugly as a hand in a glove.

Scarnici shoved his door open and it bumped against the wall. He growled, "Reino, check the street."

Tony Reino squeezed out of the passenger side and hustled over to the window. "Don't see no cops."

At the opposite end of the garage Oley and Strewl stayed out of sight as they peered through the small-paned windows in the door. Strewl called, "No one following yuhs—you're clear."

Oley spotted the broken rear window. "Anyone hit?"

Little Charlie's voice came from inside the car. "Not bad." He climbed out, holding a handkerchief over his wound and limping.

Parkin held up a blood-stained hand. "Had to punch out the back window," he said with pride.

John Oley moved in for a closer look and noted a dent on the inside of the roof. He moved around the back of the car and put his finger over a hole in the left rear fender. "Somebody got lucky," he said.

Reino pushed his way forward. "Not too damn lucky."

Oley swiped a hand across his cheek. "Whaddya mean?"

Reino stuck his pistol in his belt. "Left one lying in the street." He eased around the car. Scarnici had laid out the money on the floor in a puddle of sunshine. Reino asked, "How much we get, Charlie?"

Scarnici's voice trailed off to a mumble. "One hundred, one-fifty…"

Manny Strewl ran his finger over a dimple in the left rear fender. It bulged outward, which told him the bullet had come from inside the car. He quietly opened the car door and pushed his finger into the backseat bullet hole in the pleated black cotton seat. When he inched out, he bumped Oley's arm and cocked his head at the bullet-dimpled fender. He said, "Nerves."

Scarnici turned with a scowl. "What's that?"

"Said it was damn lucky they didn't get the tire," Strewl answered. He pointed at the small pile of money in the sunspot on the floor. "Is that all?"

Scarnici stood with hands on hips. "We got busy."

"Whaddya mean, busy?"

"The son-of-a-bitch dropped some laundry off…at a place *close to the branch bank.*"

Oley glanced at Strewl. His eyes widened. "Branch bank?"

Scarnici said, "Yeah, branch bank. You screwed up!" He held up a deposit slip. "The guy had the money alright— more'n sixteen thousand! But he did his wife a favor—dropped the laundry off to the wash ladies a coupla doors down from the branch bank and decided to go ahead and make the deposit. He only stopped by the main branch to tell 'em he'd already made it."

Manny slicked back his hair. "How the hell was I supposed to know the jackass was gonna do that?" He frowned and shook his head. "What about the vault?"

Scarnici kneeled down to resume counting. "Didn't have time—the cops showed, we had to make a break for it."

Big Joe Poffo swung the tommy gun onto his shoulder. "Yeah—and their luck ran out."

"Ran out?"

Reino pushed his hat up with his thumb. "Cops should never have opened the door. We nailed 'em good."

Scarnici interrupted his count to add, "Yeah—from here on out they won't be bothering anyone."

Strewl turned toward Oley and raised his eyebrows. He turned and kicked the rear tire below the bullet hole. "Sure as hell can't take this to New York."

Standing with his hands crossed over his chest, Manny Strewl stared at the floor. After a moment he said, "John, get hold of Angel Face, have him get the truck ready. I'm gonna go get some grub and some bandages—and poke around Rensselaer for a bit, see what's going on." To Scarnici he said, "You guys go ahead and breeze outta town late tonight. So what's the count?"

Scarnici handed him a fistful of cash. "Two grand. One-G each."

Strewl tipped his hat back and took the cash. "Damn it all! Barely enough to cover expenses on this one."

Scarnici was dealing out cash to the others. "Yeah, and a five way split." He narrowed his eyes and spoke directly to Strewl. "This Packy O'Connell of yours sure better be worth a helluva lot more than this."

Strewl pulled at his nose and peered over Scarnici's shoulder. Poffo was still cradling the loaded machine gun. Tony Reino had one foot on the rear bumper and his coat pulled back to expose his revolver while he counted his share.

Strewl knew there was no honor among thieves. He knew it would have to occur to Scarnici and the others that they could make their split bigger by killing him and Oley. He also knew he and Oley were out-gunned. It was a time for some fast talking. He would appeal to their sense of greed. He slipped his share of the cash in his pocket and said, "Don't worry, Charlie. The O'Connell family's got the bucks—and I'm damn sure Packy don't carry his laundry around."

Poffo poked his wad of cash in Manny's face. "He better be. We didn't come all this way for chicken feed."

Strewl pushed Poffo's hand aside. "We got it wired. But just in case, we'll follow Packy a while longer to make sure."

"Yuh better hurry up or—"

"Or what, Joe? You gonna pull out? You got some pressing business elsewhere? Why don't you stick your face out that door and see how far you get before somebody fingers you?"

Scarnici rested a hand on Poffo's shoulder. "Man's right, Joe. Things've gotta cool down some."

He shoved Poffo aside and gave Strewl and Oley his 'I'll handle it' look. Head cocked, one eye half closed, slight nod. "How much time we talking?"

John Oley stared up at the rafters. "Three weeks or so? Around the twenty-first of June. By then this robbery will be back page news. We'll call yuhs, you come up and get the lay of the land—and we snatch Packy around the twenty-third. By July first—we're rolling in dough."

Poffo let the tommy gun drop to his side. "We'd better be."

Strewl tugged at his ear. "John here will work on the truck, I'll get the other stuff yuh'll be needing." He looked from one to the other. Poffo, Reino, Parkin, back to Scarnici. Little Charlie, who had been slightly wounded by a bullet during the shootout, had settled against the wall in a corner and was sacked out.

Strewl pulled his hat down, prepared to leave. He said, "Not safe for you guys to go wandering outside. Just hang out in here."

***

The garage occupants had quite a wait. The truck did not arrive until about four in the morning. Angel Face Geary was at the wheel of a midsize truck with canvas covered sides. He turned off the headlights and coasted down the dark ally. Before Geary could get out Strewl appeared and spoke in a low voice. "Time's short. And remember, they don't need to know everything."

John Oley, in the passenger seat, dashed out a cigarette. "Man's right, Percy. Scarnici and the others can read it in the papers. The sooner they're gone, the better for us all. And far as I'm concerned, there's not much to tell anyway."

Angel Face followed Oley to bay six. The double doors were cracked open. He cut in front of John and said in a low voice, "Charlie, it's me—open up."

Scarnici and Reino pushed the garage doors open. Scarnici shoved his revolver back in his belt. "Was beginning to wonder."

Oley signaled for Strewl to roll the truck forward. "When yuh killed the cop yuh stirred up a hornet's nest, Charlie. Just had to wait till all was quiet, yuh know?"

Strewl left the engine running and hurried to join the others. "The Nash is hot as a stove! Some motorcycle cop got the plate number."

Scarnici said, "Ha-ha! If they ever find a Max Glub—they can have him."

Oley pointed at the truck. "There's some oil cans under the front seat, in case yuh need 'em."

The robbers filed out of the garage and into the truck. Oley added, "There's a chunk of canvas in the back to keep the wind off yuhs."

Scarnici took the driver's seat. Strewl stepped onto the running board beside him. "Two hours till sun up. Most of the cops think you already slipped out of town but there's still troopers covering the river roads, so if I was you I'd head west a little then turn south. Oh, and by the way, what about the Nash?"

Scarnici released the handbrake. "Slipped your buddy Barnett a C-note to keep it parked awhile. If he asks about the car or somebody name of Albert Sileo—just tell him ole Albert croaked in a accident. Let him keep it!"

Strewl stepped down and waved a hand. "I'll let yuh know when things cool down."

The truck disappeared and rumbled down Morton Avenue. Angel Face Geary helped close the garage doors and he and Strewl and Oley began the short walk to where John Oley's Pontiac was parked.

Strewl kicked a pebble. "Percy, anything new with Packy O'Connell?"

"Not much. Plans on joining Dan up at his lake house for a spell. Solly's still keeping his head down, mostly stays out of town. You still thinking the end of June for the snatch?"

Oley snorted. "Huh! Every yahoo in the area's got Big Charlie's description. If we still use him and his crowd we may as well wave a red flag."

Strewl lit a cigar. "Better his ass than ours. I can't wait to see the morning papers. A veteran cop gunned down in a bank holdup. And all for a lousy thousand dollars."

Oley said, "Betcha the whole town of Rensselaer's gonna shut down for the funeral." He flicked cigarette ashes into the cool night air. "Not much money for financing a kidnapping, Manny."

"I know, John. Say—yuh remember the Jersey guys we dealt with last year?"

Oley drew his palm down his face and rubbed his chin. "Yeah. Waxy Gordon and his mob. Yuh thinking to use Waxy's guys to snatch Packy? It may be outta their line."

Strewl got into the front passenger seat. "Money's one hell of a persuader."

Angel Face settled in the back seat and Oley started the engine of the maroon Pontiac. As he pulled away from the curb he said, "Big Charlie ain't gonna like being cut out of things."

"Didn't say cut him out, John. Just wanna keep our options open."

***

Strewl and Oley set their first land mine in place when they involved the Waxy Gordon mob. It had connections to the Dutch Schultz Mob. Strewl and Oley were right when they figured the Albany cops and citizens would not recognize members of the Waxy Gordon Mob, but the ensuing investigation of the kidnapping would bring unwanted attention to Dutch Schultz for something he didn't do. In January 1934 Dutch Schultz would bail Tony Reino and Little Charlie Herzog out of jail, and shortly thereafter they would be found dead. The presumption was made by many that Schultz had them eliminated.

The second land mine awaiting Strewl and Oley was put in place when fate itself caused them to switch the kidnap target to the 'Prince of Albany.'

When Strewl mentioned the Waxy Gordon Mob its name was already changing to the West Side Mob because it had lost its leader. When Waxy Gordon pushed too far into Dutch Schultz's New York territory, he disappeared. The West Side Mob operated on the west side of New York City with headquarters across the river in New Jersey. Its leadership had been split between Thomas Dugan and Charles Harrigan. They could see the wisdom of avoiding any tangle with Dutch Schultz and wisely kept their still in Hoboken, New Jersey.

Charles Harrigan had only one eye. He said he lost the other one in a knife fight and refused to wear a patch over it because he wanted to look tough. He had an ugly scar on his right cheek. Behind his back his friends whispered that he likely lost the eye to one of thirteen bullets that punctured his body when a 'competitor' sprayed him with a machine gun. Harrigan would outlive his family and his cronies. Before his death in 1982 he commented, "It wasn't worth it all."

Two days after the robbery of the Rensselaer Bank, John Oley put a call through to the West Side Mob. It was answered by the heavy-set double-chinned "Big Mac" Christy Miller.

Miller removed the cigarette he habitually kept dangling from the space where three of his teeth were missing. He handed the phone to Harrigan. "For you. Some guy named Oley looking for Waxy."

Harrigan threw his cards down on the poker table. "Auh, what the hell? I'm out. Luck's been shitty all night anyway." He took the phone. "Harrigan here."

"This's John Oley from Albany. Looking to make a deal with Waxy. Is he around?"

"I remember yuh, John, but Waxy, he uh…he ain't around no more. Me and Dugan's running things. Whatcha got?"

"Wanna clip a heavy weight. We're talking over two hundred thousand. You in?"

"Price sounds right. Meet me Thursday in the Bronx. Same place and time where you met Waxy." Harrigan handed the phone back to Miller. "Guys, we got company coming down from Albany in a few days. Make sure everything's stashed away in case I bring them here. I'm going to the shed to tell Garguillo to clean things out."

Harrigan went down two flights of stairs and out the back of the seven-story brick apartment house at 734 Adams Street and into a sixteen-by-twenty wooden shack. He pulled a handkerchief from his back pocket and placed it over his mouth as the blue-black smoke came from the open firebox below a large boiler. "Oh, hell!"

George Garguillo was a stocky man with a moon face. He looked like a six-foot man crunched into a five-foot-five body. Had a thick neck, coal black hair and dark olive skin. He was the disposal man for the mob, meaning he burned the victims to ashes—dead or alive. Warden Francis Lanagan of the Massachusetts State Prison would later remark that Garguillo was so mean even the prison guards were afraid of him, even when he was bound in chains. Their fear ended in 1938 when guards found him swinging by his neck from a bed sheet.

Garguillo walked like an ape, hunched over and swinging his arms. Harrigan fanned the air. "Wish you'd wait till the wind shifts, George. This place is gonna stink for days."

Garguillo used his shovel to open the firebox door and pull out the box. He touched his shovel to the crusted arms that crossed the man's charred face, a posture that indicated the victim was still alive when he was put into the firebox. The arms crumbled to dust in a puff of smoke. "Couldn't wait. What's up?"

"John Oley's coming to talk a deal. Gonna meet him at the Bronx place. Better clean everything up just in case I bring him here. Dugan will be in charge till I get back."

Garguillo shoveled the human dust into a bucket and placed it next to the others in the corner. "I'll need the truck. Wanna dump these in the river tonight."

Harrigan was already on his way out. He called over his shoulder. "Yeah, when Sonny gets back, take the truck."

***

Two weeks after the bank robbery Manny Strewl strolled up Albany's State Street past the bail bondsman shop and slipped into the Waldorf lunchroom. John Oley was seated in a booth in the back corner reading the *Knickerbocker Press*.

Strewl slipped into the seat opposite and noticed on the back page of the paper a sale price of $11 for men's suits. He flicked the paper with his finger. "Abe Friedman can cut yuh a better deal on a good suit."

Oley lowered the paper and Strewl continued. "Made me a suit of pure wool with a three-button coat. Hell, since you're a friend of mine, he'd probably even throw in a 59-nine-cent shirt free of charge."

Oley glanced at the ad. "Maybe I'll swing by. Angel Face might be interested in some silk shirts. He goes through 'em faster than kids eating sugar bread."

The waitress appeared. Strewl ordered coffee and apple pie.

Oley watched the waitress disappear into the kitchen. "Think we're gonna need Harrigan's men."

"Whaddya mean? Things have cooled off. Big Charlie and the boys are in the clear."

Oley rubbed his face. "Only the ones that are left." He pulled from his pocket an article from the June 10th edition of the *Troy Eagle* and slid it across the table.

Strewl waited until the approaching waitress set down his coffee and pie and got out of earshot before he began reading aloud in a low voice. "Two men were found shot to death on Purchase Street in Harrison, New York. Their fingerprints identified them as Max Parkin and Marcel Poffo, alias Big Joe Poffo. Both men were suspects in the Rensselaer Bank robbery on May 29th and the murder of Detective Stephens."

Strewl scratched his head. "That should take some of the heat off us."

Oley said, "Read the rest."

"The medical examiner determined that one bullet entered Max Parkin from the back of the right ear and exited over the right eye. A second bullet entered the back of the neck and exited through the right eye. A third bullet entered through the stomach and exited the back."

Strewl glanced up, his eyes wide. "Someone made sure he was dead."

"Read on."

"The body of Marcel Poffo had pistol shot wounds in the head and abdomen, both of which were fatal."

Strewl frowned. "I do remember Angel Face saying that Big Charlie doesn't have any *old* brash friends. Guess the split wasn't good enough for Charlie."

Oley reached for the clipping. "Maybe. But you didn't read far enough. Says here they found $221 and some change in Parkin's pocket. And $8.60 in Poffo's."

Strewl gazed out the window where people were getting off the trolley car. He said to himself in a low voice, "First the shootout, and now this. Could mean some unwanted attention turned our way. Hell, if Scarnici gets caught, cops might even hang a murder rap around our necks."

He turned back to the table and sloshed coffee around in his cup. A moment later he exhaled and caught his friend's eye. "It's too late now to cut Scarnici out. But I'm not wanting a bullet in the back of my head. Best I can figure, we better use Harrigan and his men. At least that way we hamper Big Charlie some. Will be better to bring Harrigan's men up early so they get the lay of the land."

Oley rubbed his face. "Already thought of that. They're over at the Jay Street apartment. With Percy."

"What about the landlord?"

Oley smirked. "Six months rent upfront will keep Mrs. Pierce's mouth shut. But I'm thinking we oughta use one of Harrigan's trucks to move Packy. Somebody's sure to recognize ours. We can stash him in the same place in the Bronx that Scarnici set up for the Mush job."

Strewl nodded his head side to side. "Don't think so. If Scarnici's as hot as I think he is, the cops will be watching all his hangouts. We'd best come up with another place."

Oley shook his head in agreement. "Yeah. Well, we can stash Harrigan's truck in that Elm Street spot down from your place. And let Harrigan find somewhere to stash Packy."

Strewl folded the paper. "Sounds ok—just don't mention it to Big Charlie. We'll have to string him along, buy us some time."

Oley lit a cigarette. "How much time yuh thinking?"

Strewl pulled a cigar from his pocket. "I'm thinking we get our guy near the end of June, the 20th or thereabouts, then a week for negotiations. By first of July we'll all be in fat city!" He lit the cigar and sent a plume of smoke toward the ceiling. "Any more word on Packy's wanderings?"

"Not much. Goes here and there, no set schedule. Not much for the broads, plays cards mostly. Every Friday he hits a show. Real milk-toast kind of guy."

Strewl blew a smoke ring into the air. "That's good for us. Just make sure you keep your head down. Don't want Packy to get wise to the fact he's being followed."

***

Twelve days later in the Jay Street apartment John Oley placed beer bottles on the kitchen table next to a map of Albany and stepped back to light a cigarette while Big Charlie Scarnici, Percy 'Angel Face' Geary and Charles Harrigan began studying the map.

Oley pointed with his cigarette to the square marked Capitol. "Packy works here. He brown bags it, takes lunch on a park bench on the lawn out front. That's where you guys can eyeball him. We'll snatch him late at night after his card game.

We'll box him in just like we did on the Mush job only this time—"

Oley hurried to the ringing phone in the living room. Seconds later he bellowed, "You're shitting me! No way!" A couple of minutes later he said, "I'll run it by them."

He stomped back into the kitchen where he shoved one hand into his back pocket and rubbed his face with the other. A few seconds passed before he said, "That was Manny. Change of plans."

Scarnici wiped his mouth on his sleeve. "A bit late in the game for that, John."

Oley swished the map off the table to the floor. "Son-of-a-bitch!"

"What's up?"

Oley covered his face with his hands. "Packy O'Connell died this morning. News just hit the streets. Something about his heart."

Angel Face Geary laughed at the ceiling. "This kidnapping stuff sure is easier than hijacking trucks…long as yuh don't starve in the meantime."

Oley said, "Go ahead, Percy, laugh it up! Me and Manny and you and Francis—we're gonna go to the funeral. Harrigan, best thing for you and your guys is to keep low and out of sight."

Geary said, "Why do I need to go the funeral?"

Oley raised his eyebrows and chewed his lip. In a deadpan tone he said, "New plan. Strewl says we're gonna go after Butch."

"Butch O'Connell? Solly's kid?"

"One and the same. Manny got to thinking about what Zeigler said. Butch O'Connell is a prince among three kings. Which means we can ask a king's ransom!"

Geary scratched the side of his head with his beer bottle. "Don't know, John. Gonna take some more time to—"

Oley said, "Nope—gonna cut some corners. And even Charlie's gonna go to the funeral. Manny said everything's all set up and we just have to change the mark. At the funeral Big Charlie can size up the entire O'Connell clan in one shot. No sense wasting time. Right, Charlie?"

Scarnici rubbed his hands together. "Now you're talking, John."

Geary shook his head "I...I don't know—doing business at a funeral...that's bad luck, yuh know?"

Oley chuckled. "Don't worry, Percy. If it'll make yuh feel better, I'll say three *Hail Marys* in penance."

***

At the cemetery two days later, the crowd separated to make way for the six men carrying the oak casket to the gravesite. At some distance from the main crowd of mourners stood John Oley, his brother Francis, Percy Geary and Big Charlie Scarnici. Manny Strewl came up behind them and poked John in the back. "It's me. Don't turn around."

Oley talked from the corner of his mouth. "Wondered when you were gonna show."

Strewl nudged Scarnici. "The O'Connell family is at the head of the casket. Big guy with the mush melon head that's built like a beach ball? That's Dan."

Scarnici said, "One with the white-wall-tire haircut and glasses?"

Strewl chuckled. In a low voice he said, "Yeah, that's him. The provider. He's the banker for the family. They need anything, he gets it. Money to run for office? Call Dan O'Connell. One with the banana nose is his brother, Ed. The family lawyer. Ed makes everything legit and keeps 'em all out of trouble. All of 'em live in big houses and drive big Marmon cars. Dan even has a second house on Thompson Lake."

"What's his source?"

The priest raised his voice. "Let us bow our heads and pray."

Strewl moved closer to Scarnici and said beneath the rumble of the prayer, "They were big into bootlegging. Now they own the local brewery—Hendricks Beer, and just like you'd expect, they got a lock on the market."

Oley tilted his head sideways. "Don't forget bookmaking. Word on the street is they made millions in the baseball pool scam."

Scarnici pinched his nose. "Sound rich enough."

Francis Oley rolled his gum from one side of his mouth to the other. "There's more to it. Dan uses his money to put his people on the Alcohol Board. My brother here is just as tight with the O'Connells as Mush Trachnier—but the board turned 'em both down, didn't give either one of 'em a beer license."

John said, "Yeah—didn't mean a thing, all those years I worked for the sonsabitches. They just flat out denied me a license."

Scarnici dropped his chin. "Sounds like somebody maybe oughta muscle in, take over."

John Oley whispered, "Legs Diamond tried."

Strewl's voice was barely audible. "Albany cops haven't solved that murder yet. Remember what I said about them giving money to guys that run for office?"

"Yeah?"

"Even the police chief is an elected official."

Percy Geary quipped, "So are the judges."

Scarnici snarled, "Sounds like a nice little setup. Yuh say he's called Uncle Dan?"

"Uncle to everybody on the Southside—a turkey every Thanksgiving, ton of coal at Christmas and a lamb for Easter."

Francis Oley spit his gum onto the cemetery grass. "And all yuh have to do to get your free turkey? Just vote the way Uncle Dan says."

"What about the rest of the clan?"

Strewl spoke up from behind, warning them to keep their voices down and stare straight ahead. He proceeded to answer Scarnici's question. "The old lady? She's the mother. Dan lives with her out on Whitehall Road. The plain Jane next to her is the sister, Maud. She's a school teacher across the river. The short skinny one, that's the senior John O'Connell. He's known as Solly. Stays busy getting into trouble so his lawyer brother can bail him out."

Francis put his fingers over his mouth and spoke through them. "Solly's got debt markers dropped around like grass seed. The back wall of my joint is plastered with 'em—from a fin up to C-notes. I tell Solly to pay up—his mouthpiece brother shows up, says I gotta take fifty cents on the dollar or see it all tossed out in court and get nothing."

Strewl added, "And the judge in the case, by the way, would be an *elected* judge. Solly's also known to run a little book operation, and from what I hear on the street he's not a bad shot with a .38. Wheels and deals with the bootleggers."

"Anyone I know?"

John Oley spoke up. "Way I heard it, after the Trachnier deal Solly went south and hung around Poughkeepsie. Chummed with Willie McCabe and Jimmy Amando."

Scarnici wrinkled his brow. "Is that so?"

John whispered, "Solly's got an itch for the ladies. Him and his old woman don't live together no more."

Scarnici lifted one foot and shifted his stance. "So who's the beefy buffalo with the looker on his arm?"

The priest raised his voice to a loud and solemn "Amen." The mourners by the casket began mingling.

Strewl set his hat on his head and pulled it low to cover his face. "We've just introduced you to the three kings of Albany. Dan, Ed and Solly. The beefy buffalo is our prince. John O'Connell, Junior. Friends call him Butch."

Scarnici squinted and studied the sandy-haired young man. "Big mountain of flesh—must weigh two hundred at least."

"According to the sports pages, Butch stands five-eleven and weighs in at 235."

Scarnici tilted his head. "Sports page?"

"Amateur boxer. Went the distance two weeks ago against Chip Robins. Was one helluva slugfest!"

Scarnici zeroed in on Butch O'Connell, noting how he stood in a fighter's stance even while shaking hands. Left foot forward. "He won't go down easy. Does he carry a piece?"

People were beginning to pass by. Strewl lowered his head before he answered. "Word on the street says he's lily clean. No gun."

Francis Oley chimed in. "Wears a marksmen ribbon on his uniform."

"Uniform?"

"Weekend soldier—some sort of officer in the Army Reserve. Just because he don't carry don't mean he don't know how to use. He's been through the police academy too."

Scarnici pulled his suit coat snuggly over his shoulder holster. "Well, looks like we're gonna need Harrigan and his guys. Between the dozen or so of us we oughta be able to clip the target."

Geary interrupted in a low voice. "Better tell him about Fahey."

Strewl rubbed his eyes. "Oh yeah, forgot. Mary Fahey. She's Butch's fiancée. Her old man's a cop, a sergeant in the sixth precinct."

Scarnici whispered to the ground. "To me a cop's just another target."

When the crowd had thinned out Strewl fitted his tan hat on his head and said in a muted voice, "It's settled then. We use the same plan, and Harrigan's rail truck. It has a secret compartment already built into it. He'll bring it up next week."

John Oley mumbled, "I'd better pay my respects to the family. I'll catch up with yuhs later."

Angel Face Geary stepped in front of John and his brother Francis. "Hold it, John. I gotta tell yuh…planning this at a funeral ain't right. It's breaking the rules."

John Oley scratched at his cheek. "Going soft on me, Percy? Truth is, we didn't plan nothing—just changed targets is all. And one thing you can be glad of, I worked so long for Uncle Dan I'll know what he's gonna do before he does. He's like us—a hustler. Only thing you gotta do is keep an eye on Butch, and in a coupla days I'll catch up with yuh."

Thunder rumbled in the distance as dark clouds gathered. John and Francis Oley shook hands with the O'Connell family. Angel Face Geary headed back to his car. He felt sure that even the worst mobsters avoided doing business at a funeral out of respect for the dead, yet here he was planning a dastardly crime against the deceased's family. He mumbled to himself, "Just ain't right."

***

A week later at the Elm Street garage Charles Harrigan massaged his empty eye socket as he watched Harold "Red" Crowley tie down the canvas on the truck. This Ford truck had a flat bed body and was called a rail truck. It had four 2 X 6 boards evenly spaced that looked like rails. The boards rose 42 inches above the truck floor. At the nose of the truck bed was a large plank that ran from bottom to top and was used to hold an advertising sign. Harrigan called out, "Make sure it's tight. Don't wanna leave a trail of canvas all the way to New Jersey."

Red Crowley got his nickname because of his bushy red hair and sun-burnt complexion. He was the typical Irishman with blue eyes and a bawdy grin that revealed square teeth. His medium-size five-foot-eight body was pinched at the waist and hid his street-brawl toughness. Because he was an Irish Catholic he refused to murder anyone. What he did instead was beat his target to a pulp. On his left forearm he had a tattoo of a cross and below it the name 'Katy.' He had a knife scar that ran from his adam's apple all the way around the right side of his neck. It made him wary of letting people within arm's length.

He stood on the third board, yanked the rope into a tight knot and swiped at the sweat on his brow with a rolled-up sleeve. He said, "Mine are tight. But Sweeney's no Boy Scout."

James Sweeney, alias James Doyle, was the mob's go-fer boy. He too had a scar on his head and some of his teeth had been replaced with gold ones. His average looks, including brown eyes and chestnut hair, allowed him to blend in anywhere. He was so hard to find that the O'Connell kidnap charge against him expired due to the statute of limitations. The government handled the situation similarly to what they did to Al Capone. In 1937 they would convict Sweeney of car theft and tax evasion and he would spend three years in prison.

Dugan and McGlone joined Tony Reino at the front of the truck bed where there was an advertising board. At the top the rectangular sign had faded white letters in a semicircle that read, 'Williams AST.'

Reino inspected the secret compartment. Dugan looked over his shoulder. "Heard you and Big Charlie were still kinda hot in these parts after the Rensselaer Bank job."

Reino faced Dugan. "We got it covered. Just hold up your end of the bargain. I'm just hoping this compartment is big enough.

Sonny McGlone stepped closer and curled his fists. "We don't intend to get pinched by some trigger-happy crackerjack that bumped off—"

Dugan held his arm across Sonny's chest. "Cool off, Sonny." Then Dugan squared off with Reino. "We were invited to this party, see? And we don't have the whole damn state of New York looking for us, neither."

Reino planted his fists on his hips. "Don't bother me none."

Harrigan pushed between them. "Hard to operate if yuh can't show your face." He pointed at the secret compartment. "This compartment can hold two tin of whiskey so it'll hold this O'Connell guy alright. By the way, where's Big Charlie?"

Reino wiped his palms on the back of his pants, aware that if it came to a fight he was outnumbered. "Checking things out. He'll be back shortly."

Red Crowley called out as he rolled a sheet of canvas down the side of the truck bed. "Watch it!"

When they had the canvas tied on Harrigan bumped Dugan's arm. "Gimme a hand."

They picked up the advertising board and fitted it into place. Now the advertising board looked like a natural wall though in reality it hid the secret compartment. Harrigan checked the placement of the canvas tie ropes. "We can use the tie ropes to hold this false front in place."

"Right."

Francis Oley appeared in the truck's cab. The back of the seat was down and he poked his head through the opening into the secret compartment and studied the space. He snapped his gum. "Real nice. G-men ever get wise?"

Dugan huffed. "Nope. Not the border guards, the G-men or the cops. Right under their noses and they didn't see a thing. If they'd measured they'd have found out the inside was shorter than the outside, but that's cops for yuh."

Francis Oley chomped his gum. "Suppose O'Connell tries to bust out?"

Harrigan knelt down. "Two things. Garguillo's gonna ride with him, and we'll chain up the tail gate. O'Connell won't go nowhere."

Garguillo called out, "You can bank on it."

Francis Oley pushed up his fedora. "Brother said it's best we use legit plates. We can get a cheap car with license plates up at Whitbeck Motors on Central Avenue."

Francis pulled two fifty dollar bills from his pocket. "Who wants to buy a car?"

George Garguillo grabbed the money. "I'll do it. Need a break anyway."

A short time later, across from 526 Central Avenue, Francis pointed out the driver side window of his 1931 Buick. "That's Whitbeck Motors. I'll wait down the street. Don't forget to use a fake name for the paper work."

Garguillo called over his shoulder as he crossed the street. "Got it covered."

Inside the showroom Garguillo was greeted by a slender man with curly brown hair who wore horn-rimmed glasses, a white shirt and red polka-dot bow tie. The man extended his hand. "Arthur Rose. What can I do for yuh today, Mister—?"

George Garguillo reached out his hand. "Joe Costello's the name. Need a cheap car to get me to New York and back is all—nothing fancy. Not over a hundred dollars."

Arthur Rose slipped into his coat and hat. "Well, that's a tall order, Mr. Costello. Let's see what's on the lot out back."

Outside the door Arthur Rose pointed to the rear of the lot. "Less expensive ones are back here, Mr. Costello. I think I've got just what you want. Just got it in on a trade." He pointed to a green sedan shaped like a small rectangle on top of a longer rectangle. Running boards ran along the sides, there was a sunshade above the windshield, and the headlights were bug-eyed. "This '28 Durant should fit the bill," said the salesman.

Garguillo placed his palm on the front fender and squatted down to look under the car. "Not leaking oil."

"It's got a few miles on it but the engine's good. Wanna try it?"

"Yeah, sure."

When the salesman returned with the keys Garguillo got behind the wheel and adjusted the rear view mirror. With his thumb he squashed a bug on the upper corner of the windshield and then started the car. He had to let the clutch all the way out to get the car to move forward. "Clutch is worn," he said.

He turned the steering wheel an inch before the front wheels turned. A short distance later he came to a squeaking stop after pumping the brakes twice. "It's in rough shape."

"Well, we haven't checked it out yet, Mr. Costello, but you said under a hundred and we'll—"

Garguillo held out his arm. "Tell yuh what. I'll take it as is for fifty bucks."

Arthur Rose pulled the back of his neck. "I don't know, Mr. Costello, that's awful low and—"

Garguillo held out a roll of bills. "Fifty bucks cash and I want it today."

"Sold. I'll do the paperwork myself. Where do you live, Mr. Costello?"

Garguillo latched onto Rose's outstretched hand and gave it a shake. "Done deal. 35 Hamilton Street. I'll be back after lunch to pick it up."

One hour later George Garguillo returned. Arthur Rose was next to the Durant with another man dressed in grease covered clothes who was holding a ball peen hammer, a wrench and a fist of rivets in one hand and a license plate in the other. Garguillo broke into a run with a shout. "Hold on there!"

"Oh, Mr. Costello. We're just gonna put the plates on."

Garguillo handed Arthur Rose a fifty dollar bill. "No need for that. My own mechanic can do it. Short on time, yuh know?

Here yuh go." He peeled two singles from his roll. "Throw some gas in it too." Garguillo took the license plate—3-A-8393—from the mechanic. He said, "I'm in a hurry."

Arthur Rose waved away Joe Stillwell, the mechanic. "I hear yuh, Mr. Costello. Joe, bring the car around front."

Rose handed the car registration papers to Garguillo. "If yuh look these over,

Mr. Costello, you'll see that all is in order. I'll file them myself later today. Just sign at the bottom."

As Garguillo headed for the Durant the salesman called, "We appreciate your business, Mr. Costello."

At the Elm Street garage Garguillo beeped the Durant's horn twice and Tony Reino opened the garage door. Garguillo pumped the Durant's brakes but the front bumper hit the front wall.

McGlone roared with laughter. "Can't'cha drive?"

Garguillo slammed the driver's door shut behind him. "Pile of junk!" he shouted. He pushed the license plate into the chest of Manny Strewl and said, "I ain't driving that crappie car no more. It'll kill yuh."

Strewl forced a grin. "When it gets dark we can ditch the car at the dump by Tivoli Reservoir." He turned toward Angel Face Geary. "Percy, Butch is at the brewery. You and Scarnici can flip coins to see who's gonna take the first shift to watch him."

Hours later, the moon was beginning to rise as Angel Face Geary slouched in his Chevy sedan across from Hendricks Brewery and waited for his quarry to emerge.

Chapter 4
The Kidnapping

Smoke from George Keiss's pipe drifted from the ceiling of the small porch into the canopy of oak limbs. From inside his wife called, "George, come to bed."

He called back, "In a minute, dear." The hand holding the pipe was a carpenter's hand, a callused hand that turned the pipe and tapped out the ashes. George noted with satisfaction the lone street light. It stood at the corner of his yard—a yard hardly bigger than a postage stamp. It illuminated the intersection of Van Orden and Putnam Streets, and had been installed at the request of his well-known neighbor Catherine O'Connell, who moved in with her son when she and her husband separated. Catherine said she was afraid of coming home at night to a pitch dark street.

Keiss was about to head indoors when Putnam Street became aglow with headlights. He figured it was Catherine, returning from her usual Friday night card game. Could be her son, John O'Connell, Junior. But the engine did not have the deep rumble of a big-block Buick, and this driver cut his lights while still moving along Putnam Street where it was dark.

From behind the porch column George Keiss watched. The green car, which did not belong to any of his neighbors, passed under the streetlight and continued on to the vacant house at the end of Putnam before swinging left into a U-turn.

"What's he doing?" Keiss muttered to himself. "Streets too—" He winced as the strange car sideswiped a parked car.

The car headed in his direction again and he ducked. The driver swung to the curb and parked near the streetlight. Keiss peeked over the porch railing and studied the driver as he stepped out. The fellow was tall, and he rubbed his face as he studied the houses on the opposite side of the street. Keiss suspected he was a thief, looking to do a break-in or steal a car. The guy looked tall and slim.

The night was so quiet Keiss could even hear what was said. "Let's go."

The front-seat passenger got out and followed the driver. This one was shorter but he too had a slim build. He pushed his fedora to the back of his head and made some sound. Keiss recognized the sound. Popping gum. The pair moved into the darkness but soon the shorter one spun around and took a quick look up Putnam Street. "I'm with yuh," he said, and chased after the other.

Keiss waited. It was past 11:00. He couldn't hear or see anything and he was tired. Time to call it a day—but just in case, he memorized the green car's license plate: 3-A-8393.

Just as George stepped back from the railing another set of headlights illuminated Putnam Street. This driver also clicked his lights off and continued to crawl up the shadowy street. Keiss ducked down. The car parked diagonally across the street but the engine was still running.

Keiss kept low, peeking around the corner. A short stocky man exited the front passenger seat and ape-walked around to the driver's side. The first set of men appeared again. Keiss could not make out anything that was said except a "Shush" when one of the men cautioned the females in the newly arrived car to hold down their giggles.

Another car was approaching. A voice ordered, "Scatter!"

The headlights illuminated the leaves over Keiss's head. Then the car's radiator gurgled and the driver cut the engine. It was his neighbor, Henry Tobin, who fished for his house keys while studying the strange maroon car. Seconds later Tobin entered his house and the living room lights came on.

Keiss continued his watch for a while, but nothing more happened and he decided to go to bed. As he passed through to the bedroom the grandfather clock struck 12:30. Shortly thereafter he heard the familiar deep roar of a big-block car engine. That would be the '33 Buick sedan driven by John "Butch" O'Connell. Butch was an amateur boxer. As Keiss settled in bed he thought, Butch can handle the problem—if there is one.

John "Butch" O'Connell, junior was the son of Catherine and Solly O'Connell, and the only child among the four O'Connell brothers—Dan, Edward, Patrick (recently passed away) and Solly. The brothers had always catered to Butch, making sure he had the best. College education first, then training at the Troy Police Academy, and now Butch was an officer in the National Guard.

The family was Irish and glad to support Butch's move into amateur boxing. With a muscular five-foot-eleven frame that weighed in at 212 pounds, the young man was considered a formidable opponent in the ring. His hair was an attractive sandy shade and his manners were good. The ladies saw in him an aura of Prince Charming.

Prohibition was nearing its end in 1933 and the O'Connell family had decided to make legitimate beer. They groomed Butch for running their business, called Hendricks Brewery. Butch was moderately successful at the job but not politically astute like Uncle Dan or Uncle Ed. In 1939 Uncle Dan would get him installed as the Democratic Chairman, but he would get kicked out in 1945 and die of natural causes in 1954.

On this Friday night, Butch swung his Buick around in the intersection of Putnam and Van Orden under the glow of the streetlight and brought the Buick to a stop under the oak tree in front of the two-story house at 14 Putnam. The house bordered Van Orden Street and sat across from the Keiss house. It was built like a square box—a wooden structure with a brick side chimney and a 'widow's watch' on the roof above the porch.

When Butch cut the engine the water in the radiator gurgled. He collected his hat, his cigarettes and house key and had just put his hand on the door handle when the passenger door was jerked open and a voice hissed, "Get out!"

Butch froze. He was staring into the barrel of a gun.

Angel Face Geary pushed the gun closer. "Out, I said!"

Butch's hand fumbled for the door latch and finally his door sprang open. Geary pushed the gun closer to his face, forcing Butch to the leave the car backward. His cigarettes spilled to the ground and one of his brown saddle shoes caught the door's lip and caused him to slip.

Francis Oley grasped his shoulders and righted him. Francis said into his ear, "Don't run."

Butch stuttered. "Wh-wh—"

Francis clawed his shoulder. Butch shoved against him and Francis teetered backward.

"No yuh don't," came another voice, and Charles Harrigan charged with open arms. He intended a bear hug but managed only to trap one of Butch's arms. Butch twisted and shoved Harrigan against the side of the car. Harrigan slammed against it with a thud.

George Garguillo sprang forward next and took hold of Butch's powerful right arm. Butch exhaled with an audible "Ahh-h-h" as he lifted Garguillo off his feet and shoved him against the car.

Garguillo quickly came back and Thomas Dugan joined the fray too by coming up behind and wrapping his arms around Butch's midriff. Now men were holding to Butch's arms and middle, and Harrigan reached for his throat and held it in a grip like a vice. Butch began choking. Harrigan kept his hold until Butch's feet slipped and he slumped. The ball of men tumbled to the ground.

On the sidelines stood Big Charlie Scarnici, gun in hand.

Butch was up again with mobsters dangling from him like ornaments on a Christmas tree. He pushed his feet forward and dragged his attackers along the pavement. Something at his side caught his attention and he turned his head. Whack! The cold steel of a revolver hit him and he crumpled to the ground. Seconds later, still dazed, Butch heard a car engine jump to life as he was shoved head first into the back seat of a car.

George Garguillo crawled in and jammed his knee into the captive's back and yanked his head up by the back of his hair. Scarnici plastered white adhesive tape over his eyes. Harrigan slapped handcuffs on the wrists, mindful as he did of the times the cops had cuffed him. Scarnici took one more precaution: a green laundry bag over Butch's head.

Somebody spoke in a low voice. "Let's get the hell outta here!"

Later, Butch would remember one exchange in particular. It happened soon after the engine gave a deep climbing groan and accelerated. Someone asked, "Got the machine gun?" After the question Butch heard what sounded like the snap-snap of popping gum, then whoever was in the passenger seat said, "Yeah."

A short time later Butch heard the distinct sound of a trolley's bell and the car sped over the tracks. From that point on the ride smoothed out. This made Butch pretty certain they were in Albany's downtown area.

He spoke for the first time. "What's this all about?"

"Just a chance to make some easy money is all."

Six hours later Butch was unloaded at an apartment building at 734 Adams Street in Hoboken, New Jersey. The place was used during the heyday of prohibition as a whiskey drop by the Waxy Gordon mob. The saloon on the first floor had closed as prohibition faded and in its place there was now a sweat shop where coats and other garments were made. The upper stories of the building housed apartments. The area was home to Hoboken's illegal booze trade—an area where most folks had a bathtub gin mill and trusted the mobsters more than the cops.

The kidnappers had transferred Butch to the rail truck, and at the hostage site escorted him down a walkway, up stairs and into a back bedroom. They shoved their blindfolded captive onto a creaking steel bed and handcuffed him to an iron radiator. They chuckled as Butch tugged against the cuffing but later they would find the joke was on them, for at the trial Butch would identify the cuffs by the marks he scratched on them.

Butch could not make out the mumbling words the kidnappers said that first night, but he did begin to assemble the jigsaw puzzle of the night's events. He engraved in his mind every nose and bump he had felt. The canvas that had scraped his head told him the truck was probably a six-foot rail truck. He had only to use himself as a yardstick, stretching his feet in the secret compartment and taking estimated measurements. In the hideout he immediately began etching in his mind each step he took and each turn of direction as he was led into the house.

He soon had reason to smile internally when fate handed him a prize.

The summer night was hot and uncomfortable. This turned out to be a good thing, for his sweat loosened the tape below his eyes. Now he could see a little and he began to memorize details, including the laundry mark on the pillowcase and the abnormally large feet and hands of one of his guards.

***

Three years later Butch would learn who those feet and hands belonged to: Thomas "Pivot" Burke, a luckless mobster. Burke was a thick man, only five-foot-five and well over two hundred pounds. He wore glasses and his dark hair was thinning. Burke walked with a slight limp. He could rightly be called one of the mob's foot soldiers. He had escaped from Comstock Prison in 1932 and got a job acting as a guard during a truck hijacking. His employer decided it would be cheaper to kill Burke than pay him, but during a fight over a gun Burke took several shots in the leg then jumped from the speeding hijacked truck. During that escape his roll down a steep embankment compounded his leg wounds and mangled his leg—thus the limp. His leg injury coupled with partial deafness made him of little use to the mob. To survive, he was forced to depend on Harrigan's charity and odd jobs such as guarding the captive.

During the attempt on his life he lost his gun—so afterward he always carried two guns. The FBI would capture Burke in 1936 in the Panama Canal Zone where he was working as a waiter on a cruise ship. When the newspapers heard about the two guns he carried they nicknamed him "Two Gun Burke." To get a lighter sentence Burke turned State's evidence and received four years in prison. The sentence was cut short, however, for he died in 1937 of a coronary occlusion.

The other fellow assigned to guard Butch was Frank "Dutch" Fisher—a man who looked like walking death. He was lanky and had bags under his dark sunken eyes. His face was marred with age spots and deep creases. He was born in South Africa and spoke in a low guttural voice with a German accent. It was remarked more than once that his voice sounded like a dog's growl. He too would turn State's evidence for a reduced sentence when the kidnapping went to trial. After his release he disappeared.

Soon after Burke and Fisher assumed their guard duty, fate offered Butch a second gift when a foot kicked his steel bed and a voice ordered, "Sit up."

Thanks to the loosened tape covering his eyes Butch was able to see a straw panama hat dangling from a hand, and his nose picked up a strong odor of cigar smoke. The man's pant legs appeared to be of a fine cut yet his shoes were scuffed and worn.

Butch paid close attention to the timbre of the voice as the man said, "You have to name some go-betweens—got it? We need a go-between to get messages to your family. So name some local racketeers, or guys connected with racketeers."

Butch licked his lips. "Well, uh, I don't know—I don't really know anybody mixed up in that kind of business. Only one that comes to mind is Jack Murphy. He does work for the organization and he's known to be dead on the level."

"We can't do business with people like that. Take some time to think it over. I'll be back in a bit."

The man left. Minutes later he returned. "So whaddya think?"

"There's a lawyer, Dan Prior. I think he handles cases for Diamond's mob."

"We can't do business with a lawyer. Think again."

Butch exhaled. "How 'bout Butch O'Hagan—the old fighter? Or maybe his manager, Barney Riley. There's also Mush Trachnier or Tough Tony."

"Nah, we don't know those guys."

The man left the room again but returned shortly. "Got any more?"

"Don't know. You'd have to ask my Uncle Dan or Uncle Ed. They've been around longer."

"Maybe," the man said, and turned and exited.

A short while later Big Charlie Scarnici opened the door and tossed a bundle at Burke. "Pajamas. For the kid."

Burke slipped a marble in his mouth to garble his voice and tossed the pajamas into Butch's lap with the order to strip. From the foot of the bed Burke took the blanket and fastened it on nails at the top of the window above the bed. While he was busy with this Fisher took Butch's wallet and thumbed through it. He pulled out the New York driver's license and motioned for Burke to come over to the corner, out of earshot.

Leaning close to Burke's good ear, Fisher spoke in a hushed growl. "Know him?"

Burke took the license, moved his arm back and forth until he could focus in the dimly lit room and was inclined to curse, but first he had to spit out his marble. He covered his mouth with his fingers. "Damn it! Harrigan told me this guy owed them fifteen-G's on a beer bill."

Fisher asked, "What's the big deal?"

"Who yuh think runs New York, dummy?"

Fisher shrugged his shoulders. "Got me."

Burke caught hold of Fisher's arm. "The O'Connells—that's who!"

"How yuh know?"

Burke took off his glasses. "Cause I grew up in New York—that's why. It was O'Connell money put the governor in office *and* helped Roosevelt win New York." Burke's lip rolled up and he pointed at the captive. "And damn it!—looks like we got one of 'em sitting right here."

Fisher's creased face sagged and his mouth hung open. Burke paced in a circle then stepped close again. "If this thing blows up…there won't be one flatfoot or G-man anywhere that won't be looking for us."

"Think Harrigan knows?"

Burke sucked in his lips. "Dunno. Harrigan's Jersey, this is New York."

Fisher cocked his head. "Think we should walk?"

Burke put a finger to his lips. He went over to the door, opened it and poked his head out. Garguillo was coming out of the bathroom. Burke held a hand up behind his back—signaling Fisher to wait. He stepped outside the door, pulled it almost shut and said to Garguillo, "Bring us back an egg sandwich from Skelly's, will yuh? Something for the kid too."

Garguillo nodded assent and Burke went back into the bedroom and shut the door. He went directly to Fisher's side and whispered, "If we walk we could end up at the bottom of the river—or in Garguillo's firebox!"

"So what we gonna do?"

"Only thing we can do. Play both sides. We just make damn sure this kid stays in good health."

A black ant was crossing the floor. Burke spotted it and lifted his foot and crushed it. For a couple of seconds he stared at the ant. When he lifted his head he said, "That could be us, either from Harrigan's men or the O'Connells."

Now the two guards had their own secret plan, while the ones that actually planned the kidnapping thought they had all the bases covered. What *they* did not realize was that fate was already stalking them. Two witnesses, George Keiss and Henry Tobin, would provide valuable clues to their identity. The kidnappers also made a bad mistake when they chose Butch O'Connell. He was no dummy. As soon as they apprehended him he began putting together a bundle of info—info that would eventually lead the authorities to the identity of the prime suspects and the location of the hideout.

***

Rookie patrolman Ray Joyce ran full speed up Arch Street. He paused at the bottom step of the Arch Street Police station to catch his breath. If only he could afford a car, but there was no hope of that, not on a rookie's pay, especially with a pregnant wife.

From the top step Officer John Tuffy called, "Save your strength—too hot to run in this heat!"

John Tuffy was tall, medium build, had been on the Albany police force for a number of years and would eventually become its chief. The young Ray Joyce would quit his job to take a higher paying job.

Tuffy opened the glass entrance door to the First Precinct station. "After you, Ray." They stopped before an elevated police desk and a balding man. Tuffy said, "Whatcha got, Lieutenant?"

Lieutenant Jim Mechan stepped from behind the desk and led the way to the wall map of Albany. He pointed. "Rash of break-ins on the South side. Want you and Joyce to work along South Pearl over to the line, then up Second Avenue. Elam and Daniels are working Church Street and down to the river. Check in on the hour but just remember the call box at Plum and Franklin Street hasn't been fixed yet. Elam's gonna check in on the half hour, so you check in on the hour."

Tuffy tilted his head toward the door. "Ray, let's grab some bad guys."

Lieutenant Mechan adjusted his glasses and called after them. "Leave the Friday night drunks be—t he break-ins take priority!"

Tuffy led the way to the two-door black car. The canvas roof was folded down and tucked in the back compartment. The front doors had Albany Police painted in a semi-circle and on the passenger side there was a spot beam light. Both men tucked their hats behind the seat so the wind would not blow them off their heads.

"Ready for this, Ray?"

Joyce clicked his flashlight on and off. "Ready as ever."

A short time later Tuffy rolled the police car into the gas station at the corner of Madison and South Pearl Streets. He parked next to the red sandwich sign advertising gas for twenty cents. "We'll start here and work our way west."

Hours later Tuffy glanced at his watch. "Let's head back to the station. It's almost 10:00."

They found Lieutenant Mechan sitting on the top step sipping a cup of coffee. He looked over his glasses. "Anything new?"

Tuffy removed his hat and leaned on his knee. "Nah. Pretty quiet."

"How's the kid doing?"

Tuffy grinned at Ray. "Pretty fair. Doesn't like the night shift."

Mechan chuckled. "He'll hate it by December."

A car turned on to Arch Street. The groan of the engine grew to a pitched whine. The car was accelerating—toward a police station! A man's torso popped out of the car's back window.

Tuffy shouted "Duck!" and hit the concrete.

"K-boom! K-boom!"

A Chevy. It speeded on up the street. Mechan yelled, "Get'em!"

Tuffy was already climbing in the driver's seat. The car was already rolling as Joyce pulled his door closed.

Tuffy gunned the engine and Joyce hit the siren, which sounded like a scorched cat. The Chevy disappeared around a corner. Joyce yelled, "He went left on Broad!"

Tuffy downshifted and the engine cried with pent-up power. He snapped the steering wheel and the car slid sideways around the corner onto Broad. Joyce swung the police car's spot beam ahead. It illuminated the runaway car as it rounded the next corner.

"He took Schuyler!"

Tuffy was enjoying the chase. Parked cars whizzed by like rails on a picket fence. He felt like a lion after its prey. After a few minutes and a couple more turns he came within range and pulled alongside the Chevy. Joyce drew his pistol and cocked the hammer.

Tuffy barked. "Pull over!"

Both cars glided to the curb close to the intersection of Clinton and Second Avenue. Tuffy approached the driver's side with his hand on his holstered pistol. Joyce covered the passenger side, flashlight in his left hand, drawn gun in his right.

Officer Tuffy went nose to nose with the driver. "Where's the shotgun you just fired?"

"What shotgun, officer?" The driver shrugged with palms up. "We were just going home."

Tuffy studied the two front seat men and the area around their feet. Joyce pushed his head into the right rear passenger window. His flashlight beam shone on an empty back seat. He shook his head at Tuffy.

Tuffy released his grip on his gun. "Follow me to the station."

A short time later Tuffy and Joyce marched the two suspects into the Arch Street Station House. To Lieutenant Mechan and a throng of officers he said, "Here yuh go."

Lieutenant Mechan was none too happy that they hadn't found the gun.

Tuffy said, "We haven't found it yet. Me and Ray are gonna tear that car apart. We'll find it."

"They probably tossed it," Mechan said. "I'll have the entire night shift walk the get-away route with you. I've also called in some reserves to help out."

The search was tedious and tiring. Nothing incriminating was found in the suspect's car. Along the streets the searchers looked under cars, in sewer drains, doorways, and around the Schuyler Mansion grounds.

Finally, at the corner of Fourth Avenue, one of the searchers called out, "Hey, got something." He held up two shotgun shells. "Found them in the gutter."

Tuffy was called over. He took the high brass shells and pointed to the number 8 printed on the red paper side. "Duck load. Makes more noise than damage. Maybe the gun's close by. Let's look."

He strolled around the corner onto Second Avenue and looked under the two closest parked cars. He stood up and pulled a handkerchief from his pocket and wiped his brow. And did a double take. "Huh," he said.

He called over his shoulder, "Say, Ray…" And he began walking up Second Avenue.

Joyce caught up with him at the corner where Second intersected Regent Street. "What is it?"

Tuffy rested his foot on the bumper of a 1931 maroon Pontiac sedan. "John Oley's car, I think." He took a notebook from his pocket, flipped a few pages and ran his finger down the column of license plate numbers. "John Oley's car, alright. One of them, anyway."

"So?"

"He lives over on Oakwood, northwest side of town." Tuffy peered in the back window then tested the door and found it locked. "What the hell's he doing down here?"

Joyce said, "Maybe casing a joint?"

Tuffy pointed up Second Avenue to house number 58. "Pretty stupid if he is. That's Sergeant Fahey's house. He's out of the Sixth Precinct. Oley's got real brass if he's gonna pull something under the nose of a cop."

Tuffy stood in the middle of the street and studied the unlit houses. The only noise came from the shotgun shells he was rolling about in his hand. He glanced at the shells. "Let's get these back to the station. We'll swing back by here later."

***

The morning after the kidnapping Albany's Chief of Police stepped onto Dan O'Connell's porch and the front door popped open. Chief Smurl gave his hat to the patrolman standing inside and the patrolman closed the door behind him.

The Chief was a balding man shaped like a stretched beach ball. His nose was long and thin, his cheeks drooped and his ears were big enough to put you in mind of oak leaves. His eyebrows were thick and his eyes deep set. Typically he dressed in his regulation uniform, but today he wore a light gray suit with spit-shined black shoes.

The chief had worked hard to keep the mobs out of Albany. Many of the area's insiders and old timers were convinced that he had Jack "Legs" Diamond killed—to keep organized crime out, or to eliminate a competitor in the beer business. Though the FBI had evidence to the contrary, the crime was never officially solved.

Smurl barked, "Where is everybody?"

The patrolman said, "In the kitchen, sir."

"Any word on Solly?"

"Yes sir. Major Warner sent his troopers up into the Catskills to bring him back."

Chief Smurl made his way to the kitchen where he almost bumped into Major Warner, the New York State Superintendent of Police. John Warner was a medium-built man with dust-colored hair that he parted down the middle. His forehead was high, his eyes the color of coal, and close up under his nose he kept a well-trimmed salt-and-pepper mustache. Warner eschewed the regular brass-buttoned light grey uniform of a state trooper and wore instead a suit in charcoal grey with narrow pinstripes.

Warner was a new breed of cop. He graduated from Harvard Law School in 1906 and was a renowned concert pianist who had performed in such places as Carnegie Hall. He was a man that sought excitement and to that end joined the cavalry and helped chase the bandit Poncho Villa in 1916. He was the fourth person to be sworn in as head of the relatively new State Police of New York. He had come up quickly through the ranks, was appointed Superintendent in 1923 with the rank of Major. He would serve in the post for 20 years, the longest tenure on record.

Chief Smurl nodded at Warner and stepped past him to face Dan O'Connell. These two men, the police chief and the head of the O'Connell clan, were about the same girth and both had long ears and sagging chins. The noticeable difference was that Dan had more hair on his head.

Dan O'Connell was *the* political power broker in Albany. The family was well known and reputed to operate on both sides of the law. Though it was true the family ran a lucrative illegal brewery operation, among other activities, they were virtuous in the fact that they spread some of their funds among Albany's working class. If for instance Dan O'Connell heard that someone needed a sack of groceries or new dentures, those items appeared—like magic. He did not ask for repayment, only that the recipient vote for the candidates the O'Connells wanted in office. No vote, no freebies—that's how it worked. The politicians knew it, the people knew it. Dan did not need to use guns or violence. During the Depression food or favors were bigger weapons, and the recipients knew the wisdom of not biting the hand that feeds you. To most people Dan was considered a benevolent man known as Uncle Dan.

Chief Smurl faced him. "Can you review for us what happened?"

Dan O'Connell leaned against a counter and cleared his throat. "This morning, Catherine called my office and reached my secretary. She said Butch had not slept in his bed last night. Said she saw his car with the door open when she got home from her card game, but figured he'd decided to take a walk after he took Mary home. So it was this morning before she realized anything was amiss. She went out and checked his car, found the door still open and cigarettes spilled on the ground."

He paused and shook his head as if to clear it. "We called Mary and some of his friends, and his Guard unit, and the brewery. Mary said she hadn't seen him since he dropped her off last night. Guys at the brewery hadn't seen him since he left yesterday. You knew about that threatening letter we got last March…so this time we're figuring it's for real."

Ed O'Connell stepped forward. In physical appearance he was almost a clone of his brother. He stood with his hands in his pockets and shook his head. "We never even thought they might clip Butch. Thought there was a chance they'd go after Dan, maybe Solly."

Major John Warner stroked his mustache. "My troopers should have Solly back here in a few hours."

Warner was seated at the opposite end of the kitchen table from a small pudgy apple-faced man with cream-colored hair combed to one side. This was Ed O'Connell's law partner, George Meyers. He wore a red bow tie and black suspenders.

Ed nodded toward Meyers. "George has just been filling us in."

Chief Smurl took a seat at the side of the table. "George, start from the beginning. Exactly what did the caller say?"

Meyers licked his lips. "Well, there were actually two calls. My secretary, Grace Fletcher, took them both."

"The first one, Mr. Meyers. What did they say or want?"

"Grace said it was a bit hard to understand. Voice sounded gruff and sort of muffled. They asked for Ed. Grace said he wasn't in so the caller hung up. The same voice called back shortly afterward."

Smurl bobbed his head. "About how long before the second call?"

"About fifteen minutes. Grace said it sounded like the first but easier to understand. This time they asked for Sam Arnowitz, our other partner. Since he wasn't in either, Grace gave me the call."

Chief Smurl said, "Think clearly, Mr. Meyers. Exactly what did the caller say?"

"Well, he sort of sounded gruff, like a kid pretending to be a grown up. He said, 'Tell Eddie to tell Danny we got his nephew and he'll hear from us. If they tell the police, we'll kill him.' And then he hung up."

Chief Smurl studied the ceiling for a moment. "Then what, Mr. Meyers?"

"I made the calls like they said. Dan said I should come over."

Chief Smurl got to his feet. "Dan, you said you talked to Mary, the sweetheart. And to Butch's mother, right?"

"Correct. Mary said Butch picked her up about 8:00 last night. They took in a show at the Palace and afterwards they ate at Joe's Café on Madison, then drove out to Ousterhouts for a Coke and some music—and he dropped her off a little after midnight."

"That narrows the time down. What about his mother?"

"Catherine said she got back from her card game about 12:30 or so. She saw Butch's car parked under the oak tree with the door open. Heard the radiator gurgling."

Chief Smurl shot Major Warner a raised-eyebrow look. "Gurgling," he repeated.

Dan shrugged. "She said a gurgling sound. I knew it was the radiator."

"I see." Chief Smurl frowned. "Go on."

"She figured Butch went for a walk. Until this morning. When she saw his bed hadn't been slept in she checked his car. It was just like she found it the night before. Now here we are."

"Hmm…12:30, you say. Did she notice anyone on the street? A stranger—or a strange car parked close by?"

Dan scratched his head. "Cathy didn't mention none. She did say a car almost sideswiped her skedaddling out Putnam Street. She figured it was maybe some guy got caught in the wrong bedroom."

Chief Smurl glanced at the clock above the sink. He said to Major Warner, "They got a 12-hour head start."

Major Warner tilted his head toward the door. "Got my troopers checking roadhouses along the Hudson and outlying areas. Maybe something will turn up."

Dan said, "Cheese-us, John, you gotta do better than that! They might have dumped him in the river for spite!"

Chief Smurl held up a hand. "Hold on, Dan—I'm sure Butch is safe. They got something you want, you got something they want. The snatch racket is all about money. This is only the first step."

Ed O'Connell, the lawyer brother, stepped forward. "First step?"

Chief Smurl exhaled. "Ed, you know how the snatch racket works. I take your kid, you give me money, I give kid back. No kid, no money."

Ed O'Connell hitched up his pants. "You're presuming these kidnappers are reasonable, Chief. Mush Trachnier didn't think his would-be kidnappers were going to be so reasonable. That's why he started blasting away when they came after him. Held off six of them!—from what I heard."

For a moment after this outburst no one spoke. Ed dropped his head. When he raised it he said, "Chief, for now you can pull off your guys, we'll play by their rules. They did say no cops or they'd kill Butch."

Chief Smurl reached for his hat. "I see your point. What you think, John?"

Major Warner pulled at his ear. "The repeal of prohibition isn't official in this state yet, so I'll have my troopers say they're looking for stills as an excuse to check the roadhouses along the river."

Chief Smurl headed for the door, saying he planned to talk to Catherine and Mary in case they had forgotten something. Dan looked over his glasses. "Be careful, Chief. Catherine's got a bad ticker. I'm gonna have the doc standing by."

Chief Smurl turned back and spoke to Major Warner. "Let's meet with the DA in a few hours."

Major Warner tapped his hat against his thigh. "Why not let Delaney run the show out of his office? No one will question all the cops coming and going."

"Sounds reasonable."

Smurl and Warner exited together. When they got to the chief's car, he took his hat off and wiped the inside band with his handkerchief. "Catherine heard the radiator gurgling. And some car almost ran her off the street. A radiator only gurgles a short time once the motor's cut."

"Yeah. Luck of the Irish, I guess. If Mrs. O'Connell had been five minutes earlier we'd either have two kidnap victims—or one victim and one body." He shook his head side to side. "You got somebody who can run the investigation?"

Chief Smurl tipped his head. "Detective Jimmy Hynes. My top gun. Born and raised here—knows every back door and sewer drain in Albany. If Butch is in Albany Jimmy will find him, but if these kidnappers are smart they're already gone. I'm guessing New York—with easy access and a lot of places to hide."

"If they're in New York City, we're looking at as many jurisdiction problems as there were in the Lindberg case. Maybe more."

Chief Smurl looked down at the ground and swore under his breath. When he looked up again he said, "You got any way to solve the problem?"

"Unfortunately, kidnapping is not a federal crime. So we're stuck with state law. Presuming the kidnappers are holed up in the big city, we bring in some city cops. Between them and your people and the state troopers, we'll have all the jurisdictions covered."

Smurl rubbed the back of his neck.

Warner said, "I'm thinking Joe Gannon, a detective out of Manhattan who worked with the G-men on the Lindberg case. A college man—and a straight shooter. If I can square it with the governor, I'll have Commissioner Bolan send Gannon up with his undercover squad."

"Oh, Chief Smurl." It was the voice of George Meyers, calling from the porch. Meyers trotted over. "Chief, Major— just occurred to me. The caller called the O'Connells Eddie and Danny. Only their friends call them that, and most of them are in the south end of Albany. Does that help?"

"Every little thing helps, Mr. Meyers. Thank you."

Meyers headed toward the street where his car was parked. Chief Smurl frowned. "He's right."

Major Warner arched an eyebrow. "You're saying inside job? You think maybe a friend or neighbor clipped Butch for a fast buck?"

"Worse than that, John. Solly's got debt markers out all over town. He might've set it up, snatched his own son, and is ready now to shake down everyone to help pay the ransom. A way to pay off his debts…and no one the wiser."

"That's great! Solly O'Connell. Clipping his own son. And I thought July was going to be a slow month."

Chapter 5
A Suspect

Saturday afternoon, July 8—the day after the kidnapping, Officer John Tuffy was at home when he received a summons to the Chief's office. He was to come in right away. When he stepped inside the office he was surprised to find others already present, including the district attorney. Tuffy held his cap in his hand and stood before his Chief's desk.

Chief David Smurl turned up the page of a report and tapped it with his finger, then raised his head and looked into Officer Tuffy's eyes. "Did you go back and check?"

Officer John Tuffy stood ramrod straight. "Check, sir?"

"On the car. Oley's car."

"Yes sir. But it was gone."

District Attorney John T. Delaney pulled his glasses to the end of his nose. "About what time was that?"

John Delaney was built like a penguin. He had sagging cheeks and wore frameless glasses. His receding hairline made his nose appear to stick out farther than normal. Delaney had been elected Albany's District Attorney in 1928 with the help of the O'Connell political machine, which was a subchapter of the Tammany Hall political machine. Dan O'Connell's voter "pull" put Delaney in office and kept him there until 1943 when Delaney resigned for personal reasons. Only one condition was placed upon Delaney: he was not to seek the death penalty except in the case of first degree murder. The case Delaney was now about to handle, the kidnapping of the young John O'Connell, would alter that death penalty restriction.

Tuffy said, "Maybe two o'clock or so this morning, sir."

Delaney put down his copy of Tuffy's report and held out his hand. "I'd like to have a look at your book, Officer."

"Sure, here yuh go."

Delaney rolled out his lips as he thumbed through the pages. "Where'd yuh get these plate numbers?"

"From the files, mostly. And whenever I stop a guy I take down the number—case I ever need it."

"Um-m. Seems legal."

Major John Warner reached out a hand and took the book. He flipped a few pages. "Interesting, Officer. Why keep it?"

"Faster than coming back to the station to check out a plate. Like to know who I'm dealing with right off."

Delaney, the district attorney, stood facing Tuffy with one hand folded across his chest. "So after whoever it was in the car let loose with the shotgun, how long was it that you lost sight of the car?"

"Not more than a few seconds, till we got round the corner."

Delaney peered over his glasses. "See their faces?"

"No sir."

"License plate?"

"No sir. Too much of a lead."

Delaney grimaced. "Lost again, didn't yuh?"

"Well...sort of, but—"

"But nothing. You lost'em—plain and simple. And you didn't actually see the car turn onto Clinton, did you?"

"No sir, but a pedestrian pointed—"

"Who pointed?"

"A man on the sidewalk. He pointed down—"

"What's his name?"

"Didn't get it, sir, but—"

Delaney jabbed the air with his finger. "A pedestrian pointed down an empty street to a car you can't recognize... to people you can't identify. In fact, Officer, you didn't see much of anything, did you?"

Tuffy squinted. "It—was—_late_! They had a big lead. It was the only moving car tearing down the street…_sir!_"

"Yes, Officer Tuffy. The car on the street you didn't get a good look at. And the people you did stop have never been arrested. Looks like you got the wrong man."

Tuffy's forehead wrinkled. "In all my years as a police officer I've never seen an innocent man run from the police. Now I never seen it snow in Hades, sir, but I know it don't!"

Delaney turned to the desk and said to Chief Smurl, "This officer did not flinch, did not lose his temper. He'd make a solid witness. The kid's still too green to take the stand."

Delaney glanced at John Warner who said, "John, any defense attorney would put him through a tougher meat grinder than that." Warner sighed. "On the surface of it there was good cause for arresting them—but losing them…we're going to have to cut them loose."

Tuffy opened his mouth to object but Delaney held up the palm of his hand. "The chain of evidence is broken. The fact is you lost sight of the suspect car. A potential witness that pointed out the car is not available to us. A good defense attorney could say the tooth fairy spirited away the suspect car in those lost seconds and we couldn't prove him wrong. The chain is broken."

"What about the shotgun shells?"

"What about them? You have no gun. And anyone could have dropped the shells in the gutter. When it comes to the law, we have to account for everything. One link connects to the next. That's the kind of evidence we need…and you don't have it here."

Tuffy's face went slack. He muttered, "They're guilty as hell."

Throughout this interrogation, Detective James Hynes had been on the sidelines. Chief Smurl now said, "Hynes, whaddya you make of all this?"

Lead Detective James Hynes was not a handsome man. His receding brown hair coiled like springs and made his forehead prominent. He had thin cheeks and a ball of a nose, and appeared flat-faced. He spent his youth working on the family farm but left in search of higher wages. Before joining the Albany Police he worked as a general laborer.

Hynes was slouched against the back wall. "I'm not a lawyer, Chief."

"That's diplomatic of you, Jimmy, but whaddya think?"

Detective Hynes left the wall he had been leaning against and stepped around Officer Tuffy. He dipped his head in a policeman's nod that meant 'fine job' and tossed his copy of Tuffy's report on the desk. The report was open to the back page. Hynes put his index finger on it. "Shotgun's irrelevant. Officer Tuffy solved the kidnapping right here. It's John Oley. He's—"

Tuffy interjected, "What kidnapping?"

"Hold it, Detective." Delaney arched his head toward Tuffy. "What you're about to hear is not to leave this office. That's a direct order. Understand?"

Tuffy nodded his head in the affirmative.

Detective Hynes stood to the side. Delaney and Major Warner and Chief Smurl exchanged glances. Delaney pushed his glasses up. "The young O'Connell, John Junior. He was kidnapped last night. Kidnapping took place around 12:30, and this morning approximately 9:30 the family received a phone call regarding a ransom. The caller warned the family to keep the police out of it or they'd kill him."

Delaney waved Tuffy's report in the air. "Your report, Officer Tuffy, places John Oley's car one block away from the victim's house. Chief Smurl and I have talked to your lieutenant. If you had continued your rounds of checking gas stations, you might have been on Second Avenue at the time of the kidnapping and thereby prevented it. Also, we have debated whether perhaps the shotgun incident was a ruse—to draw our police away from the scene."

Tuffy's eyes had widened.

Chief Smurl cleared his throat. "After investigating the shooting, Officer Tuffy, did you resume your rounds?"

"Yessir, me and Ray went back about two this morning, but Oley's car was gone."

Delaney pulled at his lips. "Hmm…the silver lining here. You have indeed given us our prime suspect. As Detective Hynes was about to say—John Oley." Delaney tapped the desk with his finger tips. "For now, Officer, you're dismissed."

Tuffy nodded and turned toward the door. His Chief's voice halted his step and he turned back. Smurl said, "The district attorney's caution—about keeping this quiet? That's a direct order. Keep it buttoned up."

When Tuffy had closed the door behind him the Chief shook his head. "If Oley's in on this, you better believe he's got somebody watching our cops. Hell, he's probably even bought some of our cops. We must be extra careful—so Oley gets not even a whiff that we're working on this. Otherwise, John Junior may get dumped in the Hudson."

"Well, Chief," Hynes said, "there're just too many things out of place. Tuffy's report on Oley's car. That's a big piece of the puzzle. Then there's what I saw last Thursday afternoon."

Delaney jerked to attention. "You holding something back, Detective?"

"Nothing illegal…and nothing I can prove in court."

Major Warner had been sitting quietly in the corner. Now he rose to his feet. "Just tell us what you got—don't worry about proof."

"Yessir. Well, it was last Thursday, afternoon of July 6. Howie Blackwell and me were going bowling. I saw his car coming down the street and started to wave him down—till I noticed the Jersey plate. It wasn't Howie. Was a Willy-Knight though, just like his."

"Did'ja get the number?"

"No need, sir. No law was broken. But the car rolled right by and into Oley's garage—and John Oley came prancing out of his house. But I flagged him down before he got to the garage."

"You flagged him down?"

Detective Hynes returned Delaney's cold stare. "Yessir. He lives a few doors down from me. I'm at 19 Oakwood Avenue and Oley's at 40."

Delaney's head jutted back. "What?"

"The Oleys know who I am. The whole street knows who they are—and what they do. He watches me…and we *all* watch him."

"Relax, John." Chief Smurl walked around the desk and stood next to Delaney. "Jimmy's a stand-up guy—was born here and knows the town. That's why I chose him to head up the investigation. Anything else, Jimmy?"

Hynes held his arms two feet apart. "Oley had something all wrapped up, tucked under his arm. About this long, it was. When I got close he shifted the package away from me and turned away."

Major Warner's one eyebrow arched up. "Would you say the length was maybe twenty-eight inches long?"

"Yessir. About the size of a Tommy gun."

Delaney said, "Did you in fact see a Tommy gun, Detective?"

"No, I did not."

"Did the package show an outline of a Tommy gun?"

"Couldn't really tell."

"Then for all you know, Detective, John Oley could've been carrying his laundry."

"Mister Delaney, the Oleys are known mobsters, bootleggers and all-round chiselers. It could've been his laundry, could've been a side of beef, but trust me—it wasn't!"

Delaney squinted and said, "Just bring me the evidence, Detective." He sidestepped, turning his back on Hynes. "Gentlemen, whoever it was that bagged Butch O'Connell, when they're caught you can bet they're going to have top legal talent. What I want to avoid is the shenanigans we saw at the Legs Diamond trial. No matter who's responsible for this, I'm going to take'em to the floor!"

Warner pushed back in his seat. "That's fine, John. But remember the Jersey plates. We could have jurisdictional problems. How about we call in the FBI?"

Delaney removed his glasses, reached into his pocket for a handkerchief and began cleaning them. "Former Broadcasters International? If we need a radio announcer I'll call CBS. I want Butch back alive…not in pieces."

He put his glasses on and turned back to Jimmy Hynes. "Detective, Chief Smurl has given you to me. We're going to run the investigation out of my office, in case the perpetrators stake out the police station. Now, what is your next move?"

Hynes reached over and picked up Tuffy's report. "First off, pull all the paper on John Oley and friends. But we might have a problem here."

Chief Smurl scowled. "How so?"

"Albany is a small town. Everybody knows everybody, even the cops. Will be hard to poke around and ask questions and keep this under wraps."

The Chief waved a hand in the air. "We figured as much. The governor has asked Captain Oliver in New York to send us some guys from the undercover squad. This type of thing's their meat'n potatoes." He jotted a note on scratch paper and handed it to Hynes. "Ten guys. Coming in tonight on the ten o'clock train. Their lead guy is a Detective Joe Gannon. Did some work on the Lindberg case."

Hynes cleared his throat. "Ok, but these undercover guys…well, they're out-of-towners, likely to ask embarrassing questions and step on a few toes. Could be a problem, Chief."

"Yeah, yeah, we know." Smurl glanced toward the window and then at John Warner before he said, "Jimmy…in the phone call, the kidnappers used the names Danny and Eddie."

Hynes gave a low whistle.

Chief Smurl sighed. "The O'Connells have a lot of friends on the south side, and right in the middle of it John Oley has a warehouse. On South Pearl."

Hynes shook his head side to side. "One way or another, you can bet Oley's got his finger in this."

"Why's that, Detective?"

"Way back when, Oley drove a truck for the O'Connells. Most of that work was on the south side."

Smurl winced. "Looks like the noose is already tightening around Oley's neck."

Hynes said. "I'll have the undercover guys shadow all the Oleys. John and Francis are both married and live next door to each other. Their other two brothers are single and live with John. It's gonna be touchy putting undercover cops on Oakwood Street. The neighbors will be suspicious of new faces. Oh, and one thing we need to do immediately. Pull John Oley's phone records. Any chance of tapping his phone?"

"Consider it done," Delaney said. "What else?"

"We'll see. First we get the lowdown on Oley. I'll run things by the New York guys and come up with a game plan. At some point the kidnappers will make contact with the family—and we'll go from there."

"One thing, Jimmy."

"Yeah, Chief?"

"Impress upon the undercover squad the secrecy. The caller said if we get involved they'll kill Butch. I'll personally skin anyone alive who flaps his jaws."

Detective Hynes folded Tuffy's report and slid it inside his coat pocket. "Yessir. Oh, one other thing, Chief. Butch's car. The one he drove home last night."

"A new Buick. Black sedan. The lab boys have got it. I also swung by and got a statement from his mother. It's being typed up now. Mrs. O'Connell said a car whizzed by her when she arrived home from her card game. I'm guessing it was the getaway car. It's all in the report."

Delaney rubbed his jaw. "One other thing, Detective. When you get your ducks lined up, stop by the office. Bring Gannon with you. Let me know what your plans are. I want every 'I' dotted and every 'T' crossed."

"Got it, Mr. Delaney. I'll meet with the New York guys tonight and be in your office first thing tomorrow."

Hynes started for the door. Chief Smurl followed, saying, "I'll see if they have the statement typed up."

This was not protocol with the Chief. Hynes stiffened, wondering what was going on.

The Chief pulled the door closed, walked forward a few steps and stopped at the side of the hallway. He caught hold of the sleeve of Hyne's jacket and bent his head. In a low voice he said, "Jimmy, when the New York detectives arrive tonight? Put'em to work, ok? But make sure nothing blows back on us or the department."

Hynes wrinkled his brow. "Not sure I know what yuh mean, Chief."

"Delaney can *fire us*. He *can't fire* the New York cops. If John O'Connell ends up at the bottom of the river, pin it on the New York cops. Understand?"

Hynes left the building with his shoulders sagging. Last thing he wanted was to get caught in the middle of a fight between two police departments. In just five hours the New York detectives would be arriving. Hynes would need that much time to figure how not to get caught between a rock and a hard place.

***

Edward O'Connell's secretary, Grace Sperrie Fletcher, was a Betty Crocker type with a button nose and a face framed with dark curls. She dressed conservatively and usually maintained her composure. On this Saturday afternoon, day after the kidnapping, Grace was not composed. Early in the day she had received the first call regarding the young John O'Connell's kidnapping. Now she jumped every time the phone rang.

Was it all a hoax? Maybe John had eloped with his fiancée, Mary Fahey, and didn't want publicity. Maybe…the phone rang. Grace flinched. Her fingers hovered over the phone. She took a deep breath and grabbed the receiver. "Office of Meyers, O'Connell and Arnowitz."

A deep gruff voice grumbled, "Tell Eddie to tell Danny to get a letter from his personal mail box." Click. The caller was gone.

Grace Fletcher hurried across the room and softly knocked on the open office door. "M-mister Meyers—a call, a call just came in. For Mr. O'Connell."

George Meyers rose from his solid oak desk and strode toward her. "Calm down, Grace. What did the caller want?"

She wrung her hands. "The man said—he said to, to tell Mr. O'Connell he's to go to his box—retrieve some correspondence."

Meyers's eyes widened. He forced a polite smile. "I know this is difficult for you, Grace, but…exactly what did the caller say?"

"Well, he sounded like the person that called this morning. A rough voice. Raspy. He said to tell Eddie to tell Danny to get a letter from his private box."

"Fine, Grace. I'll take it from here. You go on back to your desk and relax." He closed the door and dialed Ed O'Connell's home number and relayed the message.

Ed said, "You positive they said *private box?*"

"Yeah, Ed. From Dan's *private* box. He used the names Eddie and Danny. I told Smurl and Warner this morning—only your close friends use those names."

"You're right, George. Only our friends on the south side to boot. And not many of them know about Dan's private box."

"You want me to get—" Meyers broke off as his door opened. "Hold on, Ed."

Mrs. Fletcher was trembling and white as a ghost. Meyers said, "Grace?"

Through quivering fingers Mrs. Fletcher squeaked out, "The same voice called back. With the same message!"

Meyers tucked the receiver into his arm pit and waved her away. "Thank you, Grace. It's after four, you go on home now." He waited until the outer office door closed before continuing. "That was Grace, Eddie. A second call came in, same message as the first."

Ed sighed. "Right, George...I'll take it from here."

"Hold on a minute. Think. First call came in around nine this morning. It's just past four. Now we get a phone call directing Dan to his private mail box. A box damn few people know about. The letter had to be in the noon mail, which means the timing is awful tight. Stands to reason that these kidnappers are local mobsters. Could be trying to draw either you or Dan out in the open—might clip one of yuhs, know what I mean?"

"Yeah, George, I see your point. I'll talk to Danny about it. Say, do me a favor. Go look out the window and tell me what you see."

"Ok. Hold on." Meyers went to the window and held the drapery back. He poked his head out and looked straight down. Five stories below was State Street. No one was idling around beneath the building's ten-foot rectangular Bail Bonds sign. To his right he could see past the Albany Bank and Keeler's Restaurant all the way to the gothic-style New York Central Train Station at the end of the street. Pedestrians were on the move, stopping only to avoid traffic or window shop at Savard & Coldwell's. Up the hill toward the capitol the lights were out in Steefel's Department store. People were exiting the Waldorf lunchroom and heading for swing-shift jobs in a factory. They hurried along, did not stop to gaze into Rudolph's Jeweler's.

Phone in hand again, George reported, "Looks quiet, Ed. Everyone's closing up shop. No one hanging around."

"That's a break. What excuse did you make for staying in the office late on a Saturday?"

"Said I was working on the Hammond contract."

"Sounds good. Now hang around the office for another hour in case they call back or in case I need yuh—then go home. I'll touch base with you later. And don't forget to bill Hammond."

Chapter 6
Held for Ransom

Later that same Saturday afternoon, day after the kidnapping, a brown Marmon with white-wall tires and wire-rim wheels pulled to the corner of Whitehall Road and Holmes Court. The passenger door flew open and like a race horse from a starting gate, Solly O'Connell went flying up the front walk to 142 Whitehall. His hat fell off but Solly ignored it, jumped the three porch steps and burst into his brother Dan's home.

John "Solly" O'Connell was a contrast to his two brothers. They were big heavy-set men while Solly was short and slim. His chin was square, his nose short, and he wore glasses. By any definition he was the black sheep of the family, little more than a nickel-and-dime gangster. He ran a small-time book operation but lost most of the profit to his gambling habit. He was known in gambling houses up and down the Hudson River, from Albany to New York City, for leaving behind debt markers. As often as not he did not pay the debts, but relied instead on Dan's political clout and Ed's lawyering skills to get him out of trouble.

In local barrooms, word would soon get around that Butch O'Connell had been kidnapped. Because of Solly's habit of chiseling everyone, the opinion would be that the kidnapping was either payback or a way of sending him a message.

Edward O'Connell, the driver of the Marmon, crossed to the house as though walking on ice. He tugged at his gray cotton vest and had a gray suit coat draped over his arm. He bent to pick up Solly's hat then stood looking up and down Whitehall Road and down Holmes Court. That was Ed O'Connell's style: smooth and deliberate, seeking out all the facts. In the yard a gardener was at work. The gardener wore a traditional sun hat but also a jacket on this hot July afternoon. He raked leaves on his right with his left hand and there was an obvious bulge under his jacket on the left side.

Ed O'Connell was well suited to his profession. As in this instance, he was careful in his observations and his dealings. A shame that he did not give the same good attention to his health. Six years later, in June 1939, he died of a heart attack.

He crossed the porch and knocked once then opened the door. A voice called, "In the kitchen, Eddie."

He stopped in the hallway and deposited his hat and coat on the stand next to the phone. As he stepped through the kitchen door Solly shoved a piece of paper at him and hissed, "Take a look! They want two hundred fifty thousand dollars."

"Hell! Who do they think we are—Rockefellers?" Ed read silently at first then read aloud.

I AM BEING HELD FOR RANSOM I AM
GETTING THE BEST OF CARE BUT PLEA
DO WHATEVER THE ASK AS I THINK I
AM IN A TIGH PREDICAMENT THEY
WANT TWO HUNDRED AND FIFTY
THOUSAND DOLLARS IN FIVE TENS
AND TWENTIES AND FIFTIES THEY
SEEM TO KNOW ALL ABOUT US
SO PLEASE DO WHATEVER YOU CAN
FOR ME THEY WANT YOU TO PUBLISH
IN THE KNICKERBOCKER PRESS SUND,
ABOUT A DOZEN RACKETTERS
NAMES KNOW LOCALLY TO ACT AS
GO BETWEEN TO COLLECT THE
RANSOM HAVE IT PUT IN THE
PERSONAL COLUMN ADDRESSED
SEDGEWICK IN ORDER NOT TO MAK
THIS AFFAIR TO PUBLIC THE FOLLOW
ING SYSTEM WILL BE USED FOR
INSTANCES IF THE NAME HAPPENS
TO BE PET KLEIN IT WOULD BE UNDER
16 5 20 11 12 5 9 14
LONED IN SHORT INSTEAD OF USING
LETTERS

The hand-written envelope was addressed to Mr. Dan O'Connell, Box 1225, Albany, N.Y. In the right corner were five 2-cent Washington stamps and a blue circle around 'Special Delivery.'

Ed pulled at his lips and studied the envelope. When he looked up he said, "Since when do you have a gardener, Danny?"

Dan folded his arms across his chest. "Smurl's idea. Said I need a bodyguard."

Ed pointed to the Albany postmark and time stamp. "Eleven-thirty." He raised a hand toward the clock on the wall near the kitchen sink where the window was open. "Just past four now. Between the call this morning and this letter, and the call George just got, it's plain that whoever did the kidnapping knows the local layout. They know the timing of the local mail, and about your private mail box. They probably also know you don't use a gardener. I suggest you ditch'im."

Dan pinched the bridge of his nose. "I'll call Smurl."

Ed turned the ransom note toward Solly. "It's not Butch's handwriting. Ever see anything like it before?"

"Nope. Butch wrote better'n that in grade school."

Ed shook his head. "These perpetrators probably did not make it even that far. The gutter language tells me they're barely literate. But—"

"But what?"

"My guess Butch is still alive. And at least we know what they want—that's a start."

The ransom note lay face up on the table. Dan slapped it with the flat of his hand. "Shit! Two hundred and fifty thousand dollars! Why not make it a million?" He exhaled and nodded his head. "I'm busted."

"Busted?" Solly said. "The baseball pool made millions—what yuh talking about 'busted'?"

Dan looked over his glasses. "Two things, Solly. Our take was only two percent. And not more than eight hundred thousand at any one time. And I guess you do remember my trial in '29, when I spent a little time in jail?"

Solly scoffed. "Huh! Damn little. Three days."

Dan glared and was about to speak again when Ed interrupted. "Give it up, Danny. You're not under interrogation."

Dan massaged the sides of his head and sighed heavily. "Hell! We hand out thousands of turkeys at Thanksgiving, tons of coal at Christmas—Solly, you know the going price for an Easter lamb? Look at the books yourself. Only thing I got to show for it's the gratitude of the two or three thousand people in the South End."

Solly smirked. "And a few thousand votes, huh?"

Ed scowled. "Stop it! This is getting us nowhere. There's just one question right now. What are we going to do about the ransom?"

Solly dropped into a chair and dangled one arm over the back. "Between paying for my house and Catherine's, I'm down to the bone. Got some bucks stashed away—but nothing close to two-fifty. What about you guys?"

Dan wrapped his palm around the back of his neck. "I'm not doing much better. This place—and the lake house, mortgaged to the hilt. And to get the business moved from Troy and set up in Albany, I used the machinery at the brewery as collateral. What's more, knowing that prohibition's set to end, I paid extra to insure the brewery's up and running by the end of the summer. The money's just plain gone. I've got a few dollars, but—" He shook his head as if to clear it.

Solly exploded. "So what the hell we gonna do?"

Dan took hold of his arm. "Hey, keep it down. You know Ma's upstairs."

Ed stood at the end of the table with the palms of his hands flat on the tabletop. "Let me make some calls. Quite a few businessmen owe me favors. I'll make the calls discreet, of course."

Dan pointed at the ransom note. "Alright, suppose we get the cash…who's gonna be the bagman? Who the hell can we trust with that kinda loot—and trust to keep it quiet?" Dan paced the length of the kitchen then stopped and looked over the top of his glasses. "Solly, you touch those circles. Who yuh know that can be trusted?"

"Well, I've chummed around some with Pat Casey. He runs two speakeasies on the east side of town. And Fred Carroll's a good egg—he don't water his whiskey none. And oh yeah, I helped Tommy Lynch buy some pacers and one of 'em ran in the money! So he owes me. And he mentioned some wireless salesman that runs a bootleg operation. Think he said the guy's name is Stroll. Maybe Strewl. If we need him, Tommy can find him."

"Great," Dan said sarcastically. He retrieved a sheet from a note pad and jotted down the names.

Solly frowned. "Don't gimme that, Danny. Your friends are in the gutter too, right next to mine."

Dan whipped around and pointed with the pencil. "That's just the problem, Solly. I know what they're like...and now I have to trust'em." He glanced at the names he had jotted down. "Tommy Dyke's a good Joe. And how about Mush Trachnier?"

Ed rested a hand on Dan's shoulder. "Does Mush know you knifed his beer license?"

"No way. I had the Alcohol Board lay it off."

"Does anyone suspect that you control the Board?"

Dan shrugged. "Board members are appointed by the Governor—and my name isn't on any of the paperwork. I let them throw a few bones to the small fries, to make it look good. But Mush—he was too big, too much competition. So to answer your question, no. No one can connect me to the Alcohol Board."

Ed scowled. "Better hope no one's noticed how many votes you push into the governor's corner." He held up a hand. "I'm just saying...you could have enemies you're not aware of."

Dan averted his eyes. "We've all got enemies." He shrugged. "I'd better throw in John Oley's name. He's in the know. I can count on him."

Solly came to attention. "Oley? Have you even seen him since he went to work for Legs Diamond? I heard that John Oley was trying to pick up the pieces of that empire."

"Solly, I've known John since the early '20s. We both made lots of money. And both of us keep family and business separate. John will do me right."

Solly raised an eyebrow. "I wouldn't bet on it."

Dan scribbled John Oley's name on the note page and said, "How 'bout you, Ed?"

"I don't bump into thugs much in corporate law. Besides, the Democratic Party would take away my Chairmanship if I even got close to such guys. But, I did hear some names. Bindy Riley and Jim O'Hagan. Jack Murphy knows them. I'll touch bases with him."

For each name Dan had put on the list, he counted the letters of the alphabet out with his fingers and wrote the corresponding numbers. "That should do it. I'll run this by the Knickerbocker Press—"

"Wait a minute, Dan. Better give Smurl a call first. He might have something to say about the list."

Dan mocked a grin and went to the hall phone. He soon reached Chief David Smurl, who reported that he and Major Warner had been meeting with Delaney and decided to have Detective James Hynes lead the investigation.

Dan said, "That sounds fine, David. Is there any word yet?"

"Well, thus far we've been putting together a game plan. One thing, though—the lab's got Butch's car. They're giving it a thorough going-over."

Dan said, "Ed and Solly are here with me and we've got a letter from the kidnappers that says they want two hundred and fifty thousand dollars for Butch's safe return. Told us to put a coded message in the paper—give 'em names of possible runners, or go-betweens."

Ed tapped Dan's shoulder and waved his fingers. Dan handed him the phone. "Ed here, Chief Smurl. Listen, the cash is out. We just don't have it."

"I'll be right over."

"Wait, not so fast. The letter's postmarked Albany and the time stamp no more than a few hours old—they're probably watching us."

"You're right. Hold on, the DA wants to speak with you."

"Ed, John Delaney. Smurl says they made contact. Whatcha got?"

"A ransom note with an Albany postmark. They want big money, and—"

"And what?"

"The gutter language tells me these guys are just a bunch of cheap thugs. Probably don't have much to lose. For the moment, I'm guessing Butch is alive."

"I agree. You positive the letter is genuine?"

"It isn't Butch's handwriting, but it looks genuine."

"First off, we need some samples of Butch's handwriting. Do you know my assistant, Jimmie McGuiness?"

"Skinny guy with the drawn face and big ears?"

"That's him."

"Met him a few times."

"In case you're being watched, I'm going to have McGuiness head your way to pick up the letter. He'll take it to the lab for analysis and have copies made. And Smurl says you mentioned go-betweens."

"Yeah. Said to publish a list of racketeers, using a code, and print it in the newspaper under the name Sedgwick. It's my guess they'll pick one to act as the delivery boy for the ransom money."

Delaney said, "When McGuiness shows up, give him a copy of your list too. I'll see that it gets in the paper without any connection to you or the police."

"Be careful, John. If one of your guys shows up at the paper with a coded message it might raise a lot of suspicion. Maybe not for us, but people will wonder what you're up to, yuh know?"

"You could be right, Ed. You got someone you trust? Someone who can keep his mouth shut?"

"Off the top of my head I'd say Walt Johnson. He's the party chairman across the river in Rensselaer."

"I'll have Chief Smurl track him down."

"Sounds good, John. We'll have the list ready by the time McGuiness gets here. Oh, and one more thing. Better pull your man—the one outside Dan's house. If I can spot him as a cop somebody else will too."

"Consider it done. And that reminds me. I want you to convince Danny to go ahead and move out to his lake house— because it's more isolated and therefore easier to protect. Major Warner is having his troopers search the area to ensure it's clear.

"Shall do. Anything else?"

"No, but act quick. Deadline for Sunday's paper is just two hours away."

Ed hung up the phone and turned to Dan. "Does Ma know?"

"Haven't told her, no—not sure how she'd take it. Speaking of that, Solly, how's Cathy?"

"For the time being we've put our differences aside. Mary's with her. And I've got the doc standing by."

Ed grabbed his hat. "Let's go, Solly. Not a good idea for a crowd to be gathered here."

Dan held up a hand and went to the front window and peeped around the curtain. When he stepped back Ed had his hand on the door knob. Dan said, "Eddie, you really think Butch is ok?"

"Remember what the Chief said this morning? It's a business deal. You won't get one thing without the other."

Solly interjected, "That's the point, Ed—all's we got is empty checkbooks."

Ed sighed. "Remember two things. People always ask for more than they expect to get. That's business." He pulled the door open. "Other thing is, they don't know we don't have the cash."

Solly poked Ed with his hat. "What'll we do when they find out? Then what happens to Butch?"

Ed surveyed the street and stepped outside. "We're not there yet, Solly. One step at a time."

Dan stood in the doorway. "I'll call my secretary. Maybe Leo's heard something from the other chauffeurs."

"Couldn't hurt," Ed said as he turned toward his car. A few seconds later he was back, opened the door and poked his head in. "Yuh know, Danny—about not trusting any of those guys with the ransom? Think about it. Who would the kidnappers trust to deliver it?"

Dan's eyes narrowed. "Eddie…what you getting at?"

"Just guessing. The kidnappers have to pick a bag man they trust, so it stands to reason they're only going to pick someone they know. They ask us to list people we know that can help us. It follows that we have met or know one or more of the kidnappers."

Dan did not reply. Before he pulled the door shut behind him Ed added, "That thirty-eight Solly got you a few months back? Keep it loaded, and keep it close."

When Ed was gone, Dan stood where he was for a moment then turned to the phone and dialed. "Hello, Leo? It's Dan. Need yuh to find an old friend of mine. John Oley."

***

Detective Jimmy Hynes leaned against the wall in the shadow next to the ticket window on the platform of the Albany train station. He held his newspaper into the light to study a photo of a 1933 Pierce-Arrow automobile. He smacked his lips and thought, Oh, well…maybe after I'm Chief.

The rumble of steel-wheeled baggage carts and the clicking on of the platform lights told him the ten o'clock express from New York City was fifteen minutes away. Workmen dressed in gray coveralls stacked boxes at the far end of the platform, where the baggage cars would stop. Porters in polished black shoes and brass-buttoned white jackets waited where the passengers would exit. That's where Hynes expected to greet his New York guests, the undercover cops the DA had arranged to "borrow" to help solve the kidnapping case.

A whistle sounded in the distance. Hynes folded his paper and started down the tracks, watching the pinhole light grow larger. Seconds later the train's bell shattered the peaceful night. Once the cars came to a stop white steam engulfed the place.

Hynes stopped beneath a cast-iron lamppost. He did not know what Detective Joe Gannon looked like but the slim man grasping the handrail by the passenger car's steps looked a likely candidate. He was carrying a trench coat over one arm and gazing up and down the platform. Hynes watched him step down and look around. If he were a mobster he would have bodyguards nearby or keep one hand inside his coat pocket.

The stranger conversed with a white-coated porter. When the porter disappeared the stranger glanced toward Hynes who raised his voice above the noise and asked, "Are you Joe Gannon?" Hynes moved closer. "Detective Joe Gannon from New York?"

The stranger reached out a hand. "You must be Detective James Hynes. Captain Oliver told me about you. Glad to meet yuh."

Hynes noticed that Gannon's white cuff had a sheen to it, indicating that the shirt was made from a high quality cotton, unlike the inexpensive broadcloth of his own shirt. Gannon's light gray suit was of a linen material used only for summer wear. He would have other suits of heavier material for winter. Big city cops could afford different suits for different seasons. Hynes's blue dyed-wool suit was suitable for fall and spring. In summer he just slung the jacket over his shoulder if he got too hot. The suit wore like iron and was cheaper than linen suits.

Hynes smiled politely. "The District Attorney, John Delaney, spoke favorably of you."

"Yeah, I was told you needed some exper—"

The porter bumped Gannon's leg with a large suitcase. "Apologies, sir. Here's yuh case."

Hynes had not missed the half-baked slight. This New York guy was acting superior right off. The differences in their heights added to Hynes's discomfort. He was a full head shorter than Gannon.

Gannon tipped the porter and waited for him to walk away. "Like I said, I was told you needed extra help. Any new developments?"

"Can never have too much help. Here, let me help yuh," Hynes said, deliberately taking the smaller of the two suitcases. He led the way down the steps into the main lobby. "The O'Connells received a ransom demand late this afternoon. Postmarked Albany. Kidnappers want two-hundred and fifty thousand dollars."

"Two fifty! That's more than they wanted for the Lindberg baby. The kidnappers think the O'Connells are made of money?"

Hynes lowered his voice. "Truth of the matter is, the O'Connells are cash broke. They have property, including a brewery. But it's all mortgaged to the hilt."

Gannon set down his suitcase. "The victim's a goner. They may as well go ahead and buy him a coffin." He removed his black-banded white felt hat and wiped the sweat from the inside. "You said they have a brewery. Jumping the gun, aren't they? Prohibition hasn't been officially repealed yet—booze is still illegal."

"It may be illegal but no one is getting arrested for it. The State of Virginia even put it in the papers they were not going to arrest anyone for making booze. They predict prohibition will be repealed by the end of the year. The O'Connells are just getting ready." Hynes stretched his neck to look over Gannon's shoulder. "Say, where's the rest of your guys? Heard you were bringing up a crew."

Gannon put his hat on his head and pulled at his jaw. "Well, Detective, it's like this. My squad works undercover. They slip into town sight unseen. It's best that no one sees them."

Hynes was ready to have some fun now. Payback time for the put-downs Gannon had handed him. "I see-ee. Well, Chief Smurl booked you at the DeWitt Clinton Hotel. Tell your three undercovers over there in the restaurant that the hotel's up on State Street and they'd better tip Alice real good or she'll serve their coffee in their laps. Your guy in the balcony—" Hynes pointed over his shoulder with his thumb, "tell him the doors are locked at six. Your man on the bench across the lobby reading the schedule will find that the next train out is a freight train at midnight. Next passenger train leaves at five but usually runs late. Man in the phone booth behind you? Tell him a water pipe broke a week ago. Line's full of static. Phone next to the ticket window works better. Man out there in the Packard sedan? Tell him to roll up his windows. They start loading the grain ships at one. Lotta dust, yuh know? Hell to get off a car seat. The janitor—" Hynes turned and nodded his head at the man on the far side of the lobby mopping the floor. "The exit he's working toward is blocked. Carpenters dropped some concrete on the other side. Haven't cleared it yet." Hynes looked Gannon straight in the eye with raised eyebrows. "Is Captain Oliver an active part of your…undercover squad, Detective?"

Gannon's jaw had dropped. He gave a chuckle. "Bang, yuh got me!" He scratched at the back of his sandy-colored hair. "You choose the place, I'll buy you the biggest steak on the menu. Deal?"

Hynes offered a warm grin, a peace offering. "Deal. And call me Jimmy." He lifted the larger of Gannon's bags. "Keeler's Restaurant is up on the corner of Green and State Street. It's on the way."

"Right behind yuh. And call me Joe."

Hynes said, "Albany's a small town. Everyone knows everyone. That's why Delaney wants your undercover cops here. Wants to keep the investigation under wraps and outta the press. Kidnappers say they'll kill the victim if the cops get involved. By the way, the folks around here call him Butch." He pulled a police report from his inside coat pocket and handed it over. "That's a report from one of our beat cops. Officer Tuffy. Gave us our biggest lead on the prime suspect— John Oley."

Gannon stopped. "Oley?"

"You know him?"

"Plenty." Gannon stepped to the other side of the sidewalk under the lamp post and studied Tuffy's report. "We did a stakeout the end of April, think Oley and his brother delivered a machine gun and ammo to one Al Fisher. And Fisher dances with the Dutch Schultz mob. You might have bigger problems than you think."

Hynes set Gannon's bag down. "How'd you know Oley delivered a machine gun?"

Detective Gannon held his hands about two feet apart, same as Hynes had in the District Attorney's office earlier that day. "Package was wrapped in paper. About this long—and sure as hell wasn't his laundry. Besides, in May we raided the place and found prints, empty ammo boxes and a broken Tommie gun stock."

Hynes arched his eyebrows. "What was the exact date?"

Gannon wrinkled his nose. Thirtieth or thirty-first. Can get yuh the report. Why?"

Hynes had to check his anger before he could speak. "May twenty-ninth. Rensselaer Bank was robbed. A veteran officer…Gramps Stevens, was killed. He was fifty years on the force! Another officer…Patrolman Rabe. Wounded. The robbers had a machine gun. There are not many machine guns in these parts. We think Oley had a hand in the robbery—but we can't prove it."

"Anyone identify him at the bank?

"Nope. But I'd bet my bottom dollar he had a finger in it."

Gannon paced in a circle. When he stopped he held up Officer Tuffy's report. "Other than John Oley's car in the area of the kidnapping, is there anything else to connect him to the crime?"

"Yeah, but at best it's circumstantial. On July sixth, night before the kidnapping, I saw Oley outside his house with a package just like the one you saw. He guarded it real close. Like you said, it damn sure wasn't his laundry. Just before that a Willy-Knight rolled past me and went right into Oley's garage. It had Jersey plates. I didn't get the number, but I did include the sighting in my report."

They approached the unmarked police car. Gannon said, "I saw in this report that somebody shot up the police station. You think they're part of this?"

"Don't think so. They led Tuffy right to Oley's car."

"Yeah, I see what you mean. That wouldn't make sense…unless they were from Jersey and got lost—"

In unison the two detectives concluded, "—and went the wrong way!"

They got in the car. With his hands on the wheel, ready to step on the starter, Hynes said, "Nah. Oley's not that smart."

"You forget my stakeout and Al Fisher. Dutch Schultz *is* that smart."

Hynes stopped at the light at Broadway and State. "We can run this by the DA tomorrow. This show's gonna be run from his office. And one other thing—you can bet the Rensselaer Police will want to talk to you about that raid. Tomorrow's gonna be a long day."

Gannon rested his elbow on the open window frame. "Did the tellers get a description?"

"Best lead we got was some prints that matched up with some mug shots. Guy by the name of Scarnici."

"Scarnici! Big Charlie Scarnici?"

Hynes shifted into gear. "One of yours?"

"Oh, yeah. After our raid there were a bunch of bank robberies all over New York. The descriptions fit Scarnici and his men—and Scarnici is a trigger man for Dutch Schultz."

Hynes pulled into a parking spot close to Keeler's Restaurant and sat back in the seat. "Oley and Schultz's names and the word *kidnapping* keep popping up in the same sentence. I wonder if Schultz *is* involved somehow."

At the restaurant entrance Hynes put his hand on the door but Gannon paused to study the upper story windows along Green Street. Hynes chuckled. "Believe me, Joe. No one's gonna ambush yuh. Albany's a friendly town."

Gannon grinned and lowered his voice. "New York habit. Besides, I believe in God and a thirty-eight."

"A religious man. Delaney will love that. Beer's on me."

Chapter 7
Second List

Sunday morning Detective Gannon followed Detective Hynes up the steps of a brown stone building that looked like a church with a clock tower in the steeple. On the second floor Hynes pushed open a door. "Morning, Sheila. The district attorney available?"

"Just a minute, Jimmy. Chief Smurl is with him. I'll let them know you're here."

She pressed a button on the intercom and announced their arrival. The voice on the other end said, "Send them in."

John Delaney rose from his desk. "Morning, Hynes. And this must be Detective Joseph Gannon."

Chief Smurl was standing nearby and reached to shake the newcomer's hand. "Captain Oliver told us you did a bang-up job on the Lindberg case. We've got our fingers crossed you and your men can do the same here."

The Lindberg case had taught Detective Gannon all about jurisdiction and turf battles and made him wary of getting sucked in again. Since his arrival in Albany he had already ruffled Hynes's feathers and had no intention of making that mistake again. He said, "Detective Hynes told me about your solid leads and I read Officer Tuffy's report. Looks like you've got a helluva good start. And you've received a ransom note, I believe."

"Correct, Detective. Have a seat."

Hynes and Gannon took the chairs in front of the desk and Delaney slid a Photostat of the ransom notes toward them.

I AM BEING HELD FOR RANSOM I AM
GETTING THE BEST OF CARE BUT PLE[ASE]
DO WHATEVER THE ASK AS I THINK I
AM IN A TIGH PREDICAMENT THEY
WANT TWO HUNDRED AND FIFTY
THOUSAND DOLLARS IN FIVE TENS
AND TWENTIES AND FIFTIES THEY
SEEM TO KNOW ALL ABOUT US
SO PLEASE DO WHATEVER YOU CAN
FOR ME THEY WANT YOU TO PUBLISH
IN THE KNICKERBOCKER PRESS SUNDAY
ABOUT A DOZEN ON RACKETTERS
NAMES KNOW LOCALLY TO ACT AS
GO BETWEEN TO COLLECT THE
RANSOM HAVE IT PUT IN THE
PERSONAL COLUMN ADDRESSED
SEDGEWICK IN ORDER NOT TO MAK
THIS AFFAIR TO PUBLIC THE FOLLOW
ING SYSTEM WILL BE USED FOR
INSTANCES IF THE NAME HAPPENS
TO BE PET KLEIX IT WOULD BE UNDER
16520 1125914
LONED IN SHORT INSTEAD OF USING
LETTERS

Chief Smurl gruffed his throat. "Lab says the paper used to write the note is city stock—think it may have come right from Dan O'Connell's office."

Hynes's head jerked up. "What!? You think Mr. O'Connell kidnapped his own nephew?"

"Certainly not, Detective. The fact proves only that whoever clipped Butch was in Dan's office at some point. Since Dan was elected tax assessor in '28 any one of a thousand people has had access to that office."

Hynes cocked his head. "Tuffy's report said Oley's car was about a block or so away on Regent Street. Yuh know—Oley used to be a driver for the O'Connell family. Or should I say, friend of the family? Before he hooked up with Legs Diamond."

Gannon asked, "How long ago was that?"

"About 1920, give or take."

Delaney folded his arms across his chest. "By the mid-twenties they'd split. Oley went with Diamond, Dan into politics."

"The late Legs Diamond," Chief Smurl intoned. "You probably heard, Detective Gannon. Another mob shot him five times in the head. Killed him in a boarding house at 67 Dove Street, a couple of blocks west of here. We're still investigating."

Gannon picked a bit of lint from his trouser leg as he answered. "Diamond was in the beer business. And Oley worked first for the O'Connells then with the Diamond mob. So what business was O'Connell in?"

Delaney looked over his glasses. "Well, Detective, when prohibition passed, the O'Connells officially put an end to the beer business. But now that prohibition's about to end they're getting back in, starting up a brewery. Call it Hendricks Beer."

Delaney had not totally lied. The O'Connells quit making beer officially in Albany County during prohibition by moving their operation across the river to Rensselaer County. Well-paid officials there looked the other way. With prohibition expected to be repealed by the end of 1933, the O'Connells had moved the business back to Albany County where they could more easily control things.

Gannon gazed at the overhead fan. "Oley and O'Connell, beer. Oley and Diamond, beer. Hmm—think this could all be about beer territory?"

Delaney intertwined his fingers. "Or might be just old-fashioned greed. Either way, our prime concern is getting Butch O'Connell back."

Hynes held up the Photostat of the ransom note. "Paper stock. Familiarity. We're back to John Oley." He held up his copy of Officer Tuffy's report. "John's car was where it shouldn't have been, right in the middle of the crime scene."

Chief Smurl pointed at the ransom note. "And the post box. That letter went to Dan's private box. Since Oley was so chummy with Dan, he'd have known about it. By the way, the postmaster's put a watch on the box."

Hynes said, "Can the lab put Oley's prints to the ransom note?"

Delaney pushed up his glasses "They're trying. I've called for every bank card, contract, and driving license Oley ever touched."

Gannon arched his eyebrows. "You may have some problems down the road."

The others looked his way and he continued. "Chain of evidence. Defense cries corruption or maybe frame-up— because you've always got Oley in your sights. We've had defense counsel drag us through knotholes over stuff like this."

"Good point, Detective. So what's the fix?"

"Neutrals. Bring in some forensic guys from outside the area. Let them double-check the evidence. You indicated you were short-handed. Might be I could get Sergeant Harry Butts, our top ballistics guy in New York. And Sergeant Tom Straney is the best print man in the business. But I'm not sure Captain Oliver will be willing to part with them. And even if he should agree to loan them, the mayor won't budget any money for travel or meals."

Delaney scribbled a note and touched the intercom. "Shelia, get me the governor on the line. Tell him it's for Dan O'Connell."

The room went silent. Hynes cut the long silence by picking up the Photostat copy and saying, "My kids write better than this. Lab got a read on it?"

"Too early yet," Chief Smurl growled.

The intercom buzzed and the secretary reported that "the men from the FBI" had arrived. Delaney pulled at his tie and told her to have them wait. He turned to Hynes. "What's your next step, Jimmy?"

Hynes had begun to speak of keeping an eye on John Oley and his brother Francis when the intercom buzzed again. "Governor Lehman's on the line."

Delaney held a finger to his lips and lifted the receiver. "Hello, Governor. John Delaney." He proceeded to explain the situation. A few minutes later he said, "Detective Gannon says their experts. Think Dan O'Connell would appreciate it."

Delaney hung up and cleared his throat. "They'll be here first thing Monday."

Gannon faked a smile. This was indeed, he thought, going to be a hot case. This O'Connell family obviously had somehow or other accrued a heck of a lot of political clout.

Delaney's voice startled him. "Anything else, Detective Gannon?"

"No, sir. Ready whenever."

"Fine. Have you and Hynes seen the Sunday morning paper?" Delaney pulled a sheet of notepaper from a drawer and slid it across the desk. "Ransom note called for a list of go-betweens. In the paper the names are coded, numbers instead of letters. Recognize any of the names, Jimmy?"

Hynes chuckled. "Know all of them. Local chiselers. But nobody jumps out at me."

Gannon scratched his head. "I've never met any of them but—"

"But what?"

"One of them *is* involved."

Delaney's eyes narrowed and his brow wrinkled like a washboard. "And just how do you know that, Detective?"

"Easy. Would you trust a stranger with two-hundred-and-fifty thousand of *your* money?"

Hynes dropped his head and hid his grin with the palm of his hand.

Delaney said, "Guilt by association won't cut it. We need solid evidence."

When Hynes and Delaney exited they passed two men wearing gray suits with razor-sharp creases in the slacks, white shirts, black ties, and close-cropped hair. Standard uniform with the FBI. Before the detectives reached the outer door Delaney began speaking to the federal men. Gannon shot Hynes a look of surprise when Delaney intoned, "Gentlemen, please tell Mr. Hoover there have been no developments yet. We're just lining up our ducks."

On the stone staircase leading to the ground floor their footsteps echoed like a horse's hooves on a wooden bridge. At the bottom Hynes suggested they swing by the station and check the files on the potential go-betweens.

Gannon said, "How is it these O'Connells know the go-betweens?"

"Dunno, really. Small town, all of them businessmen—have to cross paths some place. But…if any one of them snatched Butch, there will be hell to pay."

"So Delaney would really lower the boom?"

Hynes smirked. "Didn't say Delaney." He pointed at the paperboy on the corner of Eagle Street. "Let's get a Sunday paper."

Detective Joe Gannon had just come from his first meeting with Albany's District Attorney and Chief of Police, but already he realized the nature of the sleeping political giant the kidnappers had awakened. The DA had only to refer to the name O'Connell to get the governor to pull in additional ballistics experts. And the FBI appearing right off? That was highly unusual. Gannon would have been even more astonished if he had known the White House called in the FBI.

As it was, he took note of the O'Connell family's familiarity with local mobsters and the DA's stonewalling of the FBI—and wondered who he could trust. He made a mental note to caution his undercover guys to watch their backs.

***

Across town Dan O'Connell had in hand his copy of the Sunday July 9th edition of the Knickerbocker Press. He looked again at the coded advertisement he had created.

SEDGEWICK

10-9-13-13-9-5—7-9-12-12-15
16-1-20—3-1-19-5-25
10-15-6-14—16-12-5-25
6-18-5-4—3-1-18-18-15-12-12
20-15-13—12-25-14-3-8-
2-1-18-14-5-25—18-9-12-5-25
10-9-13—15-8-1-7-6-14
20-15-13—4-25-11-5
13-21-19-8—20-18-1-3-20-14
2-9-14-4-25—18-9-12-5-25
1-13-5-19—15-2-18-5-9-14

The floor creaked under his bare feet as he headed for the telephone in the hall. His hand hovered in the air above the phone at the sound of a frail voice from an upstairs bedroom. "Danny. Is that you?"

He had not told his elderly mother that her only nephew had been kidnapped because he was afraid she would have a heart attack. He stepped to the bottom of the stairs. "Yeah, Ma. Just gonna fix some eggs. Want some?"

"That would be nice."

"I'll bring them up to you—won't be long."

He pulled the phone the full length of its cord to ensure his mother would not overhear and dialed his brother, the victim's father. "Hello, Solly? Did yuh see the morning paper?"

"Yeah, sure did, and I called Ed and Maude. How about Ma? You told her yet?"

"No—hoping to tell her after we get him back. Don't know if her heart could take it."

"Yeah, Catherine's heart isn't much better. Mary's staying with her."

"You hear anything on the street about Butch?"

"Nope—no one's seen hide nor tail of him. People ask about him, mostly about the wedding plans. I just play dumb, but I'm not sure how much longer I can get by with that. Mary's old man's got the entire sixth precinct busting down the door at every saloon and speakeasy and gin mill."

"Sergeant Fahey hasn't told them Butch is missing, has he?"

"Hell no, Danny! Says he's looking for illegal booze and gambling."

"And they buy that?"

"Old Sarg is no dummy—lays everything off on Delaney. Tells them the DA's looking to run for higher office by getting tough on crime."

Dan clucked his tongue. "Smart guy. And Smurl had his men retrace Butch's Friday night date. He picked Mary up after work and went to the Palace Theater for a show. Interesting part is, they gave CJ Williams a lift home and then Butch took Mary for a snack at Joe's Café on Madison. Solly, CJ thinks someone was following Butch."

"What!?"

"Butch dropped CJ off and a car some distance behind stopped and clicked off its lights. CJ thought it seemed to run after Butch's car, kept its lights off for a long time. But he didn't get a plate number, and his description of the car could fit any of a thousand."

"Cheese-us!"

Dan sighed. "No telling who's behind this. All I know to do is keep checking my mail."

"Danny, when was the last time you checked your box on a Sunday? You best have someone else do it."

A few hours later Leo Quinn, personal secretary to Dan O'Connell, stopped by the Albany Post Office. He was a pudgy man with white hair, neat from head to toe including a starched collar, as befitted a gentleman's gentleman. Leo marched into The Albany Post Office and inserted a key in Dan O'Connell's private mail box. He removed the typed envelope and shook his head at the four three-cent stamps in a crooked line next to the smudged Albany postmark. Too much postage, he thought. He glanced over his shoulder and tucked the envelope into his tweed jacket pocket, murmuring to himself, "Coast clear."

High above, at a sixth floor window, Undercover Detective Robert Goldstein stepped to the side of the window and chuckled. "They always overlook the obvious."

The Albany Postmaster, P.S. King, scratched his head. "How's that, Detective?"

Goldstein put his binoculars to his eyes and studied Leo Quinn and the cars parked on the street. "They never look up. They only look over their shoulder. This guy Quinn thinks he's Dick Tracey."

As Quinn gunned his engine and drove away Goldstein brought the binoculars back up and focused on the windows of the opposite buildings. "Wonder if anyone else is watching?"

Quinn zipped right along and soon reached Whitehall Road. He handed the envelope to his boss who ripped it open with his finger.

DEAR UNCLE DAN.

NAMES NOT SATISFACTORY
USE SOME RIGHT NAMES
USE SAME METHOD
USE TIMES UNION.   MONDAY
SEDGWICK

"Damn it!"

"Anything I can do, Mr. O'Connell?"

Dan covered his eyes with his palms and breathed deeply. "Hold on a second, Leo—I gotta make a call first."

Leo took a step back. "Of course, sir."

Dan went back to the phone and put in a second call to Solly. "No dice with the names on the go-between list—the bastards want us to publish another list."

After a few more exchanges between the brothers, Dan raised his voice. "Beats the hell outta me!"

"What are you yelling about, Danny?"

Dan pressed the receiver against his chest and pivoted and yelled up the stairs. "Sorry, Ma. Didn't mean to disturb you."

In the next few minutes Dan and Solly came up with a new list, to be published in Monday's edition of the Times Union. They included Solly's friend from the track, Bill Bardean, plus Dave Hotaling and Bob Parr. When Dan pushed his brother for more names he added his poker buddies, Rock Tarzio and Eddie Gorman.

"That's about it, Danny. I'm running out of friends."

"You call these guys friends? Don't you−? The paper tore. Dan had pressed down too hard on the pencil. He muttered, "Good gosh, what next?"

Solly was asking what had happened but Dan had thrown the pencil to the floor. He bent to retrieve it, bumped his head, shoved against the phone stand, and fell. In the process he dropped the phone. From the bedroom above came, "What's all that noise?"

"Nothing, Ma. Just tripped over the phone cord—everything's ok."

Quinn was at his side. "Let me help you, sir."

With the commotion over Dan picked up the phone and explained to Solly. He added, "I'm running short on friends myself. Would Mike Connolly and Willie King do us any good?"

"Connolly's getting into politics, not been so active in the rackets. But wouldn't hurt to throw his name in. If you're going that route, try Neal Ponze and Paul Carroll."

"Carroll? Didn't his place burn down some time ago?"

"That was his cousin, Patrick—part owner in the Love Nest out by Hurstville. Just remember, Danny—if Carroll helps, he'll be looking for some favors to get them back on their feet."

Dan sighed. Was he thinking about the Carrolls' bad luck? Furnaces at several saloons and roadhouses had caught fire or blown up recently. Rumor on the street had it that if you didn't buy O'Connell beer "something might happen." In the thirties, most furnaces used coal—and coal dust was extremely flammable.

"I know how to treat my friends, Solly. If they help us I help them."

"What about Oley and his crowd?"

O'Connell exhaled. "Surprised me that the kidnappers didn't pick him from the first list. Guess it wouldn't hurt to put his name in again. I've been looking for him—feel sure he'll help out."

"By the way, Danny. I heard Oley has a new partner. Stroll or Strewl—something like that."

"What about some of the guys that worked with us during prohibition?" Dan asked. He jotted down two names, Pat Coffee and Joe Leone. Solly was saying, "Dan…if something happens to—"

Dan jumped in with a reprimand, rebuked his brother for even thinking of that possibility, and hung up the phone. Almost immediately he picked it up and dialed again and soon had filled in the district attorney on the request for this second list.

John Delaney said he was glad they had already come up with the list and offered to take it from there—get the envelope in the mail as before. "Another thing, Dan," Delaney said, "we need samples of Butch's handwriting. Can you get hold of some notes or letters—even old Christmas cards, anything in his handwriting?"

Dan agreed to take care of that. He decided not to look for any in the house or ask his mother. He would get them from Butch's bride-to-be, Mary Fahey. First he would send Leo off to deliver the new list. It was while he was relating this plan to Leo that a woman's voice from above said, "Why are you sending Leo to the district attorney on Sunday?"

Dan O'Connell felt like a kid caught with his hands in the cookie jar. At the top of the stairs stood a woman with a deeply lined face, white hair brushed into a soft mound, and silver-dollar-sized eyeglasses.

Mother O'Connell had come over from Ireland after surviving the potato famine. In Albany she scrubbed floors and went without food as she raised four sons. The unexpected death of her son Patrick only three weeks earlier had brought on a heart attack. At this stage her body was frail, but Mother O'Connell herself was tougher than a fifty-cent steak.

"Mr. Quinn," she said, "I believe my son has given you an errand to perform. Please attend to it."

"Yes, Ma'm."

When the door closed behind Leo she said, "Daniel, what was in that letter?"

Dan's shoulders sank. He shuffled toward the stairs. How was he going to tell his mother that her only grandson had been kidnapped? He began climbing the stairs as if marching up to the gallows.

***

The District Attorney replaced the phone and looked across his desk to Hynes and Gannon. "What have you got on the list of go-betweens?"

Hynes leaned forward. "We're pulling all the records on all of them, but I was surprised they didn't choose Oley. Between Tuffy's report and what I witnessed the night of the sixth—thought we had a winner."

Delaney tapped the desk with his fingers. "You'll have more suspects shortly. That was Dan O'Connell on the phone, and as you heard I'm sure, the kidnappers have asked for a second list. His secretary is on his way over with it."

Gannon asked, "Is he bringing the new letter too?"

"Yup—I'll get a Photostat of it to you later this afternoon."

Gannon cleared his throat. "These, uh, go-betweens…how is it the O'Connells know them?"

Gannon caught the shifting glances between Delaney, Smurl and Hynes. It was clear that they knew the answer but were not keen on sharing the answer.

Chief Smurl had been sitting in the background. Now he leaned forward. "Albany's not like New York—it's a small town. Everybody knows everybody." He pointed at the copy of the ransom note. "You mentioned the handwriting earlier. How's that lead going?"

Hynes twisted in his chair. "Moving along. The lab's collected a bunch of signatures, mostly from the banks and driving licenses. They're wading through it all."

Delaney raised an eyebrow. "John Oley's driving license?"

"Told the lab to run it first. No word back yet."

Gannon interjected, "If any of them spent time locked up, there's a prison roster they signed. That would give you a wider sampling of the handwritings."

Delaney tilted back in his brown leather swivel chair "Wouldn't need a warrant, either. Good idea."

Hynes jumped in. "If we get something close we can subpoena financial records."

Delaney wiped the lenses of his glasses with a white handkerchief. "Already working on it."

Hynes tapped the newspaper. "If they're gonna use the newspaper to talk, we better get the subscriber lists, Chief."

"Ok, I'll give the Knickerbocker and Times Union a call. You and Gannon can stop by and pick them up."

Gannon offered, "You might wanna get the subscriber list of all the surrounding newspapers. Most of the stories go out over the wire. Kidnappers could be reading any one of them to get their information."

Delaney pushed up his glasses. "Good point."

Chief Smurl exhaled. "Whew! There's over a dozen newspapers—the Argus, Troy Eagle, Saratogian, to name a few. You guys are gonna have your hands full."

Delaney was watching Detective Gannon who had pulled the Photostat of the first ransom note and the envelope together. "Something wrong, Detective?"

"No sir, just thinking about the timing of it."

"Elaborate."

Gannon's brow wrinkled. "Kidnapping was about midnight on the seventh—less than forty-eight hours ago. Yet contacts—plural—have been made. Mailings, newspaper ads and letters. A damn quick pace. Someone's got to be walking this stuff through—and I'm thinking someone on the inside. Letters normally take a few days to get delivered." He held up the Photostat. "And you're getting replies within hours."

"We are aware of that, Detective. We think they're dropping the letters directly at the post office. But neither your prime suspect nor any of his known crowd has shown up."

Chief Smurl huffed. "John Oley's acting innocent. That makes me suspicious right there. He hasn't—"

The buzz of the intercom interrupted and soon thereafter Delaney's secretary showed in a white-headed man and closed the door behind him. Leo Quinn. As directed, he hand delivered the second list. Delaney thanked him and he left.

During the intercom exchange Delaney's secretary had also alerted her boss to the fact that the men from the FBI were still waiting. He replied that he was still in conference.

Now the second list passed from hand to hand. Chief Smurl said to Hynes, "Anybody look good to you?"

"No one jumps out at me. What about you, Joe?"

"Some of the names look familiar—but nothing screams at me."

Delaney said, "Sheila will get a copy to you. How about Mrs. O'Connell, John Junior's mother? You guys talked to her yet?"

"Not yet," Hynes replied. "I've got Joe's undercover men on stakeout around Oley's house—and we're either seeking locations for the others or watching their comings and goings. Some of McCaffey's men are kicking in doors…quietly of course. The rest of our crew's combing records. Something should turn up soon. And about Mrs. O'Connell—we'll talk to her later today. We do have two phone taps running but so far there's only been local chatter."

Chief Smurl pulled on his ear. "I spoke with Catherine briefly late yesterday. She thinks she passed the kidnappers when she returned from her Friday night social event. Said a car zipped by. She also noticed Butch's car under a tree with the door cracked open, radiator water still gurgling. I've got some uniforms patrolling out there with some BS about people complaining of noisy neighbors."

Hynes pulled at his lip. "Hmm…radiator gurgling. That can only mean she got home just minutes after the kidnapping." He rubbed his chin. "Might be better to use the undercover, Chief. If the kidnappers are local, we don't want them seeing a lot of uniforms in the area."

"Good point, Jimmy. Detective Gannon, put one of your guys close to Putnam Street. I'll keep a uniformed cop on traffic duty a block away up on Second Avenue, in case he's needed."

"I'll see to it," Gannon said, and he and Hynes rose to leave.

Delaney escorted them to the door. "Don't forget to tell your men to tip-toe around everything. The cops aren't to be involved—the O'Connells don't want their nephew back in a pine box."

Gannon and Hynes nodded agreement, the DA opened the door and they exited. Delaney called to their backs, "And keep me informed!"

Delaney began shaking hands with the men who had been waiting. The FBI affiliates always looked alike: stone-gray suits, highly polished black shoes, and crew cuts. "Sorry to keep Mr. Hoover's men waiting. I'm District Attorney, John Delaney. Come into my office."

Hynes paused before descending the stairs and pretended to be reaching for something in his coat pocket. Before Delaney's door closed he heard, "Gentlemen, this is our police chief. Sorry to say, nothing has developed yet."

Gannon twirled his hat and whispered, "There's gonna be hell to pay when those G-men learn they were stonewalled."

A short time later Hynes turned the unmarked police car onto Putnam Street. He waved at a uniformed patrolman near the two-story house with a side chimney and a brass number 14 nailed on the white door frame. He parked at the front curb.

Hynes flashed his badge at the patrolman. "I'm Detective Hynes, this is Detective Gannon. Got anything?"

"Yessir. Right now Miss Mary Fahey is with Mrs. O'Connell. A Miss Maude O'Connell left about forty minutes ago."

The patrolman pointed to the gray house with red painted windows at the corner of Putnam and Van Orden. "A Mr. George Keiss saw a fender bender the other night. Got a description of the car and occupants." He pointed again toward a two-story yellow house without a porch. "Guy named Tobin there. He heard a racket late Saturday night, but says he didn't see much."

Hynes muttered, "I bet." He straightened his tie. "Patrolmen, introduce Detective Gannon here to Mr. Tobin. Then put in a call to Chief Smurl—he's got a new assignment for yuh. I'm going to briefly pay my respects to Mrs. O'Connell, then see if I might have a chat with George Keiss."

Detective Gannon slipped his suit coat on. "Ok, Patrolman. Lead the way."

***

Gannon lowered his head over his note pad. "So you really didn't see much. Could you identify the voices? Maybe belong to someone you know?"

Michael Tobin rubbed his wrinkled bow. "Not sure exactly."

"Well suppose, Mr. Tobin, if I rounded up a few suspects. Think you could recognize the voices?"

Tobin walked to the window facing the street. He fumbled with the string on the shade. "Maybe…if you arrested someone. Maybe, behind bars, yuh know? If I listened through a door, something like that."

"Ok, Mr. Tobin. If I have any more questions, I'll contact you."

At the front door Gannon said, "You're positive it was a '33 Pontiac?"

"Right as rain, Detective. Me and the Missus went car shopping last week—thinking about buying one."

"Thanks, Mr. Tobin. You've been very helpful."

Gannon stood on the bottom step for a moment and mentally measured the distance from the street curb to Tobin's front window. He was sure Tobin could easily have overheard the kidnappers talking in the still of the night. And he suspected he could also have given a description of the people.

A voice from across the street said, "Sure is hot today."

Hynes was standing not far from George Keiss's porch. Gannon bent the brim of his hat to shade his eyes from the afternoon sun and headed toward him. They met in the middle of Putnam Street.

Hynes pointed down the street with his thumb toward Second Avenue and began walking. "What'd you get?"

"Mr. Tobin said he didn't really hear too much. A man with a grumpy voice said he was getting tired of sitting around, a couple of females giggled, and some tall guy hushed everyone up. So I asked if he could describe this tall guy and he stuttered a bit and said, 'It was kind of dark.' He says he only glanced out the window for a second or so, then flopped down in the rocker to rest his doggies and read the paper."

Gannon heaved a sigh and continued. "But, Mr. Tobin did positively identify a strange car: a maroon 1933 Pontiac. Jimmy, Tobin had the jitters. I'd bet money he knows more than he's telling."

Hynes said, "Yeah—the possibility of getting shot has that effect on people."

He grinned and held a slip of paper in the air. "How about…a plate number?"

"How the—"

"Mister Keiss gave it to Mrs. O'Connell."

Gannon grimaced. "Close enough to get a plate number means close enough to identify them."

"And smart enough not to." Hynes turned and pointed at the corner of Putnam and Van Orden. "How far you guess that street lamp is from Keiss's place?"

"Ten feet—give or take."

"And you could hear me from the across the street while standing on Tobin's property." Hynes came to a stop next to a tree. "Mrs. O'Connell found Butch's car here."

Gannon turned toward the witness's homes and was silent for a moment. He raised his eyebrows. "Yuh know, Jimmy—Tobin stuttered and stammered quite a bit. A man is only afraid of a person he knows."

Detective Hynes sucked in his lips and rocked back on his heels. "Yeah, I know. And neither of them's going to say squat till we get our suspects behind bars."

"So we twist their arms a little."

"Nah—we'd lose them for sure. Let's walk."

They turned left, up Second Avenue toward Regent Street. Hynes said, "We'll let it ride a while. Keiss and Tobin aren't going anywhere, and we've still got too many maybes in front of us to put the squeeze on anyone. I'm hoping your undercover men will turn…"

Hynes came to a stop at the corner of Second and Regent Street. He whipped his head around toward Putnam Street and back toward Second Avenue. "I'll be…"

"What?"

Hynes pointed. "This is where Tuffy and Joyce found Oley's car. There's a clear view of Putnam Street and the O'Connell House…and that house too!" He pointed to 58

Second Avenue. "That's Mary Fahey's house. Butch's fiancée."

Gannon stepped into the street and scanned both directions. "Clear view of her house and the victim's—with nobody the wiser." He pushed his hat up with his thumb. "Tuffy and Joyce just provided our prime suspect with opportunity and put them at the scene of the crime."

Hynes frowned. "Nope. They put John Oley's *car* here."

On the stroll back to their car Hynes said, "Keiss saw a green car with two people. Tobin saw the Pontiac. Drivers and spotters make it four people—maybe more. We both know you can really pack a Pontiac, four people easily. You'd need at least four men to take out Butch."

Hynes pulled the car door open. "I'll get McCaffey's guys to run the plate number. Let's check in with Delaney and the others. Might be a long night."

"Long night?"

"Yeah. We'll check with the lab to see if anything new has turned up. About midnight we can come back here, have a look-see."

"Why?"

"On the night of the kidnapping the moon was full, so the light won't be exactly the same, but I wanna get a better idea of what Keiss and Tobin could and couldn't see."

Both detectives were much aware of the need for solid proof. The evidence they had pointed to John Oley but would not hold up in court. Both were disappointed that the witnesses were unwilling to be more forthright, but understood all too well why they were holding back.

Gannon was also busy wondering why Delaney was lying to the FBI and deliberately keeping them out of the investigation. He would soon have his answer, as he came to understand more of the inside story of the O'Connell family's connection with Albany's politics.

Chapter 8
Mrs. Watkins

The next morning, Monday July 10, Detective Joe Gannon yawned in the passenger seat of the open-top unmarked police car. "Man," he said. "Sure was a short night."

Hynes up-shifted and continued out New Scotland Avenue. "At least we confirmed that both Keiss and Tobin saw enough to give us a good description *if they wanted*."

Gannon slouched back in the seat and closed his eyes. "I checked the records. Keiss's description fits John Oley *and* Francis Oley. But if our witnesses won't admit to seeing their faces—"

"They know what happened to the witnesses that testified against Legs Diamond, and they probably know the Oleys are cut from the same cloth. Keiss and Tobin are not ready to die. In the meantime, we can back-door some other possible suspects."

Gannon grabbed the top of the front window and pulled himself up straight. "Which suspects you talking about?"

Hynes touched the brakes. "Tobin said he heard female voices, right?"

"Right."

"We know from the files that John and Francis are married. Who brings a date on a kidnapping?"

"What you getting at?"

"Female voices. Wives."

"That's all we need. A few more Bonnie and Clyde teams."

"Yeah—we can talk about it after dessert."

"Dessert? What in the heck—"

On Oakwood Hynes pulled in at a house that resembled a huge doghouse. He drove around back and entered a garage with the number nineteen nailed on the door. "This is it—where I live."

Gannon grinned and walked back to the street to survey the house. It had windows trimmed in blue, a covered porch and an entrance with double doors stained oak brown. "Well, Jimmy, looks like you're doing all right for yourself."

"Me and the Missus. We get by. Got the whole top floor to ourselves. The McDermotts have the bottom floor."

Hynes pointed up the street toward New Scotland Avenue. "Late Thursday afternoon, July six…a Willy-Knight with Jersey plates breezed by me and made a beeline for John Oley's place." Again he pointed. "Down there. Number 40, on the corner. His garage is round back on Fairview. His brothers, Ed and William, they live there too—and Aggie, John's wife. Let's walk."

Detective Gannon studied the houses along the tree-lined street. The houses were similar in style: one-story shoe boxes or two-story doghouses. All had porches and yards not much bigger than a postage stamp. He pulled at his ear. "Jimmy, your report said you didn't get the plate number."

"Because there was nothing wrong. The Willey-Knight zipped right into Oley's garage. I caught sight of Oley as he left his porch to meet the car. He was holding a package in his arms, holding it like it was gold. When I got close he held it off to the side. Delaney doesn't make much of it, but I know what I saw."

Gannon said, "After Delaney reads the report on my April stakeout—where I saw both the Oleys—and the report on my Shepnick raid, he may change his mind."

"Shepnick raid?"

"We found a Tommy gun stock and empty ammo boxes."

Hynes raised his voice. "Maybe—but you never know these days."

A petite woman with a bandana wrapped around her graying hair stepped from a blue one-story house onto the porch. "Oh, Detective Hynes. Thought I heard voices out here. Home early today?"

"Just showing my friend here around. Helen Watkins, meet Joe Gannon. He's up from the big city."

Mrs. Watkins dried her hands on her apron and approached with an outstretched hand. "Pleased to meet-cha, Mr. Gannon. Come sit a while and tell me all about New York."

Gannon glanced at Hynes. The woman went right on. "Come along. You're bound to be hot out in this heat. And my pies have surely cooled by now—so you must try a piece. I insist!"

They followed Helen Watkins onto the porch where there was a small wicker table and four chairs. She disappeared inside. Gannon whispered. "Dessert?"

Hynes removed his hat and said in a hushed voice, "Jump in whenever." In a strong voice he said, "Best pie anywhere around."

Their hostess returned with a tray of plates, cups, a pot of tea and an apple pie. "He's jesting, Mr. Gannon. They're—"

"Don't be shy, Helen. I'm a detective—I know these things. Joe, her pies have won blue ribbons at the fair more than a few times."

Gannon balanced his hat on his knee. "You can't argue with that, Mrs. Watkins."

"Well, the proof's in the tasting, so I'll cut a piece for you. How's New York this time of year, Mr. Gannon?"

"Looks like it'll be the hottest July on record."

When the men raved over the pie Helen Watkins waved her hand in the air dismissively. "Glad you like it." A few seconds passed in silence as she watched them eat. Then she said,

"Jimmy, I've been wanting to ask you. Did you ever find out about that strange car last week? The one going so fast it was a wonder somebody didn't get killed? I saw you speak to John, and hoped you gave him a good tongue lashing."

Hynes swallowed a bite of the pie and arched his head in the direction of Oley's house. "We were thinking to stop by there now, but I see he's not home. You know where he went?"

"Friday morning—that's when they left. Friday morning. Filled their trunk full of groceries and headed out. Lord knows how their wives keep their figures—was enough food in that trunk to feed an army!"

Gannon came to attention. "They…uh, Mrs. Watkins, might I have another slice of that pie? It's more than delicious."

"Of course, Mr. Gannon." She reached for his plate. "Francis went with them. Took Genevieve and their child. His first, yuh know. She's a nice lady. From Vermont, I understand."

While Mrs. Watkins was bent over the table, Gannon arched his eyebrows and beamed a grin at Hynes. The grin said: *Best-tasting interrogation I've ever been part of.*

He wiped his mouth with his napkin and said to their hostess, "Sounds like Francis has his hands full. Have you known Francis long, Mrs. Watkins?"

"I've known him since he was a paper boy for the Knickerbocker Press. Used to throw the papers sidearm. Ha! Barely could hit my porch. I told him an overhand toss would give him a better aim." She smiled. "Got so he could pitch a paper through my front window there without a hitch."

Gannon glanced at Hynes. "Knickerbocker Press?"

Hynes caught the implication. The first list of go-betweens had been published in the Knickerbocker Press. "Yep, one of our bigger local newspapers."

Hynes set his empty plate on the table. "You make Francis sound like a go-getter, Helen. Know what's he doing now?"

"He's working some for John. And they say he owns part of a speakeasy over on Market Street. Started right after his brother quit working for Mr. O'Connell. Went out on his own."

Hynes set his plate back on the tray and picked up his teacup. "Mr. O'Connell is one of our leading citizens, Joe. Elected official—tax assessor." He took a sip of the tea and asked their hostess how John Oley was getting along.

She clasped her hands together. "Mighty fine, by the looks of things. Got that big house with his brothers, yuh know. Him and Aggie—he got married four months ago—bought a new car. Why they need two cars is beyond me. He could just as easily drop Aggie off at her work." The woman lowered her head. "I think it's showing off, is all. Think they're better than us regular folks."

Hynes leaned back in the wicker chair. "No doubt…and you said Aggie is working?"

"At Albany Hospital." She rolled her eyes and lowered her voice. "Don't know how long she'll last. Why, I've seen her at night. Out on the porch smoking and drinking. Betcha she thought everyone was asleep and wouldn't notice."

"No-o-o," Hynes said as if in disbelief.

"Uh-huh." Mrs. Watkins dropped her voice so low it was barely audible. "Heard she was one of *those girls.* From New York. Mark my word, that's what I heard."

"What's this world coming to?" Hynes said with a shake of his head. "How about Francis's wife? Does she work too?"

"Not sure, since the baby was born. I don't like to pry." She covered her mouth and giggled. "Think right now they're just working on a big family."

Hynes reached to the porch floor and picked up his hat. "Well, we better be getting on. Sure thank you for the pie,

Helen. I must confess I was hoping as we headed this way that you might have a fresh one. Didn't want Joe here to head back to the city without tasting the best pie anywhere around."

Gannon stood at the top of the steps. "Been a pleasure, ma'am—and the pie really is blue ribbon."

They headed toward the street and Hynes turned back and said, "Oh, Helen, my wife said she'd be over this Saturday for the final fitting and to settle up."

"Don't worry none, Jimmy. I still have some winnings left over for a rainy day. We can settle up whenever."

Gannon said, "Winnings? Don't tell me you play the ponies, Mrs. Watkins."

"Of course not, Mr. Gannon. I bought a lottery ticket on baseball. Mr. O'Connell himself sold it to me."

Gannon smiled and waved. "How fortunate you are."

Several silent steps later Gannon said to the sky, "O'Connell…lottery. She meant a baseball pool? Back in '27 or '28?"

"Yeah, same family. But he paid his debt to society."

"Few days in jail for a million dollar crime? Damn it!" Gannon turned his head to the side and spit. "In New York we give more time than that for illegal parking!"

"I don't know much about it. I didn't have this job then and no one talked to us beat cops much. But take a hard look around, Joe. People are out of work, they're hungry." Hynes stopped walking and looked up into Joe Gannon's face. "Who's gonna feed 'em? The government?"

"Better spell it out for me, Jimmy. From where I stand all I see is a million-dollar Santa stuffing his own pockets. No wonder the kidnappers are asking two-fifty. That's chump change for—"

"No, you don't understand this, Joe. Way I heard it, the O'Connells only took two percent. The big boys took the rest."

They reached Hynes's garage and stopped by its gray stone wall. With his hands on his hips Gannon said, "How the hell do you spend—"

Hynes lifted his hands in the air with the palms open. "Albany's South End."

Gannon shook his head. "I don't get it."

Hynes expelled a lungful of air. "The South End of Albany is home to thousands of poor folk. Every Thanksgiving they get turkeys. Christmas rolls around, they get a ton of coal, and at Easter a chunk of lamb. Now, Joe, that stuff don't come cheap. Hell—if what you needed was new teeth you'd just go to Dan O'Connell. He'd fix you up with cash to get them. That's where the O'Connell money goes. Back to the average guy on the street. That's why he's known as *Uncle* Dan…and most anybody's smart enough not to bite the hand that feeds you."

Gannon kicked a stone. "All that for two percent of the deal? Damn small reward!"

"Well, not exactly."

Hynes stepped inside the garage, Gannon followed. Hynes peeped outside to make sure no one was listening. He said, "The reward is a checkmark in the right box on a ballot. It's that simple."

Gannon put his hands on his hips. "So for the price of a turkey or a bin of coal—the O'Connells get to pick who they want in public office." He shook his head side to side. "Still don't make it right."

Hynes did not reply.

Gannon rubbed his chin. "Ok. Let's say the O'Connells *are* the gray knights of Albany. Why snatch one of the ones that feed yuh?"

Hynes frowned. "Dunno."

"You said the O'Connells are broke. How'd that happen?"

Hynes pushed his hat up with his thumb. "Easy. The law lowered the boom on the O'Connells' cash cow—the baseball pool. They were bootleggers for a time but the repeal of prohibition is taking all the profit out of booze. I heard that all the O'Connells mortgaged their houses to the hilt to set up this legit brewery. Between that and the South End expense...guess it's the same as if their money floated up to the moon."

"They'd be smart to sell out to one of their competitors."

Hynes huffed. "Not so long as everyone in the South End votes. All the people on the Alcohol Board are political appointees."

Gannon tapped the car with a fingernail. "I see. So these O'Connells own a brewery and the votes to control the Alcohol Board. Which means in turn they also control who gets a beer license."

Hynes frowned again.

Gannon said, "Son of a bitch! This could be more about a beer license...or revenge for not getting a license—which scenario really does make O'Connell Junior no more than a pawn in a game."

Hynes put his hand to the car door. "Hmmm. Hop in—and I'll let yuh size up Dan O'Connell for yourself. He only lives about a mile and a half away. I'll take the back way. We can be there in eight minutes flat."

Hynes headed up Oakwood Avenue. Gannon turned and peered out the back. "Eight minutes flat. Wonder if John Oley can do it faster."

Hynes slammed the car into second gear. The police car whizzed around the turn onto New Scotland Avenue toward Dan O'Connell's house. Gannon rested his elbow on the window frame. "Enough to feed an army—according to Mrs. Watkins."

Hynes said, "I'm thinking enough to feed about five kidnappers, and Butch."

"You said you think the Oley brothers' wives are in on it, right?"

"You sleep with dogs—you'll get up with fleas. I'm guessing they were there. Mrs. Watkins thinks John's wife worked the city. Can your guys run the rap sheets on her? She might have a record."

"I'll give Captain Oliver a shout. John Oley himself has got history in New York. They can back track him and his wife. You think the Oleys will show up again?"

Hynes let the car roll to a stop. "Got to, for two reasons. For one, they think they're innocent. And two, they have to keep tabs on things. I don't doubt they'll be back. Can your guys shadow them?"

"That's a cinch. In a few days we'll know what size BVDs they wear."

A car behind honked and pulled around them. Hynes slipped the car back into gear. "Not too close on Oakwood Avenue. Mrs. Watkins can spot measles on ants at fifty yards."

Gannon chuckled then asked, "So, O'Connell sold her a ticket?"

"Yeah—she was about to be put out on the street and wouldn't accept charity."

Gannon was silent for a moment. "Yuh know, if the O'Connells shook down the wrong people in the baseball pool this could be payback. Could be an inside job. You think the O'Connells are broke, so let's suppose the O'Connells scream kidnap. Let's suppose they reach out and touch all their friends to raise the ransom money. Then they head for the hills with the money and no one to blame. The victim is set free, the O'Connells have the ransom money—and no one's the wiser. Helluva set up!"

The noise of a gust of wind filled the car. Neither detective said anything. Finally Hynes said, "Guess we'd better check Dan's finances."

The hayfields they had been passing gave way to green lawns and Hynes pulled to the curb a few houses down from the intersection of Whitehall Road and Fullerton Avenue. He set the parking brake and pointed. "Number 142."

As they watched a man in brown slacks with his sleeves rolled up and a sun hat pushed back on his head moved to the side of the house and peered through a draped window. Gannon exclaimed, "What the hell?!"

Hynes said, "Let's go to work." As they approached the house Hynes shouted, "You! Hold it right there! Thinking of breaking and entering, huh?"

The slim man turned toward them with his hands in the air. "Aw, come on, Jimmy, it's me—Nat—from the Argus."

Hynes twirled a set of handcuffs. "Whatcha doing here? Looks like a burglary to me, Nathan."

"Just wanna check a story with Mr. O'Connell. Butch didn't show for work. All the cops are asking questions and looking for him. Mary Fahey won't answer her door or phone. Hell! No one will, so something's for sure going on. Maybe Butch eloped, maybe he got waylaid." Nathan shrugged. "Awful funny that no one's around, yuh know? Something's up."

The young reporter pulled a pad and pencil from his back pocket. "Wanna make a comment? Who's your friend?"

The porch door flew open. Dan O'Connell sputtered, "Get in here! All of yuhs—get inside!"

Hynes shoved Nathan through the open door. Gannon went immediately to a window and pulled the drape aside enough to see out. Then he dashed to a window on the opposite side. "Looks quiet," he said. "Don't think anyone noticed."

Nathan made a note on his pad. "Something's going on, right? Let me in on it and I'll make you famous. The public wants to know and—"

Hynes said, "Shut up, Nathan. Mister O'Connell, sorry about this. He's a reporter from the Argus. We caught him poking around outside."

O'Connell brushed past Hynes to confront Nathan. "The Argus? Who's your boss?"

"Bruce Martin."

O'Connell hustled up the hallway and grabbed the phone. When the operator answered he said, "Dan O'Connell here. Put me through to Bruce Martin at the Argus."

Seconds later he said, "Got one of your guys here, Bruce. Right in front of me—thinks he's got a story. Now listen to me, Bruce, and listen careful. You gotta call him off. Get in touch with my brother Ed—or John Delaney. They can explain."

Dan listened a moment then exclaimed, "Can it—just can it! If you print anything about us right now you'll regret it. Now get on the phone and talk to Delaney."

Several seconds later Dan handed the phone to the young reporter who listened for a moment and handed the phone back. Dan pointed to the door. "Hit it!"

Hynes waited until the door closed behind the reporter. "Yuh know, Mr. O'Connell, people *are* beginning to notice things. We can't keep a lid on this much longer."

Dan O'Connell put his hands to his temples. "Yeah, yeah— don't you think I'm aware of that? Any idiot can tell something's awry."

Gannon cleared his throat. "Uh, excuse me, Mr. O'Connell. Detective Gannon, from New York."

In an instant Dan O'Connell sized up the new guy. The fit of the suit said it all. Jacket sleeves came to just the right point on the back of his hand, trousers had a sharp crease and the

shoes looked spit-shined. This New York cop did not
appear to have come from a laborer's stock.

"Warner and Smurl," said O'Connell, "they told us they
were bringing in some outsiders."

Gannon had been busy too, taking the measure of this
Albany citizen who had just buried a top news story. Hynes
had said O'Connell got a mere slap on the wrist for running a
million dollar baseball pool—though gambling was a major
crime in New York.

"Yessir, Mr. O'Connell. That would be me and my
undercover squad."

Dan peered over his glasses. "So what can you add to all
this?"

Gannon hesitated. This bull of a man was asking for
answers no one had. "Well, sir…I think, sir, that what you have
here is a chess game."

O'Connell's eyes grew wide as Gannon asked, "Do you
play chess?"

O'Connell glanced at Hynes who shrugged. "I'm a
checkers man myself."

Dan O'Connell sucked his lower lip. A few breaths later he
exhaled and said, "I'm familiar with the game. You play it with
little horses."

Gannon suppressed a smile. "Yessir—but this is a human
chess game."

"Keep going…"

"Your nephew, Mr. O'Connell, is just a pawn. All the
mobsters want is cash. And from what I hear you don't have
that, so now each side has to maneuver to get what they want.
At the same time, each side is limited as to what they can do."

O'Connell cocked his head. "I see, Detective."

They had been standing to one side of the front entrance.
Now Dan O'Connell motioned toward a couch and a pair of
wingback chairs. Gannon and Hynes took the chairs while their

host sat on the edge of the couch. "Not sure what you mean by limited, Detective. How are the kidnappers limited?"

"First thing, if they kill your nephew they don't get paid. And, if they kill they have a murder rap to deal with—instead of just jail time."

Dan reared back. His face flushed red. "Jail time?!"

"Well, sir, the punishment for kidnapping is only jail time...unless the victim is killed. Hoffman's getting the hot seat for killing the Lindberg baby."

"Hoffman?"

Hynes broke in. "Detective Gannon worked the Lindberg case last year, Mr. O'Connell—helped get those kidnappers. He's top drawer. And we're gonna get these guys too."

Gannon leaned forward with his forearms on his knees. "Like I said, Mr. O'Connell...they've got their limitations. They've gone to too much trouble not to get some reward, but most of the time we find that the kidnappers don't expect the full amount—just a good chunk of it. One of their problems is that they can't show themselves. They'd be picked up in a heartbeat. Yet they have to communicate with you."

"And my limitations?"

Gannon shot a quick glance at Hynes and sighed. "The money. Detective Hynes says you don't have all the cash. Your second handicap is the need to do everything secretly. The kidnappers don't want the cops around, but you need them."

O'Connell dropped his head. When he raised it he said, "So...you fellas got a plan?"

Hynes cleared his throat. "For starters, we're checking the backgrounds of all the go-betweens and—"

"You think one of those bastards snatched Butch?"

Hynes drew air into the side of his mouth. "Mr. O'Connell, would you trust a stranger with $250,000?" Silence followed the question. Hynes added, "The bag man may or may not be in on the deal, but he will sure as hell know something. We just have to figure out what, and use it."

O'Connell got up and started pacing. "You said 'communicate with them.' How the hell do we do that if we don't know who they are?"

Gannon said, "You've already communicated with them. Through the newspapers."

O'Connell looked over his glasses. "All that's supposed to be on the QT."

Gannon waved a hand toward the door. "That guy from the Argus knows something's in the wind—so it's only a matter of time before the others sniff it too. Hynes here says your nephew's a popular guy around town. He disappears suddenly? People notice."

O'Connell continued pacing. Gannon added, "Keep in mind, you already know the perpetrators check the papers."

At the end of the next lap Dan O'Connell turned back, planted his feet and crossed his arms over his bulky chest. "So…what's our play?"

Hynes and Gannon met each other's eyes. Hynes nodded and Gannon said, "For the time being, play for time—try not to ruffle their feathers."

"And how do we do that?"

"Let the story break, then talk to them."

Dan's chin jerked up. "What are you talking about?"

"Tell them you don't have the money," Gannon said.

Hynes had moved over to the window and pulled back the drape enough to check the street. He turned back. "Who in god's name can come up with that kind of money, Mr. O'Connell? The thing to do is tell'em you're short but you're looking to raise it. You plant some stories, say it's hard to raise the money. And throw out a few figures—see if they bite."

O'Connell cocked his head to one side as though trying to assimilate the suggested strategy. Hynes moved to the other window and peeked out. When he stepped back into the circle he said, "In the meantime, we're busy checking every two-bit hustler from here to Florida, and checking lists of subscribers to the newspapers—especially the Knickerbocker Press."

O'Connell ran his hand over his scalp. "How do we ensure that Butch is safe and unharmed?"

Hynes winced. "Actually, Mr. O'Connell, as you know—we can't guarantee his safety. But we can give his abductors something to think about."

"Like what?"

"Tell 'em what they wanna hear, that you're not talking to the cops or anyone else. That should make them rest easy. Then you tell 'em what everybody already knows: your nephew was kidnapped at night and the neighbors saw a strange car and strange persons out in the street on that night."

"Strange car, Detective?"

"There's always a strange car on the street, sir. Wrong turns—or somebody asking directions. Thing to do is keep the details vague, let their fears fill in the blanks. If the kidnappers think they were seen that night, they'll think twice about pulling the trigger. We also suggest you let the DA help. Before you leak anything to the press, first run it by Mr. Delaney."

O'Connell shoved his hands in his back pockets and faced the New York detective. "So, if my nephew is a pawn, what does that make me?"

Gannon got to his feet and smiled. "The bishop. You can't go at them straight, have to get them by a side move."

The detectives began moving toward the door. O'Connell said to their backs, "Who's the king in this little chess game?"

Gannon spun around. "Money. Money is always king."

As Hynes pulled the unmarked car away from the curb he said, "Yuh know, Joe, it's a hell of a chance they will be taking with the newspapers. You know about the Stockberg case?"

"Not familiar with it."

"Little Alexia Stockberg. She got snatched outside her school in 1919. All the papers printed the story and her parents raised the money, but everything went cold. No word on how to make the payoff, and the body was never found."

Gannon ran his fingers through his hair. "Girl's probably dead."

Hynes slowed and waved the car behind him to pass.

Gannon said, "Maybe the case will end like the Trezke case. Kid turned up fifteen years later."

Hynes shifted gears. "There's always hope. What worries me is something like the Conway case."

"Don't know that one either."

"John Conway. Works in the Controllers office downtown. As a kid he got snatched, was held for two days. His uncle did it."

Gannon pulled at his jaw. "You think this is an inside job?"

"I wouldn't bet either way. Watkins said Oley worked for Dan for a while—and that fact does bother me."

"Too close to home?"

"Big time! The O'Connells can take their knocks, they understand business. But family? Betrayal? No telling what they'll do if it's someone they know or ever did trust. *That's* against the rules."

"Any good guesses as to what they would do?"

Hynes narrowed his eyes. "Skin him alive…with a spoon."

They traveled the next mile or so in silence. Then Hynes gave Gannon a sideways glance. "What you said to Mr. O'Connell, Joe—likening him to the bishop and the money to

the king. That being the case, I guess we're knights—
'Defenders of the Good.'"

Gannon grinned. "Guess you're right, Jimmy, if you mean
that for every two steps forward we have to move to the side—
to dodge a bullet!" His grin faded. "You think one of the uncles
clipped the nephew?"

"Again, I wouldn't bet either way. But what say we stop by
the station, see if anything's turned up? Then we can check the
phone taps."

Gannon settled back in his seat and looked at the Albany
skyline. He was intrigued by this man Dan O'Connell. Was he
really the benevolent uncle he made himself out to be? Or was
he in truth a gray knight?

The unease in Gannon's gut was palpable. He felt ill at ease
about the whole deal. As he stared out the window he realized
that for the first time in his career, he was unable to say for
sure who the good guys were.

Chapter 9
Wire Tap

Detective Hynes strolled up Eagle Street with his light-gray suit coat over his arm. Gannon was at his side. They parked a short distance from their destination, a chance to stretch their legs.

They had a copy of the July 10th afternoon edition of the Albany Times Union open to the new list of potential go-betweens. Hynes counted letters on his fingers as Gannon read the numbers. Hynes said, "That one's Bill Bardean. One more of our local chiselers."

"The next one looks easy," Gannon said. "First letter is a B and the next is a U. The eighth number is an A."

Hynes counted on his fingers. "Butch O'Hagen."

"O'Hagen. Sounds familiar."

"It should. He was a boxer –contender for the world lightweight championship? After he lost he faded away. Last I heard of him he got picked up for the Curley Murry shooting over on Beaver Street. Murry recovered but wouldn't talk. The witnesses fell down some stairs, got their faces beaten in—and bottom line was, O'Hagen was never brought to trial."

Hynes stopped in front of a gray metal door. "This is it." He pounded the door with his fist. "Told them we were coming."

The door swung open and a silver-haired man with a mustache and rolled-up shirt sleeves said, "Detectives." He closed the door after them and pointed down the dimly lit hall. "Your guy's in the fifth row."

Hynes stood for a moment to let his eyes adjust to the dim light of the telephone exchange. The clicking noise of all the phone relays sounded like a thousand beavers chomping wood. He raised his voice. "I'm betting that between the two lists, there'll be some good gossip on the lines."

He led the way but bumped into a corner rack of relays. The noise level rose. "Hope I didn't bust nothing."

A voice called from a small table in the middle of the row. "Jeez, Jimmy—glad you don't work undercover."

Hynes grinned. "Any hot stuff coming across the wires? Marty Wolf, meet Joe Gannon from New York."

Detective Marty Wolf shook Gannon's hand. Hynes stepped around the table that held the recorder and wires leading into the racks of phone relays.

Wolf pushed the play button. "Listen up. Dan O'Connell got hold of John Oley."

"Ring. Oley here."

"John, it's Dan O'Connell."

"Danny, it's been a while."

"Yeah, John. I'm in a spot, see. Keep this under your hat but my nephew got clipped last Friday night."

"Cheese-us, Danny. Sorry to hear that. Got any clues?"

"Not a damn one, John. Got a letter from the kidnappers. Says I gotta keep the cops outta this thing. That's why I'm callin'. Thinking maybe you heard something. Maybe a way to find Butch."

"Haven't heard nothing, Danny. Been trying to go legit. Got my hands full, yuh know?"

"Understand, John. But maybe you can help. Kidnappers had me make out a list of prospects for carrying the ransom. I put your name down."

"My name!?"

"Yeah, John. You're a big name around town. You know everybody worth knowing. You'd be a shoo-in. Just put the word out you're willing to help. I'm positive the kidnappers will find yuh."

"Nice plan, Danny, but you forgot my record. I spent time in the Atlanta Penitentiary, so the Albany cops have me in their sights. Hell, they'd shoot me for spitting on the sidewalk if they had the chance."

"I can handle the cops, John. I'm keeping the cops and the G-men at bay with a pitchfork. You help me out here and maybe that beer license will appear next time you apply. I know how to treat my friends."

For some seconds there was silence then Oley said, *"Yuh know, Danny, last year word on the street was the cops killed Legs Diamond."*

"No, they didn't John—that's just a rumor."

"Don't matter. No beer license is worth getting my head blowed off."

"You help me in this, John, I swear I'll take care of the cops."

"Yeah, Danny—but who's gonna take care of the G-men? They've got my number and I don't mean to give 'em a chance to dial it."

Detective Wolf hit the switch. "That's it. Dan called his brothers to let them know he'd called Oley and they were surprised Oley refused to help."

Hynes scratched his forehead. "Any chatter from the regular mobsters?"

"That's the odd part, Jimmy. They've all been real quiet. Hell, a couple of 'em even said they were gonna get outta town for a while."

Gannon fanned himself with his hat. "Jimmy, remember the Jersey plates? Could be Oley brought in outside talent. That way he calls the shots—and leaves us with our hats in our hands."

Wolf finished rewinding the recording and handed it over. Hynes dropped it in his pocket. "Keep listening, Marty. Lemme know if Oley contacts Dan."

Back at their car Hynes paused before getting in. "Joe, I'll get the recording to Delaney first thing in the morning. What you and me need is a good night's rest, because tomorrow we gotta go over the criminal records of everyone on the new list. It's the worst part of this job. I'd rather take a licking than go through another stack of records."

Gannon stood by the hood of the car and grinned wide. "Wonder how Delaney and the FBI made out this afternoon?"

"I wouldn't bet on Delaney giving them a glass of water if they were lost in the desert."

A few minutes later Jimmy pulled up in front of the seven-story brick Wellington Hotel and Gannon opened his door. "Say, Jimmy—the hotel's got stew on special tonight. If you're interested it's on New York."

"On New York?"

"Yep. I'm on expense account."

"What the hay," Hynes said, shutting off the car. "Missus is working late."

Inside a middle-aged man with gold stripes on his coat sleeves showed them, per their request, to a quiet table in the corner. While they waited for their orders Hynes leaned back, folded his arms and frowned. "Joe, yuh ever notice how horses and cows act right before a storm hits?"

"Nope. I'm a city boy, born and bred."

Hynes hunched forward. "They get skittish—nervous-like. Cows bunch up in a huddle, horses won't come out of the barn. They can tell a storm's coming. Their owners, on the other hand, don't have a clue till the storm hits."

"It's called premonition, Jimmy—a gut feeling. Where yuh going with this?"

"I keep remembering the other phone taps I listened to. Was no more than local chatter, but it didn't sound normal. A lot of stuttering, long pauses between words. And then Wolf, just a while ago at the phone exchange, made that remark about some of our suspects heading for the hills. Joe, something about it's just not normal."

Gannon arched his eyebrows.

Hynes shook his head as though to clear it. "I dunno, but sure seems like something's in the wind. That gut feeling you mentioned has me thinking those guys *know*."

Gannon unfolded his linen napkin and spread it across his lap. "Well, it has been three days since the kidnapping, and there're a lot of rumors are on the fly. Might be they know something, might be they're just being careful. Or could be they're guilty of something else and afraid their phone lines have been tapped. Guess we'll just have to wait and see—but if the mobsters are nervous, that's good for us."

Hynes bobbed his head. "Maybe, Joe, but you know these guys don't rattle easy. A knuckle sandwich here, greenback there—that's what they're used to. This coming across as skittish and nervous…it's just not normal."

Gannon tipped his head and raised his voice. "How about the Yankees?"

The man who had seated them appeared. He leaned toward Hynes. "Excuse me, sir. Mr. Delaney is on the front desk phone, asking for you or Mr. Gannon."

"Thanks. Be right there," Hynes said. He got to his feet. Before walking away he turned with a grin toward Gannon's look of surprise. "Small town, Joe. Don't worry about Royce. He served Jesus at the last supper. He knows to keep his mouth shut."

A few minutes later Hynes returned to find a waitress delivering bowls of stew. She left but Hynes did not sit down. "Joe, let it cool a bit. We're going to the kitchen."

Hynes led the way and pushed the door open. To a startled chef he said, "You got a radio in here?" The man pointed to a shelf across the room next to a boy peeling potatoes. Hynes strode across the room. "Hey kid—turn the radio to WGY."

The boy dried his hands and did as instructed. Ballroom music filled the air and the boy gave them a questioning look. Hynes said, "Got the time, kid?"

The boy pointed to a clock high on the wall. Four minutes past seven. Hynes exchanged glances with Gannon. "Guess we missed it."

Suddenly the radio blared. "We interrupt this program to bring you a special news bulletin. The District Attorney's office has just confirmed that John J. O'Connell Jr., of Albany, New York, was last Friday night, in front of his house, kidnapped. The young O'Connell's absence did not go unnoticed and has led to wild rumors as to his condition and his whereabouts. Acting on requests from O'Connell's friends, police met with his family who reluctantly confirmed the kidnapping but refused to answer police questioning or cooperate with them in any way, saying they feared for the life of the young man. Acting on his own, District Attorney John Delaney ordered Police Chief David Smurl to use all available resources to locate the would-be kidnappers and ensure the safe return of John O'Connell, Jr. Stay tuned to this station for more details."

Hynes pointed across the room. "Your clock's fast." He picked up a peeled raw potato from the sink and took a bite. "Got some salt?"

The boy turned away to get the salt. Hynes pointed the potato at Gannon. "Delaney said the newsboys broke the code, and since the dam was getting ready to break one way or the other he decided to let the story out."

"Letters for numbers wasn't much of a code, anyway."

Back at the table Hynes gave Gannon the rest of what Delaney said. "It's your job to frame out the fairy tale. He said Dan thought what you said about feeding the kidnappers information made good sense, a valid way to play for time, so they want the first fairy tale in the afternoon edition tomorrow."

Gannon put his spoon down. "Not much time. Guess we can say we have fingerprints but no name. And put out the target's description. And since it's a kidnapping it makes sense to mention the ransom—play that up a little."

"Sounds ok," Hynes said.

They ate a few bites in silence till Gannon said, "Stew's not half bad. Which reporter is gonna write the copy?"

Hynes pulled a pencil from his pocket and handed it over. "You. You write a draft, Delaney will flesh it out. "

***

Midmorning the following day at the Arch Street Station House, Detective Hynes synchronized the motion of his hands, one moving down the list of go-betweens and the other down the subscriber list of the Knickerbocker Press. He pushed back and rubbed his eyes. "Much more of this and I'll go blind. How'd that article you wrote last night go?

Gannon rested his elbow on the desk opposite to Hynes. "Gave it to Delaney. Should be in the afternoon papers."

The usual hum of noise in the precinct day room faded suddenly, replaced by stone silence. Through the glass Hynes and Gannon watched as uniformed policemen turned away from two men in gray suits. Headed their way was their own Detective McCaffy followed by the suits.

McCaffy stuck his head around the doorjamb and said, "These two say they gotta check the files"—and disappeared.

A smooth slick voice said, "I'm Agent Tamm, this is Agent Sisk. We're assigned to the O'Connell case."

Hynes and Gannon exchanged a quick glance. They knew why these two were at their door. Delaney had lost the fight to keep the FBI out of the investigation. They had received no word from the DA about sharing information. Now Hynes had to make a decision. It was his office. He did not want to engage in the turf battle, so he decided to play it neutral.

He stood up and shook hands. "Detective Jimmy Hynes." With a nod to Joe he continued, "Detective Joe Gannon from New York. Mr. Delaney mentioned you guys were in town. We were just checking the newspaper subscriber lists against the names of the go-betweens. So far we're coming up empty-handed. You're welcome to dive in if yuh want."

A thunderous crack of wood on wood from the outside room drowned out the G-man's reply. A loud voice yelled, "Put your fingers there or put your broken knuckles there. Don't matter to me."

Hynes, followed by Gannon and the two FBI agents, hurried toward the front desk where a group of uniformed policemen stood with nightsticks in hand. By the entrance were two handcuffed men. The suit coat of one of them was pulled off one shoulder and his white shirt was open. The buttons were scattered across the floor, and nose to nose with the guy was Police Sergeant Fitzgerald.

Hynes pushed his way to the front. "What yuh got, Fitz?"

Sergeant Fitzgerald snarled, "Delaney's orders, Detective—none of your business."

Hynes moved to the side so he could look into Fitzgerald's eyes and narrowed his own eyes. "If it concerns O'Connell, Sergeant, it's my business."

"Frame up, frame up, I ain't done nothing!"

Hynes demanded, "Who are you?"

Agent Tamm stepped forward. "Max Price—that's who he is. Part of the Duffy mob. He's been working outta Poughkeepsie lately. Helps Jimmy Sheehan with his speakeasy."

Hynes said, "What yuh got him on, Fitz?"

"He made a wrong turn."

Price said, "You stupid flat foot! All's I did—"

Fitzgerald shouted, "Assaulting a police officer is against the law!"—and punched Max Price in the stomach.

Price doubled over. He gasped for air and said, "Didn't make no wrong turn."

Sergeant Fitzgerald smirked. "You sure did, buster—the second you turned toward Albany!"

A moment passed with everything still. Fitzgerald growled, "Take'em in the back for questioning."

As the mobsters were led away the sergeant scratched his mustache. Then he turned to Hynes. "Detective, Delaney said question everyone and anyone who might be connected to the O'Connell case—so that's what I'm doing. Following orders." He nodded toward the G-men but did not look at them. "You hooking up with those guys now?"

Hynes stiffened and curled his fists. Detective McCaffy pushed his way between them and said, "Here's the files, Jimmy."

Hynes took the files though he was still staring at Fitzgerald. "I follow orders too, Sergeant, and it's my case."

He pivoted and marched back to his desk. The suits were at his heels. He plopped the stack on the desk and opened the top folder. "Barney Riley. Former manager for Butch O'Hagen. Hell! The O'Connells must be scraping the bottom of the barrel. Riley must be in his sixties by now."

Gannon opened another. "Tom Dyke. Nominated for Sergeant of Arms of the New York Senate. Participates in political activities in Buffalo and Brooklyn. Guy gets around."

Hynes pointed at the bottom of the page. "Not too much. He pulled his nomination from the Senate." He pulled another file. "Here's one for yuh. Ames O'Brien. Used to run the Love Nest Roadhouse out in New Scotland by Hurstville. Was making money till the place burned down." He waved the file in the air in front of the G-men. "Wanna look?"

Agent Tamm gave a wave of dismissal. "We've seen it." He pointed at the stack. "The others too. You get something new, you call us, right?" Tamm held Hynes's gaze as he asked the question.

Hynes scratched the back of his head, playing for time. How could he tell the FBI he wasn't going to take orders from them but say it in a nice manner? "Well, thing is, Delaney signs my pay check. We work for him. Anything we get goes directly to him, and I'm sure Delaney will share with you." Hynes finished with a smile. "Just call him."

Agent Tamm's brow wrinkled. He stiffened his back and gazed directly at Hynes. "And Mr. Hoover signs my paycheck, so you can rest assured that we will see what you come up with. The FBI is in Albany—on this case."

The suits turned on their heels and left. Hynes and Gannon resumed the tedious work of comparing lists.

After a few minutes Gannon broke the silence. "Seems you and this Sergeant Fitzgerald out there at the desk don't get along."

Hynes kept his head lowered. "I don't like his methods. He was point man on the Diamond murder. Day after the murder, he and his men had to replenish their ammunition."

"So?"

Hynes puckered his lips. "They had not been on the range all week."

***

Two days later, late afternoon of July 13, Detective Hynes sat back in his chair and rolled up his shirtsleeves. The over-head fan stirred the hot summer air and kept the squad room a little more comfortable but all papers had to be weighted down. He stood up and stretched and Officer McCaffy caught his arm and handed him a folder. "Troopers did the leg work on that plate number you gave us a few days ago."

Hynes read the report in silence until Gannon asked, "Whatcha got?"

"The address went to Joe Costello over on Hamilton Street who said he didn't know nothing about no car, and the salesman at Whitbeck Motors said he didn't know him. Troopers drove the salesman around the south side of town in the back seat of an unmarked car and picked up two people that looked like the buyer of the car. Descriptions were close but no cigar. Both guys had solid alibis."

Hynes turned a page. "But, you might say there's one interesting point. Back in the '20s this guy named Costello worked for John Oley." He handed the report across the desk.

Gannon took it and began flipping through the pages. "Oley again. His name just keeps popping up."

Hynes pulled another file from a stack on the desk. "And how. Read this report on Mush Trachnier. Someone tried to snatch him the first of the year. We traced a bunch of calls between Oley and some people we think did the job. We're guessing Oley was the finger man—just can't prove it. See if you can find a connection."

Gannon took the file. A moment later he said, "This Mush guy seems nice enough. Says here he's into sporting circles. Does the trotters at Saratoga and dogs in Miami, and hobnobs with political bigwigs. Easy to see why someone would want to put the bag on him. Helluva a target!"

Hynes pulled another file and leaned back on the legs of the chair and read aloud. "Percy Geary, alias John Nolan, Frank Edwards and Paul Cummings. Arrested 1916 for burglary.' He spent some time in the county jail, I'll have to send for that record."

Gannon whistled. "Says here Mush had a brewery once but was denied a license." He turned up a photo of a slim white-haired man wearing white slacks and a bow tie with a dark sport jacket. "This Mush guy cuts quite a figure. I wonder…let me see John Oley's file."

Hynes handed it over and several minutes later Gannon began reading aloud. "Burglary, bootlegging, drugs. Says here Oley moved all the way up to assault with intent to kill. I'd say he's a fast mover. The Feds got him on an interstate transient charge."

Hynes rocked the chair down on all four legs. "I remember that one. He impersonated a postal worker and hijacked the mail. He tried to silence a witness but some smart lawyer got him off—only had to serve a year. Did his time in the Atlanta pen. I sent for that record a week ago. Should be here soon. You see anything we missed?"

Gannon's eyes narrowed. "Nothing I can put my finger on, but follow me here. Mush was popular, so is John O'Connell Junior—both of them the kind somebody would be willing to pay money for. The other commonality is that they were both in the brewery business. Could be this is more about getting cash for a brewery or obtaining a beer license."

Hynes's eyebrows arched. "The theory's thin at best, Joe. Everybody's trying to open up shop with beer."

Gannon held up John Oley's file. "Maybe so—but who's got the money? You think Oley was involved in the Mush attempt. Oley's car was in the vicinity of the O'Connell house about the time of the kidnapping. This file tells me John Oley is moving up the ladder—and he's a fast learner. Let's just suppose he headed up the Mush kidnapping. He blew it there, but he corrected his mistakes. Now he's using what he learned as a blueprint for kidnapping Butch O'Connell."

Hynes leaned back in his chair and pressed his fingertips together. "Yeah, I see where you're coming from."

The phone rang. Hynes grabbed it.

"Detective Hynes? Sergeant Straney down in the lab."

Hynes listened a few minutes, hung up the phone and grabbed his suit coat. "Another letter came in. It's in the lab. They want a third list of names."

***

The lab had the Photostats of the old and new letters laid side by side. The new one had been typed. Gannon picked it up. "So this time they used a typewriter—but whoever typed it still misspelled the same words." He read aloud.

We know its no fault of yours that it reached
the papers from now on you will use the name 'Rex.;
Not satisfied with names instructions for second is as
follows in the New York Eve Telegram you will
put in the personal columm as follows
Four names for instance to an add,
as follows Dear Rex   Amin N;Y; Please get in
touchwith; name,s – 3 end up signings fourth name
Do same in Eve Journal and Sun
12 names altogether. All local
Racketters.

'REX'

The note was typed. Across the bottom of the page the name 'John O'Connell Jr.' had been scrawled with a fountain pen. Gannon pointed to the signature. "This for real?"

Sgt. Straney said, "It does appear to be his. The letter height, spacing and angle of the letters match his signature in the Christmas cards we got from the family, so I'd say it is his."

Hynes pulled the Photostat of the hand-addressed envelope closer. It had been postmarked at 1 a.m. that morning, addressed to D. P. O'Connell, Box 1222, Albany New York.

"What about the script on this envelope?"

"I'd say John Jr. wrote it," said Straney. "Conforms to the characteristics of his signature."

Hynes pointed to the Yonkers postmark. "Joe, I'd say that little article you and Delaney wrote had some effect on the kidnappers judging by this time stamp, 4:30 yesterday afternoon."

Gannon pointed at the time stamp. "It means the family knows Butch was still alive as of yesterday. It also might confirm your Jersey plate, Jimmy." He slid across the table another Photostat showing the back of the envelope which had a second postal stamp: Grand Central Station, July 12, 1933, 7 p.m. "Yonkers is only a hop skip and jump across the river from Jersey. Better have Delaney contact the New Jersey authorities for help."

Hynes pointed to the blue stamp on the front. "Special Delivery. They wanted it here fast. Any prints?"

Sergeant Straney pursed his lips and shook his head. "More smudges than anything. We expected that, since it came through the post office. But there is one peculiar item." He placed the first ransom note next to the new letter and pointed at the words. "Kidnappers spelled racketeers wrong the same way in this and the first letter. Column is also spelled wrong in both."

"What about the handwriting?"

"We know John Junior did not write the first note. We can say the person who wrote the first letter and typed this one are of the same mindset. Gutter language, misspellings and crammed typing. Whoever wrote or typed these probably never made it out of high school."

Hynes chuckled. "That covers most of the mobsters still alive. Guess we could pull the school records on the go-betweens. Might find a surprise someplace. Whaddya think, Joe?"

"A day or day-and-a-half turnaround on the letters. One marked Special Delivery. Kidnappers might be getting antsy, Jimmy."

The phone rang. Sergeant Straney answered. "Yessir, they're both right here…" He gave the phone to Hynes and whispered, "Delaney."

"Hynes here."

"Have you and Gannon looked at the latest ransom letter?"

"Got it in front of us now. Straney says Butch signed it, so we're still in the game. We've just been noting how fast they got the letter here."

"We're looking to speed up communication too. All this waiting and delay is tough on the family."

"Well, sir, the New York papers arrive at our train station about five hours before they hit the street – get here sometime after midnight. How about we meet the trains tonight? Get a jump on it?"

"Ok. I'll see that the new list of names gets in the New York papers, you and Gannon meet the trains and see what turns up."

"We can do that, sir." Hynes hung up the phone and caught Gannon's eye. "Gonna miss some sleep tonight, Joe."

***

On their way to the train station that night, Hynes remembered back a few evenings to when he had come to the station to see what Joe Gannon from New York would be like. He smiled inwardly as he remembered their rough start.

Hynes and Gannon were in the restaurant at the station when they heard the whistle of the incoming train. Hynes downed the last of his coffee. Gannon dropped some change on the table and said, "Let's see what's going on in New York."

No matter how many times he saw the sight Hynes could depend on a sense of excitement and pleasure in watching a big locomotive pull into the station. He and Gannon stood near the same lamp post where he had waited the night Gannon arrived and watched the train roll to a stop in a burst of steam. A few minutes later Hynes pointed toward the back of the train where workmen had begun unloading freight.

"Let's see what we got."

Hynes showed his badge. "Looking for some papers. The New York Evening Telegram, Evening Journal and the Sun."

The foreman glanced at the badge and nodded his head. "Just gimme a minute—be right back, sir." He carried a lantern into the boxcar and returned shortly with the requested papers. Hynes reached into his pocket but the foreman said, "On the house, sir."

The detectives moved into the nearest circle of light and began turning pages. Hynes got there first, the personals section of the New York Telegram. "Well, well, well—looky here."

> *Dear Rex: Please get in touch with 3, 8, 1, 18, 12, 5,19—*
> *23,1,3,8,20,5, 20,15,14,25—3,1,5,14,15,9—13,1,14,14,25*
> *—19,20,18,5,23,12.*
> *Willie Martin.*

Gannon rustled the pages of the New York Evening Journal. "It's here too, but this one is signed 'Al Friedman.'"

Hynes took the New York Sun from under his arm and soon reported, "Same here—but under Tom Tyndall's name. Boy! The O'Connells sure keep strange bedfellows!"

The foreman called to them. "Hey, you guys working on Butch's kidnapping?"

Hynes smiled and gave a wave of his hand then bumped Gannon's arm. "It's going to take a beer to decode these."

Gannon laughed. "Only one?"

As they headed for the lobby, Hynes turned to the sports page. "Too bad they don't have the afternoon race results in the morning papers. A guy could make some good bets if—"

Gannon stopped and jerked his head around. For a few seconds he watched as the freight handlers unloaded the remaining newspapers. When he turned back he said, "Jimmy, he's gotta be in New York."

"You mean Butch?"

"Yeah. The kidnappers have him in New York—or close by."

Hynes turned back toward the dark platform and stared at the freight handlers. "Yeah, I can see it…but what makes you feel so sure?"

Gannon held up the New York papers. "These—and the fast turnaround on the letters. The morning papers are printed the night before so they can be delivered the next day. We're reading the morning paper five or six hours before anyone else sees it. Let's say Delaney makes the newspaper deadline. All deadlines are around seven at night. By ten or so that evening the morning papers are already printed and shipped out. The kidnappers get the morning paper the night before and put their answer in the morning mail."

Hynes pulled at his jaw. "That leaves most of the time for our prime suspect to do nothing but sit around and look pretty." He tapped Gannon's arm with a newspaper. "Let's get that beer. When we give Delaney the decoded list we can suggest to him that the head of the snake is in Albany—but the body's in New York."

Tony's Saloon, across from Steamboat Park, stayed open late to serve the swing-shift dock workers. Anyone dressed in a coat and tie stuck out like a sore thumb. Hynes liked that fact, because with everyone avoiding them they were assured of privacy.

He downed a third of his beer and settled back in his chair. "The New York Telegram's got Charles Wachter, Tony Condi and Manny Strewl. What's in the Evening Sun?"

"Jim O'Connor, Dave Sherman, Joe Curro. The Evening Journal's got Fred Roma, Terry Riley and Sylvester Hess. What's the read on them?"

"I'm not familiar with all of them but they're mostly old bootleggers and sports guys. Some are boxers and some are guys who do the ponies. It's interesting, though, that Fred Roma is mentioned by name. You remember that the kidnappers used the name Roma in some of their letters."

Hynes held up his empty beer mug. "Uh-huh. And I'd say that's a hell of a coincidence."

The bartender arrived with two full mugs. Gannon took a long swig and wiped the foam from his mouth with his finger. "We're looking at something strange here, Jimmy. Been a week since the kidnapping, more than twenty names put in the papers—and still no one's been picked. I don't understand it. So far there's been no progress made on the case, and all we have against your prime suspect is circumstantial evidence."

Hynes tilted his chair back on its hind legs. "Sure is a mystery. I've also been puzzled about that recording between Dan O'Connell and John Oley. I can't figure why Oley hasn't called back." He shook his head. "Damn it. Just nothing!"

Across the barroom a man caught Hynes looking at him. The guy was at a table with another man and the two had been talking. Now the man leaned back in his chair and whispered something to the man sitting behind him at the next table, and that man whispered to the man next to him who in turn spoke to the man at the next table. A chain of words was working its way through the crowd.

Hynes plopped his chair down and set his beer on the table. "You remember, one of the letters told the O'Connells to mention some *right* guys."

"I remember. Was the second letter. Said to name some right names."

Hynes held up one of the newspapers. "Maybe not…right names. Maybe *the right name.*"

"I don't follow yuh."

"We asked Dan O'Connell who he would trust to deliver the ransom."

"Yeah?"

Hynes hunched forward. "Sure would be handy if one of the kidnappers was selected. That little twist could work out real nice for the gang. One of their own—picking up the cash! And 'the right one' could even bargain for them." He tapped the newspaper. "What are the odds of twenty names and not one satisfactory?"

Gannon poked his cheek with his tongue. "What about Oley?"

Hynes sipped his beer. "Maybe a friend of his is doing the dirty work. Maybe Oley's a front to take the heat off the real bad guys."

Gannon pushed his chair back. "Wanna bet Oley's the one we're after?"

Hynes finished off his beer and got to his feet. "You talking a for-real bet?"

"Yeah. I'll give you odds he's in there someplace. We just haven't seen him yet."

Gannon noticed that Hynes paused a moment as he put money on the table. "Something wrong?"

"Nah. Just thinking. We haven't seen Oley's finger in this thing, but I betcha we've heard him."

"Heard him?"

Hynes threw his suit coat over his shoulder. "Remember the trunk load of groceries Mrs. Watkins mentioned? The Oley brothers—*and their wives*—packing up. Also, guy across the street the night Butch was snatched. Said he heard female voices. Could be, while we're keeping an eye on the roosters, the hens are taking care of business."

Chapter 10
At the Hide Out

The early morning buzzer in the first-floor sweat shop jolted Butch almost awake and he attempted to roll over but could not because his arm was cuffed to the bed rail. He did not know at first where he was, but the buzzer, he soon realized, was one he had heard before. It came from below.

The Harrigan gang was holding Butch in a seven story building in Hoboken, the hideout a second floor bedroom. The clank of the handcuff chain was a gruesome reminder to Butch that he was not free, that the kidnapping was indeed a reality and not merely a bad dream. He took several deep breaths. The air in the closed-up room was stale.

Someone stirred nearby and he recognized the familiar clink of a chain which he knew to be connected to an overhead light bulb at the center of the ceiling. He peeked from under the adhesive tape covering his eyes. He guessed that a full week had passed since his capture.

Through the slit under the tape over his eyes he caught sight of the streaks of sweat on his pajamas. The wooden floor creaked, meaning a guard was approaching. Butch turned his head. A hand lifted his hand. He could see that whoever it was had an over-sized hand and was apparently studying his cuffed wrist. Then he recognized another familiar sound, the jangle of glass marbles.

At the trial years later he would learn it was a guy named Burke who had the big hands. Pivot Burke and Dutch Fisher served as the primary guards. They put marbles in their mouths to disguise their voices.

Burke said in the marble-garble, "Just checking."

Butch played his role of helpless victim and let his head loll to the side, a move that allowed him to see the large feet. He dared not tilt his head up lest his guards think he could see.

The voice of his instructor at the police academy rang in his head: *Details—get the details.* Butch worked diligently to gather and remember details so he could help the police find these criminals after his release. He held close the idea of release or rescue—had to keep that hope alive.

Another task Butch concentrated on was leaving details. He kicked off the sheet and scratched his foot against the foot board—making sure as he did to dig his toenail into the wood and leave identifying marks. The guards chuckled when he stretched his cuffed arm and scraped the handcuffs against the steel bedrail. He let his shoulder drop and his head tilt down, as though he had lost all resolve. Inwardly he smiled to himself, knowing that the spots on the cuffs and the scrapes on the foot board were potentially useful to a prosecuting attorney. And he was right. The marks would later be used to identify the handcuffs and link Big Charlie Scarnici to the kidnapping.

Sometime later the bedroom door hinge squeaked. Someone else was entering the room. Butch froze, not wanting to tip anyone off about what he was doing. Again there came the noise of marbles clinking and a garbled voice with an accent.

Dutch Fisher said, "Get the window."

Burke moved behind the bed and removed the blanket covering the window. White sunlight filled the room. Fisher opened the window and poked his head out and scanned the sky over Newark airport. "Where…where are they?"

He ducked back inside, coughing and choking, and spit out the marbles. He mumbled, "Hell with them."

From under his bandage Butch could see and was glad to see some bright daylight. A clear morning. A dog began to bark but a loud voice bellowed, "Jack—Jack, calm down! Ok, here yuh go boy," and the barking stopped.

Minutes later Fisher said, "There they are." Burke was also at the window to see the spectacle. There had been a big write-up in the paper about the air show, six airplanes to fly in formation. The planes kept their positions for a brief time then changed positions. Some rolled upside down and right side up again. General Balboa, of the Italian Air Force, was leading his squadron of planes in a makeshift air show near the Newark airport.

One of the guards remarked, "Boy, those wops can sure fly!"

Butch, of course, would later recall this little detail. The fact would help the authorities narrow the search for the location of the hideout.

Heavy foot stomps announced the arrival of George Garguillo who called out, "Hey! He can see!"

Burke ducked back into the room. "No, he can't. He's just listening is all."

Garguillo stomped closer. "Yes he can, damn it!"

Garguillo kicked the bed's leg so hard the bed moved. "Hey kid! Can you see?"

Butch muttered, "N-n-no."

The heavy thud of footsteps retreated but returned in a few minutes and Garguillo's fingers began jamming cotton under the adhesive tape.

Butch complained. "Ouch—you're poking me in the eye."

"Tough."

Garguillo retreated and soon afterward the air show ended. A short while later Garguillo's footsteps sounded again. All went silent for a moment after he arrived. Butch waited, listening closely. And then he froze—at the sound of a loud metal click. His military training told him a gun was being readied for firing. Sweat broke out on his forehead.

A hand yanked him to a sitting position and a heavy weight—cold steel—was dropped in his lap. His mind went blank.

"Papers say you're an Army guy."

"Well, I—I'm in the National Guard."

"Good. What's in your lap?"

Butch felt along the top of the gun. The bolt for feeding bullets into position for firing had been pulled back. He inserted his index finger into the chamber. The gun was empty so he breathed a little easier. He felt along the stock to the slot that held the round drum-type magazine. The absence of bullets assured him he wasn't about to be shot, not at this instant anyway. His hand kept moving over the sawed-off stock and along the bottom. At the barrel opening he forced in a pinky. He brought the gun to his nose and sniffed the oil fumes then rubbed his nose with his sleeve.

"Modified submachine gun. Probably .45 caliber. It's seen some use and has recently been cleaned."

No one said anything right away. The silence was broken by the noise of rushing shower water from the room above where an Italian voice sang, "'O sole, 'o sole mio, sta nfronte a te…"

In the days since his capture Butch had heard this voice many times. Sometimes the man sang something else, but this particular tune was his favorite. Close by there was a sound Butch figured was a rustle of paper bags and abruptly the machine gun was snatched from his lap and George Garguillo stomped out of the room.

As Garguillo went out "Big Mac" Christy Miller entered. Miller typically had a cigarette between his lips and his shirt tail hung out and the excess length of his belt dangled from his waist. He handed Burke three sandwich bags and crossed the room to the vanity and picked up the previous day's dirty spaghetti plates. At the exit to the bedroom he whispered to

Burke, "We get the deposit back on the plates if they ain't broke or chipped."

Burke unwrapped an egg sandwich and tapped Butch on the shoulder and put the sandwich in his lap. "Breakfast," he said.

Butch took a bite of the sandwich, thinking that these guards seemed to have bought his lie about not being able to see, but one of them had not believed so now unfortunately he could not see. But if he couldn't see, he could review. He would be careful to remember all that he had seen. The green border of sunflowers around the linoleum floor. The noise of a chain on a light bulb, the single light hanging from the ceiling. He had only seen part of the closet's double doors but he felt sure they extended floor to ceiling. He certainly would not forget the Italian singer, or the turns on the stair landing as he had been escorted into this hideout. He was certain he was on the second floor. There was a cold iron radiator to which his handcuffs were sometimes attached, and on the inside of his pillowcase a blue circle with the word 'Adams'—a laundry mark.

He hoped these details would prove useful, if he lived to tell them. In any case, concentrating on them kept him from going crazy.

He slapped at an insect—another detail about the place he was sure to remember forever. The damn bug bites. And the heat, the room stifling hot at times, plus his own stinking body odor as the days went by and he was not allowed to take a regular bath.

Dutch Fisher removed the bottle of citronella from the vanity, poured some on a rag and placed it in Butch's hand. "Wipe yourself down with this—it'll keep the bugs off. I'll get your back later."

Burke met Fisher in the middle of the room and whispered in his ear. "Bring the fan in from the kitchen. Gets ripe in here with the window closed all the time. Hot too."

Burke closed the window and put the blanket back in place then carried his chair across the room next to the door and picked up his sandwich. As he ate he thought about the folly of it, that he broke out of prison *for this*. First his leg got all shot up hijacking a truck, and now the best he could do was live off the twenty bucks of charity Harrigan threw at him. The rest of the gang didn't know it—only he and Fisher knew, but this O'Connell kid was a hot potato. The family was bound to lynch them all if anything happened to him.

What Burke wanted to do was clear out, but if he did—he figured—either Harrigan would shoot him or Garguillo would throw him in that furnace of his.

Burke crumpled the sandwich wrapping in his fist. The chain on the captive's handcuff jingled and Burke mumbled in an inaudible voice, "Who's really the prisoner here?"

Fisher came in and plugged in the fan and switched it on. He pulled up a chair and removed the wrapping from his sandwich then leaned over and whispered in Burke's good ear. "Overheard Garguillo on the phone with Harrigan. The O'Connells called Oley directly—asking for help."

"So it's done?"

Fisher wiped his mouth on his sleeve. "Nope. Oley's playing hard to get, to make it look good. He'll wait until O'Connell asks him a second time—then take the deal."

"What'd Harrigan say to that?"

"He's pissed. Says this is taking too long. Strewl's name wasn't on the first two lists, and Harrigan told Dugan if Strewl's name don't pop up soon Oley will be the go-between—like it or not."

Several minutes later James Sweeney scratched on the bedroom door and stepped inside with a jug of coffee and some writing paper. Sweeney was at the bottom rung of the mob's ladder. The errand boy. He was about five feet nine with a husky build, a square jaw and a scar on his forehead from a clubbing he got with a tree branch during his teen years on the streets of New York. He had two shiny gold teeth, one upper and one lower.

Because Sweeney served as Harrigan's gofer he needed to blend in with the locals and therefore was usually clean-shaven and fairly well dressed. He was not a violent man and in the end turned out to be a lucky man. In 1937 he was arrested on conspiracy to kidnapping, but the statute of limitations had run out and the police couldn't charge him. They got him anyway, though—by using their Al Capone trick. They jailed him on income tax evasion and car theft.

Sweeney whispered to Fisher, "Newspapers hit the streets, but once again Oley's name didn't turn up. Harrigan's steaming. We need the kid do some more writing."

Fisher's eyebrows arched. "What happened to Oley?"

Sweeney rolled his eyes. "Oley said O'Connell would call him back and then he'd accept, but O'Connell didn't call, so to avoid more delays Harrigan decided to have Strewl be the go-between."

Fisher dropped his head and mumbled, "Shit! What else can go wrong?"

"Don't worry. Oley's got his ear to the ground. Word from Albany is, there's a bunch of strangers hanging around the O'Connell mail box, so we're gonna send a letter to the courthouse—to a guy who works there. The guy knows the O'Connells, so Harrigan wants to use him—to keep the heat off Oley."

Burke wiped his glasses. "We gonna let him write like we did yesterday?

Sweeney glanced at Butch who was finishing his sandwich. "Yeah. We put him in the chair at the vanity, you two guys stand behind him to the side. I'll be directly behind him and make him look straight down. If he tries to run, we all clock him."

Sweeney took a fountain pen and a bottle of ink from the vanity drawer and placed the paper close by. He pulled Butch by his arm. "Have a seat. Keep your head down. Need yuh to write another letter. Don't get smart, we're gonna read it first. We're right behind you. You try to run and we'll queer-yuh—got it?"

Butch shook his head yes. Sweeney removed the bandages over the eyes and unlocked the handcuffs. He put his hand on the back of Butch's head and pushed it down. "Keep it there."

Butch blinked several times to adjust his eyes to the light. He focused on Burke's black shoes with shoelaces and badly worn heels. The feet were over-sized and the legs as big as tree stumps. From his boxing training, Butch understood that this guard was a husky fellow who weighed in at more than 200 pounds.

Sweeney cleared his throat. "You know a guy by the name of Connaughton?"

"Met him once or twice. Works at the courthouse."

"Good. Write him a letter. He's to take the letter to your Uncle Dan. Use today's date. It's the fourteenth."

Butch dipped the pen into the ink and wrote:

Dear God, Friday 14, 33

If you think anything of me. Please see that this letter gets to Uncle Dan unopened at once, By all means don't tell this to anyone, Silence in this case means my life.

John O'Connell Jr,

Sweeney snatched up the letter and put it in his pocket and placed a blank sheet of paper in front of Butch. "Leave the top part of the page blank. Tell your uncle to hurry up and get stuff done."

Butch thought a moment before he wrote, "Uncle Dan, they tell me this thing is coming to a close. For God's sake get it over. This is genuine."

Sweeney pointed. "Sign it 'Rex' –with your name underneath."

Butch did as instructed, then Fisher took a green laundry bag from the floor and put it over Butch's head and pulled him over to the radiator where he clamped on the cuffs. Sweeney scooped up the sheets of paper and exited.

Fisher pushed back the lock of hair hanging across his face. In a low voice he said, "Relax, kid. We'll take you to the head in a minute if yuh want."

Burke stared at Butch, thinking that there were too many cracks appearing in this kidnap plan. He recalled the day he discovered that the guy they were holding belonged to one of

Albany's political powerhouses. Right then he and Fisher decided they should keep the victim in good health. In the event they should get caught, they would want it known that they had treated the captive very well.

In a low voice Burke said to Butch, "Listen, I guess you must be bored too. I sure the hell am—so I'll make a deal with yuh. We'll let you take the blindfold off and read a newspaper sometimes—if yuh put the blindfold back on when there's a knock on the door. If you don't, there'll be hell to pay—know what I mean?"

Butch was much surprised by the offer. He wiped sweat from his face and said, "Deal."

Butch slapped at a mosquito and rubbed his arm. Burke leaned forward and focused on Butch until Fisher bumped his arm and said, "Whatcha looking at?"

Burke tipped his head in Butch's direction. "Hot as hell in here, but the kid acts like he's cold."

"Must be the breeze from the fan." Fisher moved the fan so it pointed to the middle of the room. "That'll fix him."

Burke said, "Maybe."

A big as-yet-unseen crack was forming in the kidnap plan. Burke was the first to notice but even he did not foresee what was to come. The captive's body temperature was on the rise. The junior John O'Connell was in the beginning stages of what would become a dangerously high fever.

***

That afternoon, Manny Strewl strolled down a sidewalk in Peekskill, New York, trying to act like a tourist. He glanced in all directions including at the windows of the upper story apartments before slipping into a saloon. At the bar he ordered a beer. There were few customers. He tossed some loose change on the bar and carried his mug to the unoccupied side of the room where he slapped a newspaper down on a table and dropped his white straw hat beside it. He retrieved a pencil from his pocket and flipped to the sports section. Keeping a wary eye on the other patrons, he pulled out the sheet of paper on which Butch O'Connell had earlier in the day written the date.

Strewl proceeded to write a letter—a letter to himself. He looked up frequently and took sips of the beer, casting quick glances at the patrons. He did not want anyone paying him any attention. When he finished writing he flipped the sheet over and wrote above Butch's signature:

THIS IS GENUINE BY JOHNS SIGNATURE ONLY.
"ROMA"

Sitting at the table with his head bent over an open sports page and making notations with a pencil, Strewl looked like an average guy figuring how to place his bets. He finished the writing but hesitated before slipping the page into an envelope. He decided to go to the trouble of tracing over the letters. That took some time. When he finished, he slipped the page into an envelope and printed the address in block letters. It was to go to the Beaver Clothes Shop.

He pulled out another sheet of paper, the one on which Butch had written the date in the top right corner. Strewl added this message:

DAN,
IF THIS IS MADE PUBLIC IT IS THE
END. ALL NEGOTIATIONS MUST BE
SECRET OR IT IS CURTAINS FOR JOHN.
NO LETTER IS GENUINE UNLESS IT
CONTAINS JOHNS SIGNATURE. THIS
WILL BE ENDED FAST IF YOU GET THE
SUGAR UP AND NO KIDDING US. WE

HAVE DECIDED ON A PARTY
MENTIONED BY YOU. WE HAVE
CHECKED ON YOUR LIST AND HE IS
SATISFACTORY TO US. HIS NAME IS
MANNY STROWL. WE REALISE YOUR
MAIL IS READ   THAT'S WHY WEARE
USING TODD SO TELL HIM HOW
IMPORTANT IT IS.

    WE KNOW HOW MANY CRACK WIRE
TAPPERS YOU HAVE FROM THE BIG
TOWN. BUT YOU ARE HIS GOD NOW AND
HIS ONLY HOPE TO LIVE. SO PLAY FAIR,
AND WE WILL DO LIKEWISE. OUR
CONDITIONS

    ARE – FIRST FOR YOU TO TURN THE
MONEY OVER, IF YOU CARE TO, TAKE
THE NUMBERS BUT WE WANT TIME TO
CASH IT IN. AT LEAST TWENTY FOUR
HOURS AND WE WANT YOU TO C0-
OPERATE WITH THE GO-BETWEEN AND
SEE HE IS FREE TO GO WHERE HE
PLEASES. YOU HAVE YOUR RACKET
AND CAN BE THANKFUL IT GAVE YOU
PLENTY, AND WE HAVE OURS. TO
AVOID COMPLICATIONS WE WILL
CHANGE OUR PASS WORD "REX" TO
"ROMA" FOR YOUR PROTECTION AND
THE BOYS.

Once again Strewl worked painstakingly to trace over the letters, thinking this trick would keep the cops from figuring out who wrote the note. He put the second letter in an envelope and printed the address for Todd Connaughton. He used a kid's print set purchased in Albany to print the address.

He grabbed his hat and tucked the envelopes inside the newspaper. Outside, he got in his car and headed for the Peekskill Post Office. He was thinking that all he had to do was put a bunch of stamps on the envelopes and head back to Albany, and also thinking that he wouldn't have to be wasting his time on this if his friend John Oley hadn't been so foolish. John had played at being an actor and refused Dan O'Connell's request for help, had been sure the O'Connells would very soon repeat the offer. But that hadn't happened. Hell!—they'd likely have the ransom money in hand already if Oley hadn't stalled everything with those games of his.

***

Late the next day, Saturday afternoon, Manny Strewl's black Willy-Knight two-door convertible swerved to the right. Strewl tried to avoid the swerve by jerking the wheel to the left but his maneuver came too late and the right front tire rubbed the Beaver Street curb. He pulled the car forward, parallel to the curb a short distance from the shop at 45 Beaver Street.

"Damn it!" he muttered. "If I don't get this steering fixed soon I'm gonna need a whole set of new tires."

He stood beside the open convertible and yawned, stretching his 5'9" frame its full length. All the running back and forth to New York City he had been doing had consumed a heck of a lot more time than expected, mainly because he usually stuck to the back roads. He wasn't getting enough sleep.

The afternoon was hot, a mid-July day. He fanned his face with his panama hat and watched the weekend shoppers drool over the merchandise in the store windows. He also looked in all directions to ensure no strange car was parked close by and no one he was familiar with was nearby.

He reached up and combed his chestnut hair with his fingers, fitted his hat on his head and took his gray suit coat from the front seat. He murmured to himself, "So far, so good."

Inside the Beaver Street Clothes Shop, an elderly man with a measuring tape around his neck and a yarmulke on the back of his head was stocking the shelves with men's trousers. Strewl raised his voice. "Business been good, Abe?"

Abe Friedman and his brother had opened the shop a few years earlier. At that point Strewl helped out his fellow Jews by selling them cloth at a discount. What he failed to mention was that the cloth had been stolen from a warehouse across the river in Troy.

Abe wore his usual unbuttoned vest. Its pockets held a variety of buttons, needles, chalk sticks and slips of paper. He faced Strewl with his arms crossed and noticed first his visitor's bloodshot eyes.

"I can tell you've been staying out late again, Manny. Lost some weight too. I should take those pants in. You need to find a nice Jewish girl to fatten you up. You're thirty already, right? Not getting any younger. And the pool of nice girls is shrinking."

Strewl pushed up his hat with his thumb and chuckled. "Been working late, Abe, to make a few extra bucks. A deal I made last night closed late is all." He gripped his ribs with his hands. "And don't worry about my weight none. Ma makes sure me and my brothers are well fed."

Abe grabbed Manny Strewl by the shoulders. "Always working deals, Manny. Someday you'll be rich and famous."

Abe was only half right. For the remainder of the century and into the next, Manny Strewl's name would be remembered in the area. Even in 1995, when a local news broadcaster cited Strewl's name from a historical document about the case, Strewl's descendants pleaded with the television station not to call attention to the name again because they were still embarrassed to be associated with the kidnapping.

Manny took Abe's arms and gently pushed him back. "Yeah, someday maybe."

Abe took an opened envelope from a vest pocket and handed it over. "Sorry I opened it—it's addressed to the shop."

Manny frowned. The envelope had arrived quicker than he'd expected.

He removed the inside envelope.

He held this envelope up to the overhead light and squinted at it. At least Abe hadn't opened this one, but did he suspect anything?

Strewl said, "Wonder who it's from? Gotta be from English. He's the only one knows I come here regular. Probably wants to put the touch on me."

Abe shook his head side to side. "Yeah, everybody's looking for a handout these days."

A customer came in. "Take it in the back and read it there, Manny. Use my desk."

In the back Manny closed the blue curtain that separated the sewing room from the rest of the shop and nodded a greeting to a boy who was ironing a pair of pants. He took a seat at Abe's desk and pulled the chain on the desk lamp, opened the envelope addressed to him and covered his grin with his fingers as he read what he had written the day before.

MANNY STROWL,

You NO DOUBT ARE AC-
ACQUAINTED WITH THE O'CONN
ELL PEOPLE. WELL YOU CAN BE OF
GREAT SERVICE TO THEM, WE
HAVE CHECKED ON YOU AND DE
CIDED TO PICK YOU AS OUR
GO BETWEEN IF YOU ARE WILL
ING, IN THE EVENT YOU ARE
YOU WILL INSERT THIS ADD
IN THE WORLD-TELEGRAM PERSONAL
SETTING
"ROMA"
     PLEASE GET IN TOUCH WITH
     ME MANNY.
Do THIS PROMPTLY, AND DO NOT CHANGE
YOUR HABITS, IF YOU CARE TO BE
OF SERVICE. SECRECY AT ALL TIMES IS
NECESSARY

THIS IS GENUINE BY JOHNS SIGNAT
URE ONLY.

     "ROMA"

This is genuine

John O'Connell Jr.

This should get things going, Strewl thought. He just hoped the cops didn't roust Mike Roma too bad. Roma's hotel business hadn't been too good since the cops ran off all the hookers.

Strewl touched the phone but paused for a moment. He figured he'd better tell John Oley he was going to be the go-between, but the cops probably had John's phone tapped. That's what they did in all the latest crime movies. Hell, Oley was smart enough to know if his phone had a tap on it. So far Oley had played Mr. Innocent and the cops weren't any the wiser. He would be sure to get the *real* message.

Strewl dialed Oley's unlisted number. When a voice answered he cupped his hand over the mouthpiece and spoke in a hushed tone. "John, it's me, Manny. Just got a letter at the clothing shop. Looks like it's from the kidnappers."

"The kidnappers! Cheese-us, Manny. You trying to suck me into this? Cops are already all over me."

"Yeah—sure, John, but it's not you they want. They want me to front for the O'Connells. They want me to act as the go-between."

"O-oh, shit!"

"I gotta see yuh, John—right away."

"Don't want no part of it, Manny. Me and my new bride wanna get acquainted, yuh know? I've been getting nothing but crap since my name and picture have been in the paper. If you're smart, you'll toss that letter and take a hike."

"Great, John. But if Butch O'Connell comes back in a box, both of us will probably end up in shit's creek. *At least read the damn letter.*"

"Yeah, yuh could be right. Well, slide on over then. I'll send Aggie to the store for something."

Twenty minutes later Strewl parked his car at the corner of Fairview and Maplewood and started walking. As he approached the house he darted to the side and went up the back steps of 40 Oakwood Avenue.

The door opened before he could knock and Oley hustled him inside. "Let's see the letter."

A moment later Oley slapped the letter against his leg. "This is good, Manny!"

"Yeah. Scribbled over the letters so no one could tell who wrote it, and mailed it from Peekskill."

Oley tapped his chin with the envelope. "Peekskill, huh? White Plains area. Ralph Zucco and his mob will be pissed if the cops put some heat on him over this."

Strewl shrugged. "Only if Zucco finds out it's us." He stepped over to the kitchen window and peeked around the curtain to survey Fairview Avenue. "Let the cops go after Zucco. That way they won't be after us. Did Dan O'Connell ever call you back?"

Oley smirked. "Hell no!"

Strewl paced the length of the small room. "Been over a week now. I talked to Angel Face when I was in New York. He said Harrigan and Dugan were bitching about how long it's taking. They don't like it much that you played so hard to get."

"Don't make no difference, Manny. Cops are still all over me."

Strewl drew his palm across his mouth. "Let's throw the cops a curve ball. Maybe it'll take some of the heat off yuh. We let the word out that I showed you this letter. We had an argument. You told me not to do it. I decide to do it anyway and somehow or other get hold of Dan O'Connell, show him this and feel him out. We'll see what drops out."

Oley watched a slow-moving black sedan glide past the kitchen window. "Maybe you're right. If the cops are on me they're not watching you."

Oley went to the other living room window and inched the curtain to one side. He jerked his head in the direction of the house diagonally across the street. "Broad's name is Watkins. Been watching me like a hawk. Couple of doors down is Jimmy Hynes—an Albany cop. He's always on my ass. Hell, he even stormed up to me on July 6 when Harrigan came to pick me up, when I hadn't done nothing yet."

Oley handed the letter back to Strewl. "This would give the cops an excuse to bust my balls. None of us is lily clean, Manny. Not me, my brothers—not you. Maybe it's better for me to be the decoy. That'll give you a clear path to play things out. "

"When I show this to Dan I'll play nervous and let him make the call. If he says no, we're out clean. If he says yes…I'm just doing him a favor."

"That's jake with me."

"Say John, can you put me in touch with Dan?"

Oley rubbed his face and watched as the black sedan parked across the street. Nobody got out of the car. "Not sure where Danny's at. He usually goes to his place on the lake this time of year and I don't have that number, or the address. But I betcha Tommy Dyke would know. He's tight with the O'Connells. Tommy's fond of the corn beef and cabbage at the DeWitt Hotel. Probably catch him there if yuh hurry."

Strewl picked up his hat, ready to go. Oley said, "Manny, it'd be best if you slide behind the garage before you hit the street. Be easier on both of us, know what I mean?"

Chapter 11
Court House Letters

Monday morning the detectives were on the job early. An hour or so after he arrived, Gannon was about to go again to the percolator to fill his coffee cup when a messenger arrived with the anticipated wire recording. Gannon changed his mind about the coffee because he was eager to see what they would learn from the taped phone conversation. He took his seat and Hynes reached over and started the recording.

"Hello, Danny? It's Guy Nolan."

"Cheese-us, Guy. It's been a while. Where yuh been hiding?"

"I pulled up stakes in Albany and planted them over here in Buffalo."

"Long way from the action, Guy."

"From what I've read in the papers, Danny, you've got enough action in Albany without me. 'Sides, a little blue bird whispered in my ear, said I should leave Albany for health reasons. Know what I mean?"

"Sure, Guy. I can—"

"No need, Danny. Buffalo's been good for me, yuh know. But what I got is for you."

"Better be good, Guy. I'm up to my eyeballs—"

"I know, Danny. Been reading the papers about your nephew. That's why I wanted to talk to you. I overheard some things last February—while I was in Syracuse."

"What'd you hear, Guy?"

"I was in a restaurant couple a tables away from three other guys. Didn't pay 'em no mind till I heard them mention the name O'Connell. The place was noisy—didn't hear the

*whole conversation, but I did hear one of them say
'kidnap.' Another guy mentioned something about 'big
dough.'"*

"Guy! You recognize any of 'em?"

*"Couldn't get a good look at them, Danny. They kept their
heads down. Only glanced at them a few times. Didn't wanna
look like I was spying."*

*"Appreciate your call, Guy. I'll pass it along to Smurl—
and I owe yuh."*

*"Just make sure Smurl knows it's coming from me, Danny.
I may want to visit Albany sometime."*

*"Don't worry, Guy. I'll speak to Smurl. I know how to treat
my friends."*

Hynes grinned and stopped the recording. "What yuh think,
Joe?"

The dull chatter of the police station dayroom and the
ringing of a telephone played in the background as Gannon
said, "Jimmy, who is this Nolan fella?"

"Guy Nolan. Had a finger in just about everything, mostly
nickel-dime stuff. We couldn't pin nothing big on him so we
ran him outta town."

"Sounds like he's looking to trade, give us a lead so he can
ease back—"

Detective McCaffey's voice boomed across the room.
"Hynes—Delaney's on two."

Hynes answered the second phone to his right. A moment
later he gestured at Joe Gannon, signaling him to grab his coat.

Hynes was saying, "Yes sir—we're on our way!" As he put
the receiver back in its cradle he got to his feet. "Delaney
wants to see us right away. The kidnappers made contact—and
chose a bag man."

Gannon grabbed his hat. "Who'd they choose?"

Hynes stuffed the wire spool recording in his pocket.
"Don't know, but there's another letter too, this one received at

the courthouse. Apparently the letter arrived late Friday, when everyone had left for the weekend, so Delaney didn't get it till this morning."

"What do you mean, the letter went to the courthouse?"

"Was addressed to Todd Connaughton, one of the clerks. Maybe Delaney knows why."

On the sidewalk outside the police station Gannon pulled at Hynes's arm and stopped him. "Think about it, Jimmy. If the kidnappers are bypassing Mr. O'Connell's mailbox, it's because they know it's being watched. I translate that to mean they're probably watching us too—don't you think?"

Hynes frowned but said nothing and they headed for the black unmarked police car. Seated behind the wheel, Hynes pulled his gun from his shoulder holster, clicked open the chamber and made sure the gun was loaded. As he reached to start the engine he said, "This case is starting to cook."

At the district attorney's office Sheila waved them on through. "Go right in. They're all waiting for you."

Hynes's eyebrows shot up in surprise. "All?"

"Major Warner and Chief Smurl are with Mr. Delaney. They've been here for some time."

Hynes gripped the doorknob and looked up into Gannon's face and whispered, "This oughta be interesting."

Delaney was at the window, closing it—though the July morning was already hot. The street noise faded away leaving only a soft sound of rustling paper caused by the breeze of the overhead fan. Major Warner sat on the left of Delaney's desk with his navy blue suit coat over the back of the chair. His brass vest buttons and black leather shoes were spit-shined—habits remaining from his military days.

Police Chief Smurl was not in uniform. He was seated at the far end of the desk and as he leaned back in his seat the shirt buttons strained over his wide girth. Smurl had always impressed Hynes as a man who wanted to look like a gentleman. He kept his graying sandy hair combed back neatly, and when he was ill at ease he fiddled with his tie.

In front of both Warner and Smurl were stacks of folders. In a booming voice Delaney said, "Have a seat, detectives."

A hollow feeling swam through Hynes's stomach. A hot Monday morning with the windows shut and the place as quiet as a church? What was up? To cover his nervousness he took the initiative—reached into his pocket, removed the recording and placed it on the desk. "Got this over the weekend, Mr. Delaney. Guy Nolan says he's in Buffalo—says he heard something about a kidnapping months ago. Could be a lead. And Joe here—he figures, based on the quick turnaround with the letters, that the kidnappers must be holding Butch somewhere in or around New York City."

Delaney grabbed the wire spool. "I'll pass this along to the G-men—give them something to do."

He opened a folder and pushed it across the desk to the detectives. "A Photostat there of a letter Dan O'Connell received late Saturday. It was passed along to him by Tommy Dyke. As you'll see, the kidnappers have chosen Manny Strewl."

Hynes said, "Manny Strewl, huh? Well, that's progress. Handwriting looks similar to the first letter."

"The lab's preliminary report says the same person wrote it. Turn it over. You see that Butch verified it as genuine with his signature."

Hynes slid the note to Gannon who asked, "How'd Dyke get the letter?"

Delaney shook his eyeglasses in the air for emphasis as he spoke. "It was addressed to a men's clothing shop run by Abe Friedman on Beaver Street. He's clean. No record. Abe gave it to Manny Strewl who gave it to Dyke who took it to Dan O'Connell—and Dan proceeded right away to set up a meeting with Manny Strewl, in Washington Park."

Gannon tapped the letter. "This signature. 'Roma.' Know anybody by that name?"

Chief Smurl opened up a folder and withdrew a page. "Fred Roma. Small-time mobster. Runs a motel in Schenectady. Did some driving for John Oley in the twenties. We sent some men up there to check him out."

Gannon nodded his head side to side and grimaced. "There's that name again. John Oley."

Delaney handed Hynes several more copies. "These are letters Todd Connaughton received at the courthouse. Inside the first envelope was another one addressed to Mr. O'Connell. Like I said on the phone, the letter evidently sat at the courthouse all weekend. We have advised Dan of its contents."

Hynes held one of the notes toward Gannon.

Dear Tod,   Friday/4, 33

If you think any-thing
of me. Please see that this
letter gets to Uncle Dan
unopened at once, By-al-
means don't tell this to
any one, Silence in this case
means my life.

                    John O'Connell Jr,

Hynes pulled at his lip. "Did the lab verify this is Butch's handwriting?"

"Yes, they're all but a hundred percent certain it is."

When Hynes and Gannon finished reading they put the pages on the desktop and looked up to find Delaney and Warner and Smurl with poker faces, staring straight at them. Hynes felt like he was in front of a firing squad. To hide his emotion he picked up one of the pages again and studied it.

II

But you are his God now and his only hope to live, so play fair; and we will do likewise. Our conditions are — first for you to turn the money over if you care to; take the numbers but we want time to cash it in. At least twenty four hours and we want you to co-operate with the go-between and see he is free to go where he pleases. You have your racket and you can be thankful it gave you plenty, and we have guns to avoid complications we will change our password "REX" to "ROMA" for your protection and the boys,

The room was still silent. Hynes cleared his throat and shifted in his chair. "The kidnappers aren't new to this. They said we could take the money's serial numbers. Means they intend to launder it. Interesting that the newspaper used the

name Strewl and here it's Strowl. Are we positive Strewl
and Strowl are the same person?"

"Quite sure, Detective."

Hynes read the last page aloud:

Uncle Dan;
They tell me this thing is coming to a close, For God sake if it it over, this is genuine as the people are (Rep)

John O'Connell

"At least we know Butch was alive as of three days ago."

Delaney slid another Photostat across the desk. "This is a
letter Butch's mother received last week. Dan had it delivered
here first thing this morning. Whaddya make of it?"

Wed 12, 33.

Dear Mother,

Just a line to
let you know I am
all right and every
thing will be all right
Providing you all meet
there demands. Tell
Uncle Dan and Ed to get
me out of this thing. These
people mean every
thing they say. They
have just told me
that the code word

is (Rep) so you see
you are doing business
with the right people
Please don't talk or
tell any thing. Show this
to uncle Dan and Ed,

your Loving Son,

John Jr,

Hynes said, "Handwriting is smoother than the second note. Probably a reply to the newspaper speculation that Butch may have been harmed. My guess is Butch was in good health when this was written. The other note's a bit rougher, which probably means he had more reason to be nervous then."

Gannon said, "The letter also mentions taking down the serial numbers of any ransom paid. That tells me these kidnappers are seasoned mobsters. On the one hand, that's good. They won't do anything rash."

Major Warner leaned forward. "And on the other hand?"

Gannon twisted in his chair. "It's also bad. They won't be afraid to put a bullet in young O'Connell's brain. Also, given the letter Butch wrote asking his uncle to hurry, I'd say the kidnappers want a quick deal. They want to get this thing over and done with, one way or the other."

Warner sat back. "What do you think the odds are of the kidnappers killing the victim?"

Gannon looked at the ceiling. "Right now? I'd say 50-50. I will say I'm surprised they chose this guy Strewl or Strowl over your prime suspect, John—"

Delaney hunched forward and cut Gannon off. "Oh, no. The kidnappers didn't choose Manny Strewl—I did!"

Hynes and Gannon turned toward each other, their eyes wide. The other three reached for papers in the stacks before them. The district attorney set his glasses on his nose and said, "When I saw that Dan O'Connell had put both Strewl and Oley on the first list of go-betweens, I removed Strewl's name—to see what would happen. This tactic also gave Chief Smurl time to gather more information on Strewl. And what he got surprised me."

Chief Smurl glanced at the paper in his hand. "We first got a glimpse at Strewl during the Legs Diamond trial. In 1931."

Gannon stiffened in his seat. "Pardon me, Chief. I remember reading some about that, but can you bring me up to speed?"

"Sure can, Detective, so long as you understand that what I say does not leave this room." Smurl waited until Gannon nodded before continuing. "Legs Diamond was arrested and tried here in Albany, charges of kidnapping and assault. We can't prove he bribed members of the jury or a witness, but we believe he did just that. For a few hours he went scot free. Right after the verdict was read we noticed John Oley and a stranger congratulating Legs. At the time, we didn't know who that stranger was. It was Manny Strewl."

"You say Diamond was free for a few hours…"

Major Warner held his fingers on the report in front of him as if playing a C-chord. "Yes, Detective. Diamond celebrated his release at the Rainbow Room, a local cabaret. During the party his wife, Alice, made a phone call to parties unknown. We suspect she had something to do with Jack's murder, since he flaunted his main squeeze—Kiki Roberts, a show girl—in full view of everyone. When Diamond left the party he did not have his usual bodyguard—for unknown reasons. He went to bed in a second floor apartment at 67 Dove Street. It was after midnight, last day of the year, 1931. We believe two unknown people had keys to his apartment. They put five slugs in his head. We figured the wife had him bumped off, but last year we found her body."

Warner paused and turned up another page of the report. "Diamond's wife was doing a show—about her life with him. We think the same people who killed him knocked her off to keep her quiet. The bullets matched the ones in his head—but the case is still being investigated."

Gannon said, "When they got him, how did they get in?"

"No sign of forced entry. Neighbors said they heard footsteps going upstairs just prior to the shots. "

Gannon was remembering his interchange with Hynes a few days earlier. Hynes sidetracked questions on the Legs Diamond case, a behavior that led Gannon to suspect the Albany Police had a hand in the slaying.

"How do you know there were two people involved in the Diamond killing?"

Major Warner turned up a page of the report and perused it for a moment. "After the shots, one of the tenants looked under her door. Saw two pairs of black shoes and dark slacks without cuffs headed down the hall."

"Any possibility that Oley and/or Strewl had something to do with the murder? Maybe they took out Diamond so they could take over his business?"

Smurl cut in. "That's a possibility. We now know that John Oley used to be Diamond's triggerman. As for Strewl, he stays in the shadows—uses his brain more than his brawn, though he gets in a good lick occasionally." The chief pushed a page across the desk. "That's a report from the Atlanta Penitentiary. Oley and Strewl spent a year there for impersonating a postal worker. They intended to rob the mail. The warden says he heard a rumor that Oley and Strewl ran a rehearsal on the kidnapping while they were there. He's checking on it."

Warner held up another sheet of paper. "Here's something else. Oley and Strewl attended the same grammar school. Neither of them graduated—a fact that dovetails with the poor English and misspellings in the ransom notes."

Hynes's brow wrinkled. "They only did a year for impersonating a postal worker?"

Delaney pushed up his glasses. "Strewl had a hot-shot lawyer—Dan Prior. They got them reduced sentences."

"Any luck matching the handwriting on the ransom notes with Oley or Strewl?"

Smurl leaned forward. "Still gathering samples. Here's an application for a beer license, but the handwriting doesn't matched. We're thinking Strewl's attorney probably filled it out. His name's Louis Snyder."

Hynes pulled the application closer. "I didn't know Snyder did criminal work."

"He doesn't," Delaney said. "Strictly corporate."

Chief Smurl agreed. "Snyder seems to be a straight shooter. But we did turn up some more suspects."

"How so?"

"Twice, Oley and Strewl applied for a beer license. The first time they were turned down due to their criminal records. On the second application Strewl tried using other names: his father, Ed—and Strewl's brothers, Jacob and Willie. That application was turned down too, because none of them knew a thing about making beer. When the other names popped up, I just lumped them in with the rest of the suspects—because in my opinion, Oley and Strewl have got their fingers in this thing."

Hynes rubbed his ear. "So Oley was a triggerman for Diamond, and now he wants a beer license and can't get one. You know, me and Joe were figuring…could be this is more about getting a beer license than anything else."

Warner said in a deep voice, "That theory is as good as any other."

Gannon finished reading a page of the report and tossed it on the desk. "This guy Oley sure gets around."

Delaney raised his eyebrows. "Something bothering you, Detective?"

"I was thinking about the raid we did in the Bronx last May. We pulled in a guy by the name of Shepnick, and his mob. In the apartment we found fingerprints belonging to Oley and Strewl—and Angel Face Geary. Also found gun paper, a machine gun stock and a bunch of empty ammo boxes."

Hynes twisted in his chair and looked Delaney in the eye. "Machine gun stock, gun paper—remember what I said about July sixth and John Oley's package?"

Delaney leaned forward and clasped his hands on the desk. "What else did you find in that raid, Detective?"

"That was it mostly. It was a mob hangout so we got a lotta prints. We were hoping to bag Big Charlie Scarnici but—"

Major Warner cut in. "Scarnici?"

"Yes sir."

Major Warner stroked his mustache. "Two of his boys were found dead last month in the White Plains area. When was this raid, Detective?"

"About five in the morning, May 29th."

Major Warner jerked his chin up and turned toward Chief Smurl. "The same date—the day of the Rensselaer Bank robbery. Better give the Rensselaer team a call."

The room had become uncomfortably warm and rank with cigarette smoke. Delaney loosened his tie and wiped his brow. "Scarnici's name was mentioned. Who's he tied to?"

Hynes answered. "Triggerman for Dutch Schultz. Fifty suspected murders that we know of. We also know Oley made a phone call to a Bronx phone booth—because we have his phone records. And Joe says the booth is right in the middle of Dutch Shultz's territory."

Delaney blew smoke above his head and propped the cigarette in an ashtray. "So you think Oley and Strewl and Schultz are all tied into this mess?"

Hynes shrugged. "Wouldn't bet against it. Joe can have his men follow Strewl and find out."

Gannon squinted. "If Dutch Shultz is involved—if he feels any kinda heat, he will just shoot them all."

Hynes reached a finger to the letter requesting Strewl. "I can have McCaffey pull every piece of paper Strewl ever touched. In a week's time we'll know what size shorts he wears. In the meantime, Joe's men can follow Strewl, find out where his hangouts are."

Gannon grinned. "Strewl doesn't need a shadow."

Major Warner cocked his head. "Why not?"

Gannon smiled. "Because he's the chosen one. He's the go-between. He has to stick around…till he gets the money."

Hynes said, "Yeah, Joe. I think you've got something there. We need to let Strewl run his play. All's we gotta do is break his alibi when the time comes. But Oley—he's the one we need to sniff, even press him some. And we need to figure out who else is involved."

A thick silence followed. Then Major Warner said, "I like the excuse I've got now to put the heat on good ol' Dutch Schultz. Maybe something else will fall out."

Delaney removed his glasses and rubbed his eyes. "Assuming Strewl is involved, I don't want to spook him. Last thing we want is to tip him off that we're on to him. Detective Gannon, can your undercovers keep loose tabs on him?"

"That's easy enough. But it also makes it easier for Strewl to lose the tail if he suspects anything."

Delaney said, "I understand. Just do the best you can. But I don't think Strewl's going anywhere. We just need enough detail on his actions to impeach any statement or testimony he gives us. Strewl will hang himself sooner or later."

Gannon glanced at Hynes and got to his feet. "If there's nothing else, gentlemen, I'd better get started."

Hynes took one last look at the letters. "By the way, where was the letter to Catherine O'Connell mailed from?"

"White Plains."

Gannon had turned toward the door. He spun around like a top. "White Plains!?"

That's Black Hand Territory—the Italian mob. They'd cut Butch O'Connell to ribbons if he sneezed wrong."

Major Warner nodded. "Yep. The chief there—he's having quite a time with the Ralph Zucco mob. Zucco's the main guy with the Black Hand. I'll give the department a call, put them on alert. And if you guys go to White Plains?—I'll lend you some men from N-troop."

Hynes looked perplexed. "N-troop is in the Adirondacks, Major. There are other trooper barracks closer to White Plains."

Major Warner sat ramrod straight in his chair. "N-troop is made up of

ex-lumberjacks and mountain men. If the Black Hand wants to shoot it out or duke it out,

N-troop will oblige them. You let me know when you're ready."

Gannon led the way to the door. Delaney called after the detectives, "Keep us informed."

On the courthouse steps Hynes nudged Gannon's arm. "Something bugging you?"

Gannon was rehashing in his mind the description of men thought to have shot Legs Diamond, a description that pointed to the strong possibility that it was two uniformed police officers. "Nothing much. Just thinking about who wears dark shoes and dark pants with no cuffs."

Hynes glanced at several nearby police officers. "Remember the tiff I had at the station with Fitzgerald—when he brought in Max Price a few days ago?"

"Yeah."

Hynes puckered his lips. "He worked that murder case, and his uniform doesn't have cuffs and his shoes are black."

Some seconds passed before Gannon said, "Come on, let's find Strewl."

***

While Hynes and Gannon were looking for Strewl, several blocks away a curly black-haired Jacob Strewl walked down Elm Street while perusing the front page of the Times Union where there was a large picture of a husky, bearded and very Italian General Italo Balbo in dress uniform decorated with a lot of medals on his jacket. The general, from Rome, had been at the Newark Airport and put on an aerial show with his squadron of floatplanes. Jacob stopped at the stairs to a four-story blue apartment building. The number 95 was painted in gold on the transom above the door. He balanced a bag of groceries on his hip, stuck the newspaper into his coat pocket next to several other papers and removed his keys.

He climbed the creaky wood stairs to the third floor apartment and entered. His brother Manny was asleep on the sofa next to two open widows. Jacob slapped Manny's feet with a newspaper. "Come on. Time to get up."

Manny jumped, startled from sleep.

"If yuh wouldn't tramp around all night, Manny, you wouldn't sleep half the day away. Here's the New York papers you asked for. You owe me a nickel for the World Telegram. I got some bread and eggs too."

Manny rubbed his eyes. "Yeah, sure." He pulled himself to a sitting position and opened the World Telegram to the Personal section. There it was, right on schedule:

"Roma, please get in touch with me. Strewl."

That should calm Harrigan and his New Jersey mobsters, Manny thought—but then realized that Harrigan had no way of contacting him. The Jersey guys did not have his home phone number and the phone at the garage had been taken out. Well, he would just have to make himself visible on the streets—they'd find him.

From the kitchen came the sound of grease popping in a pan. Manny called out, "Throw some potatoes in with the eggs, will yuh, Jacob?"

It occurred to him that Harrigan might have someone stop by the apartment. He would have to clear the place. He took a few dollars from his pocket and put them on the table. When his brother appeared in the kitchen doorway Manny pointed to the money. "Sold a wireless yesterday, Jacob. Why don't you and Willie and Ma go to the talkies tonight? My treat."

Jacob scooped up the cash. "What about you? Not coming?"

"Nah—I gotta meet a guy uptown. Said he needs some wireless parts, so I gotta look over his setup and see what I can order. "

"In that case, Manny, can I borrow your car? I got a job uptown at the bus garage busting tires. Just take a few hours."

Manny pulled out the keys. "Here yuh go. I'll be heading out right after I eat."

An hour later, Manny stood at the top of the apartment steps. He looked up and down the street. He pulled down the brim of his hat, a straw Panama with a black band. He preferred this style over the popular flat-top straw hat because it had more room for his thick dark brown hair. He liked the large hat brim for keeping the sun out of his eyes.

The hat would be the first nail in Manny Strewl's coffin. A few weeks later the hat would provide a clue that would finger him as part of the kidnapping gang.

He slung his beige suit coat over his shoulder and walked down Elm Street toward the Hudson River. He wandered through south Albany for hours, pausing in the darker corners of each building while he looked in all directions to make sure he was not being followed. By the time he was on Steuban Street the night sky matched the color of the shadows and the streetlights glowed like stars. Strewl leaned against the Commerce Building and fanned himself with his hat. A car honked. Tires squealed and skidded—bang!

Strewl jerked to attention. A car had run the red light at the intersection of Maiden Lane and Chapel Street and sideswiped another car. Strewl kept one eye on the fender bender and walked diagonally across the intersection toward the lights of the Ten Eyck Hotel. He noticed a man with a brown felt hat pulled down close over his eyes. Strange he thought, a man shielding his eyes from nonexistent sunlight. Guy must be an idiot, but he could be a cop.

Strewl combed his eyebrows with his fingers, shielding his face while he studied the man. About thirty, thin as a toothpick, wearing a brown suit. The man's eyes locked onto Strewl as he came close and as he passed he said, "Roma—meet me at the Mohawk, Schenectady—one o'clock."

Strewl halted his steps but resisted the urge to turn around and look after the guy. A pedestrian bumped into him. His nerves were shot. What if the guy was a cop?

He turned around and looked back at the crowd around the car accident. Where was the guy? Strewl's heart was beating like a drum in his chest. Cold sweat trickled down his cheek. He walked over to the Ten Eyck Hotel and waited in the shadows.

Minutes later he emerged from the shadows with a grin. The cops would not have asked him to meet them at the Mohawk—they wouldn't know what to ask him. Besides, Dan O'Connell had said he would keep the cops out. O'Connell had even confided that he thought his phone was tapped. If Mr. O'Connell was working with the police he would not have mentioned phone taps.

Just a case of nerves, Strewl said to himself. He stepped into the glow of the hotel's lobby lights and checked his watch.

He walked up to North Pearl Street and headed west. He was tired and rubbed his neck. A man was approaching from the opposite direction, and he looked familiar. Was he a friend? An old customer? Hell, that was all he needed, to run into someone he knew when he was about to meet with the New Jersey mob. "Probably nobody," Strewl muttered as he crossed State Street to South Pearl and made a right turn up Beaver Street.

He still had time to kill, figured he could lay up at Abe's place. Someone might be watching his own apartment. The lights were on in the apartment over the clothes shop. Just then the lights were out. "Shit," Strewl mumbled, "no sense waking him up."

He strolled back to his own apartment and flopped down on the sofa and let his head hang over the back. "Gonna be a long night," he said aloud.

Next thing he knew he was waking up to the noise of voices and jangling keys. He had not meant to fall asleep. He grabbed his hat and explained that he had to rush, had to drop off a box of parts to a customer who wanted them before morning.

Mother Strewl smiled. "Such a good boy, Manny—always working. Rest you should."

Strewl rattled his car keys. "Gotta fill this order, Ma. Could lead to a bigger deal down the road—and then we'll be in the bucks."

She kissed him on the cheek. "Be careful. No amount of money is worth losing you or one of your brothers."

At the Mohawk Hotel, Strewl burst through the revolving door. The lobby was empty except for the desk clerk and a cigar salesman dozing in his stand next to the entrance door. Strewl tipped his hat at the inquisitive clerk and eased over to the stairs that led down to the men's washroom. Inside the washroom, a faucet was dripping. He dropped to one knee. No feet showing in the stalls. So far he was hitting zero, no one on the premises looking for him.

He paused at the head of the stairs and surveyed the lobby again. Still no one. Maybe they weren't coming. He pushed up

his Panama hat and wandered back onto State Street. A
voice from behind said, "Follow me."

It was the same young man he had seen near the car
accident. Strewl trailed behind and kept an eye out, especially
in the dark spots between streetlights. The fellow continued for
several blocks and then darted into an alley. When he turned
around, he removed his hat.

Strewl said, "Damn, Sweeney—didn't recognize yuh."

James Sweeney said, "You got the dough?"

"Not yet. Dan O'Connell says it's impossible for them to
raise that kind of money, see? All's they got is fifteen or
twenty thousand—need some time to raise more."

Sweeney peeked around the corner at the empty street.
When he turned back he said, "Hell you say! It's been a week
already, time wasted with Oley playing hard to get. And
Harrigan's sure gonna be pissed when he hears this. I'd rather
you talk to him direct."

"Don't be stupid. Cops are watching anyone connected
with this thing, especially John Oley and anyone associated
with him. You tell Harrigan it's better for me to be the go-
between—let Oley play decoy."

Sweeney stood with his arms crossed over his chest. His
jaw was set tight. Strewl said, "Look, I know the fifteen won't
do—Harrigan won't take it, I won't either. They're just feeling
us out."

Strewl reached inside his coat pocket and took out a sheet
of paper. "Here's a reply I wrote to their offer. I want you to
mail it from down river—use the print set Jo-Jo bought to
address the envelope. Send it to the Beaver Clothes Shop. I'll
take it from there. When Dan gets it, he'll ante up the cash."

"Better gimme your phone number, case Harrigan needs
yuh."

"Albany 3-5042—but don't have Harrigan call it. Use some stooge to make the call. The cops probably have everyone's phone tapped by now."

"You sure of that?"

"Nah, just talk I've heard."

Sweeney pulled his hat down over his eyes. "I'll call Harrigan, tell him to get the envelope printed. He can meet me in White Plains, it'll be faster if we mail it from there. Do the cops suspect you're involved?"

"Nope. So far they're sticking with Oley. As long as John sits tight, we'll have it made." Strewl stepped back to the alley entrance and peeked around the corner. In the distance, a man was escorting a woman out the front door of the hotel and toward a car. The lady took the driver's seat. The man stood on the sidewalk and watched as the car pulled away. Strewl waited until he went back inside.

He said, "Coast is clear. Wait a few minutes before you head out. I'll call Harrigan from a pay phone to let him know how it goes. See yuh."

Sweeney watched Strewl go to his car and drive away. Then he stood under a streetlight and smirked as he read the note.

PAN.—
HEARD FROM MANNY WHAT YOU OFFERED
IS REALLY AN INSULT WHAT KIND OF PEOPLE
DO YOU THINK YOURE DEALING WITH WHAT
WE WANT IS ACTION ONE WAY OR THE
OTHER IF YOU WANT JOHN ALIVE KICKIN
TWO HUNDRED AND FIFTY G'S IF YOU
WANT HIM THE OTHER WAY WHY WE WILL
ACOMMADATE YOU WE HAVNT MUCH
SYMPATHY FOR YOUR KIND. NOW OUR
POLICY IS TO BE NICE AS LONG AS IT PAYS
AND IF YOURE GOING TO BARGAIN WHY
WERE GOING TO END IT SO LETS HEAR
FROM YOU TOMORROW HOW YOU FEEL
ABOUT PAYING THAT DOUGH WE KNOW
ALL THERE IS TO KNOW ABOUT YOU PEOPLE
SO WHEN WE ASKED FOR THAT AMOUNT
WE KNEW YOU COULD GET IT WITHOUT
ANY TROUBLE SO BE QUICK ABOUT MATTER
AS YOU ARE ONLY WASTING TIME

ROMA

MANNY IF YOU GET THE MONEY TOMORROW
OR THE DECISION HAVE ALL YOURE SQUADS
IN YOUR HOME DRAWN TO THE BOTTOM

FURTHER INSTRUCTIONS
WILL FOLLOW
ROMA

Sweeney tucked the note in the inside pocket of his suit coat. He liked his plan to meet Harrigan in White Plains. They could meet at Zucco's place. He started his car and headed south, looking for a telephone booth.

Chapter 12
Two Ton of Law

Ed O'Connell wiped sweat from his brow. On a July afternoon, a parked car was not a choice place to be. Solly O'Connell was at the wheel of the green Marmon, a short distance from the speakeasy at 18 Market Street — a speakeasy owned in part by John Oley's brother. Solly adjusted the rearview mirror for the fourth time.

"Keep doing that and you'll twist it off," Ed said.

"Tired of just sitting, Eddie. Be quicker to go in and roust Francis."

"Wouldn't accomplish much. Francis takes his cues from John so we just need to be patient."

In the 1930s, lawyers like Ed O'Connell were the new hired guns. He could manipulate the law and make a contract say anything he wanted with the help of a judge elected with O'Connell money. The legal business had taught Ed to read a man's body language. He cranked his head around to see what his brother was watching so intently. Two men were approaching on the sidewalk. As they walked they talked and their hands gestured.

"Take it easy, Solly. They've got their hands in plain sight."

Solly was the black sheep in the O'Connell family. He liked to gamble and had a habit of leaving debt markers up and down the Hudson River from Albany to New York. He ran a minor book operation, but paid off only small winners, to keep them coming back. On the big winners, he welched. Only his brothers' political connections kept Solly off the broken-leg list. During prohibition, he fronted for the O'Connell's illegal booze business, meaning he took the bad rap, which in turn meant his brothers appeared lily clean and were free to run Albany any way they wished.

Ever since the failed Mush Trachnier kidnap attempt, the O'Connells had been on edge. In March they received a letter saying they should watch their step or they could end up like Trachnier. The brothers had presumed that one of them was on the kidnappers' list, but another member of the family had been taken instead. It was now two weeks since John Junior was captured. He was the only son among three O'Connell brothers and slated to inherit their worldly goods.

Through the local grapevine the O'Connells learned that the Oley brothers had been highly upset when denied a license to distribute beer. And it was common knowledge that the O'Connells kept tight control of the Alcohol Board, granting beer licenses as they chose, with an eye to locking out competitors to their brewery.

John Oley had once worked for the O'Connells, helping them run an illegal booze operation. Times changed and the O'Connells went legitimate, while John Oley and his clan ventured into other illegal activities.

Solly O'Connell had quickly made the assumption that it was the Oleys who took his son—because it's what he would have done had the tables been turned. Dan O'Connell, on the other hand, did not believe John Oley played a role in the kidnapping. He figured his past association with John had been good enough to bridge any animosity. Ed O'Connell, the lawyer, doubted Oley's loyalty to them simply because in his line of work he had seen too many instances of a business friend turned Judas.

On this hot summer afternoon, Ed was prepared to offer a deal. If the Oleys agreed to it, Butch could be returned to his family with no loss of life and no losing face.

When a maroon Buick rolled up the street Solly elbowed Ed. "That's John's car."

Ed inched up in his seat to watch. John Oley got out, flipped on his hat, slung his brown suit coat over his shoulder and entered the speakeasy.

Ed said, "Okay, curtain's up. Just remember, Solly, this is a business deal."

Solly pulled the latch on the door. "Yeah, I know. But I want my son back in one piece."

Ed held his hand in the air between them and rubbed his fingers together. "Ante up."

"What?"

"Come on, Solly—you think we're gonna have any friends in there?"

"That's the point, Eddie. If—"

"If nothing. Oley's probably got a dozen guys in there. Last thing we need is an accidental shooting. Hand it over."

Solly removed the .38 from its shoulder holster and handed it over. Ed slipped it in the glove box. As they crossed Market Street Ed said, "Let me do the talking. We don't want to be left open to a lawsuit."

Solly smirked. "Huh! Lawsuit."

As they approached the steps Ed stopped his brother. He leaned his brown leather case against his leg and reached to straighten Solly's tie. He pushed back the brim of his black derby and gazed up at the apartments above the shops. He wanted to be seen—seen going in and coming out.

Most likely the place would be loaded with friends of the Oleys, all of them packing guns. General Custer crossed Ed's mind. His nerves were as tightly wound as Solly's, but he was banking on his ability to outwit the Oleys.

He tugged at his suit coat lapels and went up the steps. Inside, they stood motionless to let their eyes adjust to the low light—and to announce their arrival. The bartender was stacking beer mugs on the shelves behind the bar. Four men were eating sandwiches at a table across the room. Ed nudged

Solly toward an isolated table close to the door. In a low voice he reminded his brother, "Back against the wall."

To the bartender he said, "M.K., I'd like an audience with either John or Francis, if they're not busy."

"Audience? Oh, yuh mean yuh wanna see them. Yeah—sure, Ed. I'll get them for yuh."

M.K. Fitzgerald was familiar with the O'Connell brothers. Solly usually came in for a backroom poker game and lost more often than he won. Sometime later Ed O'Connell showed up to pay off the debt, either in cash or by negotiating a secret deal with the Oleys.

Ed tipped his head at the men across the room. Three of them ate with one hand and held a beer mug in the other. The fourth ate with one hand below the table. Ed returned to Solly and took a seat facing the center of the room.

When John and Francis Oley came from the backroom, the O'Connell brothers stood up. Ed extended his hand. "John, Francis—it's been awhile."

Francis raised four fingers to the bartender and took a seat. He tilted the chair back and popped his gum. "What brings you guys to my joint?"

Ed O'Connell said, "A matter of civic duty, Francis. We were hoping John there could help us."

"Now isn't that funny, Ed? That sure takes the cake, because I seem to recall that months ago, when John asked for Solly's help with a beer license, all he got was a cold shoulder. And now here you show up with your hat in your hand."

Ed knew Francis was right. His brother Dan let small timers peddle beer—just to make things look good. He did not allow any real competition for the O'Connell-owned Hendricks Brewing Company—even refused to ease the policy for a friend. Ed countered Francis's accusation with a formal lie, one that couldn't be denied: "Things are different now that prohibition is fading away. The board controls beer licenses,

Francis. It's out of our hands. Even Dan couldn't get a beer license. That's why my partner and me had to take over. Everything's going legit."

Francis rocked his chair down. His smile changed to an icy smirk. "Oh, I bet."

Ed turned his attention to John and lowered his voice. "Look, John. We could make it worth your while if you help us out. Know what I'm saying?"

Fitzgerald arrived with mugs of beer. John Oley took a swig and plopped his mug down. He said, "Danny called the other day. He asked for some help getting Butch back. I told him I probably shouldn't get involved. With my record, if anything goes wrong—poof! I'm up the river." He slouched in his chair and continued. "Other thing is, me and my brother both have a business to run, Ed. Yuh know? We don't have time for no civic freebies. But, if say, you're talking cash, well then, that's another matter."

Ed grinned like a hawk after its prey. "I think we do understand each other, John. No doubt you've read the papers and—"

Solly backhanded his brother's shoulder. "Quit beating around the bush, Eddie! Everybody knows Butch has been clipped." Solly drew a bead on John. "And I want him back!"

John lurched forward with his eyes narrowed. "You insinuating something, Solly?"

Ed grabbed Solly's forearm and pinned it to the table. "Of course not, John. My brother, well, as you can see he's quite upset. He's just stating a fact—stating it a bit forcefully, that's all."

John Oley surveyed the faces of the O'Connell brothers then glanced at Francis. "Alright," he said, "I'll buy that."

Ed lowered his voice. "What we mean to say, John, is this: we know you're a man about town. You have connections, business connections and—"

Solly broke in. "Oh hell, Eddie! Cut to the chase! John, you're a bootlegger and hijacker like the rest. What's it gonna cost to get Butch back?"

Ed grasped Solly's shoulder. "Calm down!"

Francis kept his smirk, John gulped beer, Solly dropped his gaze to the table, and Ed tried to appear calm. A moment passed in church-like silence until Francis popped his gum.

John leaned forward and zeroed in on Ed. "An upset old man goes only so far, Eddie — only so far. What I know about Butch is what I read in the papers. They said $250,000. Some people think maybe seventy-five is fair."

Ed folded his hands on the tabletop. "You're a business man, John. You understand that there are *other* things—things just as good as cash."

Francis had been working his gum like a cow chewing its cud. He stopped chewing. "Like what?" he said.

"Well, land for one, Francis. Maybe an interest in, say, a sales territory." Ed moved his gaze from Francis to John and forced a smile. "Maybe, if a person gets into trouble, a little consideration from certain sources. That could be worth a lot, if say a business deal goes bad. Right, John?"

John scratched his cheek. "Hmmm…guess it depends. Depends on how much cash is upfront and—"

Francis interrupted. "Shit, John! Why we talking money? Solly's got worthless paper hanging from here to New York!"

Solly's finger jabbed the air. "Fuck you, Francis! Way I see it, only ones dumb enough to snatch Butch is you and your brother."

John slapped Solly's hand away. "Eat shit, Solly! A chiseler like you don't come in here and throw his weight around!"

Solly jumped to his feet. "I don't give a damn whose place it is. Everybody knows you're a two-bit mobster."

Ed yanked at Solly's sleeve because his jacket was open and the dry holster visible. "Sit down, Solly!"

Solly pulled free of his brother's grasp. "Enough of this crap, Eddie. They're too stupid to understand what we're talking about. You know John snatched Butch! His fucking brother there probably helped! Now what's it gonna cost, John? We don't have 250G's—but we can sure as hell fry your balls on a skillet!"

John shot up and his chair flew back. "You accusing me of clipping Butch? Fuck you, Solly! You too, Eddie! You come in here trying to lay this crap on us? Prove it! For all I care they can make dog food outta Butch."

Solly sprang forward but Ed grabbed him in a bear hug. "Solly! No!" Ed was aware that four men across the room had turned their way and some of them had their hands inside their coats.

John pointed at the door. "Solly, take that scrawny ass of yours and the two ton tub of lard that came with yuh—and get out!"

Ed put his hat on his head. "I can see this meeting is over."

He picked up his briefcase in one hand and his beer mug in the other. He tipped the mug in a salute toward the bartender who had his hands below the bar at the spot where Ed knew he kept a shotgun. He gave the same lifted-mug salute to the other customers and put the mug to his mouth and drained the last of the beer. He set the empty mug on the table and said in a soft voice, "A tub of lard is argumentative, Mr. Oley." He lowered his voice to a muted growl and added, "But it's a scientific fact that two tons of anything can squash an ant." He straightened his bulk and turned to his brother. "Let's go, Solly."

As they were crossing the street Ed said, "What we know and what we can prove are two different things. Now get in the car before two mysterious bullets nail us in the back."

Solly got behind the wheel and reached for the glove box. Ed shoved his hand away.

Solly whined, "What the hell we gonna do, Eddie?"

"First off, you're going to take me home. Then I'm going to dust off my two ton law book. Now drive."

***

A few days later Dan O'Connell entered the building at 100 State Street, took the elevator to the tenth floor and entered his brother's office. "Good afternoon, Grace."

Grace Spierre pointed to the inner office door. "Good afternoon, Mr. O'Connell. Your brothers are waiting for you."

Inside the office Dan closed the door behind him and took off his hat. "Solly, how yuh holding up?"

Solly was seated in front of the desk. He took a newspaper from his lap and put it on the desktop. "Okay, I guess. Catherine's still a mess, complaining about shortness of breath. Mary, and the doc—they're keeping a close eye on her."

Ed, behind the desk, swiveled his chair. He pushed himself up and went to the window overlooking State Street and peered around the curtain.

Dan asked, "Anything interesting out there?"

"There's a guy slouched next to the phone booth. I'm wondering how long it takes to read a paper. And it's not the first time that blue Duisenberg has run up the hill."

Ed returned to his desk. Dan said, "After the stunt you two pulled, could be a friend of the Oleys." He took the chair beside Solly. "The day before your little circus act, I talked to John. In his place, no less."

Solly cracked his knuckles. "Lay off us, Danny. You know as well as we do Oley's finger's in here somewhere."

"You got some proof, Solly? I find it hard to believe a guy I used to drink with would stab me in the back."

"Maybe you don't know John Oley as well as you think you do."

"Maybe I don't, but at least I keep my suspicions to myself. No sense tipping them off till we get something solid. Besides, I've got my own—"

Ed pushed the newspaper toward Dan. "Drop it, you two. Dan, this is why I called you down here."

Dan glanced at the front page. "*The Pratt Tribune*. Never heard of it."

"A Kansas paper."

Dan read the headline aloud. "Lindbergh Delivers Mail to Newfoundland." So? The Eskimos get mail?"

Ed said, "So you've got a sense of humor, huh? Try the bottom of the page, lower left corner."

Dan looped his glasses around his ears and read the small print. "Walter McGee was sentenced to death by a criminal court jury which convicted him of kidnapping..." Dan looked up. His eyebrows arched.

"Keep reading."

"...kidnapping of Miss Mary McElroy, daughter of the city manager of Kansas. The case was the first in which the extreme penalty has been assessed in the nation's crusade against kidnapping." Dan tossed the paper on the desk. "Didn't that guy in the Lindbergh case get the chair for kidnapping?"

"Technically? No. Hoffman is getting the chair for *murdering* the Lindbergh baby. The kidnapping was secondary. New Jersey's kidnap laws are similar to New York's. The act of kidnapping alone would've got Hoffman only jail time."

"Yuh lost me, Ed. What's the big deal?"

"A helluva big deal, Danny. Kidnapping here is a state crime, punishable by jail time and a fine. Translated, that means if we drop the hammer on these perpetrators, it'll just bounce off them."

After a long silence Solly kicked the leg of Dan's chair. "Listen up. Eddie's got an idea — gonna hit the kidnappers with a sledgehammer."

Dan's forehead wrinkled. "Sledgehammer?"

Ed pulled several newspapers from a drawer and tossed them on the desk. "They all have reports on kidnappings. Last year's Lindbergh case made kidnapping big news. But it's the article you were just looking at that tells me people are sick and tired of all the kidnappings."

One by one Dan glanced at the papers. "So what's up your sleeve, Eddie?"

"We kill them."

Dan's arm shot up. "What! Are you two crazy? Besides, we don't know for sure who the hell they are."

"We don't have to know, Danny. We can get them all."

Dan held up his palms. "Whoa! Hold it right there, guys. You pull anything else like you pulled at the speakeasy and they'll kill Butch for sure. Solly, he's your kid. Tell me you're not going along with this crap."

Solly wagged his head side to side. "Danny, this thing started off moving along at a pretty quick pace—but it's been a while now since we've heard a thing. We know we can't raise the cash, not by a long shot, and the kidnappers could decide to take the easy way out. So please, Danny…just listen to what Eddie has in mind."

Ed stood up and held his fountain pen in his hand. "Danny, a bullet kills one person. This pen can kill thousands."

Dan scowled. "We're not in a courtroom, Eddie, so you can stop the antics."

Ed put the pen down and leaned across the desk with his palms flat on the surface. "Oh yes we are, Danny boy. We're in the world court. And Butch? He's the clean-cut kid, the military man. The kind of son every Mom and Pop wants—and he's center stage. Everyone's gonna want to help Butch."

Dan looked puzzled. Ed cleared his throat. "As I said, the act of kidnapping is a state crime punishable with jail time and a fine. The Lindbergh case was a kidnapping and murder case. New Jersey went for a murder conviction only after they had a *corpus delicti*—a dead body. But the McElroy case, the one in Kansas—it changed the rules. They got the death penalty without a dead body."

Ed paused and narrowed his eyes. He was a player in the world's courtroom now. "The girl lived. The people of Kansas brought the wrath of God down on the head of that dastardly kidnapper for the sheer act of kidnapping the woman. Danny, I wanna do the same—I wanna make the mere act of kidnapping a capital crime punishable by death, whether there's a body or not. To do that, we need a federal law—*has* to be federal, so these pricks can't jump the law by crossing state lines. And a federal law will avoid the jurisdictional problems that plagued the Lindbergh case."

Before he concluded Ed shot a glance at Solly. "Basically, Dan," he said, "I want to hit 'em with two tons of law."

Dan's brow wrinkled. "Eddie, this may be good for the nation, but it won't help us get Butch back."

"What it does do, Danny, is give the kidnappers an out. If they kill him, it's hanging time. If they give him back before the law is passed, the worst they get is jail time."

Ed reached for the phone and moved it toward Dan. "Once the law is passed, it's the chair."

Dan scratched his chin and turned toward Solly. "You okay on this?"

Solly wiped his brow with his handkerchief. "Danny, it's been weeks since this thing started. We're all tapped out."

Ed said, "Make the call, Danny."

Dan hesitated briefly then lifted the receiver. "Grace, get me Senator Copeland in Washington, and after that, Governor Lehman."

During the silence of waiting for the call to go through, questions filled Dan's mind. Would this throw of the dice save Butch's life? Or hasten his death? What else could they do to try to save him? There was no way they could raise two hundred and fifty grand.

The phone rang. Dan placed his hand on it and said, "I pick this up, there's no turning back."

On the third ring, Ed dipped his head to affirm the decision. Dan lifted the receiver. "Dan O'Connell here."

"Hold for Senator Copeland, sir."

A moment later a voice said, "Hello, Dan?"

"Yeah, Royal, it's me. I'm in Albany. My brothers are right here next to me."

"Sorry to hear about your problem, Danny."

Dan explained the situation and the proposal. The senator reported that the idea had already been discussed in committee and asked, "Do you think this is the right time to—"

Dan cut him off. "We've thought it over, Royal. If Butch is already dead it won't make a difference. If he's alive, it might make the kidnappers think twice before they plug him. Besides, Royal—you get it passed and it'll sure make you look good in the next election. If you say you're in, I'll call Heb and we'll work it from here. We can fan the fires, if you move the mountains."

Dan O'Connell hung up the phone and said to his brothers, "Ball's rolling." Minutes later the phone rang again. A voice said, "Hold for Governor Herbert Lehman."

***

Detective Hynes pulled the unmarked black police sedan to the curb on Jay Street and pointed to a three-story cream colored apartment building with the number 30 above the door. "Joe, that's Angel Face Geary's last known address. According to McCaffy's men, Geary took a hike the first week of July. No one's seen him since. I wanna see his landlord."

The water in the police car radiator gurgled for a few minutes after Hynes turned off the engine. He kept his hand below the window as he removed his revolver from his shoulder holster and clicked open the chamber to make sure it was loaded.

Gannon chuckled. "Thought you said Albany was a friendly town."

"Albany is a friendly town—but this is Jay Street and we're after Percy Geary. I'll take the left side of the street."

Hynes got out and shaded his eyes from the afternoon sun. He studied the red-trimmed bay window with white curtains in the apartment on the opposite side of Jay Street. Closed windows indicated no one was home. A closed window in summer turned those city apartments into ovens. At the corner, a young boy stared at Hynes for a moment before turning and whistling up an alley. Hynes guessed the boy was a lookout for a back alley craps or poker game, but that arrest would have to wait for another day.

From the corner of his eye, Hynes caught movement. He turned and saw two young men step from between parked cars. One had his hand behind him, apparently reaching into a back pocket. Was he reaching for a comb, blackjack or gun? No way to tell, so Hynes brushed back his coat to expose his gun. They took the hint and changed direction. The remaining people on the street paid him no attention so Hynes called out, "Clear on the left."

Hynes matched Gannon's stride and met him on the sidewalk in front of

number 30. Gannon said, "Third floor apartment. Top corner. Somebody was peeking out at us."

"That's where we're going."

Inside the building the wooden stairs groaned with each step they climbed. Gannon said, "Sure as hell no one's going to sneak around in here."

Hynes grinned. When the door to the apartment opened Hynes showed his badge to a pale old lady with sunken cheeks, silver hair, and a food-stained apron over a brown skirt.

"Mrs. Pierce, I'm Detective Hynes, this is Detective Gannon. We'd like a word with you."

Inside the one-bedroom apartment Gannon strode across the hooked rug to the window and moved the curtain to one side. "Nice view."

The old lady said, "The open window makes the hot nights bearable, Detective." She pointed them to chairs and Hynes pulled a note pad from his pocket. "Mrs. Pierce, we believe a Percy Geary and his family reside here. Is that correct?"

"Used to. Him, his wife and the child, lived at the other end of the hall. Moved out July 8, late at night."

Hynes met Gannon's gaze. They both hid their excitement. "You're sure it was the 8th?"

"Very sure, 'cause they woke me up in the middle of the night. Said they had an illness in the family—a serious illness, and they had to leave. I tried to give back some of their rent—they had paid upfront for the entire month, but they wouldn't take it. And Mrs. Geary, she said they were leaving behind some pots and pans and things and I could just give the stuff away."

Gannon faked a smile. "That was generous of them. What else can you tell us about the Gearys?"

"Not much. The missus, she worked in the laundry a few blocks over. She said they came over from Swan Street because the other landlord wouldn't fix the plumbing. I didn't see Mr. Geary much. He came and went, mostly at night. Jo-Jo—that's what people called Mrs. Geary—said he was a truck driver. Ha!"

"You didn't believe Mrs. Geary?"

"Oh come now, Detective. Mr. Geary wore silk shirts and pranced around in white sport shoes. Wouldn't last a lick on country roads. His friends weren't much better."

Hynes arched an eyebrow. "You saw some of Percy Geary's friends?"

"Not too much, maybe a coupla times. They were from outta town."

"Can you describe them?"

"Well, the hallway's dark, but one was a bit shorter than the doorway and had some scars on his right cheek. Sorta slim. Kept his hat pulled down over one eye. Other was the same size. Looked the other way when I passed them in the hall."

Gannon cut in. "I'm curious, Mrs. Pierce. How did you know they were from out of town?"

"Easy. They wore trench coats. In July?"

Hynes flipped a page on his note pad. "Did the Gearys say where they were going?"

"Just some place in New Jersey."

"Can you remember anything else they said?"

Mrs. Pierce removed her apron and laid it on the chair beside her. "Not much. Jo-Jo was terribly upset about her father's illness. Poor thing. Her hands were shaking and she could barely talk straight. Her father must have been real sick, they were in an awful hurry. Left a lot of their stuff behind."

When they left the building, the detectives stood outside the front door at the top of the steps. Hynes clutched his notes and rapped the pages against his thigh. "The Gearys said they were going to Jersey. I saw Jersey plates on July sixth. Could be a clue, could be a slip of the tongue. I want to get some guys working the street, see if anyone saw strangers here or around Swan Street."

Gannon pointed to a patrolman who was studying their unmarked car. "We got company."

Hynes pointed to three cops several buildings away. They were shoving a man in handcuffs into the back seat of a marked police car. "A bit of action down there too."

The lone patrolman looked up as Hynes and Gannon descended the steps. "You Hynes and Gannon?"

Hynes showed his badge. "Yuh got us." He pointed down the street. "What gives?"

"We're just picking up Blade Kinsella. Friend of Bindy Riley."

"On whose orders?"

The patrolman shrugged. "Delaney's."

"What's the charge?"

"Being a friend of Bindy Riley. You know, one of the go-betweens in the papers." The patrolman pointed to a red box on a steel pole half a block down the street. "There's an alert out—station wants to talk to you guys. Call box is down there."

Hynes nudged Gannon and tilted his head toward a cluster of people across the street staring their way. "Smile for the crowd. I'll see what's up."

Minutes later Hynes hurried back and pointed at the car. "We're off!"

The engine roared to life, Hynes palmed the steering wheel and the car spun like a top into a U-turn. The tires squealed like a scalded cat and left marks on the street. Hynes said, "They found the car—one that belongs to the plate number Keiss gave us. It's a Durant. Son of a bitch was right under our noses."

Hynes stomped the gas pedal. The tires screamed as they rounded the corner onto Lark Street. "Tip came in. Someone found an abandoned car at the dump next to the Tivoli Reservoir late night on the sixth. Patrolman Dean and his partner had it towed to Walters Garage on Third Street."

He hit the siren. Its wail scared the cars in front to the side. "Paperwork wasn't finished, so McCaffy's men didn't see it on their first go through the files."

Hynes slowed as they crossed Second Street and came to a stop at the corner of Oak and Third behind a marked police car. Between the sidewalk and the large wood building with splintered white paint was a car resting on its wheel hubs. Before Hynes cut the engine, Gannon stepped out to make sure. Yep, this was the place. The 2 in the number 239 hung upside down on the open double doors.

Hynes stopped just inside the doors next to two uniformed police officers, letting his eyes adjust to the low light. He spotted two men dressed in gray suits, white shirts and polished black shoes—standard FBI uniform. They were confronting a slim man dressed in grease-smudged coveralls.

Hynes whispered to the policemen, "What gives with the G-men?"

One of the cops glanced over his shoulder. "They came in right after Straney and Butts arrived to take prints. At the moment, they're grilling the driver who towed the car here."

Hynes pulled his palm across his mouth, wondering how in heck they got here before he did. When the agents looked his way he nodded slightly.

The green 1928 Durant coupe was on the opposite side of the garage by an open window with its trunk, hood and two doors open. It was a short car with a small trunk and a design that looked like something had pushed at each end and made the roof pop up. The headlights were the usual bug-eye type mounted above the front fenders. The front bumper stuck out about a foot from the car below the square chrome-plated radiator. Sunlight spilled in through the garage window and created a spotlight effect on the car.

A pair of feet stuck out of the driver's side and rested on the running board. Hynes pushed up his hat with his thumb and said to Gannon, "Let's go see if your guys have found anything."

Gannon led the way and tapped on one of the legs. "Straney, you taking a nap?"

Sergeant Thomas Straney slid out of the car. His left cheek was smudged with black fingerprint dust. He wiped his hands on a handkerchief and swiped at the sweat on his brow with his rolled-up shirtsleeve.

Straney said, "Least I'm working—'stead of prancing around in the sunshine, and I even got some prints from the bumper." He pointed to the tow-truck driver who was being quizzed by the FBI guys. "They're probably his."

Straney led the way around to the passenger side and pointed with his fingerprint brush to the car's roof. "Got some prints here. I'm thinking they belong to a salesman. They'd sit in the passenger seat during a demo ride. I'll go by Whitbeck Motors later and get their prints for comparison." He raised his voice. "Harry, you find anything in the trunk?"

Sergeant Harry Butts popped his head out of the trunk. "Nope. No torn cloth. No hair strands. No blood stains. Coupla rust holes in the floor and a lotta dirt. No sign that there was a body in here."

A voice called out, "We'd like to hear it too." The G-men approached. The one wearing a white straw hat with a red-checkered band said, "I'm Agent Bailey, this is Agent McKee. How about filling us in?"

Hynes slipped his hands in his pockets. He thought about what he'd heard days earlier when Delaney argued with Special Agent T.F. Cullen. He knew Delaney didn't want the FBI in on the case, and much disliked the idea of getting caught in a Mexican standoff between Delaney — who was his boss — and the FBI. He decided to play it real polite. "Saw your boss. Agent Cullen. A week or so ago it was, with two others. They were discussing—"

"Yeah," Agent Bailey said. "We heard. John Oley's your prime suspect and maybe there's a New Jersey connection, which makes it federal—so we're here. We went to see your witness name of George Keiss, but turned out he was willing to talk only to Delaney or to Hoover himself. People here seem real clannish, Detective. So let's just skip the small talk."

Hynes ran his tongue over his front teeth. If there was anything he detested, it was being talked down to. He glanced at Gannon and met his eye. He wanted to alert Gannon to keep quiet about Manny Strewl, their new suspect, and about the information they had just learned on Angel Face Geary.

"Always ready to help the FBI," Hynes said, and turned the corners of his mouth up in what might pass for a smile. He stepped away and faced Sergeant Straney with a frown, hoping to signal him not to divulge any information beyond the minimum.

Aloud he said to Straney, "What else, Sergeant?"

Straney sensed the chill between Hynes and the agents. He had correctly read Hynes's cue and did not want to get involved in a turf battle. "Well, like I said, I found prints on the bumper, hood and roof. I'll have to take the prints of the driver and the people at the place where the Durant was purchased— rule them out first, plus the two officers that brought the car in. And I've not yet finished going over the inside."

It occurred to Hynes that he might be able to get rid of the FBI in a nice official way. He put on a happy face and said, "Got an idea. Why don't you two take Sergeant Butts up to Whitbeck Motors and start printing the employees? They're up on Central Avenue. You get the first crack at them. Their mechanic is a guy named Stilwell. The salesman is a Mr. Rose. Me and Joe can have a chat with the driver of the tow truck while Straney finishes up—and later we can meet and exchange notes."

The silence that followed was awkward. Straney broke it with, "I've got a few hours of work yet to do here. It'd speed things up if Harry went on up to Whitbeck's and got those prints."

The two agents moved over to the car. They poked their heads inside and examined the trunk and inspected the hood and the bumper. After a bit Agent Bailey nodded his head at Agent McKee and they turned to face Hynes. Bailey said, "Okay, Detective—we can hook up at your station house. Make sure we get a copy of your report."

Hynes wasn't about to take orders from the FBI, even implied orders. He worked for the Albany District Attorney. On the other hand, he didn't want open warfare with the FBI. The issue at stake here was finding Butch O'Connell. Therefore Hynes put on his diplomatic hat again. "Soon as we're done here, we'll make our report. You can get it from Delaney whenever."

Since the two agents and Sergeant Butts were from out of town, Hynes instructed one of the Albany cops to go along and show them the way to Whitbeck Motors. As they were leaving the building, Gannon called out, "Harry, don't forget to print the bill of sale and registration papers."

Hynes removed his hat and fanned his face. He and Gannon needed to talk to the driver of the tow truck. At least they wouldn't have the FBI looking over their shoulders.

Before Hynes and Gannon finished talking to the driver Sergeant Straney yelled, "Hey! Come take a look."

The window on the driver's side of the Durant was half open and had fingerprint dust along the top edge. Straney got out of the car wearing a big grin. "Apparently the driver had some trouble getting the window rolled down. Also appears that the driver wiped down the windshield—but missed the upper left corner." Straney grinned with glee. "That being the case, I got some fine prints along the top, and a nice thumb print right here."

Gannon clapped Straney on the back. "Good work, Tommy! How about the backside of the rearview mirror? Did you print that?"

"Uh, no. Just the front."

"Let's try the back."

Straney set to work applying the dust. Gannon cupped his hand like the letter C and explained to Hynes. "People grip the mirror like this. We might get lucky."

A few minutes later a wolf whistle came from the front seat. "Looky here!" Straney had the look of the cat that ate the canary. "It's the mother lode. Three of the nicest prints I've ever seen."

Hynes's eyes showed his excitement. "The salesman wouldn't be the driver—the prospective customer would drive!" He socked a fist into the air. "Looks like we're getting somewhere."

The detectives headed back to their car, feeling terrific at the prospect of soon being able to match bodies with fingerprints. As they got close to the car Hynes said, "Ah hell!" He pointed at drops of water leaking from the radiator. "Hope I didn't crack the engine block."

Gannon said, "Let me take a look. Probably just overheated. I used to help my uncle, one the Bronx's grease monkeys."

Gannon tucked one leg under him and stretched the other out for balance. He placed one hand on the ground and the other on the front fender to keep from tipping backwards and lowered himself to just inches off the ground. "Nothing serious. Just the hose. It's rotted around the clamp. Only have to—"

Hynes gave Gannon a hand and pulled him to his feet. "You always check a car that way?"

"Sure. Only way to keep your clothes from getting dirty. Anybody that checks—"

Hynes broke into a run and Gannon followed. "Straney! Dust the front fender!"

Sgt. Straney shrugged and began spreading the powder. He shrugged again. "Nothing."

"Check the other one."

Straney dusted the right side and turned to the detectives with a wily grin. "One helluva palm print—and I know, you wanted it yesterday!"

***

The next day at the police station Hynes and Gannon were seated on opposite sides of the desk as usual when the phone rang on Gannon's side. He answered and handed the phone to Hynes. "Sergeant Straney's in the lab."

"Hynes here."

"Could be good, could be bad, Detective, depending on how you look at it. Prints on the car match the ones we pulled off the Durant's bill of sale and registration papers."

"You got a name, right?"

"Maybe. Name on the registration was Joe Costello, 354 Hamilton Street. But his prints don't match the ones on the registration. The prints don't match anybody's. Not the salesmen, the tow truck driver—or the Oleys either. Whoever owns these prints is not in your files."

"Great. Send up the report."

Hynes drummed his fingers on the desk. Gannon asked, "Good or bad news?"

"Damn it, Joe, we're back to square one. The prints don't match the suspects! First we had suspects but no evidence— now we've got evidence and no suspects."

Gannon leaned back and intertwined his fingers at the back of his head. "Could be the G-men have access to the info we need."

Hynes reached for the phone. "Delaney's gonna love this."

A short time later the detectives were walking along the street toward John Delaney's office. Gannon flipped the paperboy a nickel for a copy of the *Times Union*. He was curious to see if Delaney had put any more fairytales in the paper. The headline, when he spotted it, startled him. He read it aloud. "'District Attorney Breaks with O'Connells.' Well, Jimmy, this might buy us some time."

He folded the paper back and continued reading. "Authorities completely at sea on this case."

Gannon nudged Hynes's arm. "That ought to give the kidnappers some peace of mind. Might even keep their fingers off the trigger. I'd say we've bought Butch a few more days of living."

Gannon continued his reading in silence. A minute later he choked out, "What the—"

Hynes said, "What's the matter?"

"The Durant! It's in the paper!"

Hynes's mouth dropped open. He leaned over to see the picture. "A bunch of people could've seen it when it was towed. Maybe Delaney's trying to push the kidnappers a little."

"Maybe. But why would he put the license plate number in the paper? May as well shout from the rooftops that we've got a witness. All bets are off when the kidnappers read this. They can put two and two together."

Hynes heaved a big sigh. "I see what you mean. We might end up one witness short. I hope like hell the boss knows what he's doing."

At Delaney's secretary's desk Hynes said, "We've got reports for Mr. Delaney."

Shelia said, "Let me check. The intercom isn't working."

She knocked and opened the door to the barking of Delaney's voice. "But listen, Governor—how can I run an investigation if the G-men are grabbing headlines? Damn it!

They even listed the license plate number. That should have been kept quiet. Yuh gotta get these G-men outta here."

Sheila managed to tell her boss the detectives were waiting. She closed the door and gave Hynes a smile. "It'll be a few minutes."

Gannon was already seated across the room. Hynes joined him and said in a whisper, "Now how do I tell Delaney we need the FBI's help?"

Chapter 13
First trip to New York

Though Hynes and Delaney decided to hide from the FBI their findings on the fingerprints found on the Durant, a leak in the case was about to spring. The leak would eventually become the cornerstone of Manny Strewl's defense.

It occurred late one Friday evening at John Bradt's speakeasy on Northern Boulevard in Albany. A clang of beer mugs bouncing to the floor roused Bradt to attention. He tossed his cards in the middle of the table onto a pile of money. "Don't have shit anyway — deal me out next hand. Sounds like somebody's tearing up the place."

Bradt was second-generation German, tall and lean with a light complexion and thick black eyebrows. He kept his curly black hair cut close on the sides, which gave his head an elongated appearance and left his ears sticking out like boat oars. Countless barroom brawls had left him with a bull nose and a permanent crease in his right jaw. His strict business ethic was simple: it didn't pay to kill, because dead men couldn't pay up. Intimidation was the better way: a well-placed bullet always changed a mind.

A few years earlier Bradt and his friends John Oley and Manny Stroll (one of Strewl's aliases) took Joseph "Joey" Green for a ride. Green hadn't paid his liquor bill. It was never proved who dumped him from a car and shot him in the back. Joey survived and paid his bill. He never identified who shot him.

Now Bradt slammed the backroom door shut and surveyed the scene. At the end of the bar nearest the door, two men were rolling on the floor in a puddle of beer. They laughed and slapped each other on the back while the crowd watched in amusement. Bradt motioned to the bartender, who came over. "What gives with the two clowns on the floor?"

The bartender was known as Moose because the name fit him. He called himself Black Irish because of his dirt-colored skin, curly brown hair and barn-door-sized ears. His legs were skinny, but his trunk was as big around as a barrel and his arms like tree limbs. If he said pay up and leave, you did.

Moose's eyes twinkled. He pointed to the off-duty police officers on the floor. "Shawn's wife gave birth to twins. That makes eight, so him and Eugene are celebrating — that's all."

"Let's get them on their way. They're taking up space for paying customers."

Bradt pulled Shawn Fox off the floor and propped him up in a chair. "Come on, Shawn. Albany's finest shouldn't be mopping the floor with his shirt."

"You too, Gene," Moose said to Patrolmen Eugene Pitman.

Bradt peeled off some dollar bills from his pocket roll and stuffed them into Shawn's wet shirt pocket. "Buy the twins some milk on me."

Shawn latched onto Bradt's arm. "You're a prince of a guy, John. Not like the other bastards I deal with. But the fix is in. Their time's coming — you can make book on it."

"Yeah, Shawn. We all got it coming to us, one way or the other." Bradt shrugged off Shawn's grip and walked away, but whipped his head around at what Shawn said next.

"No one fools with the kings, John. They'll pin the rap on him and no one will be the wiser. You'll see."

Bradt stepped over to a fella seated at the bar. "See to it that Shawn and Gene get home safely — now."

Bradt waited at the far end of the bar as the two patrolmen were escorted out. There was no one else near, so he caught Moose's eye and gave a nod. Moose knew the signal and ambled over, carrying a beer for the boss. He struck a relaxed pose, to make it look like he and his boss were idly chatting.

Bradt said, "The kings? The fix is in? What's he talking about?"

Moose tilted his head close. "The O'Connell kidnapping. Shawn's been running his mouth about it all night. Says the cops know Oley's the one who clipped Butch. They're just drawing a target on him, is all."

"Cops got any proof?"

"Nah. Cops found Oley's car close to the O'Connell house the night Butch got snatched. That's all they needed. Shawn was saying that if they can't prove it, they will just make something up. "

"Why would the cops want to pin the O'Connell kidnapping on Oley?"

Moose slung the bar towel over his shoulder and rested his forearms on the counter. "I've heard things."

"Like what?"

"Maybe the kings don't like competitors. Oley was looking for a beer license, got turned down. Oley, among other things, was broke — needing some fast cash."

"Hmm. Oley must've forgot who controls the alcohol board. But you said there were other things."

"Maybe John Oley knows too well that the O'Connells control the License Board. Besides that, way I heard it, Oley shot off his mouth once too often about getting even because Diamond got bumped off. He thinks the O'Connells had a hand in Diamond's demise and that could be why young O'Connell got clipped — a little payback."

Bradt wiped suds from his lip. "Hell, the cops haven't solved the Diamond murder yet."

Moose wrinkled his brow. "Ain't looking too hard either, know what I mean? Might be the cops just don't like Oley and his crowd, so this is an easy way to take them out. And it's all legit."

Bradt pushed his empty mug aside. "Think yuh could dig up Oley? I'd like to have a word with him."

"He's been laying low since his picture was in the papers, but I heard that him and Manny Stroll are tight."

"You mean Strewl, Manny Strewl. Haven't seen him around since Joey Green…paid his bill. Make some calls. Tell Strewl I'll pick him up at eleven tomorrow morning at the corner of Northern Boulevard and Clover. Tell him it's important."

The next day Manny Strewl raised his hat high against the Saturday morning sun to peer up Northern Boulevard. Two long horn honks from behind got his attention. Bradt waved a hand above the windshield of his brown convertible roadster' Strewl hustled over and jumped in. Bradt turned onto Livingston, heading south, and began telling Strewl what he'd heard, that the police had a target painted on Oley and planned to pin the rap on him.

Strewl asked, "This on the level?"

"Straight from the horse's mouth." Bradt went on to describe the scene in the bar. "If they don't have enough evidence to put Oley away, they'll just frame him."

"But John Oley is a friend of Dan O'Connell. He wouldn't let it happen."

"Maybe yes, maybe no — but Oley's been shooting his mouth off about getting even for Diamond. Hell, half the town thinks the O'Connells were behind it. Then there's the beer license. Oley applied, but was denied."

At the next stoplight Bradt slapped Manny's shoulder. "Look at it, Manny. Oley mouthed off about revenge. He jumped up and down about not getting a beer license. Next thing, an O'Connell is snatched. Even the cops can connect those dots."

Manny slouched in the seat. "Cheese-us, John — I'm the one that got elected."

Bradt turned to stare at Manny who suddenly shouted, "Watch it!"

Bradt jammed on the brakes. As the car jerked to a stop, Manny's hands flew to the dashboard to brace himself. Bradt's head bumped the steering wheel. They missed the car ahead by inches.

Bradt massaged his forehead. At last he said, "You, Manny? You were elected?"

Manny stared into the distance with his hand over his mouth. If the cops had not yet connected him and John Oley, they would once they checked the criminal records. It was true that he and Oley and Bradt had shot and roughed up Joey Green — and silenced the witnesses — but Bradt wouldn't take the heat for something he didn't do. Bradt would see the likelihood of his furnace blowing up and the speakeasy burning to the ground — the fate of a few other O'Connell competitors. One thing Manny knew for sure. He couldn't risk telling Bradt that he was involved in the kidnapping. He would just have to play the innocent messenger.

"Yeah, John. Me. I was elected the contact man. Talked to Uncle Dan himself, I did. None of the O'Connells have the dough. The kidnappers want two-hundred-and-fifty G's. The O'Connells can maybe raise twenty, maybe twenty-five."

Bradt shifted into gear and let the car roll. "Shit, Manny! Your ass is in a crack! Mine too, maybe. If the cops can't hang it on Oley, you'd be next in line. After you, maybe me. Hell, they might even drag in all our friends."

Manny's mind was racing. What he had to do now was figure a way to cover his ass in case things went wrong. He said, "Drop me at 100 State Street."

Bradt drove the length of Broadway in silence. At State Street, he turned the corner and pulled to a stop across from a 12-story gray concrete office building. He shook hands with Manny. His words made a chill run down Manny's spine. "No one fools with the three kings, Manny — yuh know what I mean? Stop by for a beer *after* this is over."

Manny dipped his head. The inference was clear. Friends of Manny Strewl and John Oley would soon disown them. The small town of Albany was starting to get very small.

For several minutes Manny stood outside the building. He hadn't counted on John Oley talking so much about things. If the word was on the street, the O'Connells had heard it, and they could connect the dots quicker than the police.

Inside, he took the elevator to the ninth floor where he paused briefly outside the fifth door on the right to collect himself. With his hat in his hand he opened the door and addressed the secretary. "Mr. Snyder in?"

"Why yes, Mr. Strewl. Let me check."

A few minutes later a 30-something man with slicked-back hair wearing a fine cotton shirt with rolled-up sleeves motioned Manny to a seat in front of his desk and shut the office door. Attorney Louis Snyder, true to his English heritage, was always fit and proper when doing business. He walked the financially profitable fine line of a gangster lawyer. He had set up corporations for the gangster's illegal operations, but never took part in them. Due to attorney-client privilege, he knew certain things he couldn't tell the police. He himself did not participate in gangster activities such as the setting up of hideaways or jury tampering — he just did the paperwork.

Manny took the seat in front of Snyder's desk. He lifted his right leg and rested the ankle on the left knee. He dropped his hat in his lap. He wasn't yet sure what to say to Snyder. He had heard that the Albany cops had run Guy Nolan out of town. If the leak Bradt had reported was correct, this kidnapping could be the end for John Oley, evidence or not. What Manny needed now was advice on how not to get arrested because of his association with John Oley. Manny knew he must choose his

words with care to keep his attorney from knowing just
how involved he was in the kidnapping.

Years earlier, Manny had learned the best way to tell a lie:
give details that are easily verified, but never tell the whole
story.

Louis Snyder closed the folder on his desk and said, "Did
you get the letter back so I could check to see if it was Butch's
signature?"

Manny licked his lips and bobbed his head to fake
nervousness. "I didn't get the letter back, but something did
happen. Big time."

"What was that?"

Manny hunched forward and began his fairy tale. "A few
days ago some guy whispered to me while I was on Maiden
Lane. Said to meet him at the Mohawk Hotel. So I go there and
this guy comes up behind me, see, and he says we gotta take a
walk. So I walked. Man, was I scared! I was thinking this is it."

"What happened next?"

Manny bit his lip. "This guy shoves me into a dark alley
and asks about the dough. The O'Connell ransom. I tell him I
talked to Mr. O'Connell. Tell him Dan and his brothers don't
have the two-fifty, not even close — they've got fifteen
thousand now, maybe twenty or twenty-five later."

Snyder frowned. "What did this guy say to that?"

"Didn't like it. Said he'd pass it along."

Snyder tapped his fingers on the desk. "Interesting. This
man you spoke to. Could you identify him? See any identifying
marks?"

Manny licked his lips, preparing to spill his next half-truth.
"Too dark. It was after midnight. 'Sides Lou, the guy came up
from behind. Had his hat pulled down over his face. The hat
was brown."

"Hmm. Well, so far, Manny, you haven't broken any laws
— have you?"

"No, Lou, just what you already know. But John Bradt says he heard some cops say they're gonna pin the rap on John Oley. Me and Oley being friends — well, you know — could sink me too, with my record and all."

Snyder touched his fingers together and pressed them to his lips. A moment passed. He said, "Oley isn't my concern. He's not a client. You are. Remember that Mr. O'Connell came to you. You might get some bad press, but liability doesn't attach. You're not implicated or involved directly... are you?"

"No, just what I've told you. What should I do, Louis?"

"You've got two options, Manny. Either continue as a go-between or extricate yourself entirely."

"Suppose I get out of this thing and they kill the kid. What'll happen to me? What'll people think?"

"First of all, Manny, police need evidence to act. From what you say, they don't have it. A criminal attorney can spot manufactured evidence a mile away so don't worry about that. As for the press and the general population, they'll believe what they want to believe, good or bad — but after a few weeks they forget all about it."

Manny blew out a lungful of air and stood up. He pulled his hat brim through his fingers. So far so good, he was thinking. The cops might get John Oley but, according to Snyder, they couldn't touch him. He wiped imaginary sweat from his brow. "Feeling better, Lou. Yuh know, I'm thinking that after that meeting at the Mohawk, things are likely to start happening. What's the best way for me to get hold of yuh?"

Snyder jotted his home phone number on a scrap of paper. "If I'm not in the office, call me at home — but tonight me and the missus are going to the races at Saratoga. Friends of mine have a pacer running."

Back on the sidewalk, Manny paused and watched the cars breeze by. He could breathe easier now. If the cops tried to arrest him, he had an out. But, he'd best warn Oley, he thought, so he strolled down the sidewalk to a pay phone.

"John, it's me. Got time for a beer?"

"Why not? Can yuh gimme thirty minutes?"

Manny used a code any school child could have understood: "Sure, John, but take it slow. Sorta hot out."

Manny hung up the phone and bought a newspaper from the boy at the corner and headed for the local betting parlor, a place called the Jersey News Room on Beaver Street. It was known simply as the Newsroom. It was here that Manny filled Oley in on what he'd learned from Bradt and Snyder. They agreed that John would continue to act as decoy and Manny would work behind the scenes. If they were both arrested it could be shown that Oley had done nothing wrong and that Manny was involved only because Dan O'Connell had asked him to act as a go-between.

When they said their goodbyes, Oley and Strewl were feeling confident, happy to have put one over on the police and the O'Connells. But they were basking in a false sense of security. Neither Strewl nor Oley understood how politicians like the O'Connells operated. Nor did they know that their foes were, in fact, already connecting the dots on the kidnapping.

Manny stayed behind after Oley departed. It was evening now and Jerry Brody, owner of the establishment, came over and leaned close, his green eyeshade almost touching Manny's shoulder. "How yuh doing?"

Manny had the sports pages from the Knickerbocker Press and Times Union open. "Twelve races so far. About even, not counting the beers. Who do yuh like at Belmont?"

Brody pulled the Times Union closer. "Lemme look. By the way, some kid's here to see yuh." He nodded at a boy with his cap in his hand standing in the doorway between the betting parlor and lunch counter.

Manny lurched to his feet and collided with Brody. "Sorry, Jerry," he said as he tightened his tie and tried to look sober. "Maybe the kid wants to make a bet."

"Manny, are you all right?"

"Been sitting too long, that's all." As he traversed the space Manny almost stumbled. "Dewayne—what you doing here?"

"Restocking the shelves, Mr. Strewl. Mr. Friedman sent me to fetch yuh — been looking for yuh awhile."

Manny buttoned his top shirt button under his tie, rolled down his sleeves and buttoned them. He called behind him, "Save my place, Jerry. Lead the way, Dewayne."

Dewayne led the way around the puddles left by a summer rain shower. They made their way under the checkerboard of red lights from the apartment windows overhead and hastened to the far end of Beaver Street. They ignored the couples mumbling in doorways. Dewayne ignored the closed sign on the Beaver Clothes Shop door and led Manny inside. "Mr. Friedman, we're back."

Abe Friedman poked his head through the back room curtain. He told the boy to go on home and motioned Strewl into the back room where he held out an envelope. "It came late this afternoon, but I couldn't find you."

Strewl held it toward the overhead light and studied it for a moment before opening it. Friedman craned his neck to look over Manny's shoulder. He said, "Jeez, Manny. This thing ain't over with yet? A fellow like you could handle it in 48 hours. You wouldn't be afraid to handle things."

"You're right, Abe. But I'm the low man on the ladder."

"That's what I mean, Manny. Those other names in the paper are garbage. Nobodies. A guy like you is top drawer all the way. I hope you get all the credit you —"

Strewl put his hands on Friedman's shoulders. "Hold on, Abe. If word gets out what I'm doing every schmuck in the city will be asking me for a favor, yuh know? Hell, you might end up with a shop full of freeloaders. It's better if I take a backseat on this one."

Friedman pulled on his lip. "Yeah, that's what I mean. You always think this stuff through."

Strewl stepped around Friedman. "Gotta run, Abe. You ought to get some sleep. You ain't getting any younger."

Friedman began his usual speech about how he could still sew faster than any of the people that worked for him. From the door, Manny called, "You're my guy, Abe."

Strewl hurried back to the betting parlor and slipped into a deserted corner under an overhead light and took out the letter. He scratched his forehead with his thumb as he read.

DAN. — HEARD FROM MANNY WHAT YOU OFFERED
IS REALLY AN INSULT WHAT KIND OF PEOPLE
DO YOU THINK YOURE DEALING WITH WHAT
WE WANT IS ACTION ONE WAY OR THE
OTHER IF YOU WANT JOHN ALIVE KICKIN
TWO HUNDRED AND FIFTY G'S IF YOU
WANT HIM THE OTHER WAY WHY WE WILL
ACOMMADATE YOU WE HAVNT MUCH
SYMPATHY FOR YOUR KIND. NOW OUR
POLICY IS TO BE NICE AS LONG AS IT PAYS
AND IF YOURE GOING TO BARGAIN WHY
WERE GOING TO END IT SO LETS HEAR
FROM YOU TOMORROW HOW YOU FEEL
ABOUT PAYING THAT DOUGH WE KNOW
ALL THERE IS TO KNOW ABOUT YOU PEOPLE
SO WHEN WE ASKED FOR THAT AMOUNT
WE KNEW YOU COULD GET IT WITHOUT
ANY TROUBLE SO BE QUICK ABOUT MATTER
AS YOU ARE ONLY WASTING TIME

ROMA

MANNY IF YOU GET THE MONEY TOMORROW
OR THE DECISION HAVE ALL YOURE SHADES
IN YOUR HOME DRAWN TO THE BOTTOM

FURTHER INSTRUCTIONS
WILL FOLLOW
ROMA

PAN. — HEARD FROM MANNY WHAT YOU OFFERED IS REALLY AN INSULT WHAT KIND OF PEOPLE DO YOU THINK YOU'RE DEALING WITH WHAT WE WANT IS ACTION ONE WAY OR THE OTHER IF YOU WANT JOHN ALIVE KICKIN TWO HUNDRED AND FIFTY G'S IF YOU WANT HIM THE OTHER WAY WHY WE WILL ACOMMADATE YOU WE HAVNT MUCH SYMPATHY FOR YOUR KIND. NOW OUR POLICY IS TO BE NICE AS LONG AS IT PAYS AND IF YOU'RE GOING TO BARGAIN WHY WERE GOING TO END IT SO LETS HEAR FROM YOU TOMORROW HOW YOU FEEL ABOUT PAYING THAT DOUGH WE KNOW ALL THERE IS TO KNOW ABOUT YOU PEOPLE SO WHEN WE ASKED FOR THAT AMOUNT WE KNEW YOU COULD GET IT WITHOUT WE KNEW YOU COULD GET IT WITHOUT ANY TROUBLE SO BE QUICK ABOUT MATTER AS YOU ARE ONLY WASTING TIME

ROMA

MANNY IF YOU GET THE MONEY TOMORROW OR THE DECISION HAVE ALL YOURE SHADES IN YOUR HOME DRAWN TO THE BOTTOM

FURTHER INSTRUCTIONS WILL FOLLOW
ROMA

Manny hid his grin with the palm of his hand. This would surely push the O'Connells to come up with the money.

Had anybody noticed his excitement? Didn't look like it. A row of men sat close to a radio listening to the race results from the Belmont track. Jerry Brody was reading from a teletype tape and recording the race results on a wall-size blackboard.

Now, how to get the letter to Dan O'Connell? Dan had not given him his personal phone number.

Strewl crumpled the envelope and threw it in a nearby trash bin. He tucked the letter in his pocket and went over and tapped Jerry Brody on the shoulder. "I gotta see Tommy Dyke fast. Know where can I find him?"

Brody touched the chalk to his forehead. "Try the Belle Napolie Restaurant. He usually eats there Saturday nights."

Twenty minutes later, Strewl stormed into the Belle Napoli. He scanned the dining room before stopping a passing waiter. "Tell Rock Manny Strewl needs to see him."

Soon a beefy guy with pork-chop sideburns dressed in a fitted brown suit came over and shook his hand. "What's up, Manny?"

"Rock, I gotta talk to Tommy Dyke tonight. Yuh seen him?"

"Not tonight. His kids are sick. He stayed home."

Strewl paced in a circle. "Shit! I'm in a jam, Rock. Can I use your phone?"

"Be my guest. There's one in the kitchen next to the walk-in cooler."

On the third ring a female voice answered. "Snyder residence."

"Is Louis Snyder in? It's Manny Strewl. He's expecting my call."

"No, sir. They haven't returned from their evening out yet."

"Okay, sweets. I know he's at Saratoga. That should put him back here about ten or eleven. Tell him I gotta see him tonight. I'll wait for him on the corner of Beaver and Pearl Street."

Strewl hung up the receiver and hunted up Rock again. "I gotta see Dyke tonight. Can yuh reach him?"

"Maybe so, but I don't think he'll come over."

"Trust me, Rock. He'll come. Just tell him it's me and that I really need to see him. I'll be back in less than an hour."

"Sure you —"

Strewl was already heading out the door. He hurried to his Willy-Knight, raced the engine and zoomed west heading for Oakwood Avenue. At number 40 he went to the door and banged on it. "John! Open up. It's me!"

The front door opened. Strewl pulled back. "Francis! What the hell you doing here? Where's John?"

"He took Aggie to the talkies. Won't be back till late. My kid's got colic so I'm stretching out on the couch here while Gwen is handling things at home. What's bugging yuh this time of night?"

Strewl pushed through the door and handed Francis Oley the letter. "I put this letter together and had Sweeney send it up. I stopped by to tell John to be on the lookout — case the O'Connells come up with the cash quick-like. This letter will scare 'em into action."

Francis finished reading and said in a dry voice, "Would you really bump off Butch?"

Strewl put the letter back in his pocket. "Hell no! There'd be hell to pay — for everybody. The O'Connells would have Chief Smurl comb Albany for anybody and everybody that might've ever thought of doing them wrong."

Francis shrugged. "So now what?"

"I show Dan the letter. See if he ponies up more cash. Then it's up to him." Strewl pulled back the curtain and peeked at the empty street. "I'm seeing Lou Snyder too — to cover my ass."

Strewl left Francis and raced back to the Belle Napoli and double-parked in front. As he burst through the door he spotted Tommy Dyke in a wrinkled shirt. "Sorry, Tommy, but I have to see Dan tonight. Have to — no two ways about it."

Tommy Dyke pulled Strewl to the side. "Better be good, Manny. Wife's ready to skin me alive. We got our hands full right now with sick kids."

Strewl took the note from his pocket. "I heard that, Tommy, and I'm sorry — but Mr. O'Connell has gotta see this. Maybe you should tell him I should deal directly with him instead of going through you."

"Gladly," Dyke said. "I'm tired of this whole mess. Wait here. I'll see what I can do." Dyke strode over to the dining room entrance and whispered to Rock, then disappeared into the kitchen. When he returned he said, "All set. Dan will meet you at his place on Whitehall Road between eleven-thirty and midnight."

Later when Manny Strewl turned onto Whitehall Road his headlights illuminated a lone car parked in the shadow between the streetlights at the corner of Holmes Court and Whitehall Road. The car pulled off and disappeared around the corner.

Strewl coasted through the glow of the streetlight and stopped at number 42, the house owned by Dan O'Connell. He cut the motor and sat still, surveying the dark deserted street. He faked a nervous whistle. The only answer was the chirp of crickets. Several minutes later he walked up the front walk, still looking warily in all directions, and rang the bell. The house was dark. Several minutes went by. He rang again. No one answered. He twisted the knob and to his surprise the door cracked open. "Hello?"

"Come in, Manny." Dan O'Connell closed the door behind him. "Power's not on. We disconnect the power here when we're out at the lake house."

Strewl removed the letter from his pocket. "This came late today. Got it here soon as I could."

O'Connell took the letter and patted his shirt pocket, looking for his glasses. Unable to find them he went to the front window and pulled back the curtain to let in the glow from the streetlights. "Let's see." He turned the page toward the glow of light and tilted it in several directions.

Strewl stood nearby. He scratched the back of one leg with the other and began cleaning his fingernail with his teeth.

O'Connell labored to decipher the message. "Damn it! Maybe you can read this."

Strewl took the letter, leaned into the glow of light, quickly read through without hesitation or error, and handed the page back. "What should I do, Mr. O'Connell?"

O'Connell turned his back. "Dunno. Ed's touching everyone we know, but we still don't have all the cash. What we need is more time."

Strewl, intent on pushing for the ransom, decided to deliver his fairy tale.

"Mr. O'Connell, I was walking around Albany the other night and some guy bumped into me from behind. Told me to meet me at the Mohawk Hotel in Schenectady. So I did."

O'Connell's eyes widened. "Are you saying you met with one of the kidnappers?"

"Don't know that for sure, Mr. O'Connell."

"Did yuh get a look at him? Look familiar? Was he from round here? Was —"

Strewl raised his palms. "Hold on, Mr. O'Connell. I only got a glimpse of him. He got to me when I was crossing Maiden Lane after a fender bender. A crowd gathered and it was kinda dark. He just told me to meet him at the Mohawk after midnight — but again, when we met, it was on a dark street. I didn't see him good."

"What'd yuh tell him?"

"Told him 'bout your fifteen thousand offer. I'm guessing that's why they sent this letter."

O'Connell said, "No doubt."

Strewl rubbed his nose. Here he was standing beside Dan O'Connell, and he had influence with the cops. "Yuh know, Mr. O'Connell, there's some rumors floating around. Oley's picture was in the paper, and me being a friend of his and all, might be people would — might be they'd think bad of me. Could put me in a spot with the cops."

"Don't worry 'bout the cops, Manny. You're working for me. I'll cover yuh."

"Just the same, Mr. O'Connell, I'd like to speak with my attorney and see what he says."

"Who's your attorney?"

"Louis Snyder. Yuh know him?"

"Only by name. Ed's mentioned him a few times. Have you talked to him already?"

"Some, but I'm getting in pretty deep here. Makes me nervous."

O'Connell arched an eyebrow. "Well, go ahead, talk with Snyder. If he's got a problem with it, you have him call me."

O'Connell led Strewl to the door. "If you get contacted again, tell them we're working on the money, but there's no way two-fifty. If we all hocked everything we own, we wouldn't be close. Tell the kidnappers to pick a lower figure."

O'Connell walked with him to the car. As Manny opened the car door, O'Connell patted his shoulder. "Really appreciate what you're doing for me, Manny." He winked. "Just keep in mind, I know how to treat my friends."

Strewl got behind the wheel. "I'll do my best for you, Mr. O'Connell. Oh, and one thing. I'm having a hard time of it when I need to track down Tommy Dyke. Would it be alright to deal with you direct?"

O'Connell said he'd ask his brothers what they thought on that. Strewl shifted his car into gear and drove away. The Willy-Knight's taillights disappeared and O'Connell headed back to the porch with the letter in his hand. Just before he reached the bottom step he halted and glanced back at the streetlight at the corner. He reversed direction, counting his strides.

Standing under the light he said aloud, "Twenty five paces. Seventy five feet, more or less."

He held the letter toward the light and squinted, then stood with his hand on his hip and stared in the direction Strewl's car had taken. On the walk back to the porch, he noted how the black letters faded in intensity with each step away from the light.

He leaned against the porch column. His eyes narrowed and with great care he folded the letter. "Damn good eyesight, Mr. Strewl. Damn good."

***

The tires of Strewl's Willys Knight roadster chirped as he made a sharp turn from Whitehall Road onto Delaware Avenue as he left Dan O'Connell's house. Twenty minutes later, he spotted a lone figure pacing under the streetlight next to the public market at Beaver and South Pearl. He parked at the curb and jumped out. "Francis! Where the hell is Snyder?"

Francis Oley spit out his gum. "He was with friends and couldn't wait. Said to meet him at Little Caesar's on High Street."

"What the hell is Little Caesar's?"

"Beer garden. Nice place."

"Who runs it?"

Francis Oley unwrapped another stick of gum. "Moe Sanders and Pete Moran. Both are on the up and up." He pointed to his dark Buick. "We'll take my car. I know the quickest way."

Francis Oley stopped the Buick a few minutes later across the street from a door with a green awning and the number 37. Strewl got out and crossed in front of the car. Francis whistled from the open driver's window. "Say, Manny, you sure you know what you're doing?"

Strewl came close and said, "No. That's why I gotta talk to Snyder. Run some stuff by him on the QT."

Strewl checked the dark street in both directions. Inside the beer garden, he removed his hat, paused a moment to adjust to the dim light and stretched his neck to study the place. The room was full. A waiter in black vest, white shirt, black bow tie and a white apron reaching to his knees touched his elbow. "Table? Perhaps close to the band?"

Strewl looked over the waiter's shoulder. "Looking for a guy here with some friends. Name's Snyder. Seen him?"

"Of course. He's a regular. His party's at the second table to the right of the band."

"Tell him Manny Strewl needs to see him right away."

The waiter squeezed by the tables and whispered in the ear of a man with his back to the crowd. Snyder whispered in his wife's ear and headed toward the foyer. As he arrived Strewl said, "Something's come up, we gotta talk."

Snyder pointed at the door. "It'll be quieter out there." Outside, Snyder stopped under the wide awning and checked in all directions to make sure the conversation would indeed be private. "Whatcha got, Manny?"

"Got a letter late this afternoon. I just spoke with Dan O'Connell. The kidnappers turned Dan's $20,000 offer down flat. Said it was an insult. The letter I just gave Dan — well, looks like they wanna kill Butch if they don't get all the ransom. "

Snyder folded his arms across his chest. "What'd Dan say?"

"Looked worried as hell. Says the family's flat broke. Says they're putting the bite on all their friends — but twenty thousand might be all they can get, give or take."

"You got the letter?"

"Nah, he's got it."

Snyder pulled on his lip. "Hmm. Did he say anything else?"

"Told him what I heard, that people might accuse me of being involved, yuh know? He said he'd cover me. But I told him I still wanted to clear everything with you. Whaddya think?"

Snyder rubbed his jaw. "Don't like it. Kidnappers should've come off the two-fifty."

He jabbed the air with his finger. "Nothing we can do at this point. But about Dan O'Connell — his word's good. If he said you're jake with him then you're fine. If it was Eddie or Solly talking, I'd say close up shop. Did Dan say anything else?"

Strewl scratched his head. "Can't remember exactly."

"Just to be safe, I'd better get it straight from the horse's mouth, so I'll —"

"Letter said they want Dan's answer tomorrow. Maybe the two of yuh's could come up with an answer."

Snyder bobbed his head. "What about getting the O'Connell's reply back to the kidnappers?"

Strewl furrowed his brow, trying to look like he was in deep thought. "Well, the letter said to keep my shades down if I get news, so guess I could just leave them down and see what happens."

"Sounds good, but I'll have a talk with Dan myself. Where can I reach you tomorrow?"

Strewl fanned himself with his hat. "If I don't hear anything in the morning, I'll head over to the Jersey Newsroom. I usually hang out there on Sundays so they might contact me there. Number's Albany 3-3957. Ask for Jerry Brody. He runs the place. He'll find me."

Snyder shook Strewl's hand. "Okay. It'll be sometime after one."

Back in the car with Francis Oley, Strewl lit up a cigar. Francis started the engine and said, "How'd it go?"

"He says we're lucky to be dealing with Dan and not his brothers. Take me back to my car."

Oley watched Strewl spit bits of tobacco out the window. "What's eating you?"

Strewl shook his head. "The Jersey guys are pissed because the amount of money the O'Connells offered is diddly squat. And the insult letter I wrote — trying to push them to come up with the money — said we'd kill Butch if they don't come through. So now I'm wondering if Harrigan and the others would really kill the kid."

"At least we wouldn't have blood on our hands."

Strewl flicked cigar ashes out the window. "Maybe yes, maybe no. Snyder thought it odd we hadn't lowered the ransom. I'm thinking, we push the O'Connells too hard on the two-fifty they're gonna smell a skunk—maybe look closer at us."

Francis blew a bubble with his gum while they waited at a stoplight. He said, "Well, if Harrigan and his crew bump off Butch, that'll show the O'Connells they ain't so tough as they think."

Strewl twisted in the seat and shouted, "Yes, they are! That's why —"

He bit his lip and dropped his head, thinking that was why he let Francis's brother play the big man about town and get the heat, and why they brought in the Waxy Gordon mob. If this kidnapping blew up in their face, the Jersey mob was out of reach and the O'Connells would have no reason to think anybody local was involved.

Strewl tapped the cigar's ashes out the window. "Talk with your brother, Francis. He knows the O'Connells pretty good. Have him find out what they really can afford. Then have him call Harrigan. Last thing we need is for that gang to do anything rash."

They drove the remaining distance in silence. When Strewl got out of the car he leaned to the window and said, "Tell John I'll have to soft sell the O'Connells on a higher ransom number. Can't push too hard or it might look suspicious. Snyder already thinks something ain't normal, so we gotta be careful. But before long we'll all be rich and no one will be the wiser. John can make book on it."

Strewl stood watching the Buick's taillights fade in the distance. He wondered if Francis Oley's carefree attitude would get them all thrown in jail.

The most immediate problem was the Jersey mob. How much would they settle for on the ransom demand? He had heard about their reputation — heard about George Garguillo burning people alive for not paying up. And he knew that he, Manny Strewl, would not take a bullet for Butch O'Connell. Neither would the Oleys, or Angel Face Geary.

Then there was the danger on the other side. If the hostage didn't come out alive, there would be the wrath of the O'Connells to face. Somehow, Strewl said to himself, he had to play both ends against the middle. He slid his shoe across the pavement, making a sound like a fuse. He was the one holding the O'Connell bomb and the fuse was burning quickly.

***

Sunday afternoon Strewl sat in the Newsroom a short distance from the street side window. He kept one eye on his race sheet and the other on the street to see if a cop or one of Harrigan's gang was watching him. He knew his attorney already suspected something was wrong, so the cops probably did too. Just a few days ago Sweeney had been at the Mohawk, so might be there was somebody from the mob keeping tabs on what was happening in Albany. With the cops to one side and the mob at the other, Manny Strewl was straining with the pressure of the proverbial rock and a hard place.

Jerry Brody tapped him on the shoulder and whispered in his ear. "Guy by the name of Snyder called. Says meet him in his office now."

Strewl pushed his race sheet aside and grabbed his suit coat from the back of the chair. "Save my place, Jerry."

He headed out the door and down Beaver Street. Strewl made a left onto South Pearl and a left onto State Street. He hustled up the hill. When the ten story building came into view he stopped to catch his breath and stared at the number 100, five feet tall and bolted to the building's middle. He exhaled and mumbled, "Showtime."

He took the elevator to Snyder's office. In the deserted outer office he called, "Louis, yuh in there?"

"In here, Manny. Come on in. Mr. O'Connell's with me."

Snyder pointed to a chair in front of his desk. "Have a seat, Manny. Mr. O'Connell was bringing me up to date on things."

Dan's face was ashen. He coughed into a handkerchief and wiped his sweaty forehead. "I was telling Louis here what I told you last night, Manny. You're not in any hot water. You're my guy on this, I'll testify to that."

Strewl crossed his legs and asked sheepishly, "Did you tell Louis here what I heard about John Oley?"

Dan O'Connell stifled a sneeze. "We were discussing that as you walked in. John and me, we've had our differences. But he wouldn't do me wrong."

"Putting all of that aside, gentlemen, the fact of the matter is this. Mr. O'Connell, I believe you told Strewl you don't have the full amount of the ransom. I take it from what Manny has told me you made a counter offer which I also presume generated the letter Manny delivered last night. A concern of mine is that if the monetary arrangements can't be decided upon, Manny may be in jeopardy. Any possibility of raising the aforementioned sum?"

O'Connell coughed and wiped his watery eyes. "Hell! The brewery's mortgaged to the hilt. With the repeal of prohibition on the horizon, everybody's jumping on the beer bandwagon. Even Mush Trachnier applied for a beer license — and he's a horseman."

He twisted in his chair. "Right now, best we can do is $25,000 cash. I'd also agree to sign over the rights to the brewery if that'll bring Butch back. That would give the kidnappers a source of income to make up the rest."

An invisible two-by-four hit both Snyder and Strewl in the head. Dan O'Connell had just offered the family's crown jewel, the money machine that kept the O'Connells and all their friendly politicians in power.

Snyder cleared his throat. "That's got possibilities, Mr. O'Connell. Barter might work. Perhaps if, or when, Manny hears from the kidnappers he can offer up the brewery in lieu of cash."

He sat back and stared at the ceiling, his legal wheels spinning. "That might be better than cash."

O'Connell dabbed his runny nose with the handkerchief. "Better than cash?"

"Of course, Mr. O'Connell. Basic contract law. You can't literally twist a man's arm to sign a contract and have it stand up in court. There's no meeting of minds. Ed will tell you that. Ask him."

O'Connell squinted. "How's that again?"

"It works this way. Say you sign over the rights to your brewery and get John Junior back. You go to court and void the contract on the grounds of coercion. The brewery is back in your hands. Run it by Ed — see what he thinks."

O'Connell sneezed into his hand, wiped his palm and got to his feet. "I've gotta go rest up so I can shake this cold. I'll have Eddie call yuh sometime tomorrow."

O'Connell, hat in hand, pointed at Strewl. "I'm counting on yuh, Manny. Do whatever it takes to get my nephew back."

Strewl forced a grin. "Trust me, Mr. O'Connell. I'll do yuh right."

O'Connell turned to leave. Strewl called out, "Mr. O'Connell? Didn't Mush get turned down for his beer license?"

O'Connell's brow wrinkled. "Didn't hear anything about it either way."

Snyder kept a poker face so as not to reveal that he knew Dan O'Connell was lying. Snyder had heard things. His clients were some of the shadiest mobsters in Albany, including John Oley. He set up front companies for the mobsters so property could be legally transferred, and never inquired how the seller of a property ended up with bruises or broken bones. Snyder knew well that Dan O'Connell knew about everything that happened in Albany County. He was either involved in it or knew something about it.

Snyder watched Strewl. His shoulders had drooped. His eyes were averted and his tongue was poking at his cheek.

When Strewl left, Snyder rested his elbows on the chair arms and touched his fingertips together. Something about the picture wasn't right. Did O'Connell claim to know nothing about Mush Trachnier just because he didn't want to discuss the beer license activities? What about Manny Strewl, his client? His mannerisms showed a huge degree of nervousness.

Snyder began stacking the papers on his desk. He mumbled, "Not my problem."

***

On Monday morning, Strewl draped his coat over the arm of a chair at the Newsroom and said, "Jerry, you got the race results from yesterday?"

Jerry Brody stepped back from the chalkboard with its rows of horses' names and dollar sums. "Only Saratoga. Race sheet is by the coffee. Afternoon papers arrive from the Big Apple a little after eleven — if the trains are on time."

Strewl carried a Saratoga race sheet and a cup of coffee to his table. Pencil in hand, he began checking off the race results. Four cups later he was interrupted as Jerry bumped his shoulder and pointed at the window separating the betting room and dining room. "Waiter wants yuh."

Strewl took another slurp of coffee before heading that way. "What yuh need, son? Don't make policy bets no more."

The waiter pointed to the phone booth. "Somebody's on the phone for yuh. Wouldn't give his name."

Strewl slid his pencil behind his ear and made his way across the room. He grabbed the phone receiver. "Strewl here."

"Is that you, Manny? It's Roma."

Strewl stiffened. Roma was the code word, but he didn't recognize the voice. "Yeah."

"Meet me at 110th and Lenox Avenue. Five o'clock." With a click, the phone went dead.

So the Jersey guys wanted a meeting. It was risky for them to call him in Albany. What the hell did Harrigan and his men want? He had to rethink things. It did appear that Dan O'Connell trusted him. But the cops were a problem. If they pinned the kidnapping on Oley, he still might get sucked in.

He pulled at his jaw and went to the window overlooking Beaver Street. Standing to the side, he could study the street and the betting parlor. Didn't appear to be anyone hanging around. No cops in sight. Just to be sure, he went to find the waiter. "You seen any strangers hanging about? Anybody eyeballing me?"

"No sir, Mr. Strewl. Just the usual crowd."

He hustled back to his table, rolled his shirtsleeves down and buttoned the cuffs. When he grabbed his coat, his hat rolled off and onto the floor. He didn't notice because of the tapping of the teletype noise. He called, "Gotta run, Jerry. Keep my spot warm."

At the wheel of his Willys Knight, Strewl made a left onto South Pearl then a right onto State Street and headed south toward New York. He remembered what Dan O'Connell had said. "Whatever it takes to get my nephew back"—which meant he didn't have to tell Snyder or anybody else that he was on his way to meet the kidnappers. Now luck was on his side! But what would Harrigan's men think about the $25,000 offer?

His hand fumbled in the passenger seat for his hat. "Damn it — that was a new hat!"

The wheels buzzed like swarming bees as his tires rolled over the steel strips of the Hudson River drawbridge. Strewl took a right on the other side of the bridge and headed for the road parallel to the railroad track along the Hudson River. His front tire slammed into a pothole and the steering wheel began to vibrate. He up shifted and accelerated, hoping to ease the vibration. The sign he passed told him New York City was 220 miles away.

To stay on the road he had to continually counter the slack in the steering wheel. He yelled, "Shit! This ain't gonna work."

At a sign pointing toward the town of Hudson, he turned and made his way across a bridge over the river and coasted down a small hill into the town. He mumbled to himself, "Gotta be a garage around here someplace."

On Main Street he passed cafés, drug stores, clothing shops — but no garage. "Ah hell! A thousand little towns in New York and I pick the one without a garage." Then he spotted it, past the hospital, on the corner of Front Street, a tan brick garage with one bay and an apartment above where laundry had been hung out the window to dry. Strewl pulled in and blocked the entrance. He stood up in his convertible. "Anybody home?"

A voice answered from the trench under the truck inside. "Hold your horses!" The mechanic appeared and stood wiping his hands on an orange rag. "Whaddya need?"

"Steering's shot. I hit a damn pothole, and I gotta get to New York by five. What's the fastest way?"

The mechanic pointed up the street. "Train station."

Strewl held out the car keys. "Can I leave this with you till I get back? Just do what you can with it."

"Sure, Mack."

Strewl took his coat and walked the short block to the station. The Hudson station was typical for a small town: a red brick building with a shoebox shape and a large overhanging hip roof. The overhang let in the morning sun but not the hot afternoon sun. The long sides had large double doors for two reasons: easy access and a good cross breeze to cool the building in summer.

He stopped at the schedule pinned on the outside board and ran his finger down the page of departures that ended in New York City. The next Hudson to New York train wouldn't depart until 4:40. Strewl cursed and hustled over to the yellow cab at the end of the building and banged his hand on the front fender with a shout. "Say, buddy — want a fare?"

The sleeping cab driver jolted awake. "Uh, sure. Where yuh wanna go?"

"How much to New York?"

"Gee, twelve, fourteen dollars? Takes three and a half to four hours."

Strewl took a twenty from his pocket and snapped it open with both hands. "I gotta be there before five. Make it, and it's yours."

The cabdriver, a Mr. Bernhart, looked pleased. After all, it was a week's pay. "You're on," he said.

The cab burst onto the road with a cloud of smoke roiling from the tailpipe. Eight blocks later, it squealed to the curb before a gray house on a cobblestone foundation with two white beams supporting the small porch roof. "Be right back."

"Where the hell yuh going?"

"Gotta grab a jacket. It's a cold run back."

Strewl mumbled, "Hell." He slapped the seat back and noticed a cigar store across the street. In a minute, he was inside the store pointing to the jars in the showcase. "How much?"

"Nickel for the Havanas, three cents each for White Owls."

"Gimme four Havanas and one Owl."

Strewl snatched the cigars from the man's hand and dropped some coins on top of the case. "Keep it," he called. He hurried back to the cab where the driver waited. Strewl hopped into the back seat and reached over the seat to hand Bernhart the White Owl. "Let's roll!"

They raced along the two-lane river road. A tugboat was pushing a barge loaded with grain down the Hudson. The road was a checkerboard of potholes. Strewl held on as he was bouncing to the roof and sliding from side to side. He spotted a caboose ahead. Soon they were passing the train cars as if passing a picket fence. Strewl did a double take. Up ahead the tracks crossed the road, but the driver was not slowing — he was accelerating. They came alongside the locomotive.

Strewl's jaw dropped. He could see the road hump where the tracks crossed the road. "Shit!" he yelled. He grabbed the door handle. The cab hit the hump. They went airborne. Right behind them the train shot past. Its whistle bellowing like a thousand cows.

The cab bottomed out on the road. Dirt flew up as if a bomb had been detonated. Strewl's head banged against the roof. The cab swerved and threw him against the door. For the remainder of the trip, the driver gave equally close attention to getting his passenger to his destination on time. When they hit the paved roads outside New York City, the driver called over the rushing wind noise, "How far in?"

"Closest train station?"

Shortly thereafter, Bernhart stopped his cab across from the 226th Street station and pointed at the clock above the entrance. "Four-fifteen. Mark it!"

Strewl handed over the twenty, ran down the subway stairs to the map, and traced his route to Lenox Avenue. He boarded his train and exited at 125th Street. On the sidewalk, he checked his watch, decided there was plenty of time and entered a men's clothing shop. To the chubby clerk wearing a red bow tie he said, "Got a hat like the one in the window 'bout my size? Think it's six and three-quarters."

Strewl was soon on his way again, sporting a white Panama hat with a red-striped band. At Lenox Avenue and 110th, he backed up against the corner building and glanced at his pocket watch and mumbled, "With time to spare." He studied the cars passing through the intersection while fanning himself with his new hat. A few minutes passed before a familiar figure caught his eye. The guy was coming down the sidewalk with his head dipped low and his hat pulled down. The lowered hat revealed a scar on the left side of his head. Manny knew the scar belonged to James Sweeney. The suit was the same brown one Sweeney had worn when they met at the Mohawk Hotel.

Sweeney passed close by with his head low and said, "Take the Fifth Avenue bus to 72nd and go into the park." Then he melted into the busy sidewalk crowd.

Strewl looked in all directions. He saw no one he knew or anyone who might be a cop. He followed Sweeney's directions and soon arrived at Central Park. Alert for any sign as to what would happen next, he ambled along the road.

He was wondering why in hell Harrigan and Dugan wanted a meeting when a noise like footsteps walking on shards of glass came from behind. Strewl spun around. Sweeney pushed him, saying, "Look straight ahead. There's a car coming. Get in when it stops."

Strewl continued only a few more steps before a yellow LaSalle sedan slowed to a stop. The hairs on his neck stood on end. Would the Jersey guys double-cross him? The insult letter he had written hinted that Butch might be killed. Maybe the mob meant to go it alone. Would they kill him and keep all the ransom for themselves?

The back door of the LaSalle sprang open. Sweeney shoved him into the back seat and jumped in behind him. Strewl found himself sitting between Sweeney and Thomas Dugan. Sonny McGlone hit the accelerator. Hollow tinkling noises sounded as small stones hit the wheel fenders and the tires spit out the pebbles.

Charles Harrigan sat in the front passenger seat. He tossed smoke-colored glasses into Strewl's lap. "In case anyone's watching. Don't want them to recognize you."

Dugan had turned to study the road behind them. He reported, "Don't see anyone. We're clear."

Harrigan poked Sonny McGlone's shoulder. "Head for Jersey."

Strewl pulled off the glasses. "Little rough, ain't you, guys?"

Harrigan twisted around to face Strewl. "The $20,000 offer was a joke. What's going on?"

"I met with my attorney and Dan O'Connell. So far the O'Connells are turning over every leaf to raise the cash. Dan said they have $25,000 cash, plus he'd sign over the rights to his brewery — but my guess is, that's a put up job."

Dugan said, "Put up job?"

Strewl said, "Yeah. Snyder — he's my attorney, he did a bit of thinking out loud. Said even if the O'Connells signed over the brewery as part of the ransom, they could get it back in court. He said you can't twist a guy's arm for a deal and make it stand as legit — so looks like the best thing for us to do is stick with cash."

Harrigan growled. "Been over two weeks—that's too long. Time to get the dough."

"It's coming," Strewl said. "The O'Connells already upped their offer. Takes time to raise big dough. There's a depression on, yuh know? O'Connell offering the brewery tells yuh they're working hard to raise the dough. Give it time."

Dugan pulled at Strewl's shoulder. "Cheese-us, Manny — you said the O'Connells were loaded. Offering a brewery instead of cash don't sound like loaded."

"Well, they're business men. They —"

Harrigan turned fully around to face Strewl. He wore a patch over his bad eye. The other one bulged. "Business men, my ass! You told Sweeny in Albany all's they had was fifteen or twenty-G's. Sound like cheapskates to me."

"It's business," Strewl said. "And inventory —"

Dugan shouted, "Inventory?"

"Yeah, inventory. The O'Connells are legit. Beer bottles, grain, trucks — all that stuff, it's soaking up all their cash. You guys know all about that kinda stuff. Hell! O'Connell offering his brewery for the kid? Shows yuh how much they want him back. Just gonna take some more time!"

Harrigan snarled. "If we don't get the cash soon, Junior gets sent home in a box."

Thomas Dugan poked Strewl's arm. "A very small box."

Strewl gritted his teeth. He could see now that this Jersey mob would think nothing of killing Butch O'Connell. And if they did, the O'Connells would burn Albany down to find whoever did it. Hell, some of the local Albany mobsters had already got nervous and left town.

Using his best salesman's voice Strewl said, "I talked to John Oley. Cops are on him like white on rice. The G-men, too.

Shit! The whole National Guard is out looking for John
Junior. Right now all you guys are clean. Yuh hear me?
Clean!"

Strewl locked eyes with Harrigan. He added, "You kill the
kid, you turn all that heat your way. Is that what yuh want?"

Harrigan pointed his forefinger at Strewl. "Money talks!"

Strewl said, "Look at it this way. The O'Connells are
weakening. They offered you their crown jewel — the
brewery!"

Dugan said, "Sounds to me like they're broke."

Strewl waved his hand in the air. "Nah, they all drive them
big Marmon cars. Live in big fancy houses. Hell, Dan's got
two houses. But it takes time to get bank loans."

Harrigan's one good eye twitched. Strewl had seen poker
players' eyes twitch when they couldn't decide which cards to
play.

Dugan was rubbing his fingers over his coat where it
bulged. Strewl wanted to get Dugan's hand away from the gun
so he slowly removed two cigars from his inside coat pocket
and held them out to Harrigan and Dugan. "Last two. From
Havana."

Harrigan was soon puffing blue smoke. He wiggled his
thumb between himself and Dugan and said to Strewl, "You're
wasting our time. We got our own business to run. You be sure
to tell O'Connell money's the only thing that talks."

Strewl cracked his knuckles. "Give it some time. Papers
say this depression has even beaten down the Rockefellers."

They were approaching the Holland Tunnel. Harrigan
rubbed the patch over his bad eye. "Okay, Manny, we'll do it
your way for now. Sonny, head back to the park."

Sonny made two right turns and reversed direction. Inside
Central Park he stopped the car next to some large bushes. As
Strewl was getting out, Harrigan grabbed his arm. "Next time

you wanna meet, hang around the Bronx station on Riverdale about eleven at night. We'll find you."

Strewl bent close to Harrigan's open window. "Be patient. I know what I'm doing."

When the car was out of sight Strewl sprinted out of Central Park and hailed a cab. "Grand Central Station. Fast!"

In the train station, he hurried to a phone booth. When the operator connected the call and Snyder came to the phone he said, "Louis? It's Manny. I'm in New York. Just talked to the kidnappers. Can I see yuh tonight? Train gets to Albany at 10:30."

"Sure. I'll grab a beer and wait on yuh."

At 10:33, Strewl placed both hands on the railroad car's handrails and jumped to the Albany train station platform. He took two steps at a time on the station's stairs and got outside just in time to watch the last Yellow Cab drive off with a passenger. "Shit! It never ends," he said.

He shook his fist at the departing cab and walked to the Little Caesar Beer Garden on High Street. At the beer garden Strewl threw open the door and wiped the sweat from his brow with his coat sleeve. He buttoned his top shirt button and tightened his tie. He surveyed the dining room until a waiter approached and said, "Table for one, sir?"

"Nah. Gotta meet a guy. You see Lou Snyder around?"

"No, sir. Mr. Snyder did not stop in tonight. Would you like to —"

"Damn it!" Strewl exhaled and turned aside. Just then he noticed a familiar face. He made his way to the table where Frank Oley was reading a newspaper and eating a steak. Strewl pulled out the chair opposite. "Frank, you alone tonight?"

Frank Oley shrugged. "Do I look alone, Manny? Say, you look thirsty." Frank held up his hand to hale a waiter.

Strewl leaned across the table. "No time, Frank. I'm in a bind. Can I borrow your car for a little while?"

Frank Oley dug his hand in his pants pocket and pulled out the keys. "It'll cost yuh a beer when yuh get back. Whatcha got going?"

Strewl gave Frank a wink. "Can't tell yuh, can't tell nobody. Gotta run."

Frank called to Strewl's back. "Two beers if you're not back in an hour."

In short order, Strewl arrived at the home of his attorney. The maid placed beer glasses on the coffee table in front of Strewl and Snyder. Snyder dismissed the maid and began sipping his beer. "Okay, Manny. What happened?"

Strewl recounted the day's events but changed the story of the meeting in Central Park. He described how an unknown man told him to go to Central Park, how he was shoved into the back seat of a car and forced to wear smoked glasses as he talked to the kidnappers.

Snyder rested his elbow on his knee. "You get a description of these guys?"

"Not really. It was dark. Like the meeting I told yuh about at the Mohawk. Couldn't see much through the smoked glasses."

"The car, Manny. What kind was it? Did you get a plate number?"

"Wasn't looking to get a plate number, Lou. Shit, I was nervous as hell. Thought maybe they'd kill me or something."

"Understandable, Manny. Did you get a good look at the car?"

"Think it was a Chevy. Black or dark blue, I think. Why the third degree?"

"Getting you ready for the cops, Manny. They'll ask the same questions."

"What's my next move, Lou?"

"You told them they should lower their price. A counter offer has therefore been made. It's up to them. I'll call Dan

O'Connell and bring him up to speed. Where you gonna be tomorrow?"

Strewl scratched his head with the brim of his straw hat. "Things to do in the morning. Be at the Jersey Newsroom after lunch. It's at 45 Beaver Street."

"You look beat. Get some rest and I'll contact you tomorrow."

Chapter 14
"So Far, So Good"

The morning after his meeting with his attorney, Strewl stood on the top step outside his apartment surveying the street. The clanking of the horse-drawn milk wagon made the sparrows on Elm Street take flight. The sun had just peeked between the apartment buildings.

John Oley pulled his maroon Pontiac to the curb and leaned across the front seat to open the passenger door. He complained, "Too early for this."

Strewl slammed the door shut. "Ain't my fault the car broke down. I saw your brother last night."

"He told me. How'd it go with Snyder?"

The Pontiac turned onto Swan Street and turned south. Across the street an undercover cop sprinted from an alley to the police call box to make his report. "Strewl and Oley just left in Oley's car. Don't know where to."

John Oley raised his voice above the humming tires as they crossed the steel strips of the Hudson River Bridge heading for the town of Hudson. "We wouldn't have to be driving out here if you'd got your car fixed last month."

"If the county would fill the potholes I wouldn't have the problem in the first place." Strewl twisted around, looked out the back window then slouched in his seat. "Think we're clear."

He took a cigar from his inside coat pocket, bit the end off, lit up and puffed blue clouds of smoke out the passenger window. "Harrigan and Dugan are getting antsy. They don't like the fact that time keeps passing and they ain't got their dough yet. They say the O'Connells are playing hard ass. It's got me worried. Yuh think they'd follow through on the threat to kill Butch if they don't get the money soon?"

Oley did a double take and drew his hand down his face. "Gosh a'mighty! They do that—and the O'Connells will skin alive every man jack in the state of New York. Already my friends are starting to treat me like I've got the plague, because the cops stick so close to me. If they kill Butch, there won't be any hole deep enough to hide in."

Strewl rolled his eyes. "Well then, you'd sure the hell better talk to Harrigan. Tell him the O'Connells are coming up with the cash—slow, but sure. Hell, Dan even offered to throw in the brewery as part of the ransom."

"What'd Harrigan and Dugan say to that?"

"Not much they could say, cause it wasn't a good deal. Dan said the brewery is mortgaged to the hilt. I told Harrigan the O'Connells had come up with $25,000 cash. That calmed him down some. I told him it's just a matter of time before the O'Connells come up with the rest of the ransom."

Oley studied the car behind them until it turned off at a side road. "Harrigan bought that story?"

"For now."

Oley slowed to make the turn toward the town of Hudson but Strewl tapped his shoulder. "Keep going."

"Thought you said your car was in Hudson?"

Strewl blew smoke. "It is. But I wrote another letter to Dan to encourage him to get more cash. It's better if I mail it further downstate. Head for Mount Vernon."

Oley shifted into fourth gear and accelerated. "Angel Face is all set up in New York. I'll give him a call —"

"Not from your home phone!"

Oley waved a hand in the air. "I know, I know. I've been using pay phones all over Albany. Cops will never trace the calls."

Strewl tapped his cigar ashes out the window. "Yuh know, John? Would probably be better if you meet Harrigan in person. You can check on Butch too — make sure he stays in good health. Think you can give the cops the slip?"

"That's easy. They use the same black sedans they always use. I'll have Aggie use my car as a decoy. After I slip out, Francis can pick me up a few blocks over from my house and we'll hightail it down to Jersey."

Strewl pushed up in his seat. "Better pick up Angel Face too, bring him along. You can never have too many guns when dealing with Harrigan."

Strewl yawned, slouched back in the seat and pulled the brim of his straw panama down over his eyes. A short while later Oley pulled to the curb next to a mailbox in Mount Vernon and nudged him. "Here we are."

Strewl jolted awake. He took an envelope addressed to the Beaver Clothes shop from his coat pocket. "We just gotta beat this back to Albany." He got out, dropped the envelope in the mailbox and hopped back in. "Hit it," he said.

Streams of pebbles shot from the Pontiac's rear tires as Oley made a beeline for Hudson. Ninety minutes later, they crossed the bridge into the town.

Oley rubbed his face. "I think you ought to be with us when we meet Harrigan. Can you arrange another trip to New York?"

The Pontiac rolled down Main Street. Strewl pointed. "Past the hospital. Garage is on the left. Harrigan told me to hang around Lenox Avenue at night and he'd find me. All I need is a reason to be in New York. When you contact him have him send up another letter. Have Butch write it pleading for help. I'll take care of the rest."

Strewl tossed the cigar out the window. "Last night, Snyder said he'd talk to Dan this morning and be in touch with me."

"You think either one of them is suspicious of you?"

"Nah, I got both of them snowed. Cops too, for that matter. Remember what I told you after John Bradt whispered in my ear? They all think you're the finger man. That gives me a free hand. All you gotta do is play Mister Innocent."

Oley pulled up at the garage and heaved a big sigh. "So long as the cops don't frame me."

Strewl straightened his tie. "No worries there. Snyder said any defense attorney could spot manufactured evidence a mile away. So far there's nothing to connect you or me with any of this."

Strewl's Willys Knight roadster was parked off to the side with the hood up. He closed the door of the Pontiac and leaned into the window. "I'm gonna scoot right back to Albany in case Snyder contacts me. You get hold of Harrigan and tell him to be patient. Tell him you wanna meet — tell him anything! Just don't let him blow this deal and put our heads in a noose."

Hours later, at the Newsroom in Albany, Strewl closed the door behind him and stood rubbing his sleep-deprived eyes.

Jerry Brody's voice boomed, "Manny! Where yuh been all morning?"

"Had to go pick up my car. It broke down the other day in Hudson. John Oley drove me down."

"Your mouthpiece, Snyder—he called. Says he wants to meet with you today. You'd better get cracking."

"Did he say what time?"

"Hell, Manny. Am I your secretary? He said as soon as you got the message." Brody moved closer and lowered his voice. "You said you couldn't get a beer license. You got another deal going? Maybe I can get a piece of the action?"

Strewl pushed up his hat and rubbed his forehead with his thumb. "Believe me, Jerry, you don't want a piece of this action."

Brody tilted his head. "Oo-oh? Well, don't forget — you've got friends if yuh need some help."

"Got it wired, Jerry. But thanks anyway. And keep my seat warm."

A few minutes later Strewl stood outside Louis Snyder's office, removed his hat and opened the door to the empty outer office. "Lou, you in?"

Louis Snyder came to the door of the inner office and shook Strewl's hand. "About time, Manny. Where yuh been all morning? You just missed Dan."

Strewl explained that Oley had taken him to pick up his car. Snyder strolled back to his desk chair and motioned Strewl to the armchair. "Dan's still a bit under the weather. Had a fever."

"Shit," Strewl said, "that's all I need."

Snyder pulled at his tie. "Relax, Dan's on board with yuh. He said they raised some more cash. Wanna guess how much?"

Strewl sat down and crossed his legs. He dropped his head, not wanting to show any sign of his pleasure. The fact that the insult letter he had written had forced the O'Connells to raise more of the ransom money thrilled him. He looked up. "Couldn't guess. These guys say they want two hundred fifty G's, but the papers say the O'Connells can only pony up one hundred fifty. The kidnappers don't want the brewery — they want cash. So how much did they come up with?"

"Yeah. Well, uh, Dan — or shall I say the O'Connells — have $25,000 cash." He paused. "Cash in hand right now. Ready to go. "

Strewl's foot dropped to the floor. His face went white. His eyes bugged. "I'm dead!"

His hand flew to his mouth. He stared at a spot on the floor. He'd been stringing the Jersey mob along, figuring the O'Connells would find a way to come up with more money to save John Junior. Strewl's chest was tight — like it was in a vise, caught between the O'Connells on one side and the Jersey mob on the other. The only key to getting out of this tight spot was money.

Strewl drew a bead on Snyder. "Are the O'Connells trying to be cheap? Twenty-five grand is a long way short."

"The O'Connells have a problem, Manny. Dan has told everyone the brewery was worthless, mortgaged to the hilt. Most of their friends are either tapped out or got wiped out when the market crashed. The O'Connells also have it figured that these perpetrators are nothing more than a bunch of punch-drunk palookas. Mr. O'Connell showed me one of the ransom notes. The kidnappers can't write or spell worth a damn. The cops will have a field day with them."

"Field day?"

"Stands to reason, Manny. Those letters are the only direct link to the kidnappers. They find the author of those letters and I'm sure they'll rake him over the coals. Probably want to talk with you at some point."

"Me? Why me?"

"It's only logical, Manny. You're the only person that's seen the people involved and can possibly provide a description of the kidnappers to the police."

Snyder leaned closer to Strewl. "Looks like things are wearing on you, Manny. Just relax. This is routine. It's really just a business deal and has to run its course."

Manny rubbed his chin. He had written most of the ransom notes and his attorney had just said they were the evidence the police could use to link him to the crime. He had to get the letters back.

"Lou, suppose the cops try to pull a fast one. You know my record. What happens if the O'Connells leave me to hang?"

"Manny, you've done nothing wrong. Dan reassured me, said again that he knows how to treat his friends. You're golden on this one."

Strewl scratched his forehead with his thumb. "I hope you're right."

Snyder came around the desk. "Why don't you a take a break? Relax a bit."

***

A few days later, Strewl bought a paper from the newsboy on State Street and ducked into the Waldorf Lunch Room for a late lunch just as a summer rain shower started. When he finished eating, he made his way through the wispy steam rising from the damp street and stopped at the corner of Beaver and South Pearl and knocked on the wooden counter of the cigar stand. "Two of the usual, Marty."

Marty Caldwell turned to a jar on the shelf. "Two Havanas coming up."

Caldwell scooped up the change and said, "Yuh know, Manny, Abe was looking for yuh earlier."

"Did he say why?"

"Nope. But said you'd better see him."

Strewl hustled up Beaver Street to the clothes shop, unaware that a short man across the street had folded his paper and followed him. While Strewl was inside, the undercover cop window shopped.

Inside, Strewl raised his voice. "Abe, you in there?"

Abe Friedman brushed aside the back curtain and held out an envelope. "Been looking for yuh. It came a few hours ago. Figured it was important because it was marked Special Delivery."

Abe stretched his neck to study the five three-cent stamps and the Mount Vernon Postmark. He pointed at the address. "Machine printed, like the last one."

Abe Friedman was Strewl's friend, but he was nosy. Strewl decided to leave the shop. He couldn't risk having Abe recognize the handwriting. He said, "Gotta run and take care of this, Abe. Remember, mum's the word."

Strewl bolted out the door and flashed past the handful of buildings between Abe's shop and the Jersey Newsroom.

The cop had crossed to the opposite side of the street to give Strewl a wide berth. He ducked into a saloon and took a seat by the window and ordered a beer. He studied the sports section of his newspaper while keeping one eye on the Newsroom.

Strewl had taken a seat in the corner of Jerry Brody's establishment. He tossed the envelope in a trashcan and took out the enclosed envelope and smiled at his name scrawled across the top in large letters and the word 'Personnel' printed lower down. He looked at the envelope closely and mumbled, "Hmm. Better check to see if anybody steamed it open, see if anybody changed anything." He removed the two note pages and read silently.

July 19, 1933

DAN— SO FAR SO GOOD THINGS
ARE STARTING to MOVE NOW to
GET IT OVER WITH QUICKLY IS
INTIRELY UP to YOU WE HAPPEN
to BE   PATIENT AS WE
KNEW ITS NOT INTERELY YOUR
FAULT THE WAY THINGS TURNED
OUT AS WE TOLD YOU BEFORE
WE WANT TWO HONORED FIFTY
G'S TWENTY FOUR HOURS to CASH
IT ALL LETTERS PASSED BE
TWEEN US MANY TOO CONNADED
AND YOU WILL HAVE JOHN BACK
AGAIN JOHN IS GITTING RESTLES
WE ARE TAKING GOOD CARE OF HIM
AS HE ILL TESTIFY IF YOU EVER
SEE HIM AGAIN SO ACT QUICKLY

GIVE MANNY THE MONEY
DENOMINATIONS AS FIRST
INSTRUCTED AND WE WILL
GET IT AND YOU WILL GET
JOHN.
MANNY — YOU ARE BEING
WATCHED BY US AT ALL
TIMES YOUR RECOMMENDED
TO US AS A GOOD FELLIN SO LETS
HOPE FOR ALL CONCERNED
YOU ARE. IF DAN CONCENTS
TO GIVE YOU THE DOUGH HAVE
ALL YOUR SHARES IN YOUR HOME
DRAWN TO THE BOTTEM THAT
WILL TELL US YOU HAVE
THE DOUGH LATER
INSTRUCTIONS WILL
FOLLOW
ROMA·

John O'Connelly

Strewl drew his palm across his mouth, thinking it had been a smart idea to have Butch sign some blank pages. He called across the room. "Jerry, can I use your phone?"

"Yeah—but yuh make many more calls, I'm gonna start charging you."

Strewl disappeared into the back room and dialed. "Tommy, I gotta see Dan like now. Can you fix it? I'm at the Newsroom. Albany 3-3957."

Strewl hung up the phone and waited impatiently, his fingers drumming the desktop. He got up and paced the small office for what seemed forever until finally the phone rang.

"Manny, it's Tommy. Dan said he'd leave the lake house right away. It'll take him about an hour to make the drive. He'll meet you at Washington Park, same as before."

At the appointed time Dan O'Connell picked up Strewl and parked under a shade tree. Strewl handed him the letter. O'Connell lowered his head to focus on it, but he swept his eyes sideways to study this go-between guy. Strewl had slouched against the passenger door with his left arm stretched along the back of the seat. He picked his teeth with his thumbnail.

O'Connell folded the note. "At least Butch is alive, or so they imply. But we're still short on the ransom."

Strewl shifted his weight. "Well, uh, I talked to Lou Snyder a while ago. He said you had hard cash."

"That's so, Manny, but it's like pulling teeth."

Strewl said, "Well, it's a bunch of money." He shifted in the seat. "Say, Mr. O'Connell — word has it the cops might try to hang this all on John Oley, or maybe on me. Gives me the willies. Could you maybe put some words on him? Tell John everything's jake? Would mean more coming from you."

"I guess I could. Let's do it today. That'd save me some time. Joe Lieberman is a friend of mine. He's got a room at the Ten Eyck Hotel. You and Oley meet me there at four. I'll set him straight."

Strewl opened the car door. "Right, Mr. O'Connell. What room?"

"305."

"That's swell, Mr. O'Connell. Think I'll stretch my legs."

***

A few minutes before four o'clock that afternoon, John Oley pushed through the brass revolving door of the ten story Ten Eyck Hotel on State Street. He checked his watch and waited till it showed almost four on the dot before taking the elevator to the third floor. He knocked softly three times at the door with a brass number 305.

The door swung open and Dan O'Connell said, "Right on time. Manny's already here."

John Oley shook O'Connell's hand. "Glad to see yuh, Danny. You holding up okay?"

"So far. But this thing is beating all of us down."

"Bound to. You know, me and Manny been talking about this."

O'Connell removed his glasses and rubbed them on his white shirt. "So Manny said. He also said you've got the shakes."

"Who the hell wouldn't, Danny? My picture appears in the paper and all of a sudden cops are hiding under every bush around the house. They're just looking for an excuse to nail me. My friends are starting to treat me like I got the plague — and damn it, I ain't done nothing!"

O'Connell thrust his palms up. "Hold on, John. Chief Smurl does as I say. He's not gonna railroad anyone. I'd have him off the force in three days if he screwed around."

Oley paced in a circle. "What about Delaney? He's got the cops sweeping the streets and ready to pick up anybody that spits wrong. I'm always looking over my shoulder. Feel like I'm being watched. A lot of cops hanging around Market Street too, scaring off Francis's customers — even the legit ones!"

O'Connell shoved his hands in his back pockets and rolled out his lips. "John, just tell them not to worry. Delaney has to make this look good. He's got his eye on the Supreme Court. As for me and my brothers, all we want is Butch in one piece."

Oley arched an eyebrow. "You think Butch is still okay?"

O'Connell took out the letter and handed it over. "Strewl delivered this earlier today. Apparently Butch is still okay."

Oley bent over the letter and gave a whistle. "Two hundred and fifty big ones! How's that going?"

"Slow. Real slow. Strewl's been talking with the kidnappers. Offered them the brewery and cash. But they nixed it."

"How much can yuh raise?"

"Got me. Ed's calling in every favor owed him. Me and Solly kicked in our savings. We're already mortgaged up to our eyebrows. If we throw in the kitchen sink we can't make two-fifty — not even half that! No damn way."

Oley twisted his head toward Strewl who shrugged and said, "Yep. Dan offered them the brewery and they turned it down flat."

Oley drew his palm down over his face and gave a smirk. "Guess they overrated yuh — just like they did Francis. Just because my brother runs a speakeasy, people think he's worth a hundred-fifty thousand."

O'Connell's eyebrows shot up. Oley flashed the palm of his right hand. "Not even close. The place barely breaks even."

Strewl, standing to the side as Oley played his little charade, suddenly recalled what Snyder had said about the ransom letters. He licked his chops and pointed at the letter. "Mr. O'Connell, they said they want the letters back. Does that make sense?"

"Yeah, apparently it does. I talked with my brother Ed on that. In a courtroom, if push comes to shove, it's much better to have the originals. Sounds like these fuckers have been talking to a lawyer."

Strewl touched the corner of the page. O'Connell pushed it into his hand. "May as well keep it." He pulled another page from his pocket. "Here's another."

Strewl folded the letters and put them in his pocket, hiding the relief he felt at retrieving crucial evidence that could be used against him. He said, "Now what, Mr. O'Connell?"

"That's up to the kidnappers. On the next contact, tell them the money is coming in, but coming in dribs and drabs."

He shook his head and stole a wily glance at Strewl. "Well's about dry. Sure as hell won't be two-fifty. Probably not even a hundred."

With that pronouncement, O'Connell turned to the door and put his hand on the knob. "Manny, the letter said leave your shades down if you get the cash, so leave your shades down. When they contact you tell them no way it's gonna be two-fifty. Tell them to give us a reasonable figure."

Thoughts sped through Strewl's mind like lightning. He needed to know how much money the O'Connells could produce, yet Dan O'Connell kept avoiding the issue with a sideways chess move. He decided to try one last plea. "Yuh know, Mr. O'Connell, I'm taking a big gamble by leaving my shades down and not having the money. These guys could leave me in a ditch like they threatened to do. You positive you're not gonna have what they're asking?"

"Manny, I know money talks. But if we ain't got it, we ain't got it. Tell the kidnappers some money is better than none. We just need a reasonable figure. I'll be waiting for your call."

***

When his visitors were gone Dan O'Connell made his way to his car where he said to his chauffeur, "Ted, take me back to the lake house."

Ted Gorman drove in silence to Thompson's Lake, about thirty-five miles. His boss exited the car and said, "Nothing planned for the rest of the night, Ted, but make sure the car is gassed up just in case."

"Yessir."

Dan O'Connell went inside and settled in a comfortable chair by the window facing the lake. His thoughts went to his nephew. How were the kidnappers treating him? Were they harsh? Were they starving him into submission? Dan stared out at the lake and remembered fondly a day long ago, when he taught his nephew how to fish.

The floor creaked and a hand touched his shoulder. A soft voice said, "What's wrong, Danny?"

He got up. "Take my seat, Ma. I was just—"

Mother O'Connell took the seat and clasped her son's hand. "It's been over two weeks since Butch was kidnapped. You were gone all day and now you're staring toward the lake. What's on your mind?"

Dan O'Connell pulled his hand free and shoved his hands in his back pockets. "Just came from a meeting with Strewl and Oley."

"And?"

He shook his head. "Something's not right. I've got an itch I can't scratch."

"Mothers call that intuition. A message from above. You just have to be able to read it."

"I've tried, Ma."

"Tell me about it?"

Dan removed his glasses and pinched the bridge of his nose. "Had a meeting with Strewl and Oley. Half the time Strewl is jumpy and nervous, the rest of the time he's cool as an ice cube. That ain't normal."

He paced back and forth in front of the window. "Oley — he says the cops have him spooked. That he's afraid they might try to railroad him for the kidnapping."

"Can they do that, Danny?"

He shook his head. "They both know I have a lock on Chief Smurl and Delaney. Hell, I've heard about the time Oley ran a blockade in a hail of bullets — but that didn't stop him from doing it again. I saw him once go after two guys with a pipe for cheating at cards. Now he's telling me he's afraid of cops asking questions? That's not the John Oley I know — and that makes me suspicious."

Mother O'Connell dabbed her nose with a white handkerchief. "I see. What about this Mr. Strewl?"

"First I heard of him was when he decided to help us."

"Is he helping you?"

"Yes, and that's the problem, Ma."

"How so?"

Dan pulled at his lip. "For one thing, the kidnappers pushed real hard for Strewl to be the go-between. Strewl got a letter and so did a guy at the courthouse. Next thing, I offered Strewl payment in return for his help and he said he didn't want a thing. Now you and I both know, Ma, that ain't normal. Everybody wants something. Then there's the insult letter."

"The one you showed me."

"Uh-huh. Strewl delivered it to me at White Hall Road, but there were no lights on there. I couldn't read it, but Strewl, he read it without error from the glow of a streetlight—a streetlight seventy-five-feet away!"

"Perhaps Mr. Strewl has extra good eyesight."

"Incredible would be more like it, Ma."

"So what do you do next?"

Dan sighed. "All we can do right now. Wait. I gave Strewl instructions, told him to tell the kidnappers we have some cash, but they have to come up with a more reasonable amount."

"How long before you know something?"

Dan smirked. "Not long. I've been getting their letters about every other day."

Mother O'Connell stood up and put a hand on her son's shoulder. "The Lord is watching over us. I'm sure Butch will be back soon. I can feel it. You let me know when you get a reply. Right now, I'm going out for a short walk."

His mother disappeared out the door. Dan watched out the window until a state trooper fell in behind her.

***

A few days later, Dan O'Connell spread a layer of butter as thin as his bank account on a piece of toast. His thoughts were on money. He had made money on the baseball pool but now it was all gone. He and his brothers had bought nice houses. And the yearly gifts, that's what really ate up money—turkeys for Thanksgiving, hams for Christmas and lambs for Easter for the people in the south end, plus contributions to various politicians. The income from the beer business was gone and there was no way to get it back.

He sat at the kitchen table gazing out the window overlooking Thompson's Lake. The morning sun shone like diamonds across the water. Just as the coffee water began to boil, the hallway phone began ringing.

"Dan here," he said into the receiver. It was Tommy Dyke.

O'Connell listened for a moment then said, "I'll need time to get dressed and drive to Albany. Tell Strewl I'll meet him in an hour and a half in Washington Park, like last time."

At the appointed time, Dan O'Connell pulled up at Washington Park and Manny Strewl got in the car and handed him an envelope. O'Connell studied the postmark. He muttered, "Special delivery, yesterday morning. Pretty quick delivery."

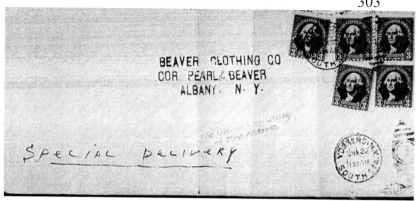

As he opened the envelope he asked, "Did you and John talk after our Ten Eyck meeting?"

Strewl glanced over his shoulder for a second before saying, "We talked some. John tried to get me to pull out but I said you wanted me—told him I was trying to do the right thing here, yuh know?"

O'Connell offered a grin. "Me and my brothers appreciate everything you're doing, Manny. We know how to treat our friends."

Strewl held up his hands. "Sure you do, Mr. O'Connell— but like I said, I don't need nothing." He nodded toward the letter. "Abe got that at the clothing shop and gave it to me cause it looked like the others. I opened it. Got it to you as fast as I could."

Friday 21, 1933

Dear Uncle Dan,

Today is Friday last afternoon, these people have been treating me very good to date. But they are getting very impatient. They tell me you are chealing Dan. they seem to know just how well off we are and they mean business, They want what they are asking for so please do it for me, and I will never forget you. I am begining to get a fever so please help me.

Yours

John O'Connell

O'Connell read silently. When he finished reading he said nothing. Strewl broke the silence. "Have you talked with your brothers about me calling you direct, Mr. O'Connell, since it's so hard to get hold of Dyke?"

O'Connell shook his head side to side. "Been busy trying to raise the ransom. It slipped my mind." He stared out the window.

Strewl cleared his throat. "Can yuh tell if it's your nephew's handwriting?"

"Looks like his."

"Whaddya think of it?"

"Sounds like he's still alive." O'Connell sighed and slapped the dashboard. "We're still short on the ransom. Hell! We offered all our cash plus the brewery—and they still won't take it!"

Strewl wondered how much money the O'Connells did have and what the New Jersey mob would settle for. Too little money and Harrigan might kill Butch. He rubbed his lips with his finger. The longer the wait, the bigger the corner he was backed into. He didn't know what to do. Then he recalled Snyder's advice. Let Dan O'Connell make all the decisions.

"What should I do, Mr. O'Connell?"

"How do you meet these guys, Manny?"

"I just hang in the Bronx late at night about midnight or so and they find me."

O'Connell removed his glasses and pinched the bridge of his nose. "Ok, so get with them, tell'em we're busted—we've offered everything."

He looked directly at Strewl and squinted. "Tell them we need a real number—before it's too late."

"What do you mean too late, Mr. O'Connell?"

Dan pointed to the bottom of the letter. "Butch says he's got a fever. They sure as hell can't call a doc. Doesn't say how bad the fever is, but it can't be good."

Strewl glanced away. Once again O'Connell had turned the tables and now he, Manny Strewl, was forced to make a decision. He wasn't sure if O'Connell was being crafty by not suggesting a ransom amount, but it was the first time Strewl had heard about Butch's fever and he too knew the Jersey guys couldn't risk calling a doctor. More importantly, Strewl couldn't risk having Butch die. He just needed time to think, time to figure a way out of this mess.

O'Connell dropped Strewl off where he had picked him up and headed for Solly's house. As he drove, he pictured Butch lying in a bed delirious with fever. No one knew for sure who was behind the kidnapping. He gritted his teeth, suddenly all too aware that he couldn't fix things.

***

The following Monday, Louis Snyder pushed the papers he'd been reading to one side and answered the intercom buzz. "A Mr. Jack Murphy on the line, Mr. Snyder."

"I'll take it." He lifted the receiver. "Louis Snyder."

A voice said, "Mr. Snyder, I'm Jack Murphy—a friend of Dan O'Connell's. He'd like to meet with you today."

Snyder had heard of Jack Murphy but was not aware that Murphy's name had been on the list of potential go-betweens published in the paper. He pulled his desk calendar closer and turned to the page showing July 24. "That'd be fine. Tell him I'll send for Strewl."

When Strewl arrived the office was already filled with cigarette smoke. Dan O'Connell was already present. Snyder pointed him to a chair and before he reached it Dan O'Connell said, "Was just telling Louis what we talked about, Manny. He agrees with what Ed's told me. No laws have been broken. You're just helping out. I was about to tell him we've only managed to raise twenty-five thousand. We've tried borrowing some, but twice now the bank's told me they won't loan money on our brewery. It's worthless as collateral."

O'Connell leaned forward and addressed the lawyer. "My brother Ed told me you deal with mugs like this all the time. What do you think the kidnappers are really looking for?"

Snyder pulled on his earlobe. "Yes, I've represented fellas like these for a long time…fellas in all kinds of rackets, but none in the snatch racket. If they were, I wouldn't deal with them. I'd even toss Manny here out if I thought he was involved, and he's one of my better clients."

O'Connell sat back in his chair and sighed. "I'm not implying you or Manny here are involved. I know you're not. What I want to know is, what would you do?"

Snyder clasped his hands and rested his forearms on the desk and leaned forward. "Play it tough. Play for time. I believe an earlier letter said Strewl was to have his shades down as a signal that he had the money. Have Manny leave his shades down and see if the kidnappers contact him. See if they come off the two-fifty. That'll also give you time to raise more cash."

O'Connell took his hat off the desk and got to his feet. "Let's do as he suggests, Manny. Ed's called in all his favors—touched all our friends, twisted the arms of others. Pickings are getting damn slim."

At the door he turned back. "You're my guy, Manny. Get with the kidnappers any way you can. Let them know we're doing the best we can."

Strewl watched as O'Connell exited the office. He figured half his problem was solved when O'Connell gave him the green light to contact the kidnappers, but why had he still not thrown out a ransom amount they could afford? But he had said they were doing their best to raise the money. That should satisfy the Jersey guys for a while. Still, he'd better ask his lawyer's opinion—in case the police questioned his actions.

He leaned forward with his arms on his knees. "Now what, Lou?"

"Nothing much you can do, Manny. If the kidnappers don't contact you when you pull your shades down, can you contact them?"

Strewl scratched his head. "Don't exactly have a schedule. They once told me to hang around the Riverdale train station in the Bronx and they'd find me."

"I see," Snyder said. His eyes became slits. "Butch isn't in good health. I think he is pleading for help, and I think the kidnappers are restless. The kidnappers also have not budged off the original ransom demand. So all in all, things are not looking good."

"So what's my play?"

In the margin of the desk calendar Snyder drew a circle with his pencil and dotted the middle. "That circle is the situation, Manny, and you're the dot. The O'Connells have offered some cash and their brewery. The brewery offer tells me the O'Connells really don't have the money. The O'Connells would not have offered it unless they were desperate. If you cut and run now the public won't blame you, but nobody in this town would loan you a plug nickel for a very long time, if ever."

Strewl bobbed his head. "That don't help me none—spell it out, Lou. What should I do?"

Snyder dropped the pencil on its point then on the eraser then the point again. "You're going to have to be a super salesman, Manny. You're going to have to sell the kidnappers on the idea that getting a smaller amount of money is better than getting none at all—and a whole lot better than fooling around with a dead body. You gotta make contact with the kidnappers. Pull your shades down. Give it some time. If nothing happens, hightail it to the Riverdale station. When the kidnappers make contact, lay it all out. Tell them the O'Connells are having trouble raising the money. This could drag out for weeks or months. Tell them if they want fast cash they'll have to settle for something less."

Strewl bit his lower lip. He'd be willing to bet the Jersey guys would go for a lower ransom if they could get a chunk of it quick, and in cash.

"What kind of dough you suggest, Lou?"

"Dunno, Manny. Best let the kidnappers pick a number. You know the O'Connells are in the twenties. Use that for starters."

Strewl smiled weakly. The ball was back in his court. "A good idea, Lou. I'll be home with my shades down. See what happens."

"I'll be here if you need me, Manny."

Strewl headed home. When he reached his apartment building he paused on the top step and looked over his shoulder. Some kids were playing stickball, but there were no adults in sight. He went to his apartment and lowered the shades.

Later, in the dark, he slipped out and went to a pay phone and dropped in some coins and dialed.

He raised his voice. "Hello, Jacob. Is Ma there?"

John Oley's voice answered. "Nope."

"Well, leave her a note for me. Things are slow and I'm running late. I'll see her later."

Oley understood the message and relayed to the Jersey gang that things were moving slow and Strewl thought they should goose the O'Connells one last time. Sweeney took the message. John Oley ended the phone talk with, "Better have Butch write it. Less evidence that way. And Strewl wants to meet."

James Sweeney left immediately for the coin-operated lunch counter where Charles Harrigan and Thomas Dugan were dining on sandwiches. Sweeney spotted them in a back corner. He leaned to Harrigan's ear and whispered the news.

Harrigan tilted his one good eye up at Sweeney. "Fine. I'm tired of this crap. Have the kid write that we're through with this fooling around. Tell'em we'll take it out on him if we have to, might even starve him if that's what it takes."

Dugan interrupted. "I vote for poison—you could mention that too."

As Sweeney turned to go, Harrigan caught him by the arm and turned him back. "You going to meet with Oley?"

"Yeah, if you want me to."

"Set Thursday as a deadline. Put a note in the letter for him to have his shades down. That'll be the signal for the meet."

An hour later, James Sweeney ran up the back steps of the five-floor apartment house at 734 Adams Street. He took two steps at a time to the second floor apartment and scratched rapidly on the door.

The door cracked open. George Garguillo's eye appeared in the crack above the brass door chain. A moment later Garguillo was leading the way into the darkened bedroom, which was uncomfortably warm. The single window in the room was covered with a blanket. Butch's clothes, hanging from the overhead gas jet, blocked light from the bulb hanging from a single strand of wire in the middle of the room. Dutch Fisher was hunched in a chair trying to read a newspaper in the dim light.

Butch, blindfolded, wore white pajamas and lay on top of a stained sheet.

Garguillo motioned to Dutch Fisher to quit reading and come to the far side of the room. Pivot Burke was dozing in an armchair and Garguillo slapped his shoulder.

Sweeney explained that the kid was to write a letter and this would be the last one. He stood studying the captive, whose head was rolling side to side. He whispered, "How's he doing?"

Fisher answered in his thick German accent. "I splashed some more citronella on him, to keep the mosquitoes away.

And did my best to shave him—but it wadn't easy. I ain't never had to shave nobody."

Sweeney loosened his tie. "What about his fever?

Burke said, "Doing better. Gave him a shot of booze and something from the drugstore. Seems to be better."

Sweeney noticed the newspaper and winced. The top of it had been cut off. "What gives?"

"Been more'n two weeks since all this started and me and Burke are bored to death and so's the kid. So we cut him some slack, let him read the paper. Cut the top off so's he wouldn't know where he is."

"Read the paper? Through his blindfold?"

"Course not. Made a deal with him. We let him take the blindfold off to read. Even let him take a quick smoke. When we knock to come back in, we tell him to put the laundry bag over his head. Then we tie the blindfold back on and stuff cotton under it to make sure he can't see."

Garguillo pushed forward from behind. "Not me! I wadn't in on it—son-of a-bitch's not gonna eyeball me. I'd plug him first!"

Sweeney tiptoed to the bedside and sniffed the stale air. He muttered, "More sponge bath."

He stepped over to the vanity and took the last few note sheets from the middle drawer. There was a matchbook on top of the vanity with a picture of a Texas state flag flying above an Esso gas station. He wrinkled his brow.

Fisher put his fingers to his mouth to mimic smoking and whispered, "Kid probably thinks he's in Texas."

Sweeney kicked the bed. "Get up. Need you to do some writing."

Pivot Burke uncuffed Butch's hand from the bedrail and recuffed it to the iron radiator. Dutch Fisher unfastened his blindfold. Butch held up his arm to shield his eyes and for a split second caught sight of Pivot Burke and Dutch Fisher. His mind matched the large hands and feet he had been able to see before with Burke's round face.

Sweeney spun Butch around and pushed him onto the stool in front of the vanity, then stood behind him and pushed his head forward and down. He kept his hand on the back of Butch's head and slid paper in front of him then deepened his voice and said, "Write what I tell you. Don't get cute—because we're gonna read it. "

Sweeney dictated a three-page letter then scooped up the green laundry bag from the floor and jammed it over the captive's head. He picked up the pages and pointed at Garguillo and they left the room.

Burke pulled Fisher over to the door and lowered his voice. "Did you hear that?"

Burked said, "You mean the part about killing him?"

Fisher folded his arms across his chest and pulled at his jaw. He leaned toward Burke's good ear and whispered, "Remember what I said about his family? Big men in Albany?"

Burke nodded and Fisher continued. "Remember Legs Diamond? Well, he tried to move into Albany. And he ain't around no more. Now here we are, with one of the O'Connells right here—and Harrigan's threatening to kill him! If that happens, what yuh think the family's gonna do?"

CHAPTER 15
Kill Threat

On July 25, 1933, Detective Ed Fitzgerald crouched on the roof of the four-story apartment house across the street from the Beaver Clothes Shop. He focused his binoculars from the roof ledge and watched Manny Strewl's trademark white panama straw hat. The detective sneered when Strewl paused at the corner and removed his hat and surveyed the people on the street.

Fitzgerald muttered aloud, "They never look up."

Behind him there came what sounded like the crunching of pebbles and glass. Fitzgerald spun around with his hand on the revolver inside his coat.

Detective Dolan chuckled. "Jumpy, are we?" Dolan held out a jug. "Figured the sun would have roasted you by now. Brought you some water."

Fitzgerald traded the binoculars for the water. "You're just in time. Strewl's on the corner."

Dolan put the glasses to his eyes. Strewl was still scoping out the street. "He must think he's Dick Tracy. Wanna bet on where he's going? The clothes shop? Or the betting parlor?"

"The afternoon race results are in, so I'd say the Jersey Newsroom."

"Well, I'm voting on the shop because the midmorning mail brought in another letter. Postmaster King gave us a call. A letter addressed to the Beaver Clothes Shop, special delivery. Both Hynes and Gannon thought Strewl would turn up here—and there he is."

Fitzgerald took the glasses. Strewl was slouched against the picture window of the shop. "Did Hynes and Gannon steam the letter open?"

"No need to. Strewl gives Mr. O'Connell the letter, he gives it to Delaney who makes copies. We'll get a copy eventually."

Fitzgerald poked Dolan. "There he goes! Let's go on down and get in position."

Dolan, already on his way to the roof's exit, grinned and said, "Don't let Dick Tracy spot you."

Inside the shop, Abe Friedman excused himself from his customer, slyly removed an envelope from his inside vest pocket and slipped it to Strewl who disappeared into the back room. The envelope had five three-cent stamps across the top and a Yonkers postmark. Strewl peeled open the envelope and read silently.

Strewl reached for the phone but pulled his hand back when he saw that there was a third page. Somebody, probably Sweeney, had dictated the words and Butch had written them. Strewl was pleased. The threat to do the captive harm was right there, just as he had wanted it. This, he thought, would make the O'Connells cough up the full ransom. He reached again for the phone and dialed. When the party answered he took several short breaths, pretending he was out of breath and blurting his words. "This is Manny Strewl—I need to speak with Lou Snyder—tell him it's important."

A moment later Snyder came on the line.

"Lou, uh, well, another letter's come. They've threatened to kill the kid if the O'Connells don't come through!"

Shortly thereafter, Louis Snyder was holding the three sheets of paper as he paced up and down by the window behind his desk. "Not good, Manny—not good. Threats of physical violence—and poison too!"

"Read the last page, Lou. Says if I can't help, I should step out."

"I read it. They're putting the squeeze on you. Are you in or out?"

"Lou, I'm about ready to chuck the whole thing. I don't need no dead bodies—specially not my own. What you think I should do?"

"Well, so far, you've been a stand-up guy through all this, so now we wait and see. Let the O'Connells make their move."

"Have yuh heard from Mr. O'Connell?"

"Not since we met a few days ago. My secretary's calling around now, trying to locate him."

"Whaddya think I should do?"

Snyder glanced at the letter again. "Says here the deadline is *Thursday!* Less than twenty-four hours! Manny, I suggest you go home and pull your shades down, as the letter says, and see if they contact you. I can get this letter to Dan O'Connell."

"Then what?"

Snyder's eyebrows arched. "Depends on him. But I suggest you make yourself available for making a beeline to New York. Okay? And call me in a few hours."

As Strewl waited for the elevator he sucked the inside of his cheek. He was thinking that he had pulled that off really well, had successfully snowed his own lawyer and Dan O'Connell.

He was the only passenger in the elevator. As the operator put the car in motion his stomach lurched. *Poison!* Would Harrigan really kill Butch? He sure as hell might. And then what would the O'Connells do?

Panic hit Stewl like a freight train. Oh shit! he thought— I've gotta talk to Harrigan, make him back off a little. He hurried across the lobby and did not notice the man by the window who lowered his newspaper.

***

An out-of-breath Dan O'Connell bolted through Louis Snyder's door. "Came as fast as I could get here."

Snyder rose to his feet and reached across the desk to hand over the bad news. "Better read this."

Dan O'Connell dropped into a chair and bent his head over the pages. When he reached the bottom of page one he gripped the arm of the chair and groaned. Again he began reading. When he looked up he exhaled deeply before saying, "The best me and my brothers can do is forty thousand."

Snyder shrugged. "You might be able to buy more time, raise your last offer another five thousand, see what they say."

O'Connell folded the letter into his inside coat pocket. "No sense monkeying around. I feel a moral responsibility to do what I can for the boy." He started to get to his feet but sat back down as Snyder began speaking.

"I just don't think this is a regular business negotiation. I don't understand why the kidnappers haven't lowered the price. To keep asking for the full two-fifty is just not normal. Manny said he told the kidnappers in previous meetings you did not have the full amount, and still they haven't budged

from the original demand. I find it very odd, Mr.
O'Connell, very odd indeed."

Snyder was in the business of reading people. Dan
O'Connell's face was flushed and his shirt wrinkled. He had
probably slept in it. His eyes kept drifting off into the distance.
Twice he wiped his forehead. Here was the iron man, the one
behind the power in Albany. More than three weeks had passed
since one of his own was kidnapped and the family couldn't
come up with more than forty grand. Maybe the O'Connells
were all show—flash and no cash. Maybe the stock market
crash wiped out their fortune. Then again, maybe they never
had a fortune.

The letter strongly implied that the kidnappers would kill
John Junior if the deadline was not met. Based on his previous
dealings with gangsters—"people of questionable character" as
he preferred to call them—Snyder had little doubt that this
bunch would kill Butch if the O'Connells missed the deadline.

"Are there any sources of revenue you and your brothers
have overlooked?"

O'Connell shook his head vehemently and growled like a
lion. "No, I tell you—no! We're all tapped out."

Snyder rapped his knuckles on the desk. "Contact has to be
made one way or the other. I'll call Manny and see what can be
arranged. In the meantime, I suggest you go home and rest up."

O'Connell reached across the desk for a pen and notepad
and wrote down the private telephone number at the lake
house. He put his hat on and took his leave, exiting onto State
Street where from the backseat of his car he said to his
chauffeur, "Ted, head for the house." A few blocks later, on
Delaware Avenue, he called out, "Pull over at the next phone
booth."

He called Delaney's office and told the district attorney to
make arrangements to pick up the newly arrived letter, then
dialed a second number. "Hello, Eddie. Strewl got another

letter from the kidnappers. I've just come from Snyder's office. They say if we don't come up with the cash, they'll take it out on Butch. They're threatening first to rough him up and then kill him."

A stone cold silence came from the other end. Finally, Ed's professional voice replied, "What did Snyder have to say?"

"The whole thing has him buffaloed. He's surprised the kidnappers didn't lower the ransom amount, but he thinks there's still a chance—some chance that Strewl might be able to work out a deal."

As he rode home Dan O'Connell stared out the window and thought back on how Strewl had read that one ransom note at his house. Read it in the dark! He recalled the times Strewl had seemed relaxed when he didn't think he was being watched, yet appeared nervous when he was talking. Why would the kidnappers choose such a person? At the Ten Eyck meeting, Oley and Strewl appeared to be friends though never once in all the time he had known him had he heard John even mention Manny Strewl.

A black thundercloud was moving across the hills leading to Thompson's Lake. The road ahead appeared to lead into a cave. Dan O'Connell removed his glasses. He recalled how he had helped Francis Oley get his speakeasy, had even kept the cops away from his door. The Oleys owed him. They wouldn't knife him in the back. But Strewl—? What about Strewl? Why was he willing to be helpful and claim he didn't want a thing in return?"

The headlights illuminated the road ahead for only a short distance. Dan O'Connell stared into the dark of the late day thunder storm and shivered. He felt a foreboding sense of moving into the dark unknown. He wondered what Strewl was doing right that moment. What exactly was this mysterious Manny Strewl up to?

***

Darkness engulfed the steps of the Arch Street Police Station where a uniformed officer missed the top step but caught the door and avoided a fall. He darted through a room filled with detectives, ringing phones and a chattering teletype and headed straight toward Detective Gannon who was sitting opposite Jimmy Hynes. Both detectives were poring over reports. The officer thrust an envelope toward Gannon. "A Detective Fitzgerald said to get this to you pronto."

Gannon sent the officer on his way and peeled the envelope open. A minute later he said, "Jimmy, you know a heavy-set guy 'bout five-foot-five with a stubby neck, dirt brown complexion and hair blacker than death? Walks hunched forward a bit."

"Not one of my guys. But sounds like half the wops on the docks. Why?"

"Got this from Ed Fitzgerald, one of my undercovers. He followed Strewl to the office of a mouthpiece name of Louis Snyder, so I had him stake out Snyder's office."

Hynes grinned. "You watching attorneys now?"

"You bet. All mobsters end up at their attorney's office sooner or later. Sunday afternoon Strewl and Dan O'Connell met with Snyder. Today, both O'Connell and Strewl met there. I'd sure like to know why."

Hynes glanced at the report. "This stranger Fitzgerald saw. He's maybe one of the

G-men?"

"I doubt it. Says here the threads were too expensive for a G-man. My guy didn't follow him because he had to stick with Strewl, who went back to his apartment on Elm Street, stayed there for a while and then made a run south to the city limits, headed toward New York City."

Hynes ran his fingers through his hair. "Probably went to New York to carry the result of the meeting to the kidnappers. How about Frank Oley? Anything on him?"

"We know it was Frank Oley whose car Strewl drove on Monday night to go out to Snyder's house."

Hynes drummed his fingers on the desk and gave a soft whistle. "Something's cooking."

Gannon asked, "How about Dan O'Connell? The G-men talked to him yet?'

"Nope. At the road leading up to Dan's lake house, the troopers turned them back."

Gannon grinned. "Didn't know troopers could be so persuasive."

One of the phones on the desk rang. As Hynes reached for it he said, "A trooper's shotgun always trumps a G-man's .38."

A few seconds later Hynes put the receiver down and grabbed his hat. "Come on. We're off to Delaney's office. The O'Connells got another note. Joe Casey, the DA's assistant, went out to Dan's place to get it."

It was a short drive up State Street. The secretary waved the detectives in and they took the empty seats in front of Delaney's desk. To the left was the head of the state police, Major John Warner, and to the right Albany's Chief Smurl. Both had duplicate stacks of paper and brown folders in front of them.

Right away, Delaney pushed three Photostats across the desk.

Tus 25, 1933,

> Dear Uncle Dan
>
> I have to write just what they are telling me If you feel like killing yourself you are crazy. you must think we are some mugs but you will realize you are mistaken, by the end of this week the kid will get Hell from now on and then if you don't see reason we are through. If you are that kind of a mug why we will have to take it out on the kid It will

Gannon asked without looking up, "This John Junior's handwriting?"

"Dan thinks so, and so does the lab."

Detective Gannon pulled the pages closer. "Starvation—poison—time's running out." He gestured toward the last two pages. "And looks like someone's trying to muddy the waters around Strewl."

Tue 25, 1933

P.S.

And as for you mr Brown why you will find your self in a dutch if you try tossing us around We won't action and if we don't get it, it will be curtains this week the trouble we went through is worth real money and we want plenty if you cant do any thing step out of the picture, Let us know how you feel about,

2) it Have your shades drawn to bottom and we will contact with you Thursday)

John O'Connell Jr

Hynes scratched his temple with his index finger. "Still seems odd to me that they haven't come down from the original demand."

Delaney pulled a sheet of paper from the stack in front of him. "Yeah, I've wondered about that too. Remember that the first ransom note was written on paper from Mr. O'Connell's office. The lab thinks letters two and three were written by the same person. The words racketeer and column were spelled wrong in both, and the reason for scribbling over top of the writing would be an attempt to disguise the handwriting. The general sloppiness, misspellings and word usage tell us that whoever wrote the notes doesn't have much education."

Detective Gannon said, "Could be either Oley or Strewl. They attended grade school together and both dropped out around the sixth grade. The only reason to disguise your handwriting is to keep someone who knows you from recognizing it."

Delaney exchanged glances with the police chiefs. "That's what we're thinking. But it's not much to go on, just circumstantial. Only thing we can say for sure is that the perpetrators are very familiar with the O'Connell family."

"That smacks of John Oley," Hynes said. "He drove trucks for the O'Connells in the 1920s. And according to the criminal reports, Oley and Strewl spent time together in the Atlanta penitentiary. Problem is, Oley hasn't done anything we can pin on him. Did you get anything back from the Warden on what he might have heard while Oley and Strewl were there?"

Delaney removed his glasses. "Another prisoner confirmed that he heard Oley and Strewl discuss a kidnapping—but there was no name mentioned."

Chief Smurl tapped the ash from his cigar. "John Oley doing nothing? That's enough to make me suspicious. Especially when you've got Strewl in the mix too." He wagged his head side to side. "The pair of them together, given their past association with the Legs Diamond mob, makes my hair stand on end."

Hynes noted the few remaining hairs on the Chief's head. In a different situation he would have joked. Instead he watched attentively as the DA held up Photostats of the previous ransom notes.

Delaney said, "Unfortunately, guilt by association doesn't hold water in court. Unless we come up with more hard evidence, these letters might be our entire case."

Major Warner pulled out copies of the ransom notes. "You'll have a tough time using these as evidence, John. You don't have the originals."

Delaney murmured. "Yeah, I know, Dan gave them back to the kidnappers."

Hynes sat up straight. "Come again?"

Delaney sighed. "Without the original copies, defense counsel can claim it can't be positively determined who wrote the ransom letters. We will claim that either Strewl or Oley wrote them, but the defense will claim the copies are unclear and suggest that we perhaps added something to them before we copied them. A good defense attorney could make the case that Jack in the Bean Stalk wrote the letters and we'd have a helluva tough time proving he didn't."

"So what's the plan?"

Delaney lit a cigarette and blew smoke over his head. "I'll have some prominent handwriting experts corroborate our findings. We'll show how the chain of evidence was not broken, and experts will testify on how Photostats are made and why Photostats we're presenting are not fakes. It'll work."

Hynes lifted his eyebrows. "What about the Durant? The one found at Tivoli Reservoir and towed to Walters Garage?"

Chief Smurl's cigar bobbed up and down. "Hold on." He shuffled through his papers and pulled out a sheet. "A 1928 Durant. Witnesses said they first saw the car parked there the morning of the seventh—didn't see any plates on it. No one paid attention to it until we came up with the plate number and started asking questions about it."

Smurl turned the page and scanned it for a few seconds. "Says here Sergeant Butts and Straney have pulled a lot of fingerprints from the car, and the prints excluded the mechanic, the salesman and the driver of the tow truck. We didn't have matches to the prints in our files so we sent them to the Feds. Did we hear anything back on that yet?

"No," said Delaney.

Smurl turned up another page and scratched his forehead as he perused it. "Whoever bought the Durant used the name 'Joe Costello.' He lives on Hamilton Street. As far as we can see his name was just the luck of the draw. We have no reason to think he's involved except—"

"Except what?" Gannon asked.

Smurl put the papers on the desktop and slapped them with the palm of his hand. "Costello admits to knowing John Oley, but says he hasn't seen him for three years!"

Gannon hunched forward. "Damn! Oley just keeps popping up. So where was this Costello guy on the night of the kidnapping?"

"Said he took his wife to a show in New York for the weekend. We're checking, but he seems to be on the level."

Hynes said, "One thing's certain, and puzzling too. A lot of the big names have left town."

Chief Smurl gave a sour grin and snarled, "Rats leaving a sinking ship! My guys have squeezed every bootleg chiseler and con man we can find — and still we're coming up empty. A lot of them have left for Canada."

Hynes wrinkled his brow. "Makes me wonder."

Major Warner leaned forward. "Speak up, Detective. You're among friends."

"In my experience, the only reason a person runs from the law is if he's guilty or about to get arrested. In this case, a lot of potential suspects have left town. They can't all be guilty—so it doesn't make sense."

Gannon said, "Well, could be we need to look at it from another direction."

Major Warner scowled. "And just what direction would that be?"

"Well, sir, my dog is afraid of thunder. When a thunderstorm approaches he hides in the corner a good thirty minutes before the actual storm arrives, so he's like a fortuneteller. Now let's just suppose that all these mobsters who've left town are innocent of this particular crime."

Chief Smurl smirked. "Hell, detective, we know they're guilty of something—we just haven't caught them yet."

"Correct, Chief. But suppose these same guilty parties are innocent of a particular crime and think they might get swept up in it. They're not willing to risk getting arrested for something they haven't done."

"And?"

Gannon leaned forward. "Well, we all know how prominent the O'Connell family is here in Albany. And the victim himself, very well liked around here. This latest letter implies that the kidnappers may very well kill one of the O'Connells. So it's like my dog—sensing an approaching storm, you see? The mobsters leave because they see trouble coming. They have nothing to gain by staying around, and maybe everything to lose if they stay."

Hynes bobbed his head. "Makes a lotta sense. I heard that Mr. O'Connell himself commented that Strewl is acting nervous about his part in all this—yet so far Strewl is still hanging in, and acting like such a *nice* guy."

For a moment, quiet reigned around the desk. Gannon raised his eyebrows. "Could be Strewl's waiting for payday.

And could be John Oley's waiting for payday, too—just as we all suspect he is."

The district attorney leaned back in his chair and intertwined his fingers over his belly. "Makes a great story, Detectives. All that's missing is the proof."

Hynes bobbed his head. "We're working on it."

Gannon said, "The paper of the first note—you said it came from Mr. O'Connell's office. Have we checked his business associates?"

Chief Smurl grunted. "That's a tall order, Detective. Includes about every man in Albany County. But yeah, we're checking—and so far, they're clean. What about Oley? Any of the undercovers come up with anything new on him?"

Hynes pulled a paper from his coat pocket and put it on the desk. "So far, Oley seems to be standing pat. Doesn't make many phone calls, but he does receive a lot of calls from New York. Here's the list."

Gannon chipped in. "Those pay phones on that list? They're in Dutch Shultz territory. Captain Oliver's hauling in anybody that touches those phones, but nothing's turned up yet."

Major Warner turned toward Gannon. "In your opinion, Detective, is Dutch Schultz involved in this thing?"

"I wouldn't make a bet either way. But since it's been three weeks since all this started, I would expect Schultz—if he's involved, is cutting his losses by now."

"You mean, shooting his losses?"

Gannon shrugged. "Same thing. Captain Oliver is using the premise as an excuse to push Schultz really hard. As for John Oley, he's given my men the slip a few times. Twice, by accident, we stopped his wife."

Major Warner's expression soured and the Chief's cigar bobbed up and down.

Hynes grinned. "Chief, may I see your papers?"

"Be my guest."

Hynes fished through the stack and pulled out a report. "When we interviewed Butch's neighbors we met George Keiss. Lives next to Butch at 21 Putnam Street. He gave me the plate number. We also talked with the guy across the street. Henry Tobin. Both of them said they heard women giggling on the night of the kidnapping. As Joe has said, you don't usually bring along a date when you set out to do a kidnapping, so we're thinking the kidnappers are keeping this a close-knit deal. Probably made their wives accomplices."

Delaney tugged at his tie. "Well, if so, the wives will swing with the rest."

Gannon glanced at the Photostats of the envelopes. He laid them out side by side. "Did you notice these postmarks? The first note came from Albany. Number six, from Peekskill, nine and ten from Yonkers. They're working south! The letter Catherine O'Connell received a week ago came from White Plains."

Major Warner said, "I've talked again to Chief Miller, in White Plains. He hasn't heard anything new—says Ralph Zucco is sitting tight."

Gannon shrugged. "Doesn't take much to drop a letter in a mail box—or keep an eye open. Presuming the kidnappers are in New York City and getting the morning papers the night before, they could hand a letter to a member of the Italian mob and have it mailed upstate to throw us off. There's a real short turnaround on the time stamps."

Delaney's brow furrowed. "But why do it? What's in it for the Italian mob?"

"Money," Gannon answered. "It's been about three weeks now and the kidnappers have not lowered the ransom demand. It's looking like a lot of mobsters are involved in this, so our suspects need a large payout to cover expenses."

Delaney looked over his glasses. "Sounds plausible."

Hynes bent over a Photostat. "Look at this envelope. Strewl's name is spelled with an O."

Delaney pulled Manny Strewl's criminal record from his stack. "I remember noting that. Through the years Strewl has spelled his last name several different ways. With an E or an O— sometimes a double L."

Major Warner tilted his head to one side. "That'll give you problems on the stand, John."

"What kind of problems?"

"I had a case where the defense counsel said the average man knows how to spell his own name. If you are going to base part of your case on the person's handwriting, you'll have to show consistency. A last name spelled two different ways could give a jury reasonable doubt on who wrote what."

Detective Hynes held up Strewl's file. "Sir, I've seen hundreds of criminal histories with last names spelled all kinds of ways—because mobsters can't spell! Besides that, they try to hide their identity by spelling their names different ways. It's a pretty common trick with them."

"Well, maybe we'll let you explain that to the jury."

The intercom on the desk buzzed and the secretary's voice came through. "Special Agent Cullen is calling from New York."

"Put him through." Delaney put the receiver to his ear. "Agent Cullen. Anything on those prints we sent down?... I see. Well, I'll be waiting. If anything turns up... Yes, I'll send down a Photostat of the last ransom note. So far, that's all we have. Nothing else new."

Delaney hung up the phone. Even as he was talking to Cullen he had noted the way Hynes propped his elbow on the chair arm and covered his eyes with his hand and Gannon stared at the ceiling. Delaney blew air between his teeth and addressed the detectives. "When I gave the Durant license plate to the FBI, it ended up front page news. I had to ask Chief

Smurl to put some uniformed cops over on Putnam Street
in case anybody decided to try to bump off Keiss or Tobin. I do
not intend to have any potential witness disappear or get shot
or killed—just because the FBI wants to grab some headlines,
and I'm sure as hell not going to have my evidence on the front
page of the paper so the defense counsel gets a chance to pick
it apart before I'm ready. Now…anything else?"

CHAPTER 16
Ransom to New York

While Delaney and the detectives discussed the case, Manny Strewl was on his way south toward New York City. He drove slowly so he could think. Were the O'Connells playing coy, or were they really broke? Maybe, after all, they really weren't wealthy. Snyder had said the O'Connells had come up with $40,000—in cash, but still less than a quarter of the ransom they'd demanded.

Strewl worked at coming up with a good excuse, some way to convince Harrigan's mob to accept the O'Connells' latest offer even if it was a lot less than they'd expected. It was a cash offer, and it didn't look like they would get much more even if they delayed and kept Butch longer. Besides, too much time had passed. They needed to make a move.

A car honked its horn and passed Strewl, leaving him to eat a trail of dust. He was ahead of schedule, did not need to be in the city until late evening, but he was antsy, tired of hanging around the house. He checked behind him to ensure he wasn't being followed. He figured he was safe enough, because both Louis Snyder and Dan O'Connell had told him to contact the kidnappers. And that's why he was going to New York—he had been ordered to go. That's what he would tell anyone who asked.

He smiled as he recalled what his attorney had said. Copies of the letters were not as good as originals so far as evidence was concerned. And he had been smart enough to hold on to the originals, so there was little to worry about.

At the trial, Strewl would learn otherwise. It would come as a surprise to him that not all copies of the ransom notes were equal.

A sign at the side of the road said New York City was still ninety miles away. John Oley and Angel Face Geary were supposed to be there when he met with Harrigan and he sure hoped they were, in case Harrigan should come up with the idea of making his split bigger by killing him off—the way Scarnici had done with Poffo and Parkin over the Rensselaer Bank robbery money.

A glance at his watch made him moan. "Ah hell."

He had a lot of time to kill. He stopped across from the Yonkers RKO Picture Theater where the marquee read "Emergency Call." Seeing the show would be a good way to pass some time, so he went in, but about thirty minutes later he exited. He didn't like the picture. He drove down Broadway and parked six blocks from Joe's Spaghetti House, a place where he had eaten numerous times, but this time he did not dine. He headed for the nearby subway entrance where the clock read 7:00 pm. He took a train to 41st Street. When he was again on a sidewalk he checked his watch and mumbled, "Still early."

He slung his coat over his shoulder and ambled along the street. At the Palace Theater he studied a picture of Edward G. Robertson and paid for a ticket and went inside. Some time later, he came out and immediately bumped into a man on the sidewalk.

"Manny! Manny Strewl! What the hell you doing down here? It's been a while—you know Sammy and Tommy, don't yuh?"

Strewl's eyes locked onto his old friend Sollie Levy who was dressed in his usual gray suit and brown derby. Strewl offered a weak smile. "Sollie. Long time no see."

Strewl looked past the other two men, thinking that his luck had changed. Could be these guys were working for the cops. He tried to make a show of relaxing but played the meeting cautiously. "Yeah, I know Sammy and Tommy." He reached his hand to them. "Nice to see you guys." After they all shook hands Strewl wiped his brow with his coat sleeve and tried to think of an excuse for being in New York.

"Been reading the papers about you, Manny," Sollie said. "Got the dough with yuh? Got any inside dope for us?"

A cold shiver went up Strewl's spine. If Sollie Levy knew about his involvement in the O'Connell case then most of New York City probably knew—including the cops. "Uh, no, Sollie."

Strewl stole a glance over his shoulder. No one came running up and no one approached from behind Sollie Levy. The coast was clear. Anyway, except for the fact that his name had been on the go-between list, nothing else had been written about him.

Sollie's belly jiggled with laughter. Strewl decided Sollie was just pulling his leg. It was time to make a fast exit. He said, "Got a deal up town in half-an-hour and—"

"Still wheeling and dealing, Manny? You oughta take a break."

Benny Tomkins, better known as Tommy, interrupted. "Say, when yuh going back?"

Strewl locked his teeth. "Tonight."

"Why tonight Manny? Why don't—"

Strewl exclaimed, "Why the hell you asking me like that, Tommy? I have to get back is all."

Tomkins held up both palms. "Right."

"Hold on, guys," Levy said. "Manny, we're on the way to my office. When you get through with what you gotta do, stop in and we'll get some suds."

Strewl spoke to his watch. "Hell, its 9:30—I'm late! If I get a minute, guys—I'll be there." He hurried away and hailed a cab. To the driver he said, "Seventy-ninth and Broadway."

At his destination he ran down the steps of the subway station to a large wall map and traced the route to 207th Street. He took the next train. At his destination he slipped into a diner. To the waiter he said, "Gimme a ruben sandwich, Mack—piled high, with lots of mustard. And a glass of water."

When Strewl finished the sandwich he hailed another cab. "Bronx line station on Riverdale."

At the entrance to the Bronx subway station he paid the fare and was soon puffing cigar smoke and pacing in a circle. There were few pedestrians but he studied them all as they crossed under the streetlights. A cigar later, he spotted the familiar tilt of the approaching man's head. James Sweeney once again had his hat pulled down over his eyes.

Sweeney passed him by, holding to the brim of his hat and saying, "Walk two blocks down on the left then take a right. A car will pick you up." Sweeney crossed the street and disappeared.

Strewl waited a moment before he tossed his cigar into the gutter and did as instructed. Shortly thereafter a yellow LaSalle's headlights approaching from behind blinded him when he turned around. The car stopped and James Sweeney burst forth and shoved Strewl into the back seat and jumped in behind him.

Sonny McGlone was in the driver's seat. Strewl asked, "Where're the others?"

McGlone shifted gears. "Oley said we all should talk. Everyone's gonna be at the Adams Street place."

Strewl lit a cigar. "So what's on everyone's mind?"

"Ransom. Oley thinks the O'Connells are coming up short and Harrigan's pissed—everyone is, for that matter."

Strewl sat back and removed his hat. "Hell, we all knew we weren't gonna get 250 grand. You have to ask for twice what you want and settle for half."

Sweeney said, "Shit, Manny! According to you the O'Connells are loaded, but according to Oley we won't even get half. Hellfire!—it costs dough to hold a prisoner and run back and forth to Albany all the time."

McGlone remained silent until he turned into the Holland Tunnel leading to New Jersey. "Dugan might buy your speech, Manny—but Harrigan, or Garguillo? No way. Harrigan says we should've stayed with John as go-between—says Oley would've had the full amount by now."

Strewl pulled himself closer to the front seat. "It's working out better this way. Cops are all over John and Francis. As long as they sit tight, it'll keep the cops off the rest of us."

McGlone exited the Holland tunnel and turned onto the cobblestones on Jefferson Street. "Great. Tell that to Harrigan."

At the corner of Eighth and Jefferson, Saint Ann's church bells were ringing. McGlone pointed to the left, up 8th Street. "This is the back way in." He parked at the side of the building with the car facing Adams Street and opened the wooden gate. They retraced the path along which the captive had been guided several weeks earlier. At the bottom of the eight concrete steps, Strewl paused and listened. A tenor voice was belting out a song.

McGlone jerked his head toward the upper window. "Don't mind that, it's Vito Calvino—owner of the building. Harrigan promised him five hundred for letting us use it."

Inside the building they turned left toward the old saloon on the ground floor. McGlone led the way around the sweatshop's now silent sewing machines and into the main barroom. He called over his shoulder, "Everyone's in here."

The chairs were upside down on the tables. The saloon had not been used for some time and blankets blocked the windows. Many of the overhead lights were burned out too, so the room's atmosphere was gloomy. Strewl made his way to two round tables that had been pushed together. Harrigan, Dugan and Garguillo sat at one, and at the other were the Oley brothers and Angel Face Geary. McGlone and Sweeney pulled up chairs behind Harrigan. Strewl took a chair between the two groups. The straight faces and slow slurping from beer bottles told him they were all on edge.

John Oley slid an open bottle of beer across the table. "Wet your whistle. I've just been explaining things to Harrigan."

The eyebrow over Harrigan's one good eye arched up. "From what John says, the O'Connells seem to be broke— either that or playing real hard to get. But either way, this whole deal's already dragged out way too damn long."

Strewl said, "There's a depression on, and we're talking a lot of dough here. It just takes time. The O'Connells have already come up with more cash. Just—"

Dugan cut in. "Just nothing—talk's cheap. The first offer was fifteen thousand, then twenty—so it sure don't sound to me like they're loaded."

Harrigan rocked his chair back. "If they don't ante up the dough, I'll cut Junior's ear off and send it to them. If that don't work, I'll send up his leg. If they still hold out, I'll send him up in small pieces as a warning to others who want to hold out on paying ransom."

Dugan nodded his agreement. "Very small pieces."

Strewl held up both arms. "Hold on, Charlie. The cops are tearing up Albany and every town within fifty miles looking for Butch. You do what you're threatening and a steamroller of trouble will come down the river. None of us needs that kind of heat. Sure it's slow going. But this is big leagues—and big dough." He pointed his beer bottle at the Oleys. "Right now, we're taking all the heat. You guys don't have the cops peeking in your windows like John and Francis do. Hell, Angel Face had to get out of Albany lest the cops arrest him for spitting on the sidewalk. The way we see it, it's easy playing baby sitter. Least you ain't got the cops nipping at your heels."

Harrigan rubbed his eye patch. "Still taking too long."

Strewl raise his eyebrow at Harrigan. "One of the letters said Butch had a fever."

Harrigan nodded. "Yeah. Kid got the shivers, but we fixed him up. Dugan got some stuff from the drug store. That and a shot of whiskey took care of it. Now what about the dough?"

"Alright—you want fast cash, we'll get fast cash. Pick a number. The O'Connells were up to twenty-five thousand last—"

Harrigan slapped his beer bottle on the table. "Twenty-five? That's all?!"

Strewl snorted. "Yeah, and that's up five G's in two days. A heck of a lot better than hijacking a truck loaded with booze—and there's more coming. I heard they plan to raise another ten—maybe twenty—in a week or so."

He snapped his fingers. "We lower the ransom enough, we get the cash just like that. All we gotta do is pick a number in easy reach."

Dugan pulled out a cigarette. "A hundred is a nice round number."

Strewl studied each man's face. He decided to con the conmen.

"Was thinking that myself. But me and Oley had a meet with Dan a few days ago at the Ten Eyck Hotel. He said the market crash hit them pretty hard. They're all mortgaged to the hilt—even the brewery's worthless far as the banks are concerned."

Harrigan growled, "You got some number in mind?"

"Well, we could hold on a few more weeks for the big bucks—but why wait? We're all tired, so I say $75,000."

Harrigan and Dugan exchanged looks but Strewl held up a hand. "Here's what you gotta consider. This'll wipe out the O'Connells' inventory and let you guys move in with your beer and take over all their territory. And—it will all be legit."

Harrigan's eyebrows shot up. "Legit?!"

Strewl leaned forward. "Of course. The cops think me and Oley are guilty—but they can't prove it. And they don't even suspect you guys, so besides your share of the dough you get the whole northeast beer region."

Strewl pointed to the Oleys and Angel Face Geary. "And with our share, we take a nice long vacation. Everyone wins."

John Oley smirked. "Except the O'Connells."

Strewl's biggest concern was to head off any possibility that Harrigan and his gang might kill the hostage. He thought he had done a good job of heading them off. He tossed some cigars on the table. "Havanas—nothing but the best."

John Oley raised his beer bottle in a silent toast. He understood what Strewl had been playing for and wanted to move the meeting along and give the New Jersey mob no time to think about what had been said.

Oley rubbed his cheek and said, "While we're here, mind if we see the goods?"

"Suit yourself," Harrigan said. He led the way up stairs lined with bead board and along a hallway with a checker-board linoleum floor. He scratched on the apartment door several times and Christy Miller opened the door a crack.

Harrigan barged in. "The Albany crowd is here. They wanna check on the kid."

Strewl entered the bedroom and tiptoed over to the hostage who lay stretched out on a bed. Harrigan's head bumped against the single bulb light suspended in the middle of the room.

Butch tilted his head toward the mumbling voices. From under the blindfold he caught a glimpse of the panama hat that Strewl was holding at his side.

Strewl stepped back and pointed to the adhesive tape holding cotton patches over the hostage's eyes. He whispered to Dutch Fisher, "Can he see?"

"No, only time that blindfold comes off is when they have him write letters."

Strewl wiped his forehead with his sleeve. "Hot in here."

Dutch Fisher whispered, "Gets ripe in here during the day. We bring the fan in from the kitchen when it gets to be too much. Been wiping the kid down some to help get rid of the smell."

When the visitors had left the room and pulled the door to behind them, Dutch Fisher dropped onto the vanity seat next to the bed and popped two marbles in his mouth. He kicked the bed's sideboard and asked in slurred words, "Say, kid, you know Manny?"

Butch said, "I know a Tom Manning. Sells fire extinguishers. Why?"

"No matter."

Dutch sat for a moment until he saw Burke place his ear to the bedroom door. He got up and met Burke in the middle of the room where he took the marbles out of his mouth and whispered, "Hear anything?"

"Can't make it out clear, but it don't sound good."

***

Charles Harrigan rubbed at his eye patch as he led Strewl and the others down the back stairs of 734 Adams Street. At the bottom he paused with hands on his hips. "Say, Manny—how long does it take you to drive back to Albany?"

Strewl pulled a cigar out of his shirt pocket. "Four hours or so, depending if I take a break."

Harrigan guided the group into the dark alley between the apartment building and the shed. "That puts you back in Albany about six in the morning. We may as well get this thing over and done. Tell the O'Connells if we get 75 grand by midnight Saturday, we'll release the kid 24 hours later."

Thomas Dugan studied the deserted 8th street up to Adams Street and left down to the stop light at Jefferson Street. "All clear," he said.

Harrigan gripped Strewl's shoulder. "We clipped the kid on the seventh and now it's the 28th. Impress upon the O'Connells that this thing will not—will not—drag into August. Capiche?"

Strewl took the cigar from his mouth. "Money's in the bag."

"It better be. Sonny will drive you back to your car."

Less than an hour later Strewl was zipping his way through Yonkers, where he had a bit of trouble with the car's starter. Getting that taken care of took up about forty minutes, so when he was on his way again he went full throttle to make up for lost time. In Poughkeepsie, his car bottomed out in a pothole and he lost control and slid sideways onto the roadside in a cloud of dust. The car stalled and jolted to a halt. Coughing and choking on the dust, he pulled back onto the road. At the next roadside diner he stopped and downed a quick coffee. When at last he made it back his tires hummed as they rolled across the steel drawbridge over the Hudson, announcing his arrival. At his Elm Street apartment he set the alarm clock for nine and dropped into bed without taking off his clothes.

When the alarm jolted him awake he shut it off and went into the living room to the phone and dialed. "Hello, Lou. It's Manny. Met with the kidnappers last night. Got a real ransom number."

"How much?"

"Lou, the lowest they'll go is seventy-five."

"Right, Manny. I'll call Mr. O'Connell. Can you be at my office at eleven?"

Strewl, on time for the meeting, breezed by the empty desk in the outer room and into Lou Snyder's private office. The attorney motioned him to a seat next to Dan O'Connell and said, "I was just telling Mr. O'Connell that you returned from New York this morning after meeting with the kidnappers, Manny. Tell him in your own words what transpired."

"Well, Mr. O'Connell, I went to New York and hung out on Riverdale. About midnight this guy contacted me and right after that I got tossed in a car—and I told them what we talked about."

Dan pushed his glasses up. "Did you get a look at them? Get a plate number?"

Strewl slowed up, aware that he needed to make his next lie sound real. "Couldn't. Made me wear smoked glasses. And besides, I was too scared—yuh know?"

He rubbed sweat from his brow and stole a peek at Dan O'Connell. Was the man buying his story? Better not to let him think about it too long. Strewl cleared his throat and launched into his fast-talk salesman's pitch. "Got the kidnappers way down from the two hundred and fifty thousand, Mr. O'Connell. But man, was I nervous!"

O'Connell rolled out his lips and nodded. "So…Lou here says the kidnappers gave you a number?"

"Right, Mr. O'Connell. Said they'd take $75,000 if they could have it by midnight Friday—and twenty four hours after that, they release your nephew."

O'Connell looked over his glasses. "That's less than 12 hours away. Do they—"

"I told them, Mr. O'Connell, that wasn't much time so they said if the money is delivered Saturday they'd release Butch Monday."

O'Connell slapped his knee. "Now we're getting somewhere. At least we know what they want." He stood up and headed for the door, saying as he went, "I'll get together with Ed and Solly. Stay by your phone. I'll call you about two."

***

The loud clicking of the wall clock's big hand moving straight up to 2 o'clock caught Lou Snyder's attention. His fingers drummed the desk for a moment before he picked up the phone and called Strewl's number. "Hello, Manny? It's Lou. Did Mr. O'Connell call you yet?"

"Nope."

"Looks like a waiting game. If he calls, let me know."

Snyder hung up the phone and sat tapping a pencil in his palm. After a few seconds he turned his attention back to the papers on his desk and began reading another contract.

When the clock showed five o'clock he said to himself, "Something must be wrong." He pulled at his jaw. If the O'Connells did not raise the money, what should he advise Strewl to do? If he advised him to return to New York empty-handed, both he and Butch O'Connell might be killed, as earlier notes had implied. If he advised him to stay in Albany, Strewl would be safe but chances were high they'd kill Butch O'Connell.

Snyder mumbled to himself, "But the O'Connells are not my clients."

The ringing phone startled him. He answered, listened and said, "Good to hear from you… How much?"

Snyder tilted back in his leather chair and stared at the ceiling. "I'll call Manny and tell him."

Snyder hung up and dialed Albany 3-6042. "Hello, Manny—just heard from Dan O'Connell. Hurry down to my office."

Strewl burst into Snyder's office panting like a dog. Snyder pointed him to a seat.

Strewl could feel that something was wrong.

"Manny, the O'Connells have raised $42 and a half thousand—in cash."

Strewl exploded. He threw up his arms. "Cheese-us! It's useless talking to these people."

He wiped his brow and began pacing in a circle. This time his case of nerves was real. Harrigan was not going to be happy with just $21,000 and would most likely kill the hostage.

Strewl threw his hat into the chair. "Damn it! That's ridiculously low! I don't think the kidnappers will take it. And they'll probably kill the hostage."

He stared at the floor. His mind showed him a picture: Butch being sliced into pieces. He hung his head. "I can't go down there with that offer, Lou. One thing I forgot to tell you. They said there'd be no more contact after Saturday."

Snyder dialed a phone number. "You can tell Mr. O'Connell yourself." Into the phone he said, "Send a cab to 100 State Street for Louis Snyder and Company."

A short while later they were standing on Dan O'Connell's porch on Whitehall Road when Dan's Marmon swung to the curb. Dan jumped from the back seat and hurried up the steps as he pulled keys from his pocket. Before he opened the door he looked back at the street. "How'd you get here?

"Cab."

O'Connell popped open the door. Inside he said, "Be a minute," and disappeared up the stairs. He returned shortly with two bundles. "Small denominations like they wanted— $42,500."

Strewl turned bug eyes toward him. "Mr. O'Connell, I… I can't go down there with that."

"Why not?"

Strewl stole a glance at Snyder. He'd already protested to him about the low offer but Snyder wasn't talking. Strewl rummaged around in his head, trying frantically to find a way out of a precarious predicament he had brought on himself. He was afraid he'd give himself away if he attempted to negotiate for more money, but he dreaded facing Harrigan's wrath if he arrived in New York with less than the $75,000.

"Well, the money. And I'd be alone. Something could happen."

O'Connell rolled out his lips. "You'll be all right, Manny."

"No, I mean... Mr. O'Connell, yuh know—there's been talk, yuh see?"

Dan O'Connell stood with his hands on his hips and roared like a lion. "Take it down there and throw it in their faces and bring the boy back!"

He lowered his voice then and said with a sigh, "That's all there is."

Strewl studied the packages of money. "Mr. O'Connell, this is a lot of money. If a cop stops me... with my record... well, he might think I stole it. Might take me in. Then what would I do?"

"Hmm. You're probably right about that." He took a piece of notepaper from the phone stand and scribbled some lines. "Take this. Says you're working for me." Then he reached in his back pocket and pulled out the last ransom letter. "Take this. They wanted it back."

Strewl took both notes and tucked them into a money package. "Suppose I give them the money and they don't give the kid back?"

Strewl could feel Dan O'Connell's eyes. They were burning right through him. He knew he was not going to avoid the trip so he decided to try to get Dan O'Connell to take the trip with him. He was thinking that if the big fish of the clan showed, Harrigan could snatch him and then they'd be sure to get the full ransom. And Harrigan would probably be more reluctant to murder two people.

Strewl pulled on his jaw. "Suppose I do get stopped? Then I'm in a tough spot. Yuh think someone should go with me?"

"Got anyone in mind?"

"Well—"

O'Connell interrupted. "How about you, Lou? If you go, I owe yuh one."

Snyder pulled on the back of his neck for a moment. He'd never gotten so directly involved with his clients, but this situation was different. It might mean saving a person's life. It could also be to his benefit to have the most powerful man in Albany owing him a favor. On the other hand, he needed to be careful, needed to protect himself.

"Guess so—if it'll help. But if we're going to have all that cash we need some protection. You got a gun?"

From the hall stand O'Connell pulled a .38-revolver. His brother Solly had given it to him after the Mush Trachnier kidnap attempt. He clicked open the chamber to show it was loaded then snapped it closed and handed it to Snyder. "What else?"

Strewl swallowed hard and tucked the package under his arm. "Mr. O'Connell, I won't give them the money at first. They might take the dough and then ask for more. I'll meet them first—tell 'em what's what."

O'Connell held the door open. "Do whatever, Manny. Just bring my nephew back. My chauffeur can take you to your car."

Ted Gorman took them to Snyder's home. As they rode Snyder loosened his tie and said, "I'd better check my oil and tires. We'll have to stop to fill up. While I get cleaned up, I'll have my wife fix yuh something to eat."

Strewl was figuring on an excuse for why he needed to talk to his partner. He needed to talk to John Oley, tell him what had transpired and let him make the arrangements for the meeting. He said, "It's a long ride to New York, Lou, and I'm supposed to meet these guys around midnight. Why don't I borrow John Oley's car? It's newer, bigger and ready to go. I can have him run it over—save some time." Snyder agreed to the plan.

After Strewl made his call to Oley he waited in the kitchen with Mrs. Snyder. She fixed them a bag of sandwiches to carry along, and a few minutes later Snyder came hurrying down the stairs with a brown leather bag for carrying the cash.

Oley had been waiting to hear from his pal Manny Strewl. He came right over. Louis Snyder reached to shake Oley's hand. "Thanks for letting us borrow your car. We can drop you off on the way."

Oley rubbed his cheek. "I want this thing over quick as you guys do—so's the damn cops get off my back."

Strewl was frowning. "Yuh know, Lou—me and John, we was talking about this cash. The kidnappers already turned down 40 grand—and another 25 hundred ain't shit. Sounds like I'm selling a car or something. It just don't make sense."

Oley drew his palm down his face. "I agree with Manny, Lou. If these mugs are as big as they say, 25 hundred is peanuts. If I was them, it wouldn't budge me."

Snyder proceeded to John Oley's Pontiac not knowing it was the same car that had been used in the kidnapping. Strewl got in the driver's seat, Snyder in the passenger seat and Oley in the back. Snyder said, "You guys are probably right. No sense showing them all our cards at once."

Hours later, Strewl pointed to the corner of 230th Street and Broadway. "Pull over there."

Snyder pulled to the curb a short distance from the intersection and turned off the headlights. Strewl stepped out. "Supposed to meet these guys up on Riverdale. They better not see you—might scare 'em off. Wait for me here."

Strewl strolled to the curb and hailed a cab. At 260th and Riverdale Strewl got out and checked his watch: 11:30 p.m. He jammed his hands in his pockets and whistled as he paced up and down the sidewalk.

A familiar shadow appeared. As usual James Sweeney had his hat pulled down over his eyes. "Took yuh long enough. Got the cash?"

Strewl held up both his hands. "Got what they got, $40,000—that's it. The boy, for the cash. Final offer."

Sweeney scoffed. "Bunch of hard-asses."

Strewl followed Sweeney a half block to Harrigan's yellow LaSalle. Sweeney said, "I'll have to check it out with Harrigan." He dropped Strewl off on Broadway a short distance from where Snyder was waiting. "Meet me at 174th west of here. Beat it."

Strewl hopped out and trotted the remaining distance. He said to Lou Snyder, "Think we got him. Go up to a hundred and seventy-fourth."

Snyder gunned the engine and a few minutes later rolled to a stop. Strewl took the leather bag full of money, said, "Wait for me in the lobby of the Taft Hotel," and disappeared into the shadows.

Strewl inched along 174th Street, eyeing every nook and cranny for possible danger. Suddenly from behind a mailbox, a hand grabbed him. "In the car!"

Hands rammed Strewl into the back seat floor. Dugan put his foot on Strewl's back. "Stay down."

The yellow LaSalle sedan roared off. Dugan raised his foot and said, "You're late."

Strewl pushed himself off the floor. "Took time to get the money."

"Only $40,000. Hardly worth it."

Strewl took a bead on Harrigan's good eye. "It's the easiest dough you'll ever make. All's you guys had to do was babysit a while."

Harrigan shouted. "Strewl, we got expenses! Trucks, cars, that apartment and all—twenty grand will barely cut it."

"The O'Connells took a hit in the market—like everyone else. Would take weeks before they get the rest of the cash, if they could get it—but now, we got some cash. We take it—and it's over. No more cops for us, and you get on with business."

Harrigan growled, "You got the money?

Strewl held out the packages. "Sure I got it. Right here."

He opened the bag and Harrigan took a package and peeled off the wrapping. He fanned the edges with his thumb and returned it to Strewl. "Take it back."

"What?!"

"You heard me—take it back. It's marked."

"How do you know it's marked?"

"It always is. Cops think we're all stupid. Everybody knows they record the serial numbers. That's why we need the 24 hours before we release the kid. Need time to wash the dough. Anyone come with yuh?"

"My attorney. Lou Snyder. Got him pretty well snowed. Figured he'd make a good alibi, maybe a witness too. Told him I'd catch up with him at the Taft."

Harrigan tapped Sonny McGlone's shoulder. "Head for the Taft."

To Strewl Harrigan said, "Too late to do anything now. Better make sure you weren't followed. Pick another hotel and check in. You can exchange the money tomorrow. Small denominations. Just make up a story. Meet us on 174th and Broadway after lunch. That should give yuh enough time."

McGlone zigzagged through the streets of New York, checking for tails. Three blocks from the Taft Hotel, he pulled to the curb.

As Strewl got out of the car Harrigan caught him by the arm. "Don't forget. I even smell a cop and the kid will join the typewriter and print set—at the bottom of the Hudson."

Strewl pulled away. "Don't worry."

Chapter 17
Released

Strewl waited for the LaSalle to disappear into the night.
Minutes later he burst through the revolving door of the Taft
Hotel. The door kept spinning as he paused to catch his breath.
The lobby was deserted except for Lou Snyder who was sitting
on a large red doughnut-shaped sofa opposite the elevators.

Snyder had dozed off but he jarred awake as Strewl
approached. He whispered, "How'd it go?"

Strewl glanced back at the desk clerk who was inserting
bills into room slots. The elevator boy was dozing in a chair
beside the elevator. "Pretty good," he bragged. "They took the
forty, so I saved the O'Connells $2,500! But there's one hitch."

"Which is?"

"They think the money's marked and want it exchanged for
the same denominations."

"Aw hell! At three in the morning?" The elevator boy
jolted awake and Snyder reached to smooth back the hair on
the side of his head. "Come on, let's get outta here."

On the sidewalk Strewl handed the moneybag to Snyder.
"We'd better call Mr. O'Connell about this. Supposed to meet
the kidnappers about one this afternoon."

"That means we have one morning to care take of it. For
now, we'd better find a place to stay."

Strewl held open the passenger door of the Pontiac. "We
can get a good rate at the Empire, over on 63rd."

At the hotel Strewl asked for a room with two beds. The
clerk handed him a registration card and turned to get two sets
of keys.

The clerk glanced at the card and said, "Here you are,
Mister Silverman.

Room 229. Elevators are around the corner. Any bags?"

"No, we missed the train is all—and we need a wake-up call, eight o'clock."

The clerk made a note. "Yes sir."

The next morning in the hotel's dining room, Strewl wiped the egg yolk on his plate with buttered bread. In a low voice he said, "Was thinking we can call Mr. O'Connell from Penn Station. It's closer to downtown, and there're more banks down there—depending on what he says."

"Fine by me," Snyder said as he finished his coffee. "Banks will be open at nine. If we hustle, we'll beat the crowds."

Strewl waved for the bill. "Let's get this show on the road."

Twenty minutes later he pushed through the door of the train station and pointed across the lobby. "Phone's over there."

Snyder tucked the moneybag under his coat and Strewl dropped coins in the phone. Snyder waited with his back glued to the booth. A woman attempted to enter the phone booth next to the one Strewl was in but Snyder held out his arm. "It's out of order. Try the next one down."

Strewl exited the booth saying, "Orders are to wait till we hear back. Mr. O'Connell asked for the number here, said he'd call back shortly."

Two cigars later Strewl answered the ringing phone.

"Is Snyder with you?"

"Sure is."

"Go to the Bank of Manhattan. Ask for a Mr. Keenan. He'll take care of you."

The wall clock at Penn Station read 10 o'clock as Snyder and Strewl boarded a taxicab. Two hours later they were back at the train station. They entered the front door and exited by the side entrance where their car was waiting.

"Gonna be close," Strewl said. "—supposed to be there by one."

Strewl ran most of the red lights between there and Dyckman Street and double-parked on 230th as he let Snyder out. He said, "Wait here till I get back."

Strewl melted back into traffic and headed for 174th Street. He parked the car, tucked the money bag under his jacket and headed for Broadway. He arrived on time and leaned against a coffee shop. He fanned himself with his hat as he waited. Before long a familiar figure came skulking down the sidewalk.

James Sweeney held to his hat. "Got the dough?"

Strewl pointed to his coat. "Right here."

Sweeney stepped into the curb with one hand waving and almost immediately the yellow LaSalle roared up and the back door opened. Before Sweeney could close the door behind them Sonny McGlone shot the car into the traffic.

Charles Harrigan looked in all directions. "Don't look like yuh was followed. Sonny, head for the G-W."

McGlone spun the steering wheel. Harrigan raised his voice above the noise of tires crossing the steel rods of the George Washington Bridge. "Got it with yuh?"

Strewl held out both packages. "Here it is. Had the bank divide it up."

Harrigan took one package of cash and flipped it like a coin. McGlone made a right turn off the big bridge and took the back way to the Adams Street apartment.

McGlone pulled in at the back. "How we gonna get the kid outta here?"

"After work," Harrigan said. "Oscar's running another shift for winter coats. Last thing we need's for the sewing machine broads to see anything."

Harrigan led the way into the wooden shack where James Dugan was sitting in a chair smoking a cigarette and reading a newspaper with his feet propped on a steel drum.

Dugan dropped his feet to the floor. "What took yuh so long?"

Strewl tossed his cigar into the bucket of ash. "Took the bank longer'n I thought it would to change the money—but I got it."

Harrigan tossed Dugan a package of money. "Take a look."

Dugan sliced open the wrapping with his thumbnail and pulled out a twenty and held it up to the sunlight coming through the window. "No pinholes, and the ink's all the same color." He held the bill at eye level. "No raised edges." He snapped the bill using both hands. "It's good."

Harrigan took the bill back and used it to scratch his jaw. "Twenty grand's hardly worth it. Oughta send him back in pieces just to teach—"

"Hold on there, Charlie," Strewl said. "Cops are still all over Oley and sniffing round me. It took longer than planned—but you guys are in the clear."

"Yeah," Harrigan said without enthusiasm. He pointed the bill at Sweeney. "Get hold of Miller. Have him bring the truck around tonight. After we move the kid you and him can break the apartment down."

Harrigan counted out two thousand in tens and twenties. "Have either Burke or Fisher come down. Tell 'em it's payday."

To Strewl Harrigan said, "Where yuh holed up?"

"Me and Snyder took a room at the Empire."

"About midnight, cruise 230th Street. We'll drop the kid off. After that—he's your problem."

From behind came a noise of popping gum. As he came through the door Francis Oley pushed up his fedora with his thumb. "Heard you were back."

Strewl handed Francis Oley the money packet. "Take care of this. What's your brother doing?"

Francis Oley tucked the money under his arm and laughed. "He's doing nothing and it's driving the cops nuts. By the way, Angel Face is all set up in New York. This'll come in handy."

Pivot Burke sniffled while dragging his heels through the door. "You rang?"

Harrigan held out a thousand dollars. "Good faith money. You'll get the other half when we dump the kid. Get him dressed and ready. Have Fisher drop down."

He pointed at Strewl. "Whenever you're ready."

Strewl took two cigars from his inside coat pocket and gave one to Harrigan. He used matches from his pants pocket to light each cigar. "Me and Oley will have to lay low awhile, till this thing cools down."

Harrigan blew a ring of smoke at the ceiling. "In a week, this'll be yesterday's news."

"Sounds jake. Is the kid feeling all right now?"

"Seems to be better—stopped shivering. Looks like the pills did the trick."

"Sounds good. Lemme take a look before I leave."

At the entrance to the apartment Strewl took off his hat and scratched the door's frosted glass window. Christy Miller opened the door. Strewl held his fingers to his lips and entered the room. He stood inside the door, studying the body on the bed. Butch had a white bandage covering his eyes and wore suit pants and a white pajama top.

Dutch Fisher had Butch's shirt slung over his arm. He mumbled, "Here's the boss."

Butch turned his head at the approaching footsteps. Through a slit in the gauze he could see Strewl's dark hair and slim build, and he sniffed the aroma of clothing saturated with cigar smoke.

Strewl pulled Butch's feet from the bed, forcing him to sit up. He sat next to him and said in a low tone, "You know what

this is all about. If you do anything, you know what you're
in for. You may get one or two of us, but you'll never queer us
all."

Butch nodded his head.

Ninety minutes later Strewl was blowing the car's horn and
waving at Lou Snyder who was studying men's suits in a store
window on 230th Street. Snyder hustled toward the car,
ignoring the honking horns of the cars backed up behind
Strewl.

"I was beginning to worry," he said. "Where's John?"

"It's all jake. We get him tonight at midnight."

"Jesus Mary and Joseph!—that's more than six hours to
wait."

Strewl made the next right turn. "What can I say? We can
check back in at the Empire and rest up. Could be a long
night."

Just before midnight Strewl pulled up beside a coffee shop
on 230th Street. Next to the shop was a gas station. He switched
off the headlights but kept the motor running and looked in all
directions. "This is it. Wait right here till I get back."

Snyder took the gun from the glove box, checked it and put
it back in the glove box. "Be careful," he said.

Strewl nodded and drove south. At 220th street, Sweeney
stepped into the circle of light under a streetlamp and waved
his hands. Sweeney got in the car. He said, "Round the corner
on Riverdale."

A few blocks later Sweeney pointed. "That Ford coupe—
between the street lights."

Strewl pulled to the curb behind the Ford and in front of
Harrigan's LaSalle. Dugan and McGlone raised the rumble seat
of the Ford to pull Butch from the trunk.

A voice called, "Give us a hand here."

Strewl and Harrigan hurried over and wrapped their arms
under Butch's shoulders. As Butch started to bend down to

enter the car, his shin touched the running board and he stumbled.

Harrigan roared, "What are yuh? Dumb?"

Strewl ran around to the driver's seat and hopped inside to help guided the blindfolded Butch into the front seat. "John, I'm Manny Strewl. It's alright."

Harrigan leaned into the car and barked orders at Butch. "Keep that bandage on for half an hour—and stay away from the cops!"

Strewl waited until the tail lights of the other two cars disappeared into the distance. He nudged Butch and said, "You can take it off now."

"No…wait."

"It's alright, John—they're gone."

Strewl started the car and pulled away from the curb. Butch put both hands to his face and yanked the bandage off.

Strewl said, "Be careful of your eyes." Strewl was wondering if Butch would ever be able to retrace his steps, locate the hideout. Playacting, he said, "I just don't know where I'm at. Do you know where you are, John?"

Butch hid his eyes. He thought the driver's voice sounded familiar. He blinked as they passed street lights. When he spotted an intersection sign at Johnson and 230th Street he said, "Bronx, maybe."

Strewl up-shifted and hid his delight. The guy did not know where he was! "Got it. Say, you know a guy by the name of Louis Snyder?"

"A little. Enough to say hello."

Strewl turned onto Fieldstone Avenue. "Well, he's down here with me. Gotta pick him up at a coffee shop."

A few blocks later Strewl slowed and bent his neck out the driver's window, studying the people in the coffee shop's window. Two people with bottles in their hands sat next door on the gas station steps. Strewl muttered, "Where the hell is he?"

He coasted down Broadway and froze when he spotted a policeman at the call box on the corner. At Dykeman Street he made a U-turn. "Cheese-us, where is Snyder?"

As he cruised back up Broadway Strewl saw in the distance a lone figure strolling up the sidewalk. He punched the gas pedal and swung to the curb across from the gas station he had just passed.

Snyder opened the passenger door. "Saw a guy in a parked car back there. Think he had a rifle or something. Let's move!" Butch slid to the center and Snyder climbed aboard.

Strewl accelerated. "Think we should call Dan? Let him know?"

"Let's get outta here first. At least above Yonkers."

He extended his hand. "You've been through a lot, John. How yuh doing?"

"I've been better, Mr. Snyder."

"John, do you know Manny Strewl there?"

"Don't think I know Mr. Strewl. But I've heard about him." A moment later Butch added, "If you wanna make a call, Miller's Restaurant in Peekskill is on the way. There's a phone booth in it."

Snyder bent around Butch. "Should be safe enough. Yuh hear that, Manny?"

"Gotcha."

During the long ride, Butch more than once slouched forward in his seat and gazed at the stars overhead. He was much aware of the odor on the clothes the driver was wearing. A strong smell of cigar smoke. The driver's voice sounded familiar too.

The voice said, "Say John, how long of a ride was it from where they held yuh to where I picked you up?"

"Seemed like an hour or so."

"Do yuh know—know where yuh was held?"

Butch was sure of it now. This man's voice was familiar. "Near Italians. Heard them singing."

"Yeah, they like to do that. By the way—how much yuh think they paid to get yuh back?"

"Couldn't guess."

Strewl held out a roll of money and spoke in his practiced business tone. "Forty-grand. But I saved your uncle 2500 dollars—right here."

An hour later, Strewl pulled into the parking lot at the Miller Restaurant. He and Butch waited while Snyder went inside to make the call.

Snyder returned within a few minutes. "Couldn't get Dan, but my wife's gonna keep trying till she gets hold of him. John, the kitchen was closed. I'm guessing you're hungry. Need something to eat?"

Butch shifted his position to make room for Snyder. As he did he caught sight of a white panama straw hat on the back seat—a hat like the one he'd seen from under his bandage. "No-o-o," he said, "I'm fine."

"Well," Snyder said, "I sure could use a beer. Manny, pull over at the next road house you see."

***

"Car coming," called a voice from the bushes that lined the gravel road leading to the O'Connell house on Lake Thompson.

It was four o'clock in the morning and New York State Trooper Lieutenant McGarvey knew whoever was driving the car was not arriving for a social visit. He clicked off the safety on his pump shotgun and waved two other patrolmen to positions on either side of the shrub-lined driveway. Seconds later, he saw the car lights and heard the deep roar of an engine. The lights rounded the corner onto the gravel drive.

McGarvey could tell it was a big car—big enough to hold several armed men. He flashed back briefly to the time he and his men got into a shootout with members of the Jack "Legs" Diamond mob on a similar backcountry road. He brought the shotgun to eye level and stared along the barrel.

There was a sudden high pitch whine of the engine and a deep rumbling noise which told him the driver had down shifted and was slowing. Maybe this was the car they had been expecting. He yelled, "Cover me."

McGarvey laid his shotgun across his chest, creating a black "X" on his chest with the black gun barrel and the black leather uniform strap that ran from his shoulder to his black waist belt. He knew his men hidden in the brush had their fingers on the triggers of their guns. He stepped into the glow of the headlights. He waved his gun up and down to signal the driver to stop and stepped to the side of the car as it slowed.

Strewl stopped abreast of McGarvey and poked his head out the car window. "I'm Manny Strewl. This is Louis Snyder. We've brought John O'Connell back."

McGarvey tilted his head around Strewl. The man with the haggard beard, shaggy hair and blood-shot eyes offered a meek grin. McGarvey had seen Butch box and at the police academy during his training. He returned the grin. "Welcome back, Mr. O'Connell."

McGarvey stepped back and yelled, "It's Strewl—with Mr. O'Connell. Let them through."

Strewl shifted into first gear and let the car roll forward at a snail's pace. He couldn't see the other policemen but he guessed there were likely a dozen guns pointing directly at him. He parked next to the five cars in front of the lake house and got out. He waited for Snyder and Butch to join him before he approached the house. Before he could open the screened door, a hand, in a dark blue Albany police uniform reached from out of the dark. An Albany policeman opened the porch door. "Everyone's expecting you, Mr. Strewl."

Strewl removed his straw panama hat with a smile, "Just glad to help." He nodded a greeting to Chief Smurl as he passed through the main entrance.

Chief Smurl tipped his head. "Good job Mr. Strewl."

Smurl waited until Strewl and others were surrounded by the people waiting inside before stepping onto the porch and whispering into the dark corner at the hidden policeman. "Check the car."

Detective Hynes touched the patrolman's arm. Silently, the patrolman and Detective Fitzgerald followed Hynes out to the Pontiac that Strewl had arrived in and began to search it. In no time, Hynes had discovered the pistol that had been given to Strewl and Snyder by Dan O'Connell hours earlier. He sniffed the barrel and opened the bullet chamber. He saw all the bullets in place. "Never fired it."

Fitzgerald called from the back seat. "Nothing here."

The patrolman called from the trunk. "Same here."

Meanwhile, inside the O'Connell house, a throng of people enveloped Butch. Dan O'Connell pushed through the mob. He grabbed and shook Butch's hand. He gave him a bear hug. "You're a sight for sore eyes. Glad you're safe."

Butch's shoulder sank in relief. "Glad to be back." A moment later,

"Uncle Dan −"

Delaney cut off Butch by giving him a two-handed handshake. "John, it's over."

Butch closed his eyes for a second and nodded yes. He opened his eyes and looked Delaney directly in the eye. "But I wanted to tell −"

Delaney lowered his head, but arched up his eyebrows. "Later, son. You look spent. We also got Doc Conway right there to check you out."

"Yeah, I am pretty well spent. But—"

A female voice interrupted. "John!" Mary Fahey sprang from the crowd. She wrapped her arms around Butch's neck and gave him a kiss and a hug.

Delaney whispered to his assistant, Joe Casey. "Me and Captain Oliver will question Strewl in the bedroom. You and the Chief can take Snyder out to the porch."

Delaney saw Hynes quietly enter the living room and stand at attention by the door. He dipped his head and patted his side coat pocket, indicating he had recovered the pistol.

Delaney gave Doctor Conway a poke in the ribs and the doctor followed him as he pushed through the crowd around Butch. Delaney shook Butch's hand and bobbed his head. "John, the doctor wants to rub you down with alcohol and help you clean up. You don't want to look like a hobo for the rest of your life."

Delaney added in a low voice, barely moving his lips, "Don't say a thing." Then he raised his voice and said, "Take care of him, Doc—this man's been through a lot."

Delaney waited until the doctor disappeared into the bathroom with Butch before moving closer to Strewl. He pulled on his lip for a moment. "Mr. Strewl, you did one helluva job. If you could answer a few questions, it might help us locate the place where they held Mr. O'Connell."

A hand pulled Strewl by the shoulder and turned him around. Another hand shook Strewl's hand like a water pump. "I'm Captain Oliver from New York. The family owes you a lot of gratitude, Mr. Strewl. We'd like—"

Snyder stepped forward. "Not without me you don't—I'm his attorney. Manny, don't say a word unless—"

Strewl smiled. "Got it covered, Lou." He took a roll of money from his pocket. "Saved Mr. O'Connell $2,500. Right here. Only took out a bit for expenses."

Delaney took the cash and handed it to Joe Casey. "We'll need this for evidence." He pulled Strewl by the arm toward the bedroom. "Sure you weren't followed? That was a lot of cash to be carrying around."

"Don't think so."

Snyder raised his voice. "Manny, I'm telling yuh—yuh don't have to talk to them."

"I'm fine, Lou."

Captain Oliver closed the door after Delaney escorted Strewl into the bedroom. He moved the vanity chair next to the black steamer trunk at the foot of the bed. "Have a seat, Mr. Strewl. This won't take long."

Strewl took a seat and crossed one leg over the other. Captain Oliver sat on the trunk facing Strewl and leaned forward. "Tell me about these guys you met, Mr. Strewl. How tall were they? What kind of complexion did they have? Any scars? Did they speak with an accent of any sort?"

Strewl rubbed his forehead for a moment while he stared at his feet. He had to tell Captain Oliver something, but not anything that would connect himself to the kidnap plot. "Well," he said, "it was dark mostly. Didn't see much."

Captain Oliver sat up straight. "Thought you made the money exchange yesterday afternoon."

"Well, yeah. I thought you meant the first time in Albany. It was late when I met them."

"The first time, Mr. Strewl? So you met them in Albany and New York City—on several occasions? How many times did you meet them?"

Strewl licked his lips. He had already told both his attorney and Dan O'Connell he had met the kidnappers. Better keep the answers vague, he thought. "Met them a couple of times, but only once in Albany. The rest were in New York. Usually around midnight."

Delaney, who was standing behind Strewl, nodded his head, indicating that he wanted Captain Oliver to press Strewl further. Oliver continued. "Let's go back to Albany, Mr. Strewl. You said you met one of them here. Can you describe this person? His size, his hair or eye color? Anything unusual about the guy?"

Strewl dropped his foot to the floor and looked at the ceiling. He knew he had to be careful because the police would check out his story. "Well, it was on Maiden Lane one night. There was a little car accident. Guy comes up behind me and says meet him at the Mohawk Hotel at midnight."

Captain Oliver clapped his hands. "That's great, Mr. Strewl. So you met this guy face to face. What'd he look like?"

Strewl's eyes opened wide. He'd been caught. He had just admitted he met a kidnapper and had a conversation with him. Now he had to dodge the question on what James Sweeney looked like. "Well, like I said, in Albany he came up from behind me so I didn't see much. At the Mohawk, was late at night—and he kept his hat pulled down over his eyes."

Strewl noted Captain Oliver's expression, how he half closed one eye. It was a look of disbelief so Strewl threw him a bone. "I can tell you he was a tall skinny guy. Wore a long coat and talked in a low voice. He sounded like an American. I was sure nervous. Thought maybe the guy was going to toss me in a ditch like what one of the letters said they'd do, yuh know?"

"Yes I do, Mr. Strewl. It's unfortunate you can't give us a better description."

Oliver listened to the rest of Strewl's story of the Mohawk Hotel meeting while he thought about who to send to Schenectady to check out the story. He wanted to determine what the late night visibility would allow one to see from the streetlights on a summer night. It sure sounded strange that Strewl could see street signs but couldn't give a better description of a person an arm's length away.

Strewl finished his Albany story and began fanning himself with his hat. Captain Oliver reached over and tapped his knee. "Good work, Mr. Strewl. We'll check with the hotel clerk. Maybe he saw something. Now tell me about your New York meetings."

Strewl scratched at his eyebrows. He didn't know what the Mohawk hotel clerk saw or would say. Then he remembered and felt huge relief. Sweeney had not entered the hotel and the clerk would confirm his alibi about being in Schenectady. Neither the clerk or elevator operator would have come out of the hotel, so Strewl figured there was no one to contradict his version of the events. He'd been interrogated by police on other occasions and knew they would check out his story so he decided to tell Oliver things about his New York trips that would confirm his story and make it believable. He did not notice when Captain Oliver flicked his nose with his finger.

Strewl loosened his tie and began his story with information he'd seen in the newspapers and what the ransom notes had said, for he presumed Dan O'Connell would have discussed that with everyone. "Well, the letters said keep my shades down as a signal. Sometimes I got a call at the Newsroom on Beaver Street. Then I'd—"

The bedroom door creaked open. A tall medium built man with a charcoal gray suit coat draped over his arm came in and stood next to Strewl. Captain Oliver stood up. "Mr. Strewl, this is Detective James O'Connell. He is my most experienced detective when it comes to mobsters and kidnappings. He came up with me early yesterday morning. He was born and raised in New York City so if you give him some landmarks as to where you were we might be able to find out where the kidnappers were hiding Mr. O'Connell. It's the hideout we're looking to find."

Strewl faked a smile. He needed time to think. He said, "Say, Detective—are you related to Dan O'Connell?"

The detective took a pad and pencil from his coat pocket and grinned. "No—not that I'm aware. Don't mind me, Mr. Strewl, I just want to take a few notes. I don't want to forget anything and go off in the wrong direction."

Strewl glanced at Delaney, standing beyond the detective's right shoulder. The district attorney had his arms crossed, his bottom lip turned out, and his glasses halfway down his nose. He looked like a schoolteacher.

Strewl licked his lips. "Been a long day, yuh know? I might be a bit fuzzy."

Delaney pushed up his glasses. "Not much longer, Mr. Strewl. Just a few facts to get us started—then we'll let you go and get some rest. You deserve it. You've been doing a great job here and we all appreciate it."

Strewl began with his first trip to New York and how he had broken down and had to hire a cab. He described his second trip to New York, but forgot where he parked so he added in a place he had visited before. "On one trip, I parked in the lot next to Joe's Spaghetti house. Was early, so grabbed a bite and saw a movie. Bumped into some friends. Got their address if you want them."

Detective O'Connell scribbled a note. "Very good, Mr. Strewl. That's a big help. Sounds like you spent a lot of time in New York discussing the payoff. How many men were there?"

"Four or five, I guess."

"What'd they look like?"

Strewl pulled at his ear lobe. He knew he couldn't describe any of the New Jersey guys or his own friends. He dodged the question. "Cheese-us—it was dark, I tell yuh. I always met them about midnight. Never got a good look at them, cause they shoved me into the back of a car."

"A car you say. What kind of car? Could you make out the make or model? Maybe the color?"

"Well, it came up from behind and blinded me by the headlights."

"Really?"

Strewl watched as Detective O'Connell exchanged glances with the others. He didn't think they were buying his story but he continued. "I think maybe the car was dark blue, maybe black. Think it was a Ford, but it had big headlights like a Chevy."

Assistant District Attorney Joe Casey entered the room. "Troopers swept the area. They weren't followed."

Captain Oliver cleared his throat. Strewl turned his back to Casey. He didn't see Casey tip his head at Detective O'Connell telling him it was his turn to interview Louis Snyder and compare stories.

Oliver scratched his jaw. "Tell me about the other trip to New York, Mr. Strewl."

The change of topics made Strewl rest easier. Maybe these guys were buying his fairy tale story of the first meeting with the kidnappers.

"My attorney *and* Mr. O'Connell said I should meet these guys, so I did. This time they made me wear smoked glasses."

"Terrific, Mr. Strewl! That means you must have seen them for a few seconds while you put on the glasses. Were they the same people as before? Can you describe them for me?"

A big lump formed in Strewl's throat. He'd been trapped into admitting he could have possibly seen the kidnappers. He said to himself, just give them a few nuggets of information, and keep it vague. "Well, some little guy shoved me in the back seat from behind. Never really saw him."

"The driver then. You had to have seen him."

He thought about Sonny McGlone for a second. "Sort of. Just a little in the mirror. He had big eyes and thick black eyebrows."

Oliver pointed. "That's exactly what we need, Mr. Strewl. Good job. Any little detail can help. Now if there was a driver like you said and a guy shoved you from behind, it stands to reason there were others in the car. How many others were there?"

Strewl picked his teeth with his fingernails for a moment. Oliver had just boxed him in so he had to provide a reasonable answer. "There was another guy in the back seat. He was slim. Because the little guy shoved me in and onto the back floor I only saw the back of the head of the front seat passenger. Didn't—"

"What color hair?"

"Don't—"

"Was he old?

"Like I said, I didn't—"

"An Italian then."

"Whaddya mean Ital—"

"Was the guy a Jew?"

Strewl shrugged. "Who's to say what a Jew looks like?"

"Before they forced you to put the glasses on, Mr. Strewl—did you see a plate number?"

The questions were coming at Strewl like spitfire. He cried out, "Plate number! These mugs threaten to kill me—dump me in a ditch! Who's thinking about a plate number?"

Oliver's head dropped. The detective was an old hand at this work. He knew that the momentum had been broken, the interrogation was over. He sighed. "See your point, Mr. Strewl. It's late. You should rest, freshen up your memory."

He escorted Strewl back to the living room where Louis Snyder was waiting. "Mr. Strewl was most helpful. We just need to have his statement. A steno over at the courthouse can take it down tomorrow, after you both rest up some. For now, I'll have an officer escort you back to Albany—first class all the way."

The detectives stood outside and watched as Strewl got behind the wheel and Snyder took the passenger seat of the Pontiac. An Albany police car swung out in front and the driver waved his arm out the window, signaling Strewl to follow.

District Attorney John Delaney stepped over to Detective O'Connell. "What'd you get?"

The detective held his notepad in the air. "Strewl left Snyder alone most of the time, so there's not much there. The point of most interest is that Mr. Manny Strewl, bootlegger and burglar, does a favor for the O'Connell family even though the kidnappers threaten to kill him. And though he spent a lot of time with the kidnappers, he claims he did not see or does not remember most anything we ask him—doesn't even know who shoved him into a car. He's got a pat answer for everything. I'd say he's either part of the three blind mice—or guilty as hell."

Delaney huffed. "All's I got are the eleven letters in Strewl's name from his driver's license, which do look similar to the writing on the letters, plus his association with John Oley. I can prove he's part of the three blind mice, but not that's he's guilty—damn it!"

Captain Oliver placed his hands on his hips. "Can't prove it yet. But wait a while. Strewl will make a mistake. All we gotta do is squeeze him a little. In the meantime, the escort I sent along will keep an eye on him while we check his story."

Delaney shook his head side to side. "A rubber-hosed confession won't cut it in court."

Captain Oliver stepped forward and let out a deep rumbling chuckle. "Mr. Delaney, that's why I brought up Detective James O'Connell. He has a way with suspects. He'll trip up Strewl."

Delaney looked Detective O'Connell in the eye. "So what's your plan?"

O'Connell gave a wide grin. "I'll use the soft sell."

Part II
The Trial

Part II – The Trial
Chapter 18
Evidence or Frame Up

Butch was returned to his uncle's lake house on the first day of August. Two days later, with the weather hot enough to fry eggs on the sidewalk, a policeman galloped up North Pearl Street and stopped next to a man reading a newspaper at the bus stop. Gasping for air and wiping sweat from his face, the patrolman huffed, "Detective O'Connell...Mr. Delaney...sent me. They broke Strewl's story. Said the parking lot, next to Joe's Spaghetti House, where Strewl said he parked his car? Said it's been closed for a while now. They want you to pick Strewl up for further questioning. Oh, and Mr. Delaney said something...something about a soft sell."

Detective O'Connell waved his paper in the air. "Follow me."

Across the street, Detective Dolan quit looking at the men's clothing in the store window and moved closer to the man some little distance away. "You're Manny Strewl, are you? Guy that's been in the papers?"

Strewl backed away. "Buzz off! I'm tired of reporters."

Dolan caught him by the arm. "I'm Detective Dolan of the—"

Strewl shoved Dolan aside. "Right! And I'm John Rockefeller!"

Dolan yelled, "Hey!"

Strewl cocked his fist and took a swing. Dolan ducked but came up quick and slammed Strewl against the window frame. The window rattled like thunder. Strewl body-slammed Dolan backward, sending him against a phone booth. Dolan bounced right back. He socked Strewl in the stomach and shouted, "I said—I'm a detective!"

Detective O'Connell rushed up and hollered, "Hold it!" He grabbed Dolan's raised fist. "Mr. Strewl, are you all right? And by the way, this fella is a detective."

Strewl looked a bit wobbly on his feet but his voice was clear. "Yeah, guess I'm all right."

"Glad to hear that, Mr. Strewl, because we need your help. There's some stuff we need you to check out. How about coming along with us to the courthouse?"

"The courthouse?"

"Mr. Strewl, we need your help. And tell you what...we'll take you in the back way, so there won't be any reporters to bother you. No one will know you're helping us." Strewl still looked undecided so O'Connell put some bait on the hook. "Bet yuh Albany will be willing to treat you to a nice steak dinner, to help settle your stomach."

O'Connell turned, still making eye contact with Strewl, and when he took a step forward Strewl fell into step beside him. Dolan and the patrolman followed. Strewl glanced over his shoulder with narrowed eyes and growled, "Better be a damn big steak."

When they trooped through the back door of the Albany Courthouse it was Detective Dolan who pulled the door shut and thus symbolically closed the physical phase of the kidnapping of John O'Connell, Junior. From here on out the action would consist of quite a few battles—and all of them played out in words between opposing attorneys.

Lawyers would argue over whether Dolan and Strewl had a fight or a shoving match. They would argue about whether Strewl was under arrest. They would argue about who wrote the ransom notes. The only thing no one would have reason to argue about was what happened on this day. It was, undeniably, the last day Manny Strewl was a free man.

He was led down the back hallway to a small room furnished with one table and a couple of chairs. There were bars on the window. Detective James O'Connell motioned Strewl to take a seat at the table. "Need some water?"

Strewl turned down the offer. O'Connell rubbed his forehead. "Mr. Strewl, I'll have this officer keep you company so no one bothers you, and I'll go order that steak I promised."

Strewl gave the patrolman a sideways stare. "Want a baked potato, too. And I like my steak rare."

"You're my kinda guy, Mr. Strewl. Be right back."

O'Connell closed the door behind him. In the hallway he met Detectives Gannon and Hynes and told them he needed some writing paper. Hynes stopped a passing patrolman. "Bring us some writing paper, will yuh?"

Gannon lowered his voice. "Jimmy, have you met Detective James O'Connell? From our homicide division."

Hynes scratched his forehead with his thumbnail. "Yeah. Met him briefly the other night out at Dan O'Connell's lake house." He reached to shake O'Connell's hand. "Pretty ritzy of Delaney, having a homicide detective work the case before a murder has occurred. Strewl's not even dead yet."

Gannon chuckled. "Jimmy, this guy happens to be the best con man in the department. He's pulled more confessions from suspects than you can shake a stick at, and best part is, they hold up in court." Turning to the detective he was praising Gannon said, "So tell us, what do you have in mind for our good citizen—Mr. Manny Strewl?"

James O'Connell took two steel pens from his inside coat pocket. "One of these is a fine point, the other a stub. Delaney wants a larger sample of Strewl's handwriting. I'll have him write a story, and Delaney's assistant is coming over later, bringing Photostats of the ransom notes."

A patrolman rushed up and handed Hynes a stack of blank writing paper. O'Connell said, "No lines. Yeah, these'll do."

The patrolman started walking away but O'Connell called him back. "Was about to forget. I need one takeout order. Deliver it to the interrogation room nearest the back exit. One steak and a big baked potato. And make sure the steak's rare."

The patrolman left and Gannon and Hynes exchanged puzzled looks. O'Connell grinned. "A condemned man always gets a last meal," he said and turned and strolled back down the hall. As he opened the door he raised his voice and called out, "Make sure it's rare."

He closed the door, set the stack of paper on the table and took off his suit coat. "Be awhile on the steak," he said. He stood at the end of the table where Strewl was seated. "Is it true what I was told? You were the one delivered all the ransom notes to Mr. O'Connell?"

"Most of 'em. Kidnappers wanted them all back."

O'Connell tilted his head. "That's bad for us, since we can't prove who wrote them."

Strewl's eyebrows arched but fell again when O'Connell added, "But we can prove who didn't write them, Mr. Strewl. We just need a sample of your handwriting to show that you were not involved."

"But I'm not."

O'Connell waved the pens. "We all know that, Mr. Strewl—but you know how lawyers are. To make sure they know I told you to write, I'll place my own initials on the back of the paper. Watch me."

He printed *JOC* and flipped the page over and slid it in front of Strewl. "There you go. Now everyone knows I watched you write. Here, use my pen. I'll tell you what to write." He moved behind Strewl and began dictating a letter.

MY BROTHER LOUIE IS DOING VERY G
AND HE EXPECTS TO BE OUT OF THE HOS
SOME TIME NEXT MONTH

WOULD YOU BE KIND ENOUGH TO FIND OUT H
IT WOULD COST TO BUY A NEW CAMP UPON S
LAKE
WEN

WHEN YOU SEE JACK SOLOMON WILL YO
KIND ENOUGH TO ASK HIM ABOUT THE NEW
THAT HE BOUGHT LAST SUMMER AS I WO
LIKE TO KNOW HOW GOOD THE MOTOR ST
UP THIS WILL GIVE ME SOME GOOD PO
I MAY SAVE MONEY TO THE EXTEND OF
BY SAVING THIS G I WILL GIVE YOU
OF ONE HUNDRED AND FIFTY DOLLAR
AT ONCE BECAUSE IF I BUY THE CAMP
SARATOGA LAKE I WILL MEET THE MOT

ONE TWO THEE
MY ADDRESS IS NUMBER 16 25 RICHARD
ALBANY NEW YORK
RENEE DEVOE WAS OVER TO THE HOUS
WNTS TO BE REMEMBER TO YOU DEWE
A NICE GIRL FOR A GOOD F AND
THAT SHE WILL NOT GET MIXED UP WIT
OF THAT CROWD UP AT GLENS FALLS

1234567 8910
12 7890

1234 5 7891

O'Connell took the written paper and smiled. "A little hard
to read, Mr. Strewl. Let's try another but use the other pen. It's

got a better point." He initialed the back of another blank
sheet. "Try writing this," and again he moved behind Strewl.

PLEASE COME OVER TO MY HOUSE AND
BRING WITH YOU THE PACKAGE THAT I
LEFT ON THE PIANO IN YOUR LIVING ROOM
LAST SUNDAY NIGHT IF YOU CARE TO BRING
GEOTGE WITH YOU PHONE ME AND I WILL
PREPARE A NICE DINNER FOR ALL

I DONT KNOW IF I TOLD YOU THAT THE
RADIO IS OUT OF ORDER AND THE NEXT TIME
THAT YOU SEE GOS TELL HIM THAT HE WAS A
FINE MUG FOT STICKING WITH A FINE PIECE
OF JUNK I DID NOT EXPECT GUS TO STICK
ME WITH A PIECE OF JUNK AFTER PAYING HIM
THE TOP PRICE
GUS KNOWS HOW WELL I TREATED HIM WHEN
WE HAD THE TRUCKS WORKING AND FOR YOUR
INFORMATION I SPILT WITH HIM TWENTY
G'S IN MY OPINION HE IS NOTHING BUT A
CHEAP CHISLER AND IF HE DONT MAKE GOOD
ON THIS BUM RADIO I NEVER WANT TO MEET
OR SEE HIM AGAIN GUS BROTHER IS A DECENT
FELLOW AND I WAS ONLY TO GLAD TO GIVE HIM
THE LOAN OF 2 G'S TO OPEN UP THE JOINT
AND IF HE NEEDS TWO MORE G'S TO FIX UP THE
BEER GARDEN I WILL ONLY BE TOO GLAD TO
LET HIM HAVE THIS MONEY

O'Connell took the writing and studied it for a moment.
"This should do, Mr. Strewl. I'll have copies made so—"

A soft knock sounded at the door. O'Connell opened it slightly then pulled it wide and admitted Assistant District Attorney Joe Casey and Detective Edward Fitzgerald.

Casey had been in the District Attorney's office for a number of years and was a younger and slimmer version of his boss, John Delaney. He wore the same kind of frameless glasses, had a chin that was beginning to sag and was short in stature. He was also careful to buy suits unlike the ones his boss wore.

Casey beamed a smile and said, "We're about to make an arrest."

They all stared at Strewl. A chill gripped his body and he sank his fingernails into his thigh to keep from screaming out his fright. His throat tightened as he exchanged looks with the two detectives, but they were not reaching for the handcuffs he knew they carried, they were just staring at him, probably trying to trip him up, get him to admit he'd done something wrong.

Strewl decided they were waiting for him to react so he broke into a grin. He chuckled and said, "Who yuh gonna arrest?"

They brought in some more chairs. Detective Fitzgerald took a seat next to Strewl who gave him a sideways glance. Strewl's main attention was on Joe Casey who was seated across from him.

Casey said, "Got some people downstate for you to identify, Mr. Strewl."

Strewl relaxed his grip on his thigh. So they weren't after him, they were after other suspects, and the wrong ones at that. "Glad to help. Who yuh want me to identify?"

Casey knew Strewl was not likely to say anything that would give him away. "Mr. Strewl, do you know the Grossi brothers? Or a Frank Russo?"

Strewl covered his mouth to hide his glee. "In my business I run into a lot of people. Can't remember them all."

"Understand, Mr. Strewl. Unfortunately, they're downstate—in Monticello. It's a long drive, so you can stay here overnight and we'll get a real early start in the morning."

"Hey, wait a minute! Am I—"

"Just a material witness, Mr. Strewl."

Strewl locked his lips. This sure felt like a trap…but they couldn't prove anything.

Detective O'Connell stepped forward. "Don't forget, Mr. Strewl, your steak is on the way."

O'Connell moved behind Strewl again and said, "Mr. Casey, Mr. Strewl wrote out these sample stories. I initialed the backs so there will be no confusion about anything. I'd like to have these Photostatted and have Mr. Strewl recheck them, so there's no slip up."

Casey took the prearranged hint. "Good idea, Detective. We sure don't want to convict the wrong guy. Which brings me to my visit."

Casey handed Strewl one of the steel pens. "We need a few more samples of your writing, Mr. Strewl. Please write, 'Manny Strewl, Personal.'"

Strewl did as instructed. Casey looked over the writing. "Hard to read. Do it again, but this time spell your name S-t-r-o-l-l—and underline it."

Strewl followed instructions. He recalled how Detective O'Connell initialed the earlier writings so he pushed the new sample to Detective Fitzgerald. "You get to initial this, so we all know who had me to write it."

Fitzgerald wrote his initials and abruptly Detective O'Connell leaned over the table and said, "Just to make sure there's no confusion, Mr. Strewl, I'll add my initials too."

Casey gave Strewl another blank sheet. "Try this, Mr. Strewl. Write a letter to Mr. O'Connell, telling him everything is alright."

Casey watched as Strewl scratched out 'Dan.' Pointing to a space below the word, Casey said, "Start here and write, 'So far so good. Things are starting to move.'" He proceeded to dictate the exact words of the ransom note later identified as Exhibit Number 8.

Strewl was more than a little uneasy. Some of the wording sounded familiar. Was it one of the letters he wrote? He couldn't voice his thoughts because the letter had gone to Dan O'Connell—and Dan hadn't showed it to him.

He slid the page to Fitzgerald and said dryly, "Make sure your initials are clear." Over his shoulder he said to O'Connell, "Yours too."

As O'Connell penned his initials he told Strewl not to worry. "We'll all say we told you to write these."

Casey gave Strewl another blank sheet. "Just a few more, Mr. Strewl. Don't want to confuse your handwriting with that of anyone else. We want to compare it to samples from the Callegari brothers."

Casey dictated the ransom note that would become Exhibit Number 1. "Write, 'I am being held for ransom. No period. I am getting the best of care but—"

Strewl jerked his head back. "Hey, wait a minute! I saw this in the papers. It's one of the ransom notes. You're trying to frame me!"

Casey threw open his arms. "No, we're not, Mr. Strewl— these detectives will vouch for you. They even put their initials on the backs. There's no way to frame you for writing the ransom notes. As a double check, I'll let you look at the Photostat when we're done, and tomorrow the Callegari brothers will get their turn. You'll see."

Strewl touched a finger to the paper. "I guess it's okay, since the detectives signed."

Casey pointed to the space below the words 'I am held.' "Start the line here. Write, 'please do whatever they ask...'" At several points Casey gave instructions about spelling: racketeer with two T's and one E, column with two M's. When all the remaining ransom notes had been dictated, Casey handed them to Detective O'Connell with instructions to have them Photostatted and returned to the room so Mr. Strewl could inspect them.

O'Connell nodded and exited. In the hallway he found a patrolman holding a large white folder standing next to Detectives Gannon and Hynes. He passed off the job of getting the pages copied to the patrolman, who hurried away to get the job done. Then Detective James O'Connell leaned against the wall and let out a lungful of air. He now held the white folder, which he held up. In a low voice he said, "These are Photostats of the real ransom notes. Will be interesting to see if Strewl can tell the difference. We're taking him to Monticello tomorrow to identify some possible suspects. That'll give the lab the full day to check out his handwriting samples and let Delaney make a decision."

Another patrolman came hurrying down the hall with a covered tray. O'Connell said, "Strewl's last supper. Give me a few minutes before you deliver it."

Back in the interrogation room O'Connell said, "Here yuh go, Mr. Strewl." He spread the Photostats of the real ransom notes on the table, careful not to let Strewl see that there were no initials on the back. "Now, can you tell me who wrote these notes, Mr. Strewl?"

Strewl bent close. When he looked up he leaned back and stretched his mouth in a wide grin that revealed his cigar-stained teeth. "I'd stake my life on it. That's my handwriting."

There was a knock on the door. O'Connell opened it. "Your steak has arrived, Mr. Strewl. A just reward."

The next day, at the Third Precinct Police Station, Detective Hynes was reviewing the statements of George Keiss and Henry Tobin when Gannon walked up to the desk and said, "Nothing new from my undercovers. Any word on the Grossi brothers, or Strewl's handwriting samples?"

Hynes arched his back and stretched his arms. "Nah, not yet. But you should have seen the parade this morning. Albany Police cars, State Trooper cars. One car full of G-men, and Joe Casey leading the way, all headed for Monticello. If anything, it'll at least put the Grossi brothers on notice they're being watched, maybe slow them down some."

The phone rang and Hynes reached for it. "Albany Police Department. Detective Hynes speaking…Yes sir."

Hynes handed the phone to Gannon. "DA named Clinton, from across the river. Wants to talk with you."

Gannon took the phone. "This is Detective Joseph Gannon of the New York City Police. How can I help you, sir?"

A moment later Gannon said, "I'll have to clear it with Captain Oliver and Mr. Delaney, but with a chance to bag Big Charlie Scarnici it shouldn't be a problem."

Gannon hung up the phone and whistled softly. "City of Rensselaer wants to borrow some of my guys to work their bank robbery case. Said they found Big Charlie Scarnici's fingerprint on a counter."

Hynes stuffed some papers into a folder and put on his new cotton suit coat. "Was on my way to Delaney's office with these papers anyway. We can put it to him."

The secretary waved them through to Delaney's office and Hynes dropped a file folder on the desk. "Reports on the Dewaynesburg lead. It was a dead end. But we discovered that Abe Friedman's brother works with Strewl's attorney, Louis Snyder, so we instructed our guys to back off on him. We also got a call from the Rensselaer County DA's office. Mr. Clinton wants to borrow some of Detective Gannon's men to work last May's bank robbery."

Delaney turned his gaze to Gannon. "If you don't need the men, I'm good with that idea."

Hynes asked, "How about Strewl, Mr. Delaney? Any word about him?"

"Still waiting. No word from Casey and his adventure in Monticello either. For now, it's a waiting game."

The intercom buzzed. "Mr. Delaney, Agent Cullen on the line, says he has some new information and it's urgent that he talk with you."

Delaney sighed. "Just what I need. Well, put him through."

The phone jangled and he reached for the receiver. "Agent Cullen. I was just discussing the case with my detectives. Our lab is still examining Strewl's handwriting samples. And so far I have no word from Joe Casey, or from your agents who accompanied him to Monticello."

A few seconds later Delaney's eyes bulged. "Well, Agent Cullen. We've hit the mother lode. Where is Gross now?...Ok, I'll send Detective Gannon back down. He can bring you up to date and give you a hand. If it all comes together, I expect to be ready for trial by mid-September. Look for Gannon sometime tomorrow."

Delaney hung up the phone and bit his cheek to keep from smiling big. With a straight face and deadpan tone he said, "The Feds got a witness who heard and saw Strewl and Oley planning the kidnapping."

Both Hynes and Gannon arched their eyebrows and Delaney continued. "A guy by the name of Sam Gross told the U.S. Consulate General in Canada he witnessed the planning of the O'Connell kidnapping in a New York City hotel room. Said both Strewl and Oley were there, plus a guy named Phil Zeigler. And he said Strewl appeared to be the ringleader.

Gannon, the Feds are bringing this witness back to New York and want you there when they question him."

Hynes smacked his lips. "We got him!"

Delaney held up his palm. "Almost. I'm still—"

Another phone rang and Delaney reached for his direct line to the crime lab. "Yeah....Ok. That's all I needed."

When he hung up he faced the detectives and narrowed his eyes. "Now we got him. Sergeant Butts says the lab can prove Stewl wrote the first two ransom notes. They're still working on the rest."

"You want us to arrest Strewl when they bring him back?"

Delaney shook his head. "No. First things first. When Strewl sets foot back in Albany County we'll arrest him for mail fraud—since the ransom notes were mail. That'll make it a federal crime with a long jail time. The lab said he wrote at least two of the ransom letters. I'll have three other experts confirm their results. Assuming this witness Sam Gross pans out, I'll add in the charge of conspiracy to commit kidnapping. The kidnapping charge will be the bow that ties the noose on Mr. Manny Strewl."

Delaney had his secretary call Dan O'Connell. When she confirmed that he was at home the district attorney said to the detectives, "Grab your coats. Dan's gonna be thrilled to hear the news about an eyewitness."

An hour later they arrived at the lake house and Delaney threw up his arm in greeting to Butch O'Connell, who was sitting under a shade tree near the lake. Inside, the visitors found Dan O'Connell in a tee shirt and wrinkled pants and bare feet. He had been reading the paper. He switched off the tabletop radio and greeted his visitors. "Good to see you. I'm guessing you've come to interview my nephew again?"

"No, Dan," Delaney said, "I've come to bring you some good news. I've issued an arrest warrant for the ring leader of the kidnap gang."

Dan was still holding the folded newspaper. He dropped it. "Well, that is news. Who is it?"

"Manny Strewl. We have evidence—"

"What?!" Dan's yell was so loud it rattled the windows. His face turned beet red and he took a deep breath before he could speak. "You're telling me…Manny Strewl? The guy who helped me get my nephew back, the guy who pretended to be my friend—you're telling me he was one of the *kidnappers*?!"

"Actually, we believe Strewl planned the entire episode. We also believe—"

"I'll kill him!" O'Connell reached for the table drawer. "Where's my gun?!"

Hynes and Gannon lurched forward and caught hold of him. They crashed into the table, which busted apart and all, including the radio, landed on the floor.

Hynes was on the bottom. He yelled, "Get the gun, Joe, get the gun!"

Gannon snared the revolver from the table's rubble and hopped across the room. O'Connell pushed himself to his feet. Hynes sprang up and grabbed hold of him and was pulled him across to where Gannon stood.

Delaney sidestepped in front of O'Connell and put his hands on his shoulders. "No, Dan! Let me handle it. We'll get Strewl the legal way. You have to trust me on this—we're going to get him!"

A tense moment passed before O'Connell's arms dropped limply to his sides. "Maybe you're right. There's a better way to handle it." He ran a hand over his brow and exhaled. "My apologies. I was upset."

Hynes said, "No problem, Mr. O'Connell. I'd be upset too if it were my kin that got kidnapped."

Gannon put the revolver in his pocket. Hynes straightened his rumpled shirt and wondered to himself about what Mr.

O'Connell had said. Was there something implied in the words 'a better way to handle it'?

Delaney ended the odd silence. "Well, I'm sorry, Dan. I came out to deliver good news, didn't mean to upset you. I *will* *get* Mr. Manny Strewl and Company. As a matter of fact, the FBI called just before we left and said they now have solid evidence against Strewl *and* John Oley."

O'Connell's head jerked up. "Oley too?"

"Afraid so. The Feds have a witness, so I'm sending Detective Gannon here back to New York to work with them, to make sure we get an airtight case against both of them. Now I suggest you get a bit of rest. We'll keep the gun for safekeeping, and if I were you I'd stay out of Albany, in case Strewl has friends we don't know about."

O'Connell put his hands to his head and slicked back his hair. "Yeah, sure. That's good advice." When his visitors left he watched from the window until their car disappeared, then crossed the living room and kicked at the broken table. He lifted the telephone receiver and dialed. "Hello, Solly? Got some news for yuh."

"Good or bad?"

"Depends on how you look at it. Just talked to Delaney. They're arresting Strewl for the kidnapping. Also sounds like John Oley was involved but Delaney didn't say he was going to arrest him yet."

"Those bastards! I know the cops down at the station. I'll get them to see that Mr. Manny Strewl gets a taste of Irish law."

Dan's chest was tight. He gripped the phone. "No, Solly. Delaney will convict, but I'll be the one to decide on the punishment. What I want you to do is get hold of Theodore Washington Dunn. He owes me a favor. Tell him I need a jury foreman."

"Sure thing, Danny."

"Mr. Manny Strewl is going to get a taste of O'Connell law."

O'Connell Law or Irish Law? Whichever it was, there was no doubt that Strewl suffered a severe beating, yet according to court records the answer to the question of who administered the punishment was never determined.

And in the end, the rigmarole of having Strewl copy all the ransom notes played against the prosecution. The assistant district attorney's misjudgment landed Delaney's 'solid case' in quicksand.

The defense argued that telling a person where to start, stop or how to spell words in a writing sample undermined the validity of the handwriting analysis. Only eighty words were used in comparison in the courtroom, and that was legal, but when the case went to the High Court someone did the math. Turned out those eighty words comprised a small percentage of the total. Did such a small percentage warrant sending a person to jail or execution? No, the High Court decided—and sided with the defense counsel.

Chapter 19
Scarnici Talks: The Inside Story

Defense Attorney Daniel Prior was built like a pine tree. His ashen gray hair was white at the sides. His black patent leather shoes sounded like a hollow cup on wood as he marched up to the third precinct desk sergeant. He removed a paper from his fitted navy blue sport coat and snapped it open with a flick of his wrist. "Writ of habeas corpus for Manny Strewl. Produce him now."

"Let me see if this is all in order, Mr. Prior."

"You've horsed around for the last couple of days, Sergeant. This is a court order!" Prior leaned over the desk and pointed to the judge's signature. "He's an Appellate Judge—and he does not live in Albany County."

"So I see. Better have the Chief take a look—we do want to follow proper procedure." Sergeant McKinney turned aside as he put the receiver of the desk phone to his ear. After a few muffled mumblings the sergeant announced that the Chief would be coming out shortly to personally take Mr. Prior to Mr. Strewl.

Minutes later a uniformed Chief Smurl rounded the corner and slipped on his glasses. "Good day, Mr. Prior. I was told you have some papers for me."

Prior glanced sideways at Sergeant McKinney and wrinkled his brow before handing the sheets to the Chief. "Yes, writ of habeas corpus for Manny Strewl. And no more stalling around, please."

Chief Smurl took the paper and read as he walked. "Stalling? Come now. With our limited space, we had to ensure Mr. Strewl was, uh, adequately taken care of." He held the paper in the air. "This seems in order."

Prior snatched it. "Damn right it is."

Chief Smurl stopped in his tracks. He lowered his voice to a crackling growl. "Mr. Prior, you're no longer a judge. I no longer have to laugh at your jokes or kiss your ass. You're in my house now. I make the rules here." He pointed at two patrolmen standing in front of a door down the hall. "He's down there."

Prior scuttled down the hall. At the door to the interrogation room he paused and looked back. "Trust me, Chief. You don't make all the rules."

Prior put his hand to the knob of the door and pushed. Inside he cried out, "God A'mighty, Manny! What the hell…?"

Manny Strewl was at a table with his head laid across with an outstretched arm. The other arm dangled lifelessly. He barely raised his head off his arm at the sound of Prior's voice. A brown circle at his left eyebrow faded to yellow as it extended to the middle of a swollen cheek. His blood-stained left eyelid drooped over his eye. On the right cheek there was a dark red blood blister. The right eye was swollen shut.

Prior rushed to Manny's side. Over his shoulder he yelled, "Get me a damn doctor!" He put a hand to Strewl's head and rubbed gently. "The cops do this to yuh, Manny?"

Chief Smurl came bustling in and stood near the table. He leaned toward Strewl. "What the hell—what's happened? Who did this? Just gimme a name!"

Strewl shimmied away from the Chief's voice and muttered, "Nobody – nobody!"

Prior went nose to nose with Smurl. "What kinda place yuh running here, Chief?"

"Counselor, this is news to me." He yelled to the patrolmen, "Get a doctor in here fast!"

Strewl gurgled, "It's a frame-up. They're trying to frame me. Made me write stuff—and switched 'em."

Chief Smurl stabbed the table with a finger. "Don't worry. I don't put up with this kinda stuff in my precinct. I'll personally investigate it."

***

Agent Cullen slapped his desktop. "Damn it all to hell! Those Albany cops—why, they could blow this whole case."

NYPD Detective Gannon shook his head. "Can't prove the cops did it."

Cullen waved a hand in the air. "Come on! People aren't that stupid. Guy has the hell kicked out of him in jail – and they don't know who did it?! A good defense attorney can get any statement the defendant says thrown out because of police intimidation."

Gannon said, "Yeah. Well, I checked with my undercovers. They said the Albany guys gave them the cold shoulder. I've sent them on home—except for three on loan to Rensselaer."

T.F. Cullen had been one of the initial hires by J. Edgar Hoover when the FBI was founded in 1919 and was now the FBI agent in charge of New York City. He had once been a lawyer, but craved more excitement. His time with the FBI had delivered more excitement than he'd bargained for. During a raid on a still he had been wounded in the stomach. Cullen was exacting in his work, careful to dot all "I's" and cross all "T's"—because he had seen local authorities bribed or bought off and suspects set free. Because of this distrust of small town policemen, he went out of his way to make sure he did not hand any defense lawyer a technicality that could let a suspect go free.

Gannon hefted a briefcase onto Cullen's desk. "In here you've got everything we have so far on the O'Connell kidnapping."

Cullen dialed two digits on his phone. A few seconds passed and he said, "Got something for yuh." Shortly thereafter a man knocked at the office door and Cullen handed him the briefcase. "Compare this to what we have."

During the silence that followed Gannon watched Cullen snap open a revolver and check to see that it was loaded. Cullen holstered the gun and said, "Don't get comfortable. I just spoke with your boss. You're working with me now—and we're about to head over to the Hotel New Yorker. We've got Sam Gross setting up a meeting with Phil Zeigler. The meeting's in room 3220 and we're right next door."

Gannon ensured his gun was loaded. "I've heard about Zeigler. What's he got to do with all this?"

Cullen grabbed his coat from a hook on the wall. "We set up a trap to snare the entire O'Connell kidnap gang in one swoop. Gross told us that Zeigler knows how to contact the various gang members."

"How straight up is this Gross character?"

Cullen set his hat on his head. "Tells a good story. Says he hosted John Oley and company for a few weeks last year in Canada. He overheard them talking about some big-time kidnapping. Then the first of this year Gross met Zeigler here in New York at the Century Hotel. Was in need of some help on a business deal."

"So who did Zeigler get?"

Cullen half closed an eye. "Among others, John Oley and Manny Strewl."

"That'll tie the two together!"

"There's more. Gross didn't think much about it till he saw the pictures of Oley and Strewl in the paper then he remembered something odd. Remembered that Zeigler said, 'Why get the old man? Get the kid. He's the prince among three kings.' So, Gross put two and two together and contacted the American Counsel in Windsor, who contacted the FBI. Gross has already convinced me and Mr. Hoover that he's on the level."

The wheels of Gannon's police mind were turning. "Sam Gross. Playing the good citizen, putting his friends behind bars. And he's doing this with no thought for himself or a reward? That'll go over good at trial."

Cullen snickered. "We told Gross the FBI has no authority regarding reward money—that's up to the family and the courts. We do, however, sometimes overpay expenses—if you know what I mean. Thing is, an eyewitness account trumps anything...including any Irish law the cops dish out."

They found the lobby of the Hotel New Yorker buzzing with activity. A well-dressed man folded his newspaper, left his chair and joined them at the elevator door. In a low voice with his head lowered the man said to Cullen, "Nothing new. Haven't seen anything of the west side mob, nor any of Dutch Schultz's men."

Cullen tipped his head toward Gannon. He also spoke in a low voice. "Detective Gannon, Agent Sisk." The two men shook hands, than Cullen said to Gannon, "The Durant car? Turns out the prints belong to George Garguillo. He's with Charles Harrigan and the Westside mob. They chum around with Dutch Schultz. We think they're probably involved somehow."

Gannon pushed up his cream-colored hat. "Yeah, I've mixed it up with some of Harrigan's men. Betcha they have Jersey plates."

"Yep. I read Detective Hynes's report. He saw Jersey plates on the night of July sixth. That's why you're here. You know the O'Connell case, plus Harrigan and his gang. We're gonna double-team Harrigan and Schultz. This O'Connell case may break them both."

They took the elevator to the thirty-second floor. When the door opened two men waiting to ride the elevator nodded at Cullen. In the hallway Cullen softly stepped by room 3220 and knocked gently at the room just beyond. The man who cracked the door and peeped out at them wore an exposed shoulder holster and a white shirt with rolled-up sleeves.

Cullen whispered over his shoulder to Gannon. "Keep quiet—a doctor's office."

Once inside, Gannon understood the joke. At the wall adjoining 3220 three men had stethoscopes plugged in their ears, listening at the wall. Gannon recognized one. Detective George Salayka was one of his own undercover cops.

Across the room, a man sitting on the bed next to the nightstand motioned them his way. The nightstand held a phone and a wire-recording device. The agent pulled back one earphone and whispered, "Zeigler just called Gross. Said Scarnici is hiding out due to some bank job. Wants to meet Gross at a saloon on Forty-ninth and Seventh. We sent two men to stake it out."

Cullen looked puzzled. Gannon pulled at his jaw and whispered, "Scarnici...bank job—yuh know, they found Scarnici's prints at the Rensselaer Bank and Trust. A cop was killed. That could be the reason Scarnici's hiding."

Cullen's eyes gleamed. "So, Big Charlie Scarnici, might be implicated in the O'Connell kidnapping and a bank robbery. We already know he's tied to Dutch Schultz. Maybe a triple play?"

***

Months later in early January 1934 the front tire on the police car dropped into an iced-over mud hole. Gannon braced himself by holding to the dashboard. Hynes maneuvered the police car past the snow banks and slowed for the turn onto the slick road called Broadway that would take them to Rensselaer, New York. Gannon had been recounting the details of a raid the previous September on 1448 Webster Avenue.

"It was Gross," he continued, "who set up Big Charlie Scarnici. It was apartment 5E. Scarnici had company that evening, some of his buddies over for a visit—including Zeigler and Tony Reino." Gannon chuckled. "Captain Oliver tackled Reino when he was set to jump out a window. Took both of us to haul him back in. It wouldn't have mattered much if Reino had got out; we had cops on every fire escape. So that's how it went, Jimmy—that's how we came by the cuffs and the dark glasses we handed over to Delaney."

Hynes said, "Do you remember, Joe, in one of Strewl's statements? He said when he met the kidnappers he was forced to wear dark glasses—so he wouldn't be able to identify them? Well, Delaney said the pair of glasses you found are circumstantial, can't really be linked to Strewl. But the handcuffs, there we have something. Delaney showed them to Butch O'Connell and he identified right off. The kid was smart—marked the cuffs with some scratches, and even identified two rust spots."

Gannon shook his head. "Some big time crooks. Between them, Scarnici and Zeigler had only ten bucks when we arrested them."

Gannon spotted more potholes ahead and reached for the dashboard again. "Anyway, in that raid last September, Dolan took Scarnici into the bathroom and closed the door. Don't know what happened, but everybody on our side heard Scarnici scream, 'I can give yuh O'Connell—for some consideration!'"

Hynes said, "Looks like Scarnici talks a lot, but I'm not convinced that what he says amounts to much."

A car coming toward them splashed slush onto the windshield. Hynes clicked on the windshield wipers. "We've had him locked up already five months and he's said nothing. But who knows? A little more jail time may soften him up."

Gannon sneezed and pulled out his handkerchief. After a bit he said, "On that same day of the raid, we got Charlie Herzog across town. Fool was using an alias: Little Charlie Shore. Also nabbed Freddie Plental. Scarnici led us to Ralph

Zucco in White Plains. The G-men raided the place and got him talking. He's the one said Scarnici was pissed at Oley for holding out on him, and that Oley and Strewl were in on the kidnapping together."

Hynes downshifted. "Uh-huh, probably the reason Scarnici offered to talk on the O'Connell case "for some consideration." He knew his goose was cooked either way. Too bad the Troy jury acquitted Shore and Reino. Because Reino was ready to talk before his attorney showed up. I'm hoping you guys can get him to talk before the O'Connell trial begins."

"You don't—? No one told you?

"Told me what?"

"They're dead. Reino and Shore. They're dead! We think Dutch Schultz had them rubbed out."

Hynes hit the brakes. A moment later when the friction had dried the brakes, a loud squeal sounded just like the warning that Mush Trachnier had heard the year earlier. The car stopped. "Shit! Reino was about to talk. He was one of our best leads."

Hynes faced Gannon with a wrinkled brow. "How do you know Dutch Schultz did it?"

Gannon shrugged. "We don't. Reino's attorney, name of Winters, bailed both of them out. Next day, they were both found dead. Winters works for Dutch Schultz, so we just put two and two together. You recall last year, when we met with a Mrs. Watkins and I said Schultz wouldn't take any undeserved heat. Reino, Shore…there yeah go."

A passing car splashed a rain of ice pellets onto the police car. Hynes shifted into gear and continued toward Rensselaer. As they reached the city limits he clicked his tongue and said, "At least Rensselaer has Scarnici in custody until his new trial."

"Right. I was much surprised that the jury acquitted Reino and Shore on the bank robbery charge. Seemed odd, like they were set on charging Scarnici. But at least bail wasn't set for him."

Hynes wagged his head. "No telling." A moment later he chuckled and said, "Yuh know, Joe, a few minutes ago the tires squealed when I stopped? I remember talking to Mush Trachnier. He said a squeaking tire outside his house about this time last year alerted him that guys were after him. The noise saved his butt! Maybe it's the same for us."

Gannon buttoned his winter coat as Hynes slowed and parked in front of Rensselaer's City Hall. "You mean like an omen, Jimmy?"

"Yeah."

As they approached the entrance Gannon said, "What's the district attorney's name?"

Hynes pulled the door open. "Henry Esmond Clinton. Locals call him the Gray Fox. Dunno why."

When Clinton's secretary showed the detectives into the district attorney's office, Gannon and Hynes knew immediately why the moniker fit the man at the desk. He had gray hair, a long pointed nose, small pinned-back ears and large dark eyes—just like a fox.

Clinton was reaching into a folder. He pulled out a sheet of paper and slid it between two books stacked on the corner of the desk.

He had been Rensselaer's District Attorney for a number of years. Most of the crimes he prosecuted were robberies. Very few had been murder cases. Hynes had wondered about Clinton's lawyerly ability when the jury acquitted Reino and Shore for the Rensselaer County bank robbery, but at least the bigger fish—Big Charlie Scarnici—was still in custody here. Hynes was looking forward to seeing this Gray Fox nail Scarnici at the retrial.

Clinton stood up. He shook hands and gave the detectives a letter before he sat back down. "That's a copy from the G-men.

It was smuggled out of Danamora Prison and given to Mrs. Lottie Coll."

Gannon looked up with a puzzled look. "Coll. That name's familiar."

Clinton rested his elbows on the chair arms and pressed his fingertips together. "Should be. Her husband was Vincent Coll. G-men found his body in a burnt-up car in White Plains. Think Big Charlie Scarnici did it."

Hynes whistled. "Says here that Scarnici is Dutch Shultz's star killer. Fifty or more bodies to his credit. Is this going to make your robbery case against Scarnici any easier?"

"Not my case, Detective. Yours." Clinton pressed the intercom button. "Send them in."

Clinton pointed to chairs against the wall. "Have a seat over there. Delaney won't put Scarnici on the witness stand. Who would believe a bloodthirsty killer? But I want you to hear this, might point you in the right direction."

Shortly Big Charlie Scarnici entered. He was handcuffed and with him was his attorney, the guy named Winters. Two uniformed police officers followed. Clinton asked them to wait outside.

Scarnici stood before Clinton's desk but looked toward Hynes and Gannon with a look of amusement. "Come to see the show, did yuh? I know who Gannon there is, been giving him the slip for years. Who's the other flatfoot?"

Clinton waved his hand. "Doesn't matter. They're here to witness your confession."

Winters blurted, "Immunity still in place?"

Clinton held up a sheet of paper to Winters but kept it out of reach. "Signed, sealed, and almost delivered. I held up my part of the bargain, now it's your turn."

Gannon and Hynes jumped to their feet. Gannon demanded, "What bargain? What kind of a deal did you make with this killer?"

Clinton tilted his head. "The bank robbery. Kidnapping too."

Hynes shouted, "What! You letting this bastard off the hook?"

Scarnici laughed aloud as Clinton waved his hand in the air again. "There are bigger things at stake here, Detective. I gave Mr. Scarnici full immunity for the Rensselaer County bank robbery and his part in the O'Connell kidnapping—in return for his information."

Attorney Winters cut in. "Don't forget the Trachnier episode."

Clinton nodded in agreement. "And information on the attempted Mush Trachnier kidnapping."

Hynes sat back down and slapped his leg. "Cheese-us! You paid too high a price."

Clinton shrugged. "Listen to what Mr. Scarnici has to say." He faced the prisoner. "Now, Mr. Scarnici, it's time for you to uphold your end of the deal. Tell us all about the O'Connell kidnapping."

Scarnici beamed a wide grin at the detectives, enjoying his moment in the limelight. "Well," he began, "was Strewl that planned the whole thing, set it all up—since Oley's crack at Trachnier was a big flop."

Hynes hunched forward and said, "Oley planned the Trachnier kidnapping?"

Scarnici shrugged. "Yeah. Right there on Market Street, at his brother's speakeasy, he came up with the plan. Strewl wadn't in on that one—he just helped plan the bank job. Oley too, but neither of 'em took part in any of the rough stuff."

"Why the Rensselaer bank?"

Scarnici cackled. "That's where the money is! Takes cash to run a kidnapping."

Hynes leaned back. He covered his face with his hands and muttered, "Cheese-us!"

For the next hour Scarnici gave his account of the Mush Trachnier and O'Connell kidnapping. When he came to the end of the confession he said, "That's all I know."

Gannon cut the still air. "You said Harrigan and Dugan were in on it. Recognize anyone else?"

"Nah, there were some others, but I only knew Harrigan and Dugan."

Winters held out his hand. "If you all are satisfied, I'll take that immunity agreement now."

Clinton glanced at the detectives who kept their silence, and handed it over. "Of course. Signed, sealed and now delivered."

Winters tucked the paper inside his black suit coat pocket and said, "Let's go." As Scarnici exited he called over his shoulder, "Pleasure doing business with yuh, detectives."

Clinton tilted back in his chair, fingers pressed against his lips, staring at the closed door. Hynes and Gannon left their seats by the wall. Hynes planted the palms of his hands on the desk. "Hell've high price to pay for that information."

Clinton rolled his eyes. "We'll see."

Gannon was about to speak when outside there was a commotion, someone shouting. Clinton reached to the corner of his desk and retrieved the paper he had hidden earlier between two books and said, "Wonder what all the commotion is about?"

In the hall a crowd was gathered around Winters and Scarnici. Clinton pushed through followed by Hynes and Gannon. Two uniformed police officers held Winters by his shoulders. Four officers held Scarnici's arms. The surrounding officers stood with their night sticks drawn and several had their hands on their gun butts.

Clinton waved at the officers restraining Winters. They released their hold. Winters stepped in front of the district attorney and said, "We had an agreement!"

Clinton turned a dead-meat stare toward Scarnici before turning a poker face to Winters. "We do have an agreement. I'm not charging your client with kidnapping or bank robbery." Clinton thrust the paper in his hand into Winters chest. He said in a voice for all to hear, "I am charging your client, Big Charlie Scarnici, with the first degree murder of Officer James Stevens, and the attempted murder of Officer Fred Rabe."

Clinton stepped back. He ordered, "Take him away!"

Scarnici began howling. "I didn't kill him! It was Reino—he was at the door. Was his gun—we exchanged guns in the car!" As the officers shoved Scarnici down the hall he shouted, "I wanna make a deal!" When the door leading to the jail closed behind them, silence reigned.

A few seconds passed. Gannon and Hynes stepped up on either side of Clinton. Gannon cocked his head. "You gonna make a deal with him?"

Clinton exhaled, and headed back to his office with Gannon and Hynes in his wake. As he walked Clinton said, "The G-men are digging up bodies all over White Plains. Scarnici will run out of breath before they run out of bodies." Back in his office he stood behind his desk facing Hynes and Gannon. "You two played your parts well."

Hynes said, "Whaddya mean?"

Clinton grinned. "I needed you two detectives to act angry over the immunity deal. It took everybody's mind off the happenings at the bank robbery—and helped sell the deal to Scarnici."

Gannon asked, "Mr. Clinton, I'm wondering. How do you know it was Scarnici that killed Stevens?"

Clinton rolled out his lips. "Elementary, Detective. Scarnici's the only one left alive."

Gannon exchanged a dumbstruck gaze with Hynes.

***

Since Scarnici gave his account of both the Trachneir and O'Connell kidnapping the authorities had a first hand account of what happened. They also knew a jury would not believe a blood thirsty killer on the witness stand. It always a questionable tactic on putting a known criminal such as Scarnici or person of shady dealings such as Sam Gross on the witness stand. The cops now knew what happened they just had to prove it.

It's unknown if the jury pool was tainted by the beating Strewl received. Strewl had taken a "right guy". The man whose family fed the residents of South Albany during holidays and warmed them in the winter. Some say Strewl deserved it. Some called it Irish Law.

Either way Scarnici got his in 1935 when his "deals" ran out and he was executed in Sing-Sing for the murder of Officer James Stevens.

Chapter 20
Opening Statements & Sam Gross

Albany's District Attorney, John Delaney, felt confident that he had a sure thing going as he headed into Manny Strewls's trial. He was banking on the confession of Big Charlie Scarnici, plus the testimony of Sam Gross and handwriting experts. Eight months had passed since Strewl's arrest, and Delaney had evidently forgotten the concerns Major John Warner expressed about the problem of not having the original ransom notes. He also, apparently, failed to take into account the ability of an attorney like Louis Prior to engage in smear tactics.

The trial would last three weeks. Delaney, and everyone else, would be surprised by the fire works ahead.

On the morning of March 2, 1934, light entered the drab mahogany-furnished courtroom through frost-covered windows. The only colors in the room were high on the walls, with the seal of New York set between the blue globes of Lady Liberty on the left and Lady Justice on the right. The flags of the United States and New York State stood at the corners. Spectators began to arrive at 9:30 that morning, as Deputy Sheriffs Frank Stanton and Charles McCarthy escorted Manny Strewl and his attorney, former judge Daniel Prior, to the defense table. The deputies took seats in the first row behind the railing and directly behind the accused.

At 10:00 an officer in a blue uniform with brass buttons down the front trumpeted, "Hear-ye, hear-ye—the Court of the State of New York is now in session. The Honorable Judge Gallup presiding. All rise."

The ashen hair and pale skin of the man entering through a side door was in stark contrast to the black robes that hid his physique. He took his seat and those close enough to see may have noted that his dark eyes behind wired-rimmed glasses seemed like rifle shots when he aimed them your way. Judge Gallup rapped his gavel and roared, "Courts in session. Mr. Delaney, begin."

Delaney adjusted his glasses and approached the jury box as flash bulbs flared from the cameras of reporters. He began. "The charges against Manny Strewl arise out of his participation in the seizure of John O'Connell, Junior, approximately eight months ago on July 7, 1933." For the next ten minutes he recounted the kidnap story, much of which had been in the newspapers.

Then it was Dan Prior's turn. Prior appeared to pose for the cameras, to accentuate his tall lean build as opposed to Delaney's penguin shape. Even the common spectator could tell that this man's suit was finely tailored while Delaney's was right off the rack. Prior placed his hands on the railing of the jury box and paused dramatically as though on a world stage. At his wrists gold cuff links gleamed. "I will show," he said, "that unknown kidnappers chose my client, and that Mr. Dan O'Connell chose my client's name from *a list he himself provided*. He begged my client to help him. Mr. O'Connell entrusted my client with forty thousand dollars to get his nephew back—which my client did. The O'Connells got their nephew back. And what did Manny Strewl get? NOTHING! Not a thanks, not a red cent. In fact, Manny Strewl is the victim of one of the worst plots that ever has come to my attention—a plot to railroad a boy off to prison for the rest of his life. The police say Manny Strewl wrote the ransom notes. They have copies. But *they* dictated those notes to Mr. Strewl. They told him how to write them, spell them—even where to put the letters on the paper."

Prior let that sink in before he dropped the bomb. "Now I can tell you this. Something you have not seen in the newspapers. My client was beaten. A bag was placed over his head, he was thrown into the bottom of a police car and driven out to the lake. There he was kicked, punched and hammered with blackjacks. They threatened to throw him in the lake if he didn't confess. I can't prove Mr. Strewl was beaten—but the bruises! Bruises still visible after *ten days*! In fact, one news photograph does show my client with a black eye."

Prior returned to his table. "Ten days with those bruises, in custody, and still no confession." He paused again and looked up and down the rows of jurors. "I will show you that my client is innocent of the charges."

Delaney's assistant, Joe Casey, leaned over and whispered to his boss. "Whaddya make of that?"

Delaney whispered back, "He's put the police on trial. Strewl's statements—"

A voice interrupted. "The prosecution may call your first witness."

Delaney leaned toward his assistant again. "Take Sam Gross—so I can size up Prior and see how he's going to proceed."

The teddy-bear-faced Joe Casey pushed his glasses up. He rose and sank his voice to a bass. "The prosecution calls Samuel Gross to the stand."

All eyes focused on a plump squat little man making his way toward the witness chair. His gray suit was perfectly fitted, which was unusual in the working class society of Albany, New York. Sam Gross smiled meekly, took the oath and sat down in the witness chair.

Casey took a notepad from his table and began to read questions from it. "Mr. Gross. Do you know the defendant, Manny Strewl?"

Gross crossed his legs and cleared his throat, betraying his uneasiness. Finally he answered in a Russian-Polish accent. "Yes, I do."

Casey took a step back as though to give the witness room to ease his nerves. "When did you first meet the defendant?"

Gross took a deep breath then spoke in his immigrant English. "I met him in the middle of the month of November 1933 at the Century Hotel in New York City."

"Who was in the room besides the defendant?"

Gross dropped his head for a moment to think before he answered. "Was Phil Zeigler, Al Fisher, Benny Holinsky, Manny Strewl and John Oley."

"Do you recall a conversation between Phil Zeigler and Manny Strewl at the Century Hotel?"

Gross shrugged. "Phil didn't mention his last name. Just called him Manny."

Casey raised his hand. "Fine. Just tell us what you heard as best you can."

"Well, Phil you know, smoking the pipe."

Casey stroked his forehead with his fingers. He did not want information on how Sam was associated with drug users. He leaned back against the prosecution's table but stayed to the side, allowing John Delaney a clear view of the witness. "Yes, that's alright, just tell the Court what they did or said."

"Alright. Phil said, Manny, how old is the O'Connell? Manny said he was about fifty years old. Then Phil said, what do you care for the old man O'Connell? Get the kid—he's a prince among three kings, and his uncle will pay any amount—without the law, without the public, shall know."

"How did Mr. Strewl reply to that, Mr. Gross?"

Gross pulled his lip. "He said, maybe you're right, Phil. If he will be taken then the uncles will pay any amount of money without police knowing and without the public shall know. Just what I want from you, is to get the spot and the boy. The money I will produce."

"Was anything else said, Mr. Gross?"

Gross licked his lips. "We left the hotel room. And then Manny, he said to Phil, if we can't take the old O'Connell we will take the young O'Connell."

"Now, Mr. Gross, was there anything further said about the O'Connells?"

"We was all walking on Broadway and Manny told Phil, I'll give you three days time to get the spot and the boy. If not—I'm gonna look up a different mob. That's all I heard, cause I crossed the street after that."

"No further questions."

"Mr. Prior. Your witness."

Dan Prior stood up. "Thank you, Your Honor." He drew his finger down the paper on his table. He wanted to make Sam Gross think he had a lot of information. He wanted to rattle the witness and make him think he would be on the witness stand a long time. "Where do you live, Mr. Gross?"

"I was living Detroit. Fourteen years."

Prior strolled toward the witness. "Ever been convicted of a crime?"

"No sir."

"What was your business while in Detroit?"

Gross puffed out his chest. "I was the owner of Fleisher Knitting Mills."

Prior gave a one-eyed look. "Interesting. How's business?"

Gross's head sank. "Not good. Doing retail in Toronto."

Prior smiled like he was about to eat the canary. "How often had you met Zeigler in New York?"

"I was in New York in 1933 three or four times. Every time I came to New York I met Zeigler pretty near daily."

"Did you discuss the O'Connell family of Albany during your visits with Zeigler?"

"Not before the visit at the Century Hotel."

"Later on, did he mention the O'Connell family?"

"Yes."

"And when did you visit the Century Hotel, Mr. Gross?"

Gross wiped the dampness from his brow. "Was August. 1933."

Prior put a hand to his mouth and turned back to his notes. "August, 1933? Earlier you told the court it was November, 1933. Isn't that true?

"Uh...yes."

"Why did you tell this court it was August?"

Gross's accent became more pronounced. "Because August I remember I came to the Department of Justice and I remember the date. That is why I was getting mixed up."

"Do you have a record of that, Mr. Gross?"

"I've got no record, but I remember that."

"Ahh, yes. Just your memory."

"You met Phil Zeigler in New York. Do you know his business?"

"Yes. He is connected with big mobs."

Prior moved close to the witness stand. He leaned toward Gross. "One of these big mobs that you just said Zeigler was connected to. Was one of them the Purple Gang of Detroit?"

"Don't know."

"Do you know what I mean when I speak of the Purple Gang in Detroit?"

"No."

Prior frowned. "You mean to tell me you never heard of the Purple Gang of Detroit?"

Gross rolled out his lip. "Well, I heard in the papers."

"So you have admitted you associate with mobsters and kidnappers, Mr. Gross. Do the Detroit police think you are legitimate? I remind you I can get the record."

Gross bristled. "Legitimate I always was."

Prior cocked his head. "How long have you known Phil Zeigler?"

"Six years."

"So Zeigler said he was connected to big mobs."

"Yes."

"Were these kidnapping mobs?"

"Well, he mentioned kidnapping mobs. Kidnapping too."

"So, Mr. Gross, you've known Phil Zeigler six years and met him in New York several times—knowing he was a kidnapper, is that correct?"

"Right."

"Knowing he was a gangster?"

"Right."

Prior took some papers from his desk. "You told the police you hosted Holinsky, Zeigler and Fisher in your house in Toronto, is that true?"

"Yes."

"When did you learn they were connected with kidnapping mobs?"

Gross shrugged. "Holinsky told me."

"How long did they stay with you, Mr. Gross?"

"About three weeks."

"Do you have a family, Mr. Gross?"

"Yes."

"To be clear, Mr. Gross—is it true you hosted known gangsters and kidnappers with your family for a period of three weeks?"

Gross bobbed his head. "Correct."

"While they were in Toronto at your house, Mr. Gross, did they talk about kidnapping John O'Connell?"

"They been talking kidnapping a fellow named Mush Trachnier."

"Did they talk about kidnapping young O'Connell?"

"I don't remember."

"Did you tell authorities about the Trachnier kidnapping after you heard about it?

"No."

"After hearing about the plot to kidnap young O'Connell, at the Century Hotel. Didn't your conscience feel rather guilty?"

"Not when I been reading the papers about it, no."

"When did your conscience begin to feel guilty, Mr. Gross?"

"When I saw this man's picture in the paper and with the story or statement of President Roosevelt that everybody should try to get the kidnappers of John O'Connell. That is the time I feel guilty."

"So you heard the plotting of the O'Connell kidnapping approximately February of 1933, read about it in the papers in July when the kidnapping occurred and did nothing until contacting the American Consulate in Windsor in August 1933. Is that correct, Mr. Gross?"

"Yes. I tell Mr. Vance. He send me to New York to meet the FBI to help."

Prior rested one hand on the witness stand. "Listen to this, Mr. Gross. I suppose you're going to tell us you were playing private detective."

"No."

"Oh. You weren't playing private detective?"

Gross wrung his hands. "I was trying to help out a friend. Joe Swartz in some particular case."

"You testified earlier, Mr. Gross, that you heard Phil Zeigler and Manny Strewl discuss the O'Connell kidnapping. Now listen carefully. Did you and Zeigler discuss the kidnapping after February 1933 and before John O'Connell was kidnapped?"

"He talked to me about it right after the visit with Manny Strewl."

Prior gave a surprised look at the jury. "So you knew that John O'Connell was to be kidnapped, Mr. Gross? Yet you didn't tell anybody about it?"

Gross's head sank. "Not at the time, no."

When Sam Gross was dismissed he stepped lightly from the witness box and left the courtroom. Judge Gallup said, "Call your next witness, Mr. Delaney."

"Prosecution calls Daniel O'Connell to the stand."

While the court officer retrieved O'Connell, Delaney whispered indignantly to his assistant. "For four months he admitted, four months he knew about the kidnapping and he told no one! Then he comes forward to be a good citizen. Do you believe that?!"

The sound of the closing courtroom door brought everyone's attention to the husky build of Dan O'Connell as he marched to the witness stand and was sworn in. For the next long while Delaney led Dan O'Connell through a summary of the kidnap story for the jury.

And then it was Defense Attorney Louis Prior's turn and the people in the courtroom held their breath. Prior had been a judge, until he was kicked off the judicial bench by the O'Connell political machine. Astute people knew this was not going to be a usual cross-examination. It would be a grudge match.

The snake known as Dan Prior uncoiled himself and handed out copies of ransom notes to the jury but gave none to the witness. Prior then faced the mongoose named Dan O'Connell and tossed out his first chunk of bait. "For the record. You are Daniel O'Connell. The most politically powerful man in Albany County?"

"No."

Prior smiled like the Cheshire cat. "You're not Daniel O'Connell?"

O'Connell's brow furrowed. "Dan O'Connell, yes. Politically powerful, no."

"Come now, Mr. O'Connell. Isn't it true that no one can get a public job in this county without your blessing?"

O'Connell pointed. "Not hardly. My brother Ed, there, he's head of the party, I'm just his assistant."

"Be honest, Mr. O'Connell—"

John Delaney jumped to his feet. "Objection! Counsel is attempting to characterize the witness."

"Sustained."

"Isn't it true that nothing happens in this county without your say so, Mr. O'Connell?"

"Definitely not! Check the records. I just schedule meetings and run errands."

Prior's eyes narrowed. "Do you recall a meeting you arranged in room 305 at the Ten Eyck Hotel which you arranged on or about July 20th 1933 in which Manny Strewl and John Oley were present?"

"Yes. Manny Strewl told me that his friend John Oley was upset about the whole thing. Thought the police would pin the rap on him or Strewl. Wanted me to talk to Oley, so I did."

"In your own words, Mr. O'Connell, what transpired in that conversation?"

"First off, John said Strewl was nervous because he thought the cops were following him. He'd heard rumors that the cops would railroad either him or Strewl for the kidnapping. Wanted me to say something on their behalf, get the police to back off."

Prior placed one hand on the witness stand, the other on his hip. "Did you not say that you could have Chief Smurl tossed off the force at any time?"

O'Connell shrugged and held his hands up palms forward. "Couldn't. Chief Smurl works for the D.A."

Prior bobbed his head. "And the D.A., Mr. O'Connell. Did you not say you had him in your vest pocket, that you could get him to back off?"

Again, Dan O'Connell held up his hands. "Can't. D.A works for the governor."

Prior stepped back and glanced at the jury. "I'd like to remind you,

Mr. O'Connell. Perjury is a serious offense. Would it help your memory if I put a witness on the stand to help your memory?"

Dan O'Connell sat back in his seat and checkmated the intimidating question. "I'd say call them. I told the truth."

Prior's left eye twitched. He knew both of the Oley brothers were on the run and he wasn't about to put Manny Strewl on the stand. Dan O'Connell had just reversed the tables and Prior knew he would have a tough time getting out of the corner he'd just been pushed into.

He said, "In due time, Mr. O'Connell."

Prior pulled at his lip and turned to the side. He spotted a copy of the July 31, 1933 issue of the *Times Union* and an idea dawned on him, a way to counterattack Dan O'Connell's testimony. He stepped forward again.

"Mr. O'Connell. I handed out a copy of peoples' exhibit five to the jury. It's a Photostat of a ransom note that starts out, 'Dan: Heard from Manny. What you offer is an insult.' Do you recall such a letter?"

"Yes."

"Did you read it?"

"Yes. Several times."

"You read it carefully?"

"Very carefully."

Prior sprung his trap. "So you read the note carefully, Mr. O'Connell. What is the punctuation after the word 'Dan'?"

O'Connell reached for the copy Prior held in his hand. "Let me look."

Prior pulled back. "No sir."

"Objection your honor. Witness cannot testify to something he can't see."

Prior showed the Photostat to the judge. "Your honor. The witness just testified he read this ransom note carefully several times. I have the right to test his memory of events."

Judge Gallup made a note. "I agree. Objection overruled."

Prior tucked the Photostat under his arm. "I'll repeat the question, Mr. O'Connell. What is the punctuation after your name on this ransom note?"

"Well…I can't say."

"So you did not read it carefully?"

"No, I did, I just…"

"So you can't recall, is that correct?"

O'Connell shrugged. "Who looks at punctuation?"

"So you don't remember anything—"

"Objection! Counsel is attempting to character assassinate the witness."

Prior waved his hand. "Withdrawn." He reached back and took hold of the newspaper. "I now show you a copy of the *Times Union* dated July 31, 1933. There is a picture of you and your nephew with the caption—"

Delaney sprang up. "Objection, Your Honor! Counsel is introducing items not in evidence."

Judge Gallup twirled his gavel between his hands. "Yes, I agree. However, I'll allow the witness to read the article silently to refresh his memory before he's questioned."

Questionable looks were exchanged between the spectators as O'Connell scanned the article. Prior said, "Is that a photo of you and your nephew, Mr. O'Connell?"

"Yes."

"Is it true the article quotes you as saying neither you nor you nephew can identify any of the kidnappers?"

"Well, I never saw them. Butch said—"

"The article says he could not recognize anyone. Is that true Mr. O'Connell?"

"Yes, but—"

"No buts, Mr. O'Connell." Prior raised his voice. "It says right there in print that your nephew could not recognize any of the kidnappers and you agree with him in the article. Isn't that true, Mr. O'Connell?"

"No-o! We didn't say those things."

***

For the next hour the attorneys stuck with the argument over what was said or not said. In the end it was a wasted hour, for arguments back and forth could not erase the simple fact that the statements printed in the local paper had opened a trap door that would undermine the district attorney's case against the defendant.

Chapter 21
Butch O'Connell and Detective O'Connell

The third witness for the prosecution was the star of the show, John 'Butch' O'Connell. Everyone present had read the papers but now they would get the story right from the horse's mouth. All the spectators, including Sheriff Charles Stanton and Deputy Fred McCarthy seated on the other side of the railing just behind Strewl, turned their best ear forward.

"The prosecution calls John O'Connell, Junior, to the stand."

The six-foot boxer was built like a cinder block and moved toward the stand with a military swagger. He sat tall in the chair and during the next two hours under the questioning of Prosecutor John Delaney related the story of his kidnapping step by step.

"For the record, Mr. O'Connell. Would you identify the person who entered your car on the night of July seventh, 1933?"

The witness's voice was strong and showed no hesitation. "It was Percy Geary. The police call him Angel Face Geary. After I was released the police showed me mug shots. I was also able to identify John and Francis Oley as the ones who attacked me."

Delaney held up a police report. "In this report, Mr. O'Connell, it says you were blindfolded yet you gave various descriptions to the police. How was that possible?"

"Well, uh, the bandage over my eyes came down to about the middle of my nose, and I could see out of each corner. It was also real hot and the sweat loosened the tape after a while, so I could see under it at times. When they had me write letters they'd take off the blindfold and I'd get a peek at the guards too."

"Was there a light in the room at the time?"

"Yes."

"You know what other furniture was in the room?"

"Yes."

"For the jury, Mr. O'Connell. Please tell us about the furniture."

For the next twenty minutes Butch described the contents of the room in which he was held and gave a general description of the two people who guarded him most of the time.

"Now, Mr. O'Connell. You stated at the time they were the only ones you saw and heard. Was there anyone else?"

"Yes. At some point—I think it was evening—a man came in and sat on my bed. He asked me to name some go-betweens—men that were in the money, and some local racketeers."

"How could you see him, Mr. O'Connell?"

"I could see him from under the bandage on my eyes."

"Can you tell the jury, Mr. O'Connell, who that man was?"

Butch rolled his palm over and pointed at Strewl. "Him. Sitting right there."

Strewl's head bolted back. He lurched forward. "You're a goddamn liar! I saved your life!"

The deputy jumped over the railing. Defense Attorney Dan Prior yanked Strewl back and admonished him. "No, Manny! Hush!"

Strewl lunged forward over the table. "You son of a bitch! You're trying to hang me!"

Judge Gallup pounded his gavel. "Quiet! Quiet in the courtroom. Guards!"

Dan Prior cried out, "That won't be necessary, your honor."

The judge waved his gavel in the air, motioning at Strewl. "Nothing more out of you. I'll put an officer right along side of you. Guards, move up."

Deputies took seats an arm's length away on each side of the defense table. Judge Gallup twisted in his seat. "Mr. Delaney. Any more questions?"

"No, Your Honor."

"Mr. Prior. Your cross."

Attorney Prior took some papers in his hand and stood up. He looked to be trying to figure how to proceed. This was not what he had expected. His client's outburst had provided clear evidence of an innate wild streak, and guards seated at either side of him added to the bad impression. For the next few minutes Prior attempted to move past this bad beginning by having Butch O'Connell recount the events prior to the kidnapping, starting with his departure from the brewery and then taking his fiancé to the movies.

He followed this with the question, "Now, to be positive, Mr. O'Connell. Did you see or not see Manny Strewl outside your house on the night you were kidnapped and stuffed into a car?"

"No. I did not."

"You told the police that while you were in the getaway car you heard someone pat a machine gun. Did you see it?"

"No sir."

"But you swore that someone did that?"

"Yes sir."

"How can you swear to something you didn't see, Mr. O'Connell?"

Butch intertwined his fingers. "I spent a lot of time on the gun range in the Army. I know what flesh on metal sounds like."

"And you were blindfolded the entire time, correct?"

"Yes, but I could see—"

"Don't volunteer information, Mr. O'Connell! I'll get to that. The report states you were blindfolded, yet you said you could see. Was it through the blindfold?"

"No. It was tape and—"

"Listen up, Mr. O'Connell! I want to get at the truth. Answer yes or no."

"But I was—"

Prior sneered in Butch's face. "I need a yes or no, Mr. O'Connell. Could you see through the blindfold or the tape you mentioned?

"N-no."

Prior slapped the witness stand. "Finally an answer!"

Prior tilted his head at Butch. "Only a small glimpse out the sides as you just told the court."

"T-true."

Prior turned up a page on his police report. "Says here you gave the police the size of the truck and size of the compartment you were transported in. Correct?"

"Yes."

"Did you have a yardstick?"

"No. Just my feet."

Prior raised his voice. "Pay attention! Don't embellish. I didn't ask about your feet, Mr. O'Connell!"

Delaney jumped to his feet. "Objection! Counsel is badgering the witness."

"Sustained."

Prior raised his voice. "Tell the Court how you were able to provide the police a description of the truck and compartment *without*...actually seeing it?"

Butch's shoulders relaxed. "Well, uh, I'm six foot tall. When I walked across the truck bed my head breezed the canvas top. By law, the top can't exceed eight feet. I had to duck to get into the compartment so I guessed the door was five foot high or so. Waist to my feet is maybe four feet give or take. I slung my feet around to measure till some guy shouted at me."

Prior caught sight of juror number five. The man was leaning on his elbow with his fingers at his lips and he muttered, "Ingenious."

"Let's move on to the go-betweens. The mobsters you associate with."

Delaney rose up. "Objection, your honor. Counsel is attempting a character assassination."

"I'll rephrase. The go-betweens *you mentioned*. What names did you provide, Mr. O'Connell?"

Butch swiped at the sweat on his brow. "Just names I'd seen in the paper. There was Butch O'Hagan. Ames O'Brien. And…"

Prior poked his head forward. "Forget already?"

"No. There was Barney Reilly and Mush Trachnier…"

"Was that all?

"N-no."

"Well, tell the jury then!"

"I gave them your name."

A roar of laughter rolled across the courtroom and Judge Gallup banged his gavel. "Order! Order in the Court!"

Prior sank his head. "Surely you don't think I'm one of those kinds of people."

Butch shrugged. "No. Let me explain."

Prior rolled his eyes toward the ceiling. "Go ahead."

"They were just names I'd read in the paper. Some said you defended Legs Diamonds and his mob is all."

Prior's left hand pushed back his jacket and he planted the hand on his hip. "Well, it was lucky I wasn't one. Since my name never appeared in any of the lists, can we presume they didn't want me?"

Butch shrugged. "Guess so. Said they couldn't do business with lawyers."

With this, some of the jurors put their hands over their mouths to stifle laughter. Prior took another stack of papers from his desk. "To be sure, Mr. O'Connell, you did not mention Mr. Strewl's name. Correct?"

"Yes sir."

"And the person who asked for the go-betweens did not mention Mr. Strewl's name, is that correct?"

"He did not."

"Think back, Mr. O'Connell. Did any of these people mention Mr. Strewl's name?

"No. Only the short guard. Once."

It was an answer Prior had not expected. He shot back, "A yes or no is all I want, Mr. O'Connell!"

He paced a few steps and came back to the witness stand. "The short guard. What'd he say?"

"Asked if I knew Manny—said the only Manny I knew sold fire extinguishers."

Prior raised his voice. "And when did he ask this, Mr. O'Connell?"

Butch rubbed his forehead. "Don't know exactly. During the first week."

Prior's voice took on a scolding tone, like a schoolteacher running short on patience with a student who can't come up with the right answer. "Was it before or after Mr. Strewl's name appeared in the papers?"

"Don't know. Couldn't see a paper."

Prior took the police report in his hand and pointed it at the witness. "Hold it, Mr. O'Connell. Moments ago, you told this Court you saw Mr. Strewl in the room with you. Now you say you couldn't see." Prior raised his voice. "Could you see or not see?"

Butch stuttered. "Out the—the sides."

Prior jabbed his finger in the air. "Didn't you just swear under oath, right here, that you couldn't see what time you discussed the go-betweens?"

Beads of sweat ran down Butch's face. "It's true. I couldn't see the time—"

Prior slapped the railing in front of the witness stand. "Finally!"

"—cause I didn't have a watch!"

Again Prior jabbed his finger in the air. "Answer only the questions I ask, Mr. O'Connell! You told this Court it was dark. Too dark to see. *Didn't you?*"

"It—it *was* dark."

"Too dark to see?"

"No. Saw his—"

Prior went nose to nose. "Don't embellish!

Delaney interrupted. "Objection! Counsel is badgering the witness."

Prior moved back a few steps. "So now it isn't dark, Mr. O'Connell. Can you make up your mind? Was it dark or was it light?"

Butch's face went beet red and his voice trembled. "It was dark, only one light in the room."

Prior sneered. "Yes! A single strand light." He flipped a page of the report. "Let's jump to the night of your release. Were you bound in any way?"

Butch bit his lips. "No. Just blindfolded."

"When did you remove the blindfold?"

"After a couple of minutes. Mr. Strewl said it was all clear, that he was there to help me."

"After that, Mr. O'Connell. How long did it take for you to pick up Mr. Snyder?"

"Not positive. Guess maybe thirty minutes."

"And on the way, is it true you saw a policeman?"

"Yes. On the corner of Dykeman Street."

"Also according to the police report you made a call from a restaurant in Peekskill. How long a drive was it?"

Butch pulled at his jaw. "Well, I think a few hours."

"Is it true that you told the police you recognized Mr. Strewl's voice as belonging to one of the kidnappers?"

"Yes."

As he spoke his next words Prior stepped closer and closer to the witness. "So in brief, Mr. O'Connell. You rode for hours next to a person you thought was one of the kidnappers—yet you made no attempt to flee. Is that true?"

"Well, uh, I was nervous. Didn't know if I was free or it was the end. Killed."

"Understand, Mr. O'Connell. But you did see a cop, didn't you?"

"Y-yeah."

"Again, you didn't try to yell out?"

"Correct."

"You didn't try to escape?"

"True, but—"

"To make it clear to the jury, Mr. O'Connell. You were not restrained in any manner. You saw a cop. Spent hours riding next to a person you thought would do you harm…and yet you did nothing? No attempt to escape—or scream for help?"

"Yes, but—but I wasn't sure until—"

"Not sure? Son, a man's life is at stake! You have to be sure!"

"I am! I am sure now."

"*You're sure now*—after the police arrested Mr. Strewl. *But you were not sure then.*"

Butch leaned forward. "It…it was his voice. I know it. I heard—"

Prior snapped the report shut. "That's right. You claim to have heard Mr. Strewl's voice twice in your life. Now you're ready to hang him on a not sure or maybe."

"Objection! Counsel is making a speech."

"Sustained. Save it for closing, Mr. Prior."

"So please tell the court, Mr. O'Connell. After riding for hours next to a person you were frightened of, a person you thought was one of the kidnappers…why you didn't jump out and say something like, 'Hey, that's one of them right there—that's one of the kidnappers'?"

Butch swallowed hard. "Well, no one asked."

"Did you tell them the next day?"

"No."

"When did you tell the detectives you thought Mr. Strewl was involved?"

Butch coughed. "Tuesday following. I was played out. Spent two days in bed."

Prior took the July 31, 1933 issue of the *Times Union* from his desk. "Two days later. On a Tuesday. Because you were in bed. Resting."

Prior flicked open the paper. The prosecutor jumped to his feet. "Objection. Counsel introducing items not in evidence."

Judge Gallup peered over his glasses. "Mr. Prior?"

"I use this only to refresh the witness's memory and to verify what he has stated."

"I'll sustain the objection in part. I'll allow the witness to read the newspaper in silence so the jury does not hear it and allow the witness to refresh his memory. Counsel may then question his recollection of events."

After Butch looked at the article Prior pointed to the front page photograph. "Who's that sitting in a chair on the front lawn of your uncle's camp?"

Butch's jaw dropped. "Me. Next to my uncle."

"And these two people in the background?"

Butch licked his lips. "Captain Oliver and Detective O'Connell—of the New York Police."

Prior leaned an elbow on the witness stand. "What date is that right here?"

"Monday, July thirty-first, 1933."

"Not in bed, are you?"

"No—but I did get up to—"

"To what, Mr. O'Connell? Pose for the camera?"

"No! To—"

"Score some political points?"

"No-o!"

"Come now, Mr. O'Connell. You just lied about being in bed. Two cops nearby, and still you didn't finger Mr. Strewl as a possible kidnapper."

Delaney pounded his table. "Objection! Move to strike! Counsel is verbally mugging the witness."

Judge Gallup pointed his gavel at the stenographer. "Sustained. Strike out the last remark, Frank. Continue, Mr. Prior?"

Prior turned the page of the newspaper. "A moment ago you said you recognized Manny Strewl, is that true?

"I did."

Prior held the paper wide open. He pointed to a paragraph. "Did you tell the newspaper that you did not recognize any of the kidnappers?"

"No-o-o."

Prior cocked his head. "You didn't tell the newspaper that you did not recognize the kidnappers?"

"No—neither me nor my uncle said those things."

"Are you telling this Court that the newspaper printed...lies?"

"No, but what I meant—"

Prior snatched the paper back. "No further questions, Your Honor."

"Witness is excused."

The next witness sworn in was Detective James O'Connell. The Assistant District Attorney, Joe Casey, questioned the detective on how Strewl was taken to the police station after the "scuffle" occurred, and how sample writings were obtained.

Defense Attorney Prior started his attack by questioning Detective O'Connell about the places he had lived during the past twenty years. With each minor error or hesitation from the witness, Prior jumped at the chance to say the detective had a faulty memory.

Prior's next line of attack focused on the scuffle between Manny Strewl and the two detectives (O'Connell and Dolan) when they first picked him up and escorted him to the police station. Prior sparred over the details and attempted to show how brutal the detectives were to his client. He went nose to nose with Detective O'Connell. "So tell me, Detective. How could my client have gotten the black eye?"

"How should I know? Maybe Dolan gave it to him."

"Wait a minute, Detective. Be honest."

O'Connell's face was already red. Now it turned purple. "I am telling you the truth!"

Prior jabbed his finger at O'Connell with each word. "Give it up, Detective. You just said Dolan didn't punch him and now you say he did. I want the truth."

Detective O'Connell arched over the rail and spoke between clenched teeth. "Are you calling me a liar?"

"I want you to wake up, Detec—"

O'Connell spun around. "That's it!" he muttered. And just that quick he was out of the witness stand.

Joe Casey waved at the retreating witness and yelled, "Don't!" One of the guards intercepted Detective O'Connell while the other took a position beside Dan Prior and Manny Strewl.

Judge Gallup pounded his gavel. "Order—order in the Court!" A moment later when all was calm, Judge Gallup struck the gavel again and announced, "Court's in recess. Counsel, all yuhs—in my chambers! Now!"

While the attorneys went to the judge's 'woodshed' the question on everyone's mind was whether a man trapped in a car with two strangers and fearful for his life would have yelled for help.

***

Once Butch was safely back home, Attorney Delaney himself ordered the victim of the crime not to mention or in any way implicate Strewl. First of all, Delaney did not want to scare Strewl off. So long as the guilty party was free to roam, the prosecutor felt sure they stood a better chance of building a stronger case against him. Delaney was playing for time. His decision to stall, however, ended up providing a good stroke of fortune for the defense.

Strewl's temper tantrum in the courtroom provided proof that he was capable of violence. But the point was offset by the fact that both Dan and Butch O'Connell were quoted in the paper as saying they were unable to identify any of the kidnappers. Though most everyone in town had read the article, the questions went unanswered. Had both Dan and Butch O'Connell really said they did not recognize the kidnappers? Did the newspaper perhaps get the facts wrong or maybe even embellish the story? What would the jury think?

The fact that Strewl had been badly beaten played a huge factor in the outcome. He did indeed suffer bruises that lasted ten days. But who gave Strewl a beating? The question was never answered, though most people suspected the police. To some degree the question tainted all the prosecution's evidence.

The prosecution and the defense had to work around these land mines once they were uncovered. And one land mine went unrecognized. That July 31 newspaper was not "introduced" into evidence.

Years later at the Appeal Trial, these land mines would explode and Manny Strewl would be granted a new trial. And what would the new trial bring? New land mines, of course.

Chapter 22
"It's a Photograph"

In the Albany Police Department's lab, the day after the trial recessed for the weekend, John Delaney reached down to adjust the valve on the radiator. March temperatures made wild swings, and now that it was late afternoon Delaney wanted the water in the pipes hot again.

When a gurgling noise sounded he recalled the one like it that Catherine O'Connell heard last July, when she got home from her card game and discovered Butch's car under the oak tree. The car's radiator had gurgled because it was cooling. Catherine had no way of knowing it then, but that sound marked the beginning of the kidnapping of her son.

"Here you go," Joe Casey said, interrupting Delaney's thoughts. Casey had pushed together several tables and laid out the Photostatic evidence and various lab reports. Because the defense counsel had poked gaping holes in the testimony about the handwriting, Delaney much needed to find a way to do the same on his end.

He rolled his sleeves down and peered at the evidence. "What else we got?"

Casey bent low over the papers and as he did his tie dragged across the papers and slid them out of place. "Damn this thing!" he said, and pulled the tie off, then bent again over the copies of the letters and ransom notes. "Maybe we could focus on the spacing *between* the lines and letters. Osborne's report said they're similar in both the originals and the samples we had Strewl write."

Delaney paraded around the table like a general studying a battle strategy. "Could be a hit, could be a miss. Detective O'Connell told Strewl where to begin, so defense counsel could claim the defendant was forced to cram words close together. And then he'd likely kick in the lack of free-will writing—so all we'd accomplish would be planting more doubt in the jurors' minds."

Casey stood straight and ran his fingers through his hair. "We didn't do it all the time. When we took Strewl to Monticello we—"

The lab door opened and in came Detective Hynes followed by a neatly dressed balding man who was unmistakably a high-ranking FBI agent. He was modestly built and only a bit taller than Delaney, but he wore mirrored black shoes, an expensive white cotton shirt and a well-fitted three-piece gray suit. A beige trench coat hung from the same arm that held a brown leather brief case.

Hynes said, "Sorry to interrupt you, Mr. Delaney. This is Special Agent Charles Appel. Got him here as fast as I could."

Hynes stepped to the side, ignoring the others and studying the evidence on the table. Agent Appel first introduced himself and then said, "Detective Hynes here has already filled me in— said you're pressed for time, and I've already read Osborne's report."

Delaney removed his glasses. "What'd you think?"

Appel chuckled. "Very thorough. He even checked the emulsions of the pen ink. Hell, I wouldn't have thought of that. So how is the old coot?"

Delaney's eyes shot sideways toward Casey, indicating to Casey that he wasn't about to tell this acquaintance of Albert Osborne that Osborne's testimony was sinking their case. He said, "Mr. Osborne's testimony was very exact."

Appel shrugged. "So what do you need me for?"

Delaney licked his lips. He didn't want to embarrass himself or cast a dark light on the handwriting analysis. "We're reassessing our theory of the crime and are in need of a tertiary opinion on the ransom note evidence to help formulate a new hypothesis."

Appel rubbed the bare spot on his head. He stood at Hynes's side and took a look at the Photostat Hynes was holding. His brow wrinkled and he glanced back at Delaney. "What?"

Hynes mumbled to the Photostat—forgetting that the concrete room would amplify his voice. "Defense is kicking his ass, he needs you to bail him out."

Appel pulled back, his eyes as round as ping-pong balls. Casey's mouth fell open. The gaffe was followed by a thickening silence.

Delaney pursed his lips. "Thank you, Detective…for that layman's explanation."

Hynes drew his palm across his mouth. "Yeah. Well, I may have missed something in my notes. I'll go check'em." He left the room.

Delaney pointed to a chair. "You can toss your stuff there, Agent Appel." He leaned over the table and swept an arm over the papers. "This is our evidence. As you know, we have Photostats of the ransom notes but not the originals. We need a second opinion. The question is, how is the handwriting on the ransom notes and that on Strewl's sample writings similar?"

When the agent dropped his trench coat and briefcase in the chair and removed his suit coat, Joe Casey grinned. "What, no gun?"

Appel said, "I'm not a field agent, I'm a scientist. Chemical compounds, equations and scientific analysis—those are my bullets."

Casey slid a Photostat that started with 'Dan" next to Osborne's report. "How's this? Osborne says the letter D in the ransom notes is peculiar. It looks like a P here and in other places."

Delaney picked up the report and read aloud. "The stroke of the letter is made with a fullness at the top, which makes it look like a P.' And here he says the 'W's and M's were made much the same way. Each with four strokes, but the pen was never taken up when the W was made.' Well, that's certainly a peculiar detail. Make a note of it." He turned up another page and continued reading. "'In all the writings there were no small G's, F's or M's.'" He stroked his chin. "I'd say that's a unique characteristic. I wonder..."

Agent Appel bumped Delaney's arm. "Sorry to interrupt. Do you have a duplicate photograph of this? I don't want to work from an original."

Delaney drew his palm across his mouth and mumbled, "We gotta stop these mistakes." He raised his voice. "Yeah, I can get you a copy. But when I put you on the stand I want you to identify the evidence properly. They're Photostats."

"This one's not. Look at the background."

Delaney's head shot up. Casey jerked his head up.

Appel pointed with his pinky. "This image is so sharp you can see the pores of the paper. That's called depth of field. A Photostat machine is incapable of getting that kind of detail, only a camera with a good lens can—so it's definitely a photograph. But as I said, it's the only—"

"So it's on the negative too?"

Appel shrugged. "Sure."

Casey pinched the photograph. "It's in evidence, but it was never made public."

Delaney looked over his glasses. "And Strewl looked at it and swore it was *his* handwriting. Joe, get the Photostatic operator, get the photographer, get the stenographer too—I wanna review the testimony."

The door slammed behind Joe Casey and Agent Appel scratched the back of his neck in wonderment. "I only need a copy. What gives?"

Delaney smiled. "Defense counsel stressed the point that Photostats are not the same as originals, and your friend Osborne testified that reproductions are not as good as originals. But a photograph's negative? Why, that's something else entirely—different as night and day. You can't fake a negative."

Delaney smiled and patted the FBI agent on the shoulder. "Mr. Appel, you have just convicted Manny Strewl."

***

In March of 1936, almost exactly three years after the first trial, Detective Jimmy Hynes pulled his top coat closed against a gust of cold air. He paced through the sidewalk slush, leaving over-sized footprints, and as he walked he read the headlines. Parts of Johnstown, Pennsylvania had been slammed by fourteen feet of floodwater. His own feet were cold and he thought to himself that a little cold was nothing to complain about, not when some folks had drowned in floodwaters.

"Jimmy."

Joe Gannon was approaching. Hynes folded the paper, shoved it in his coat pocket and said, "About time you got here."

Gannon blew warm air on his reddened hands. "Wouldn't miss it for the world. Three years since the kidnapping—one of my longest-running cases."

They climbed the steps of the tall granite building and paused before entering. Hynes grinned. "You should have seen Dan Prior's face when Delaney sprang the news that he actually has a photograph of one of the notes. Thought Prior was going to drop dead right on the spot."

Gannon gazed up at the name carved in stone: New York State Supreme Court. "Well, Jimmy, looks like this is the last stop for all us—including Strewl. You got a read on this?"

Hynes pulled at the thick oak door. "Nope. Didn't have a chance to get up here much. Strewl was convicted, and then lost his first appeal—as I'm sure you know. Two outta three, that's what we've got so far, but no telling how the chips will fall this time."

Inside, Gannon turned and peeped through the window in the door. A black sedan marked Police rolled by, followed by a large black sedan filled with six men. The barrel of a shotgun protruded from one of the back windows. He turned back and said, "Yeah, and sure would be something, wouldn't it, if this court trumped the others? At any rate, should be a good show."

Hynes mumbled. "Just what I was thinking—but at least we have Harrigan's mob on ice, plus we still have our ace in the hole."

Gannon removed his top coat and chuckled. "Harrigan's mob? Yuh mean the ones that haven't committed suicide yet?"

Hynes led the way past some bystanders and to the courtroom. "It's only a matter of time. The G-men *will* pick up

Geary and the Oleys. Hey…looks like it's standing room only."

Before stepping inside Hynes whispered, "I heard Strewl got a new attorney. Does Winters sound familiar?"

Gannon's eyebrows shot up and he grinned wide. "Sure does, but he didn't do any good for Tony Reino, or Freddie Plentl or Shore—whatever his name was, nor for Scarnici. They're all dead as a doornail. So if Winters is here, that's good—might just work in our favor."

The two detectives sidled up against the back wall. Gannon arched his head above the crowd. Sure enough, there was Strewl and the new attorney, and Delaney and Casey. He whispered, "Odd thing is, there's no sign of the O'Connells."

Hynes had no chance to respond for at that instant a door opened and in walked a policeman with shiny brass buttons on a dark blue uniform. He bellowed, "The Supreme Court of the Sate of New York is now in session. The Honorable P.J. Hill will read for the majority."

Five men filed in, each like a clone of the others, with graying hair, long black robes and expressions similar to ones on the mug shots on view at the post office. When they were all seated, Judge Hill leaned forward and said, "The crime for which the defendant is indicted, namely kidnapping, is a continuing crime. The preparation for the crime began by the seizure of John J. O'Connell, Junior, July 7, 1933, and ended upon his release on or about July 30—the crime having been committed for the purpose of paying ransom. The prosecution based its case chiefly upon the evidence of witness Sam Gross. While the past record of witness Gross leaves much to be desired, we agree with the lower courts that his contradictions and polluted sources are as obvious to the Appellate Court as they are to the jury. There can be no reversal without breaking down the barrier between the separate functions of the Appellate Court and the jury."

Hynes popped out a finger on his left hand. Like an umpire calling strike one, he indicated that the judges seemed to be leaning toward upholding Strewl's conviction.

Judge Hill's voice droned on. "It is also to be remembered that in fixing the blame for such a crime, the State is not likely to discover witnesses of high character."

Hynes popped out another finger. Two marks against Strewl.

"On direct testimony, witness Gross affixed the first meeting in November 1933, four months after the kidnapping. Then the witness says he heard the plot to kidnap the victim in early February 1933 and made his first visit to the Century Hotel in August 1933. Finally, he says he was mixed up. Gross also stated that Zeigler, Fisher and Holinsky visited him for three weeks during Easter of 1933. He overheard them discuss kidnapping Mush Trachnier. When asked what they talked about, he said they talked about the O'Connell kidnapping. If this man's evidence is true, for months he had knowledge of the proposed kidnapping and made no disclosure to prevent the perpetration of this most serious crime. The reason he gives for finally telling the story is illuminating."

Hynes's right hand began a count. One finger for the defense. Maybe Strewl would win after all.

"We next look at the handwriting experts called by the people. The number of samples is a matter for the legislature and this Court will not comment on how sufficient a sample must be taken. However, it is shown that only eighty samples were observed as similarities compared to the thousands in evidence. And it should be noted that in the whole, there were more dissimilarities in the samples than similarities."

Hynes showed another finger 'for' the bad guys.

"We next look at the actions of the defendant. We find it difficult that a defendant would act as of free unobstructed will when there are bruises still visible after ten days of confinement."

Hynes popped out another digit for the defense and stared at his hands in astonishment. The count was two against Strewl and three in his favor.

"We next turn to the identification by John O'Connell, Junior, and his contradictory statements and his failure to give vital information when he had it. The victim stated he saw a policeman shortly after entering the vehicle upon his release, yet he did not cry out for help. Upon his arrival at his uncle's residence—where he was surrounded by police, he still did not alert them to his suspicions. Next, there were statements printed in the newspaper dated July 31, 1933, saying that he could not identify his captors while being held. Yet at trial, he contradicted himself by stating he recognized the defendant both while he was held captive and in the car upon his return. His statements to the press were denied. Why the reporter or newspaper editor was not called as a witness is conjecture. The fact remains that either the statements were made or that a reputable newspaper is guilty of an intentional misstatement."

Judge Hill paused a few seconds and continued. "We next look at the testimony of the detectives. There were several detectives in the room while the defendant made his sample writings. The prosecution failed to call additional detectives to the stand for sake of judicial economy stating it would be repetitive testimony. We disagree."

Hynes locked his lips and stared at his hands. Two to five—in favor of the bad guy! He whispered to Gannon, "He's gonna go free. We're gonna need that ace."

Gannon hurriedly vanished from the courtroom as Judge Hill continued with his list of reasons that favored the release of Manny Strewl. Hynes ground his teeth in disbelief. He had missed a few sentences but his ears perked up again when he heard, "The magnifying glass permitted in the deliberation room which was not in evidence is misconduct."

What the hell! Inwardly, Hynes fumed. This was the first he had heard about a magnifying glass. He put a hand to his chest. His blood pressure was rising.

Judge Hill said, "One of the most serious crimes has been committed. It is important that the perpetrators be apprehended and convicted. It is equally important that the defendant shall not remain in prison for the remainder of his life unless his guilt can be established beyond a reasonable doubt, after a trial without errors here mentioned. I favor a reversal of the conviction and a new trial, in the interest of justice, because of the errors assigned."

"Damn it!" Hynes muttered.

He stepped sideways to the policeman by the door. Leaning to the cop's ear he ordered, "Have Strewl funneled out the side exit."

For the next several minutes, Hynes sat in the large arched window overlooking Eagle Street. Two men in handcuffs huddled among the many uniformed policemen holding shotguns and men in plain clothes holding submachine guns. Those would be Feds, he knew, for they were the only ones who could afford machine guns. A voice interrupted his thinking and he got to his feet.

Strewl's attorney was escorting him out of the building. Winters gave a cackle of a laugh. "What's the matter, Detective? Feeling lonesome?"

Hynes smiled and stepped around in front of them to prevent their progress toward the stairs. He pulled a newspaper from his jacket pocket. "Just wondering about your two friends, Manny."

Strewl had his eyes fixed on the window. "Burke and Fisher aren't my friends."

Hynes reached the newspaper forward and tapped Strewl's chest. "I didn't mention Burke or Fisher, now did I? But they sure as hell know you. I heard they've been having a long chat with the DA—and the G-men."

Winters jabbed his finger at Hynes. "That's entrapment!"

Hynes touched the newspaper to the attorney's chest. "Not my case, Counselor."

Winters snatched the paper. "This could be assault!"

Hynes took a step back and held up his palms. "Could be your lucky day, Counselor. I'd read page five if I were you."

Hynes continued to back away. "Me? I'm going ice fishing." He mocked casting a line and winked. "Maybe I'll catch a big one."

Winters snapped open the paper and mumbled, "What's he trying to pull?" His mouth dropped open when he spotted the headline. Death Penalty for Kidnapping Bill.

Strewl reached over and looked at the page. "What is it?"

Winters stepped back, out of the way of traffic in the hallway. In a low voice he began reading aloud. "Governor Lehman signed the bill into law…making kidnapping a crime that calls for the death penalty if the victim is under sixteen and life in prison if over sixteen."

Winters pulled at his jaw. "I'd heard that Senator Royce Copeland moved a similar bill out of the Senate. The President is expected to sign it."

"So?"

"Manny, used to be that kidnapping was formally counted a misdemeanor. Today it's a felony."

"What's all that mean? I'm getting a new trial, right?"

Winters glanced away and saw Hynes, who was still standing in sight, touch his fingers to his hat brim in a mock salute before pivoting and hurrying away. Winters said, "Yeah, Manny, you're getting a new trial. With new laws. You also have two new witnesses that will testify against you. I'm guessing they have first-hand information that will help the prosecution." He held up the newspaper. "The best you'll get is life in prison. The worst is the death penalty."

"But—but they can't!"

"Oh yes they can, Manny. And it's damn likely."

Some time later, back at the Arch Street Police Station, Gannon and the FBI Agents followed Hynes to his desk. He dropped his hat on the desktop and removed his coat. "Well," he said, "that's all we can do."

Hynes handed the FBI agents a folder. "Here's a copy of the statements from Burke and Fisher. They put Strewl at the hideout. Delaney is scheduled to talk with them again later today."

FBI Agent Merrick took the folder. "We'll hang around. We have some questions for them too, about some New York bank robberies."

Gannon opened his topcoat. "Be interesting to see what—"

The phone rang. Hynes reached for it and identified himself and a few seconds later he chuckled. "Is that so? Only an attorney would think of that." He gave a thumbs-up to the men standing before him and chuckled again. "Sounds good to me. Jail time is jail time."

Hynes hung up the phone and clapped his hands. "We got him! He cut a deal with Delaney. Strewl will plead guilty to extortion by mail if they don't press the kidnap charge. He's looking at fifty to sixty years of jail time."

Gannon grinned big and shook his head side to side. "Death is a motivator."

Agent Merrick cut in. "So, technically…we didn't get Strewl for kidnapping."

"True," Hynes admitted, "but Strewl did get in the last lick. Said to save his honor and not drag his family through another trial he'd plead guilty to the extortion charge since that doesn't carry the death penalty like this new kidnap law does. And with the death penalty off the table, he did admit to writing two of the ransom notes. Your agent Appel sure hit the target. And like I said on the phone, jail time is jail time. Serving time for kidnapping or extortion—same thing in my mind."

Gannon said, "Yuh know, Jimmy, must be luck of the Irish to have the kidnap law become a death-penalty crime."

Hynes smiled. "Remember way back? When we discussed O'Connell's money after we talked to Mrs. Watkins?"

"Yeah."

"Governor Leham's from Albany and so is Senator Copeland. Both elected officials, both Irish. You catch my gist?"

***

By late 1937, John and Francis Oley and Angel Face Geary had been arrested by the FBI, and the remaining O'Connell kidnappers were at last behind bars. In 1934 Harrigan's mob, along with the Oleys and Geary, had committed the "crime of the century" when they robbed an armored car outside the Rubel Ice Company. By the time the case against the Oley brothers went to trial, the still-alive members of Harrigan's mob were already serving time for that robbery.

The Oleys and Geary were also convicted. The following editorial, from the Buffalo Times, provides an interesting summary:

LAST OF THE KIDNAPERS

The trial of the kidnapers of John J. O'Connell Jr. of Albany has been concluded at Binghamton with conviction for the ten prisoners after a trial that has lasted all summer.

Probably few of our readers have had the patience to bestow more than a passing glance upon the daily dispatches we have been printing recording the progress of the case. The attempt to sustain interest for 11 weeks in the sequel to something that happened four years ago is a bit too much for most of us.

Nevertheless, we hope that the outcome of the trial will be carefully noted by the public and especially by those whom it may concern, if you get what we mean.

We don't quite see the distinction between the 77-year prison sentence imposed upon John Oley, for instance, and the 58-year-term meted out to Manning Strewl (Oley by our reckoning will get out of prison at the age of 113 and Strewl at 93) but if the court feels that it is important it is all right with us.

The essential fact is that the Federal Government has demonstrated once more, and in unmistakable fashion, that kidnaping does not pay.

Epilogue

Manny Strewl's trial began March 2, 1934. It ended three weeks later with a conviction. For the next three years he remained in custody, awaiting his appeal, totally unaware of the land mine the O'Connells were planning.

John and Francis Oley and Percy Geary had refused to give Big Charlie Scarnici his share of the money, saying they had to hold on to it for Strewl's defense and appeal. Scarnici decided he would talk, or so the newspapers reported, and at this point the Oley brothers and Percy Gearing went to New York City to hide out.

A few months after Manny was convicted, a small time crook named John Manning contacted the Oleys and Geary about a potential robbery of an armored car. They figured fortune had smiled on them and proceeded with the robbery, which netted a cash intake of $427,000. Local reporters dubbed the robbery of the Rubel Ice Company "the crime of the century." (See "Robbery in Brooklyn," *The New Yorker,* May 13, 1939).

Following the robbery Francis Oley made his way to Denver, Colorado, where he took an assumed name. In January 1937 the authorities received a tip from a resident named James McGuire who had recognized Francis from a photo in *True Detective Magazine*. The police followed Francis for several days and quickly became convinced he was a crook because he was casing the Denver mint. The police arrived at his house and questioned him and were not satisfied with his answers. Though still not positive of his true identity, they ordered, "Ok, you're coming with us. Get your things."

At that point his five-year-old daughter blurted, "Oh Mommy, does that mean the photos under the pillow?"

A search of the bedroom turned up an envelope under the mattress stuffed with photographs. The return address was in New York City and inside there was a note from Uncle John and Auntie Aggie—along with vacation photos of John and Agnes Oley. A few days later the FBI arrested John Oley, Percy "Angel Face" Geary, and Harold "Red" Crowley.

It's presumed that Francis Oley, knowing he faced a long time in prison for his involvement in the O'Connell kidnapping and the Rubel Ice Company robbery, committed suicide. His death occurred on April 2, 1937, in the Utica Jail. He was 28 years old.

John Oley, Percy Geary and Harold Crowley were tried and convicted in Binghamton on August 12, 1937. Oley and Geary each received 77 years of prison time and a $10,000 fine (equivalent to more than a million of today's dollars). Crowley got 28 years since he did not participate in the Rubel Ice Company robbery.

While they were being held in the Onondaga County Penitentiary they escaped, but were recaptured three days later. This time Oley and Geary were rushed off to Alcatraz and Crowley to Leavenworth.

John Oley offered to talk for a reduced sentence but the offer was rebuffed. In 1959, when he was 58, he was granted a medical parole due to terminal cancer. A year later he died in Ballston Spa, New York. His wife was at his side.

By the time he was 62, in 1959, Percy Geary had spent much of his life behind bars. He pleaded with prison officials not to free him because he feared the freedoms on the outside. They did not heed his request, so two weeks prior to his scheduled release he threw himself under the Atlanta Penitentiary's laundry truck and thus committed suicide.

Harold "Red" Crowley served his time in Leavenworth. In 1957 he was transferred to the State of New York to serve time for various State crimes.

Charles Harrigan's truck linked him to the O'Connell kidnapping. He and his gang used the same truck that had transported Butch O'Connell to rob a mail truck in Fall River, Massachusetts, in 1935. They carried away $129,200. The FBI quickly caught up with them and each of the robbers got 25-year prison terms, but because the truck linked them to the kidnapping each one got an additional 77-year sentence. Harrigan served his time in Alcatraz and was paroled on July 8, 1959. As time passed, he realized he had no family or friends left on this planet. Word was at the nursing home where he lived in Long Island City, Queens, New York, that Harrigan often repeated, "It wasn't worth it." He died April 20, 1988, at the age of eighty-eight.

George Garguillo was so mean that while he was imprisoned in the Massachusetts State Prison the guards kept him chained much of the time and heavily guarded. Most reports give the impression that Garguillo was little more than a wild animal. He couldn't abide prison restrictions, and on March 9, 1939, committed suicide by hanging himself with a bed sheet.

By 1937, Butch's two guards—Frank Fisher and Thomas Burke, had been arrested. Since they were minor members of the mob, they turned State's evidence in return for a reduced sentence and got four years each. Before his short sentence was up, at the ripe age of 36, Burke died of a heart attack in Lewisburg Prison. Frank Fisher served his time and faded into history. Rumor had it that upon release he returned to South Africa to once again take up diamond mining.

Thomas Dugan ended up buried in the Alcatraz prison cemetery. He served only a fraction of his 77-year term before dying of heart disease at age 44 in 1946.

The vicious John "Sonny" McGlone served most of his time in Alcatraz. As he watched his friends die out, he mellowed. Over the years he worked in the prison infirmary and became a capable technician. He was paroled on April 21, 1960, and died 22 years later at Briarcliff Manor, Westchester, New York.

James Sweeney was the lucky one. He successfully evaded capture until the statute of limitations had run out—thereby avoiding a kidnap charge, but he was arrested in November of 1937 for stealing a car and given a three-year sentence. In 1939 it was reduced to a year and a day. Afterward, he faded into history.

"Big Mac" Christy Miller was arrested December 28, 1936 in Hoboken, New Jersey, and transferred to the Albany County jail. The authorities attempted to make him talk but he cut them short by hanging himself. He left behind a wife and two kids.

"Big Charlie" Scarnici was held for the murder of Officer Stevens. After describing to the authorities what occurred in the O'Connell kidnapping, he continued to talk as he tried his best to avoid the inevitable. He had been a triggerman for Dutch Schultz and had too many bodies to atone for. Therefore, on June 17, 1935 he was executed in Sing-Sing Prison's electric chair.

The record does not indicate who did it or why, but Tony Reino and Little Charlie Shore were assassinated in January, 1934. Speculation had it that after the mob's attorney got them out on bail, Mob Leader Dutch Schultz ordered them killed to keep them from pointing attention in his direction.

Albany folklore had it that the O'Connell family had the Albany Police kill Jack "Legs" Diamonds because he attempted to claim some of their beer territory. A book entitled *Jack Legs Diamond: Anatomy of a Gangster,* by Gary Levine, alludes that Diamond's wife Alice may have been sufficiently unhappy regarding her husband's long time affair with Kiki Roberts that she was involved in his killing. The truth may never be known since Alice met the same fate when she was murdered by an unknown assassin in June 1933.

Strewl's appeal decision was handed down on March 17, 1936, almost exactly three years to the day after his first trial. He listened with glee as Judge Rhodes, of the New York Appeals Court, read for the majority and struck down the pillars of evidence Delaney had so carefully built.

The first was the testimony of Sam Gross. The judge summarized how Gross had hosted three mobsters for several weeks and overheard them talking kidnapping. He recounted Gross's story of what he had heard in the Century Hotel room and his reason for being present. The judge found it "illuminating" that Gross knew about the kidnap plans for months and told no one, but had a sudden change of heart in August 1933 and decided to tell authorities his "fantastic" story. Gross had also confused various meeting dates, and he associated with people of "low character" (mobsters). Given all this, the judges decided his testimony was not credible.

The second pillar to fall was the testimony of the victim, Butch O'Connell. The judges ignored the fact that Strewl lurched over the defense table when Butch testified that Strewl had been present in the room where he was held. The judges concentrated on the Times Union newspaper article that quoted both Butch O'Connell and his uncle stating they could not identify any of the kidnappers—statements they both denied making. The dissenting judge, McNamee, pointed out that the majority didn't believe Gross because of his "low character" yet now they did not believe a person of high moral standards—meaning the victim, who had served in the military and attended the police academy.

The judges also questioned why Butch, who had ample opportunity to tell the authorities about his suspicions that Strewl was one of the kidnappers, did not tell for several days. (The fact that John Delaney had indicated to Butch that he should delay telling never made it into the trial testimony or trial transcripts.)

Next on the list were the incriminating statements attributed to the defendant, Manny Strewl. Again the judges ignored the fact that the witness Detective James O'Connell jumped out of the witness stand to attack Dan Prior when the Defense attorney implied he was lying. They focused instead on Strewl's bruises, which had been visible at least ten days. The judges figured a person would say anything to stop a beating, and therefore tossed out all Strewl's statements to the police—without accusing the police of anything.

The other evidence was the handwriting samples. The judges noted that the experts checked only a small percentage of the writings and in essence found more dissimilarities than similarities. The judges suggested that a closer and more thorough examination of the writing samples was needed.

A majority of the judges on the appeals court concluded there was "reasonable doubt" concerning Manny Strewl's guilt. They reversed his conviction and ordered a new trial.

Strewl's victory, however, was short-lived. A new trial meant new evidence could be introduced, and in 1936 the FBI had discovered that one of the ransom notes was not a Photostat—it was a photograph. The FBI had also captured Burke and Fisher, who would turn State's evidence.

Strewl would also have to face the land mine the O'Connells had managed to put into effect: the brand new State of New York Kidnapping Law. The others arrested for the O'Connell Kidnapping had been tried under the old law, meaning they served prison time. Under this new law, which the O'Connells had rushed through the legislature, Strewl would face a possible death penalty if convicted.

This was a gamble Strewl was not willing to take. In a plea deal "to save his honor and prevent his family the embarrassment of another trial," he pled guilty in 1936 to extortion by mail. He admitted writing two of the ransom notes. For this crime he was sentenced to 58 years in the Atlanta Penitentiary.

Unlike the other guilty parties, who were mobsters, Manny Strewl had not been sought on prior charges. This fact saw his sentence reduced to 28 years.

Strewl was paroled in 1958. For a time, he worked the docks in Orange County, New Jersey. In the 1970s he moved back to Albany and married Ethel Miller. He died on December 19, 1998. He was 95, and had never discussed the kidnapping with any reporter or historian.

The ransom was never recovered. It is reported that John Oley did not give Scarnici his cut of the ransom because they needed it for Strewl's defense. This author also speculates that since the mobsters had no employment, they either spent it for living expenses or for other illegal activities.

Photo Gallery

Theodore W. Dunn (author's grandfather) being sworn in as jury foreman. Hand picked by Dan O'Connell. At the time of the trial the penalty for kidnapping (presuming the victim remained alive) was jail time. His instructions were to give Strewl the death penalty (could not be done under the law at the time). The law was later changed due in a large part to the O'Connell political muscle.

Manny Strewl. Also thought to be a "finger man" in the Rensselaer County Bank robbery. Sentence reduced to 28 years and paroled in 1958. Worked the docks in Orange County New Jersey. In the 1970's he returned to Albany and married Ethel Miller. He died at the age of 95 in 1998 without ever discussing the episode with reporters or historians.

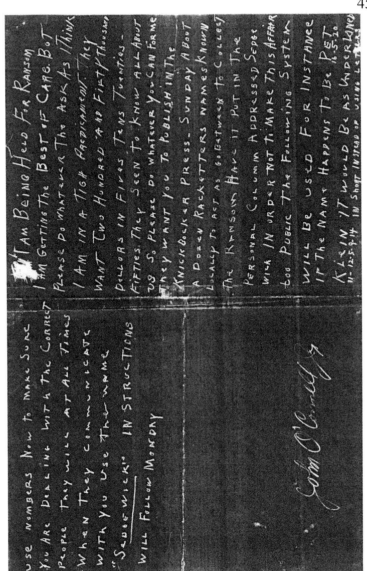

Copy of the original Held for Ransom note.

I AM BEING HELD FOR RANSOM I AM
GETTING THE BEST OF CARE BUT PLEASE
DO WHATEVER THE ASK AS I THINK I
AM IN A TIGH PREDICAMENT THEY
WANT TWO HUNDRED AND FIFTY
THOUSAND DOLLARS IN FIVE TENS
AND TWENTIES AND FIFTIES THEY
SEEM TO KNOW ALL ABOUT US
SO PLEASE DO WHATEVER YOU CAN
FOR ME THEY WANT YOU TO PUBLISH
IN THE KNICKERBOCKER PRESS SUNDAY
ABOUT A DOZON RACKETTERS
NAMES KNOW LOCALLY TO ACT AS
GO BETWEEN TO COLLECT THE
RANSOM HAVE IT PUT IN THE
PERSONAL COLUMN ADRRESSED
SEDGEWICK IN ORDER NOT TO MAKE
THIS AFFAIR TO PUBLIC THE FOLLOW
ING SYSTEM WILL BE USE FOR
INSTANCES IF THE NAME HAPPENS
TO BE PET KLEIX IT WOULD BE UNDER
16520 1) 125914
LONED IN SHORT INSTEAD OF USING
LETTERS

Duplicate written by Strewl under police supervision for comparison purposes. A key clue was the misspelling of the words "racketters" and "columm." At his new trial and plea bargain, Strewl admitted writing it.

Sunday 14, 33

MANNY STREWL;

You NO DOUBT ARE AC-
ACQUAINTED WITH THE O'CONN-
ELL PEOPLE. WELL YOU CAN BE OF
GREAT SERVICE TO THEM, WE
HAVE CHECKED ON YOU AND DE-
CIDED TO PICK YOU AS OUR
GO BETWEEN IF YOU ARE WILL-
ING, IN THE EVENT YOU ARE
YOU WILL INSERT THIS ADD
IN THE WORLD-TELEGRAM, PERSONAL
SECTION
"ROMA"
    PLEASE GET IN TOUCH WITH
    ME. MANNY.
Do THIS PROMPTLY, AND DO NOT CHANGE
YOUR HABITS, IF YOU CARE TO BE
OF SERVICE. SECRECY AT ALL TIMES IS
    NECESSARY

THIS IS GENUINE BY JOHNS SIGNAT-
URE ONLY.
    "ROMA"

Copy of original Strewl accepted as the go-between. Letters were scribbled over to disguise the handwriting.

MANNY STROWL   (2)

You know doubt are ac-
quanted with the O Connel
people, well you can be of
great service to them, we
have checked on you and de
cided to pick you as are our
go between if you are will
ing, in the event you are
you will insert this ad
in the NY World - Telegram Personal
                                    Section
"ROMA"
        Please get in touch with
            me,

                MANNY

Do Bthis promptly, and don't change
your habits, and if you care to be
of service. secrecy at all times is
                    neccasary

Duplicate dictated by police to Strewl for comparison purposes.

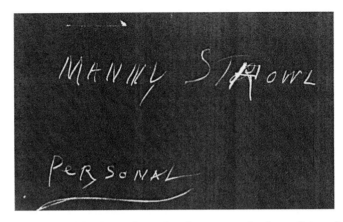

Copy of original envelope the above came in, later determined to be a photograph copy and not a photostatic copy (like the other ransom notes). At his new trial this fact destroyed Strewl's claim that the police faked the evidence.

One of many dictated duplicates written by Strewl under police supervision for comparison purposes.

Copy of ransom note stating Dan's offer of $20,000 was an insult.
During the first trial the defense attorney severely questioned Dan as to
the punctuation marks (Dan could not remember them).

John O'Connell house (2007 photo)

George Keiss house (2007 photo)

Morris "Mush" Trachneir House, #4 Kate St.

John Oley. Alcatraz #455

John Oley 1937. Given 77 years and a $10,000 fine. He was sent to Alcatraz. Medically paroled from the Atlanta Penitentiary in 1959 and died of cancer in 1960 with his wife at his side. Buried in Ballston Spa, New York.

Agnes "Aggie" Oley (about 1937), wife of John Oley

Francis Oley (approx 1937)

Francis Oley, 1937. On April 2, 1937, while in the Utica jail he cleared out the cellblock by claiming he had TB. He then hung himself with a bed sheet. Left behind a wife and child (Patricia).

Genevieve Oley (wife of Francis)

Francis Oley House. #40 Oak Wood Ave. (2007 photo)

John Oley's House, 50 Oak Wood Ave. (2007 photo)

Percy "Angel Face" Geary about 1920

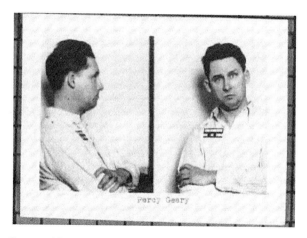

Percy Geary, Alcatraz # 456. Sentenced to 77 years and a $10,000 fine. It's presumed, since he spent most of his life behind bars, that he could not face the outside world. Upon hearing about his parole he pled with officials to keep him in prison - to no avail. On July 16, 1959, he threw himself under the prison laundry truck, committed suicide.

Josephine "Jo-Jo" Geary
Bought the print set used
for ransom notes

#19 Oak Wood Ave. Home of Detective James Hynes – who was
credited with solving the kidnapping (2007 photo)

Rensselaer County Bank, 1933 photo. At the corner of Partition
Street and Broadway in Rensselaer, New York.

Rensselaer County Bank Robbers: Tony Reino (left), Leonard "Big Charlie" Scarnici, Charles "Little Charlie" Shori, and Phil Zeigler

Tony Reino: Following his acquittal at his Troy, New York trial for the bank robbery charge in 1933 he was bailed out of jail by Dutch Schultz's attorney and found assassinated in early 1934.

Charles Scarnici, known as "Big Charlie," was a known trigger man for Dutch Schultz. Participating in both the bank robbery and kidnapping, he "talked" to the Rensselaer County District Attorney for a reduced sentence for his part in the kidnapping. That charge was dropped, but the DA then arrested him in the shooting death of Detective Stevens during the bank robbery. In 1935 he was executed in the Sing-Sing electric chair.

Charles Shori known as "Little Charlie," and alias Charles Herzog. He also was acquitted at the bank robbery trial in Troy in 1933 and bailed out of jail along with Tony Reino - and assassinated alongside Reino.

Phil Zeigler (far right) served time for various unrelated activities.

The Nash getaway car, found in September 1933
at a garage at 148 Morton Ave.

Back of the Nash, showing bullet holes in the rear fender. One
bullet went through the rear window and into the roof.

Typical Ford "rail truck." The secret compartment was behind the advertising board.

1937 photograph of the hideout at 734 Adams Street, Hoboken, New Jersey. St. Ann's steeple can be seen on the lower left. Its bells were a clue to the location of the hideout.

734 Adams Street, the hideout in Hoboken, New Jersey (2007) - now a
garden apartment house

St. Ann's Church (2007)

Charles Harrigan. Alcatraz #255. A known lieutenant to Dutch
Schultz, he shared leadership (with Thomas Dugan) of the Waxy
Gordon Mob - also known as the West Side Mob. Paroled in 1959.
Died April 20, 1988, in Long Island City, New York.

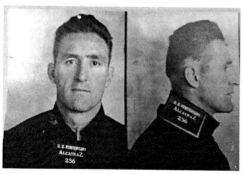 

tutional Rule Violations

Thomas Dugan. Alcatraz #256. Shared leadership with Harrigan
and also had close ties to Dutch Schultz. Died while in prison in April
1946 of heart disease.

George Garguilo. In 1934 and 1935 he was a "second boxer." He
was so mean the prison guards were afraid of him and kept him
chained as much as possible. Arrested for robbing a Boston Bank in
1935, he was given a 35 year sentence in addition to his 77 year
kidnapping sentence. On March 9, 1938 he committed suicide in the
Massachusetts State prison.

Frank Fisher, one of the guards. Turned State's evidence in return for a reduced sentence of three years. Presumed to have returned to South Africa diamond mines.

Harold Michael Crowley

Harold "Red" Crowley, was given 28 years at Leavenworth (#52393). In 1937, along with John Oley and Percy Geary, he escaped from Onondaga County Penitentiary and was captured three days later. He offered to talk for a reduced sentence. In 1957 he was transferred from Federal Prison to the New York State prison system to serve time for various state crimes.

Thomas Burke, nicknamed "Pivot" (FBI#304764). He guarded John O'Connell. After his arrest the papers called him "Two Gun Burke." He was recovering from a mangled leg received during a truck hijacking and was partially deaf, so he was mostly useless to the mob. Turned State's evidence in return for a three year reduced sentence. Shortly after entering Lewisburg Prison in 1937 he died of a coronary occlusion.

"Big Mac" Christy Miller. Low ranking member of the mob, he was noted as always looking like a slob. In February 1937 he committed suicide in the Albany County jail, leaving behind a wife and two kids.

JOHN McGLONE

John "Sonny" McGlone. Alcatraz #252. Known as a hothead, he was so feared in New Jersey that when he murdered a man in front of 14 witnesses including two police officers no one would testify against him. He mellowed in later years and became a physiotherapist in prison. He died in December 1982 at Briarcliff Manor, Westchester, New York.

James Sweeney (alias James Doyle). Arrested in 1937 for car theft and income tax evasion. The statute of limitations had run out so he served a year and a day in prison.

David Smurl,

Chief of the Albany Police from 1926 to 1940.

John Tuffy. While on patrol, Officer Tuffy and partner Ray Joyce discovered John Oley's car "in the wrong place," and thus provided the authorities with their prime suspect.
Tuffy later became Chief of the Albany Police.

Jack Legs Diamond, killed in December 1931 in a rooming house on 67 Dove Street, Albany. Folklore had it that the O'Connell family had him killed because he was attempting to move in on their beer territory. Another theory was that he was killed by one of a long list of enemies who were perhaps aided by his wife, Alice. The case was never solved.

Major John Warner, Superintendent of the New York State Police at the time of the kidnapping. He was a Harvard graduate, a lawyer, an accomplished concert pianist, and also rode against Poncho Villa.